To Fenn

The Strong and Steady Waves

Ebonene Charles

May waves of love caress you daily.

Bogach Books

Ebonene Charles
IV 25 23

Bogach Books
Canada

ISBN 978-1-7387093-0-4 (paperback)
ISBN 978-1-7387093-1-1 (ebook)

First Edition: April 2023

Foley's Rest is a completely fictitious place. Although some of the
cities, towns, or villages exist in Canada, the sites mentioned
within are entirely fictional, as are all the characters in this story.
Any resemblance to real places or people is entirely coincidental.

This is a work of fiction. The views expressed may not reflect
those of the author.

Cover artwork by markanthonystudio.com

Dedicated to those who love the Canadian landscape.

The Strong and Steady Waves

Ebonene Charles

1

The up-and-down motion of these waves is nauseating. It makes me feel like I'm riding in a high-rise elevator for a never-ending ride.

I wonder how long it's been, but time passes differently here: slow. Here, there is nothing except time itself. Even though there haven't been that many nights or days, I still can't seem to count them for some reason. So, it seems like I've been out here for a week, but it may not have been.

My phone doesn't work. Swimming wasn't good for it.

I suppose I can be grateful that if I had to go without food, at least I'm in a place where I cannot get hungry–my stomach is so queasy that I never think of food. But I am beginning to get weak and sitting up makes me dizzy.

The rain here is something else. I've been through a couple of storms that are impossible to put into words. This suit cost me eight thousand dollars, and now it is nothing but garbage. And no dry cleaner in the world will be able to save it.

I wish I had never booked that trip because I didn't need new clothes anyway. If I'd only known how this journey would end before it even started.

It sure is a good thing there is no mirror here because I would hate to see myself at this point. And my hair, what on earth would it look like? I rub under my eyes often in case my mascara is smudged, but I imagine that there is no longer any trace of my makeup left.

I think I'm all dry after the last rain, but perhaps not completely. Likely I haven't been for days. And thank goodness it's August, for if it was January or something, I would've died from the cold. The North Atlantic Ocean has a reputation for being pretty chilly.

I often imagine the survivors of the Titanic floating around, waiting to be rescued. Of course, that happened in April, so it would have been much colder for them. And probably no one was alone and entirely all by themselves for miles. Or, I should say kilometres, since I'm Canadian.

At least I was able to drink some water when it rained. The positive side of the torrential downpour was that by laying on my back and opening my mouth, I had to gulp just to keep up. But that's all that is keeping me alive now.

Of course, I'm cold. A sheet of some kind of plastic protects me a bit, but I'm quite surprised that I am not frozen solid. Also, this funny yellow thing I'm floating in is not very insulated, so the chill of the water is beneath me all the time. Why isn't this raft fully inflated anyway? It must have got punctured somewhere along the line. And my synthetic cover could be another raft that was never inflated at all.

I know my life is hanging in the balance because one wave could just tip me over, and I would no longer exist. But there is nothing to swim to and nothing else floating around.

Why are there no rescue planes, boats, or helicopters? I'm not looking forward to another plane ride, and a boat doesn't interest me either, but a helicopter might be Ok. From time to time, I went on a cruise, but I never had the same respect for the ocean as I do now.

I must have drifted far away from the plane crash, because I had seen no rescue efforts. Yet it doesn't appear like I'm going anywhere. Without any reference points, it seems like I'm just staying in one place.

The scenery never alters, and there are only two things: the sky and the ocean. It's so weird to look at the horizon in all directions and see nothing but water. However, the colour changes often and can be a variety of shades of blue depending on the sun, perhaps, and the time of day.

There was a powerful wind on the afternoon of the crash, and it seemed to drive me far away, as the debris got smaller and smaller and then disappeared completely. Back then, I felt I was being carried elsewhere by some unknown force. And now here I am. Nowhere.

I have way too much time to think, and that is remarkably depressing. Floating around aimlessly, I know no one is looking for me. Hundreds of people were missing from this crash, but I never saw anyone after. Unlike me, they must all have dozens of family members and friends, sometimes sobbing at the news, and at other times, being hopeful that the phone will ring with the announcement that their beloved is still alive. But not one person is missing me.

Sure, I had people over many weekends and went out sometimes, but I had no friends to speak of: no family, no husband, and no boyfriend. I don't think I've ever loved anyone. I must not have, otherwise, I'm sure I would be thinking of them now. And it would be such a waste to die, never having loved or been loved. A shame for a life to end without a single tear shed.

I had a promising career and thrived on the excitement.

Then I would shop. There are a few stores that import some quality garments from Europe, including shoes. Of course, there are also places in Paris that I can buy from directly and get my purchases delivered, but it was always more fun to do in person.

Yet I just served myself. Anything I ever did on the pretence of helping others was only to be noticed. I loved attention and never left my place until I looked perfect.

Everything was such a waste.

The ocean was calm now, and bright fluffy clouds seemed to mock my dire situation. As blue stretched on endlessly in every direction, it made me feel even more alone than in the world I had created for myself.

If I'm going to die, the likely end of this all, I hope I can do so peaceably in my sleep and not violently in a storm or shark attack.

But if I'm going to live, I want to learn to love and if I could just once have someone love me back. Maybe get married because I am getting tired of being alone. How does one make friends exactly?

No one at my work would be a good choice, as they're all like me.

If I live, I will simplify my life and not be so after money. I even made a personal proposal, sort of. First, I will quit my job, sell my condo and car and try to live a quality existence as a normal person. Then I will give more to others and do so from my heart because I care about someone other than myself. Sometimes I'll wear my hair down and buy casual clothes. Part of my plan involves walking into a discount department store and staying for half an hour, watching people and trying to understand. I'll stop spending so much on myself and even look at stores in a regular shopping mall. Finally, I will make a friend.

If I live, but probably I won't. No one cares, and why should they?

I am so weak and can't think straight anymore.

Sometimes I hear different things. Who knew there could be such sounds when there was nothing around? So, I used to sit up at each in the hope that it was someone, someone looking for me, or at least someone who happened to see me. Now I know there is no one, just noise.

It is night again, and I try to sleep through the up-and-down motion by imagining that I'm in my elevator. Not that I've ever slept in a moving elevator before, but at least it's something that I can relate to, something close to home.

IT'S FINALLY morning and the water's very rough once more. Should've been in France. Should never have left... stayed in Toronto. If only I had picked a different destination. Should've chosen the earlier flight. Was even a bit cheaper. Don't love planes anyway. Wanted to buy clothes from Paris... Stupid...

Should be married. Normal people get married. Could have kids. Don't need kids. House maybe. Have a nice condo but empty... cold.

Can cook, though, even Japanese. Sushi! Lots of fish here... but never learned to fish. Never learned anything truly useful.

The Strong and Steady Waves

Look! I'm on my very own island. Tiny yellow island. No washroom, no table, no food, no bed. Very primitive. My island. I'm the queen of my island...

Maybe I'm by Greenland or Iceland by now. Maybe Norway. Back to Canada? Newfoundland? Maybe. Probably right smack dab in the middle of the Atlantic Ocean.

My mother died. They phoned me and told me so. Wonder if she was ever sorry.

Too loud. Ocean's too loud... Too tired of opening my eyelids.

Feels like I don't have legs or arms... I'm like a fish: smelly and flailing. I have my purse. A fish with a purse. A fish that can't swim away but has a credit card...

More noises... different? Probably only... heavy things... Can't move anyway... Have plastic over me still...

"Hello! Is there someone there?"

Voices. Just a dream? They're going to take me away. More sounds. Can't move. Don't leave me! Must move. Could be my imagination. *Help! Please!*

"Oh, man! Are you Ok?"

I manage to lift my arm. *Don't go! I'm here. Please help!*

I hear a bang, then silence. *Don't forget about me!*

More noises, some splashing. My plastic's gone. Gone! Taken.

"Hey! Are you alright?" the voice booms.

There's a man. Open eyes. Open! Heavy eyes. First Nations man. Copper skin, black hair. Concerned eyes. Red buffalo plaid jacket...

Ouch! He pulls and drags me. My head is heavy. Neck is weak. Then I'm hanging. My feet dangle and blood rushes to my skull. Guy's got me with one arm. Climbing with another. Going up... His pants are wet. Then carrying me with both arms. Down now. Narrow staircase inside a boat...

Very dark. Lacquered wood, plaid fabric, bed. Blankets... So many blankets. I don't have so many blankets. He puts me down on a bed. Beds are nice. They're soft and dry.

He gets a mug of water and pulls me to sit. *Ouch.*

"Here, drink a little water." Calming deep voice... Holds cup for me. Must gulp. That's Ok. I'm used to it. Eyes don't stay open.

"How long have you been out there?" I try to shrug, but shoulders won't move. How long? I open my mouth, but tongue is stuck.

"Few days," I spoke. Maybe not. Doesn't resemble my voice.

"You've drank some rainwater?" he asks.

Can't drink seawater. Too much salt. "Yes."

"Have you had anything to eat?"

Food. Food! "No." I sound like a frog. Frogs don't speak.

Dark brown eyes. Puts a blanket on me as I lay down. Went away... back.

I hear chopping, a pan, and some sizzling. Soothing sounds.

I'll be Ok now.

"HERE, HAVE some fish." I startle awake. And he makes me sit again and wraps something around my shoulders. This man feeds me, and I've never been fed before. Maybe as a kid. But probably not. Always wanted a guy to feed me as it's supposed to be romantic. Romantic fish with blankets and red buffalo plaid jackets.

He has a denim shirt. Where is the jacket? It's on me! So, that's why I am warmer. This is my first time in a red buffalo plaid jacket. Being a North American thing, it seems so at home in the wilds of Canada. I pull it tighter around me, but don't have the energy to put my arms through the armholes. Although the loud red and black squares are not like anything I've ever worn, it's soft, and smells of wood.

First very good fish. Tastes like butter. Looks terrible, but I don't need to be picky now. "Thanks," I manage to say.

"I need to get you to land, but I have to go up to steer the boat. You going to be Ok here for an hour?" he asks.

Feel like sleeping. I'll just sleep. Warm blankets.

"Yes," I say.

He leaves. What if he wants his jacket? Must look better on him...

NOISE STOPS. Motor? Some banging. Steps. He's back! Picks me up and carries me out. *Ouch!*

Land! Finally, land! We are docked on the coast. Indigenous people, a dozen or so women. A few kids all looking at me. Small village with colourful homes side by side. Blue, red, yellow, and green townhouses on stilts. Circle of houses together with wood boardwalk all around, leading to each. No trees but hills behind them. Big rock hills. Lots of rock. He's taking me toward a home in the middle and an older lady now walks alongside him.

"Found her in the sea," he mutters.

"My goodness," she says as she opens the door of a yellow home.

It's nothing expensive, but a dark house with wood walls. He puts me on an old couch while another lady rushes in.

"Urma, we better get her in some fresh clothes," she says.

"That seawater can't be good either. She must have been splashed with the waves all the time. She needs a bath," Urma, says.

"I'll come and check back later," the man says and leaves.

"We're going to help you take a bath," Urma says to me. "What is your name, child?"

"Adelle."

"Adelle. That's pretty. I'm Star and this is Urma's place," the other lady says.

They led me up to the second floor. And the stairs were a little tricky because I kept feeling like I was going to fall over. But we did get into the bathroom, which was pretty clumsy, and eventually, they managed to take my suit off and helped me into the bath. It would have been painless if I wasn't helped to discover all my bruises. I didn't even realize I had gained such a collection during the crash. Next, they undid my hair, which was still sort of up somehow, and then they washed it.

The warm water ran down to the bottom of my hair as one poured from a bucket, and the other held my head back. My long, dark brown hair fell into the water. It was wonderful, and I imagined I was in my very own spa and had two attendants. I was ridiculously rich, and these were my bath servants, and I was in a vast garden oasis with a mineral pool in the centre.

Even my bathroom at home would be nice. My tub has clean, smooth lines and a slanted back. There I would slowly, luxuriously, sink deep inside, surrounded by the scent of lavender and millions of bubbles. Fresh fluffy white towels would be warming in my towel warmer, and relaxing music would softly flow in.

This, however, was different. Instead of the smell of essential oils and luxurious tropical fruit hair products, there was a scent of wood and baking. The soap and shampoo smelled like... soap. Talking and laughing with themselves, they created an ambience new to me. Neither tried to hide the fact that they had never bathed an adult before.

Urma must be in her fifties or so, and Star was younger, late thirties, perhaps. My rescue man would be around my age, late twenties.

Although I could not continue with my spa daydream, this was... I don't know... something. Here they were very gentle and caring. The warmth they had you could never find in any spa. Because no one there cares about anyone else. Not like in this strange place.

Next, they helped me dry off and put on some clothes that they found. I wonder where. It was a dress with long sleeves, a lengthy wide skirt and a tie back at the waist. Also, it was full of tiny blue flowers. Dressed this homely, it was worse than even what I wore as a child. Oh well.

Finally, they bundled me up with blankets on the couch. It was so good to be warm and not starving. On top of me one cover was light blue and crocheted, but over the years, the stitches had welded themselves together. The other was a dark green duvet which only really had its stuffing left in the corners, but the fabric still lasted. Also, it had small red flowers on it.

Nothing in the house matched, I noticed as my eyes slowly gazed around. Everything was clean but kind of cluttered and very old, yet somehow warm, like how I imagined a grandmother's home would be. I've never had a grandmother. But there was something cozy about this place.

Where is that man's jacket? I looked for red and black. But it was not with his bedding folded up on the other couch. Finally, I saw Star carrying it. And she was telling Urma that she would wash it for Tom.

Tom. That must be his name.

His blankets didn't look so old. The first was grey wool and the other was a blue comforter which still had all its stuffing as it towered tall when folded up. So, that must have been the soft one I had felt against me, though my memories weren't clear.

Urma put a coffee on and brought me a little food and water. Although my arm was shaky as I ate the meatloaf and mashed potato, the taste was incredible. I had no idea meatloaf could be so good because it always sounded like a recipe gone wrong to me.

Then Urma went outside, and all was quiet as I fell asleep with the smell of coffee, supper, and baking all around me. It smelled as if someone had made a cake with cinnamon.

I could hear the ocean.

I WAS disturbed later by a guy with a stethoscope, but I could not wake up completely. He was acting like a doctor and checking me. Still checking things... poking me...

"I got a feeling you will be alright. You just need to rest, and Urma will take good care of you," he said. "I'm going to put you on an IV, as it'll speed your recovery."

"Shouldn't I go to a hospital?" I asked.

"There are none here, dear. But no, I think that after we get some nourishment in you and you rehydrate, you'll be back to normal. Anyway, my name is Mac, and if you need anything, just send for me."

Is he a doctor? I wondered. Then he talked to Urma, but I couldn't really stay awake.

Soon he returned and was struggling to put up the IV pole. Had it ever been used before? All the humidity in the air no doubt caused a little rust on the ends, and it probably got dropped a few times as he moved it from corner to corner in a dusty storage room. Finally, it was standing relatively straight, and Mac attached it to my arm. Funny, it didn't hurt at all after he put a hole in the top of my hand.

There were more men in the house now. And I'd never been with so many First Nations people before, but I still couldn't keep my eyes open for long.

I almost woke to the sound of cutlery on plates as they were eating, yet it was more like a dream than anything else.

Later, I woke to the sound of Tom's voice. He was talking with Urma and another man, who must be her husband.

I could touch the curls of my long hair, which form locks when I leave it to dry. It was so soft. But I always wore it up because it looked more formal. In fact, this was the first time it's been down since I started working at my firm. When I was sick at home, I still put it up so it wouldn't be in my way. Now it was down and curly. Man, had it ever grown! It looked healthy, even a bit shiny. And it seemed happy to be released and floating around free and bouncy in long locks.

Tom came and sat beside me, and the couch springs creaked.

"How are you doing?" he asked in almost a whisper, with a genuine look.

"Alright. Sore, tired." I ran my hand through my hair. "Thank you for saving my life."

"No problem," he said, as if he pulled people from the sea every day.

"Where am I?"

"Foley's Rest, Newfoundland. It's a tiny remote community on an island. We are three hours away from St. John's by boat."

"Oh."

Of course, I had never heard of this place before. I've never even been to Newfoundland and Labrador, but I was glad I was at least in the same country. But it might as well have been a different continent because life here seemed nothing like it was in Toronto. Canada is a big country, and I'd never made it out of Ontario.

If I was alright, which the resident doctor implied, then this was much more interesting than a hospital, but I was utterly stuck here by the sounds of it.

My boss had me visit a hospital once, and I couldn't stand it. There was one benefit of not having any real friends: you didn't have to see them in there.

I wasn't used to people dressing this casual. Never before have I seen so many loose jeans, chords, and sweats. Everyone I work with is in a suit, and whenever I was doing something recreational, the guys usually wore nice, pressed khakis and crisp shirts, leather belts, and brand-new shoes. So, they always looked like they could be on the cover of a glossy magazine.

Tom's clothes were clean but somewhat wrinkled. Of course, I was likely the cause of that. He had wool socks, grey with cream patches at the toe and heel. And his one toe was close to being able to come out. His jeans were bigger than usual and worn at the knees, but not yet with holes in. As well, a blue T-shirt was under a lumberjack-style flannel button-down that did not exactly match the shade.

His clothes were not perfect, and neither was his hair. You could tell where it was supposed to be, but it wasn't going to conform entirely to where it was parted. Obviously, not held in place by anything, no gel or spray, it was neatly cut, short, and very black.

But his eyes carried a determination, and he smelled like his boat, the smell of a wet piece of plywood.

"Are you up to a few questions?" he asked me. "I, besides fishing, work with law enforcement here, and I have to file a found persons report. As opposed to a missing persons report." He smiled, got up, and returned with an old clipboard and a pencil. "How did you get cast at sea?"

"The plane I was on crashed," I said. "I was flying from Toronto to Paris."

"That happened Friday."

"What day is it?" I asked.

"Tuesday. That's a long time to be at sea. They never found anyone," he said, tapping his pencil to his upper lip. *Who still uses orange-coated pencils with pink erasers on top?*

"Then they certainly were not looking very hard."

"There aren't usually any survivors when a plane that large crashes in the ocean. However, there were lots on the search crew. Did you see any other people?" he asked.

"No. No one. I never saw anyone alive or otherwise."

"When I found you, you were way farther than the reasonable search lines," he said. "How did you get out of the plane?"

"It crashed," I said. *What did he mean?*

"Yes, but how did you get out of the wreckage? Do you remember how you got out?"

11

"I held onto the seat." *I could remember the screaming and the very loud creaking of the metal, probably bending where it shouldn't. The wind was crazy intense. Then a large item came flying at me.* "I had to let go, and I fell into the water." *That was a forceful splash, yet I couldn't focus on that because, just seconds later, there was the bang of the entire plane hitting the ocean.* "I swam." *Of course, I had to do something to stay afloat, but then thankfully, somehow, there was this tiny yellow half-inflated thing with plastic over it.* "I got into that life raft. It was the only thing I saw… floating."

I was trying to recall more, but I could still hear the noises, the screaming, the deafening sound of the water, the sound of the plane… splitting, maybe? Dying. It was the sound of dying.

"Do you remember clearly?" he asked.

"I don't remember what I did, really. Somehow, I think I kind of fell out," I said.

"I see you managed to keep your purse with you the whole time. Can I see if your ID is still there? I can probably get everything I need from it."

"Sure," I said, and soon Tom was writing down information from my driver's license.

"Who of your family should I call?" he asked.

"There is no one to call. I have no family," I said.

"Is there anyone else you would like me to reach?" he asked.

"No." He looked at me strangely.

"I have to get this in right away. I'll come back a bit later," he said.

I watched him leave. He was quite tall and had an awkward, rather abrupt way of moving. But here in this wild and rugged place, he fit.

Shortly after, Urma brought me a little more food. My arms did not want to move, the muscles were sore from my bruises, and I still shook because I was so weak, but I was doing it myself. Her cooking was delicious, and I enjoyed more of her mashed potatoes and gravy with some carrots and peas. I never ate food like this, yet I had to admit that I'd been missing out.

I looked around the room. Here the couches were brown with orange flowers, well, two of them anyway. The other was green. Yes, green, and guess what? It had blue flowers on it. Next, the coffee table was exactly what you would see if you drove down some of the roughest streets of Toronto and happened to glance by the garbage bins. But the floor was wood and seemed pretty new. The walls were wood too and covered with shelves which were full of things: toothpick holders handmade from play dough, mussel shells glued together to form… something, and a cup and a saucer that I would have hidden instead of displayed, even if it was worth thousands. Lastly, there was an old globe on a broken stand, tiny brown and orange flowers in a ceramic vase, a little framed mirror, a fake plastic pear and a banged-up jewellery box.

This house was tiny. I had a small loft condo, but it was just for me, and I liked the minimalist style, not like this, where things were jammed into every possible corner. Though I didn't have a bedroom, this home was even smaller than my place. From here, I could see the stairs that led up to the second floor. And the kitchen was right behind the couch. You could barely squeeze between the dining table and the sofa.

Urma and her husband came into the living room and sat down.

"I'm Bill," the man said.

He had on blue and white striped overalls and a red T-shirt. And his brown socks definitely had holes in them. Urma wore a big, worn, light green apron. It used to have a pattern of strawberries on it, one day, a long time ago. Also, she had dark pink pants which were polyester, the kind with an elastic waist. Her blouse was navy, and she wore white socks, which were now mostly grey. Everything was wrong. Yet it all seemed to fit somehow.

However, at this moment, I don't look much better.

I could hear the waves crashing on the rocks not far away. It was a steady, consistent beat, like a heartbeat. So, I just listened for a while before I drifted off again.

I WOKE up when I had to go to the washroom. And I managed on my own, thankfully, but Urma was less than an arm's reach from me as I walked.

My legs were sore, and I felt light-headed. The IV pole was at least something to hang onto, though it looked pretty flimsy as I had to drag it with me. And it was no help with the stairs.

My reflection in the mirror showed my cheeks were flushed. Additionally, I didn't recognize myself without makeup, with my hair down, and wearing this dress. I appeared like a character from a movie in a land far away. One that lived by the sea and would walk along the shore at night singing softly. Secretly, that was something I loved to do at home when no one was around. Anyway, this still was not me. How can I be me when I look like someone else? I continued looking for a while. Who am I?

My reflection had betrayed me. Here it had me camouflaged to blend in. So, a strong feeling spread throughout me, the sense that there was a side to me that even I didn't know yet.

Perhaps Tom would like my hair. Now it fell softly around my face and swayed as I walked. It was kind of pretty, and a lot of girls get perms to look like this.

By the time I got back to my spot on the couch, I was already exhausted.

I propped up the cushions and blankets to be able to stay in a sitting position.

"So, tell me about the history of this place," I said.

"Hmm..." Bill grunted. "Well, someone lived here a long time ago." *This was helpful and interesting.* "Then they left... Someone else came, and they left too." *To have him as a history teacher in school would've made things so much easier to remember.* "They all fished. More people came, First Nations, and then were all wiped out by smallpox. I heard about this place from someone that the fishing was good, so I came, but there were lots of problems. Some people here were causing problems, and the houses kept falling apart. Then Tom came. He was sent but volunteered to go. He got rid of all the trouble-makers and then got the government to give us the supplies to make good homes. We all built these," he said proudly as he pointed around him.

"Tom is from Haida Gwaii on the other side of the country. Different ocean. He came all this way. He was fishing there before," Bill added. "He's been here about five years now. Good guy. We all like him."

Then there was a knock at the door, and without anyone having to answer, Tom came in.

2

"Hey," Tom said and came and sat in the living room. "Well, Addy, you look more alert."

He called me Addy. No one has ever called me anything but Adelle. Oh well, I don't need to fix that right now, I guess.

"Yes, I am feeling better," I said as Bill got up and grabbed a beer from the fridge for both of them.

"You drink beer, Addy?" he called out.

"No," I said. "And knowing the shape I'm in, a beer would knock me right out."

Also, I don't drink beer. Because ladies do not drink beer. A martini would be nice, with one olive, but not today anyway.

Besides, my name is Adelle.

"No beer for you," Tom said, smiling at me.

"How'd your day go?" Tom asked Bill.

"Y'know, not bad," was the reply.

"Bergs are better."

"Yup. Not like that baby I had in June," Bill said.

"Took a while to fix your vessel after that one."

"Yeah, well, gotta expect that every few years."

"Could've been worse," Tom said. He turned to me. "The icebergs come floating down here. Quite the show in the spring."

"You've had a busy day," he said to Urma.

"Yeah, you should take care of your own catch," she said, smiling.

"I'd love to, but I'm not as qualified," Tom said.

"One can't live on fish and wieners alone," she said.

"Hey, my fish and wiener dish is where it's at," he said, and Bill laughed.

"Thankfully, I'm saved from all those batching meals," Bill said.

"And my fish and rice dish is where it's at," Urma said.

"Can't argue with that," Tom said.

"So, you got lots to do with Addy?" Bill asked.

"Yup. Nothing like that's ever happened before here, so I'm digging through all these boxes of forms. Finally found it. Guess what paper it was beside? The complaint form for if you don't like the smell coming from your neighbours."

"That could come in handy," Urma said.

"Yeah, if someone forgets to do his laundry," Bill said.

"The new guys, they don't believe you when you tell them you gotta wash your clothes right away when you get back," Urma said.

I relaxed and listened to them all talk and chuckle occasionally. Yet this had to be one of the funniest conversations I have ever heard. This was such a different world.

Urma answered the phone, returned with urgency, and turned the TV on.

"Becky said you're on the news," she said excitedly, almost out of breath.

But by the time we found the channel, nothing remained on the subject.

"They couldn't possibly have much to say," I said.

"Becky said they showed more footage of the search boats and helicopters and had a picture of you in the corner."

"They didn't even find me. Sounds like false advertising."

"Becky said they seemed to have the details right, from what she knew."

With the excitement over, everyone settled back on their chairs or couch.

A warmth permeated here. And I didn't understand why, but this whole place was one warm, fuzzy blanket. They were like... family. At least, this is what I always imagined a family to be like. A child would want to come home to this.

I always saw kids take off at elementary school as soon as class finished. They would run all the way home sometimes. But I would go to the park, even in the winter. Then, slowly, slowly, as it became absolutely necessary, I would walk to the place where I lived.

Home never really fit, as it couldn't be the right word to use. However, I shouldn't complain because they fed and clothed me, being much better than the alternative. So, chores for food and clothing were not exactly a bad trade-off, while it lasted anyway.

I watched Tom. He smiled a lot, laughed often, talked softly, and drank his beer. Slowly, I dozed off again.

I WOKE up when they stood up. Still, it was light out.

"Hey Addy, I'll see you tomorrow after the boats come in," Tom said. Whatever that means.

"What time is it?" I asked.

This day would still not end. I had arrived today, and yet it seemed like a day or two ago. So, it felt like it must have been late, but the sun told me otherwise.

"Must be around seven-thirty," Bill said, but no one had a watch.

"Yes, it's seven-forty," Urma called from the kitchen, where she had actually gone to check the clock on the microwave. It is still early.

"Did we have supper?" I asked.

"Are you hungry, dear?" Urma asked.

"No, but I thought you all ate a long time ago," I said.

Tom laughed. "We do things a bit differently here. Since all the guys come back at two in the afternoon, that is when we have dinner. Then, we go to bed around eight in the evening and take off at four in the morning. That's when the fish are out," he said.

"Then breakfast is when?" I asked.

"Three-thirty." He smiled. "See you."

I watched him leave. He had an abrupt way of leaving because he was in the house one second, and the next, he was out. There was no in-between from opening and closing the door. There was no walking towards the door. There was no leaving. Only in and out. Of course, without a knob on the door, you just had to push it. I looked at the couch where he sat a moment ago and marvelled at his clumsy, yet somehow smooth, way of moving.

The wooden door had a screen on it. And the spray of the ocean almost came through. But the air was different here. Humid but clean, every breath carried a salty yet fresh and sweet taste.

"So, how big is this island?" I asked.

"Not big at all," Bill said.

"About how far up are we?" I asked. I loved his history lesson, so I couldn't wait for my geography one.

"Not up at all. This is like the most south you can get," he said. "We are even a little south of St. John's. We are basically in the middle of the Atlantic. This is the only island inhabited out here, though there are two more west a bit. But hard to anchor there. We have to take a boat to the big island to get anything."

"I see," I said. I had heard of St. John's but couldn't picture the exact location on a map. Nevertheless, this sounded rather isolated.

I got up, had some water and brushed my teeth. And thankfully, someone found a new toothbrush for me. Without any need to take off my makeup and none of my usual skin products, it took little time for me to get ready for bed.

Urma set out some pyjamas for me. Being old, flannel, and plaid, they had been worn thin at the elbows, shoulders, and knees. These were not even worthy of donating to a homeless shelter. Nevertheless, I wanted to put it on and go to sleep, but how was that possible with this thing stuck in my hand?

As I tried to figure it out, Mac sauntered in, removed it for me, and waited while I went to change. Then he hooked me back up with a replacement bag and hollered a good night to us all.

I straightened the pillow and blankets on my couch and crawled in.

I fell asleep immediately despite it still being light out, and I'd slept all day. There is something about the quietness here. Because everything was perfectly quiet, no sound existed except the sound of the waves.

I WOKE up when Urma entered the kitchen to put the coffee on. Still being dark, I sat up and watched her after my eyes adjusted to the bright fluorescent lights. She pulled out an ancient but huge orange plastic container. Slowly, she took off the lid and grabbed the scoop inside. Plastic would make the coffee taste really gross. Next, she took a paper filter out of a glass jar with a rusted lid and put it in a coffee maker, which must have been around way before my time. They don't make those anymore.

I was amazed at how slowly she moved as she got breakfast started. She had a kind of rhythm, and her arms worked methodically. Her coffee got finished at about the same time as it would take me to make it back home, but how could that be when she wasn't rushing as I always did? When Bill surfaced, he moved slowly too. He poured his coffee like a Sunday on vacation.

"You drink coffee, Addy?" he asked.

"Yes." But afraid of this stuff, I hesitated.

He poured me a cup as I got up and headed to the kitchen. It took only about five steps, but pretty awkward ones because I was stiff.

The appliances looked like they were from the sixties, and I couldn't believe they still functioned.

Everything was ugly. The sugar bowl had a cracked lid with a chip in it. Cream in colour, it had a brown flower on it. Don't they know flowers shouldn't be brown because that's a bad thing? The teaspoon looked like it had been dug up in the dirt, an ancient artifact of a past civilization. Also, the frying pan Urma had was scary because it had so many scratches on it. The creamer was another old plastic container that probably used to be clear but now was yellowish. I think there used to be a marking on the one side, but it was so faded that it could no longer be seen.

"How are you doing today, Addy?" Urma asked. *And I like how everyone is just calling me Addy. That is not my name. No one even asked if that was Ok.* "You seem to be getting around a bit easier."

"I'm still weak and sore, but definitely better," I said and left to brush my teeth first.

It was delicious when I finally mustered up the boldness to fix and sip my coffee. It had a sweet taste to it. Perhaps it came from the plastic container. But it was very mellow and really quite perfect.

I tried to ignore the looks of my mug. Yet some worn-out company logo sat on the front, and not one of their mugs looked the same.

The coffee smelled better here. It filled the house and made it seem like a holiday. I always thought that coffee tasted so much better on vacation against the fresh air, and this was exactly the same. It was strong but not acidic at all, like mine, even though I imported it right from Italy.

Mac came in again.

"You are looking good. Big improvement," he said, staring at me intently. "Do you feel stronger? Not as dizzy?"

"Yes. I am more stable today. Much better than yesterday."

"I don't think you'll need any more IV. You seem hydrated again, and you've eaten. No problems with digesting?"

"No. Everything seems fine," I said.

"Any lingering pain that seems worse than bruising? Any shooting pain?"

"No."

"Then I'll disconnect that, and you can enjoy your breakfast. I smelled it coming down the walk."

"You should stay. There's always enough for another," Urma said.

"Tempting as that is, Jac's got ours started already. I think she's just making porridge, though." He wrinkled his nose. "But I promised I'd be back for it."

Breakfast was also incredible, but I had to close my eyes to fully appreciate the flavours because the plates and cutlery looked awful. More of a yogurt and granola person or a bagel and cream cheese fan, I found it a treat to have an all-out breakfast. There was bacon and huge pancakes. Also scrambled eggs with cheese. A wonderful mixture of blueberries and whipped cream accompanied the pancakes. There were sausages and orange juice as well. Furthermore, I couldn't remember the last time I had breakfast like this. And how did she make all this so quickly when moving so slowly?

A breeze blew in from the screen door. It was cool and fresh, so I took a deep breath.

Urma and Bill were all dressed, but I still had my pyjamas on.

After Bill left, Urma took a bath. They did not have a shower, only a tub.

I decided to try washing my hair in the sink afterwards, but it was too long. I soon had a pile of hair spilling all over, being hard to rinse. Besides that, my back and arms were killing me. So, from now on, I will stick to washing it in the tub.

Then I took a bath. Even though the bathroom was as mismatched as the rest of the house, and the tub was rough and scratched, the warm water felt comforting. There was something wonderful about it and everything here, but I couldn't figure out what.

I put on another dress that Urma provided. This one was white. It was also long and wide, but it had some embroidery, and almost pretty in a homey way.

I sat back on my couch, already tired, and drifted off for a little nap.

A KNOCK on the door woke me, and then a non-Native lady and two kids came in. There were white people here. Notably, these guys all had blond hair.

"Addy, this is Becky and her kids, Roxy and Ryan," Urma said.

"I'm so glad to meet you," Becky said. "If you are too worn out for company, I would understand completely," she added.

"No. This is fine," I said, and the kids looked at me with huge eyes. "Where are you from?"

"We're from Norway," she said as Urma put on some more coffee.

I figured that I must be the tourist attraction of the summer, because what else could possibly happen here?

"How are you feeling?" Ryan asked. He was cute and had a way of looking like he was up to something.

"Not too bad," I said. "How old are you?"

"Eight." He kind of squirmed around. "Were you really in a plane crash and stuck out at sea?" he asked, completely intrigued.

"Ryan! I told you not to bring that up today," Becky scolded him.

"But I just have to know," he told her.

21

"It's alright," I reassured her. "Yes. It's all true. I was taking a plane from Toronto to Paris, France, to go on holiday. It was early morning, and we were flying over the Atlantic Ocean. I was flipping through a magazine and drinking champagne and orange juice.

"All of a sudden, there was this loud bang, followed by a strange hissing sound. A few women screamed. Everyone frantically looked around. Then the plane started to rock side to side. People fell out of their chairs, and bags of luggage fell on people's heads.

"Then the pilot got on the speaker system and told the passengers he would try to stabilize the plane and find out what happened. The flight attendants came up to the front. People searched for those inflatable things and the air masks.

"Next there was a loud ripping noise—like the loudest zipper ever imagined.

"Then we fell. We couldn't move. All of a sudden, this gust of wind, stronger than any on earth, shot through the plane from somewhere and ripped the wall apart. I was hanging onto a chair, and my feet were blowing in the air. But I had to let go because something large flew towards me.

"I hit the water pretty hard, but heard the plane hit the water right after. As I kind of swam along, I saw this yellow thing floating by, and I climbed onto it.

"Everything went quiet with only the sound of the sea left. So, I laid on the yellow thing, and the wind carried me away on the ocean for four days before Tom found me."

"Wow!" Ryan said. "That's so cool that you survived. No one else did."

"Good thing Tom found you," Roxanne said.

"Yes. I was getting pretty sick," I said.

"Were the waves making you throw up?" Ryan asked.

"Yes, but I was also rather cold and sometimes wet, and of course, I had nothing to eat," I said.

"You should've caught some fish," Ryan said.

"I don't know how to fish."

"Oh, everyone here does. I catch mostly crab. Would you like to learn?"

"Yes. I could handle that, maybe," I said.

"It's good because you don't even need a boat. So, till I get my own boat, I'm the crab hunter round here," he said, making me smile.

"If you're better, I can show you tomorrow," he said.

"Sure. It's a deal," I said.

I never got to be around kids. In fact, I knew none by name. I thought I would hate them, but I found myself surprisingly at ease with Ryan and Roxanne.

"So, what else do you guys like to do?" I asked them.

"We have a telescope," Roxanne said, "and we can see the boats when they are very far away and the bergs and whales too."

"Oh really?"

"I also like to play princess," she said softly.

"How about tomorrow, if I'm feeling good, I'll show you different ways to braid hair?" I asked.

"Alright," she said as her face lit up and a big smile formed.

Urma brought coffee and cake.

"I hope it didn't bother you to talk about the crash," Becky said.

"No. It was good, I think. It helped it to be clearer in my mind, more like a fact of history than just some bizarre nightmare," I said.

"You seem to be recovering very well," she said.

"Yes. I feel not bad, considering."

"Emotionally, I would be completely torn apart,"

"Well, I imagine that is better than not having any emotions to tear apart," I said.

"Oh, don't be silly. You're very strong. That's all. Your family must be worried sick about you."

"No. No fear of that. I don't really have any."

"Oh?" she asked. "I'm sure many people are missing you already."

"No. I was supposed to be on holiday anyway," I said.

This cake was excellent. It had only cinnamon to flavour it? And it was so soft. My bakery doesn't make anything like this.

After a while, Urma moved to the kitchen and started cooking lunch. Becky joined her, and I must have fallen asleep again, but woke from the kids' laughter from time to time.

We had lunch, and then Becky had to drag the kids out with promises that they would see me tomorrow and they seemed to be looking forward to it. The kids had such a contagious laugh that you just had to laugh with them.

How slow and easy everything was here. When people dropped in, you fed them.

In Toronto, no one ever dropped in to see me. I thought for a second about how ridiculous that would seem. So, the doorman at my building certainly was not getting a lot of work from me.

My mornings were always panicked as I grabbed my yogurt, granola bar, and fruit. I would have my granola bar wrapper clenched in my teeth as I made sure I had everything in my case before the elevator arrived. Next, I would run to my yellow sports car and then drive to my favourite cafe for my cinnamon coffee latte to go.

There was a tension in the air that was tangible through the lingering smog. Everyone rushes to get to work because that is what defines you. Even if you are a wife or mother, the world judges you by your career alone. There was something about the traffic in the morning. Being an exciting kick-start to the day, it was full of anticipation as to what lay ahead. So, after battling it for half an hour or so, I finally arrived at work.

My day there would begin with my secretary running alongside me, going over my day's schedule: the meetings I had, who I would have lunch with, and who I had a dinner meeting with. It was always one rush to the next, one panic or two, or even three at a time. However, I loved the action. And just thinking about it made me excited.

I would have on an expensive suit with a knee-length skirt, my hair done up, and sexy shoes. I loved shoes.

When I left my apartment each morning, I always knew that I looked my best. Of course, there was a definite satisfaction in that, and it was missing here.

My work had a sense of purpose, yet here the women didn't seem to have a purpose. They stayed home and only cooked and cleaned, so really, they were just glorified slaves. It was like feminism never even happened, and there was no equality. So, at the end of the day, what did they have to be proud of? To be relegated with nothing more than to serve your husband? What kind of life was that?

They have probably done so for so long that they can't see how things could be different. True, the possibilities here were slim, but certainly, an Internet business was a possibility. And perhaps it was up to me to bring it up and make a suggestion.

Urma was doing laundry and cooking, but I felt a bit run down, so I took a nap. I woke to find her taking off her old apron and fixing her hair with her fingers in the hallway mirror. I sat up.

"You wanna see the boats come in?" she asked.

Did she mean the men coming home from work? So, what on earth is so great about that? Boy, it sure does not take much to amuse the people around here.

Nevertheless, I got up and intended to follow Urma out of the house onto the boardwalk. Her place faced the ocean right in the middle of the cul-de-sac kind of layout. Now many women were doing the same. Those that lived a little farther in had walked out so they too could stare out at the sea.

Not having any shoes, I hesitated. Whatever happened to my heels? I think I took them off on the plane, and now they are probably at the bottom of the ocean. I suppose it wouldn't kill me to be on the boardwalk barefoot. Yet it seemed so weird, and the finest dust had gathered on it. The smoothness was foreign to me. Everything was built just five years ago, so the homes' exteriors, boardwalk, and rail all looked pretty new. My toenails still had their polish on and were a darker blue with a gold dusting on them. I chose that because it reminded me of a starry night.

My fingernails were usually in a French manicure style, so they didn't stand out too badly. Back home, I never wanted them to clash with my suits or be distracting. So, I kept them not too long so they wouldn't get in my way. I had my nails done before my trip, but it was a misfit here.

Every minute, more women would join. They were mostly Indigenous, but not all. Becky, a few houses down, also stood on the boardwalk watching and waiting with her kids. But Star had come out to the centre as her place didn't face the ocean and was more on the side.

"Where does Tom live?" I asked Urma.

"His is the blue right in front of us, facing the water. We can only see the back from here," she said.

25

As there now seemed to be women everywhere, I asked her, "Is everyone here married?"

"Everyone except Tom." Then that must be the only place where no one is waiting. "Oh, and Gregg's wife died. He is the one over there on the only boat left on the dock."

"He doesn't fish?"

"No. He takes all the fish the guys caught, pays them, then takes it right away to sell it in town. Makes a round trip every day."

There was a pattern to the colourful homes. Red, blue, yellow, and green, and then it repeated.

Here there was nowhere to go. The houses stood against the rock. A spot to my left had a little grass, and then the rock shot up again. Truly, there was only the ocean and this one circle of townhouses.

All the women were here. It was strange, and what exactly were they all waiting for? Yet there was a tension in the air, one of excitement and eager anticipation. You would think the fair was coming to town, or a celebrity, or someone carrying a considerable fortune for all. Everyone was silent too. Usually, these women were real talkers, and you would always hear laughing and talking in the background, but not now. Now there was an eerie silence. And even the children were quiet. They were restless but silent. The women shuffled their feet a bit, swayed from side to side, and moved to the left or right to get the best view.

Then finally, you knew something was spotted, as everyone was now standing motionless. No one stirred at all. After a bit, something appeared on the horizon—just dots, as they were still far away. But slowly, very slowly, they came closer, and you could tell they were boats, and they were all in a line moving together.

"Tom's is the third one on the left," Urma said, pointing excitedly, "and Bill's is the fifth one from the right."

This was quite the observance, and they do this every day? It is rather pathetic but kind of cute.

As they got closer and closer, the figures of the men became obvious. Although unable to see their expressions, they all stood proud and tall. They had provided for their families, and because of them, the community would survive. You could see it in their faces even more as they got closer. There was such a look of

26

contentment and pride. It was almost primal: the men coming home from the hunt. Yet it wasn't that way at all. They looked happy to have their wives anxiously waiting for them. They were happy to be appreciated for their hard work and happy to be happy. I was trying to figure this out.

There was something about this. I could feel it in the air. What was it? It was like watching a movie you never planned to see, and maybe you even thought it was stupid, but you find yourself watching anyway and being completely glued to it.

Some were waving back and forth now, husbands to their wives and wives to their husbands.

It was like some kind of race, and you just got all caught up in the action and had to cheer someone on. But yet, it wasn't a race. They were all coming in one straight line at the exact same speed.

I watched Tom, as he was the only one obviously not being watched, and I somehow felt sorry for him missing out on this event.

No. I am lying. That is not why I was watching him. I was watching him because I couldn't help myself. He did have a commanding figure.

Tom dressed much the same as yesterday. He leaned against this pole-type thing with one arm, and the wind brushed against the ends of his plaid shirt and ruffled his hair. There was pride in his stance and confidence.

He was looking at me as well. And I wanted to look away but was unable.

There was some kind of feeling swelling up inside me that was unfamiliar to me but accompanied by an increase in blood pressure.

He did not wink nor wave, but continued looking at me.

They broke up the formation slightly for all the boats to dock.

As they arrived, each man tied his boat up, came to the dock, and grabbed empty wooden crates that were piled up there. Then they went back on their boat and started filling them with fish.

Tom threw his rope with one easy toss, and it wrapped itself around the wooden pole. Without delay, in a kind of jump, he was out of the boat and, in one swift moment, made a knot to anchor it. Then, in just a couple of steps, he grabbed a few crates and was back in his boat. No, I was right about his figure.

One by one, the men would bring their crates full of fish onto Gregg's boat, and he was weighing them and scribbling on paper. After they brought their last one, he would also give each of them a receipt or something. They would stuff it in their pocket.

Those crates must have been heavy because each of them had sweat on their brow as they stepped off the pier.

Lastly, each one walked quickly but not entirely running, into the arms of his wife. And you would think they'd been parted for months or even years by the warm embrace they received. They kissed. They all really kissed, and not briefly. It took quite some time for them to finally walk hand in hand to their home.

Roxanne and Ryan grabbed onto their dad the second he came close. They were all over him with hugs, kisses, laughter, and screeches as he picked them up and swung them around with all the delight in the world. Then they ran off so Becky could greet him as well.

This was quite an amazing ritual. No matter what you had discussed with your husband the previous night or the morning before, you couldn't possibly be mad at him now. So, I discovered that I was very touched.

I was still watching Tom intently and everything else I saw from the corner of my eye. Now I wished he would come my way. This was not me. This was not my life, so man, would it ever be alright if he came to me. It was not so weird, I told myself. If any other woman were here in my place, she would want the same. Whatever these guys did, it worked. And boy, did it ever work. If this were a movie, the girls would drool. Trust me. I had never felt like this before, and it was an incredible high.

He was still looking at me. Tom looked at me the whole time. I would know, as my eyes were glued on his. But when he started walking this way, my insides jumped into my throat. His home was over there, but he was not going that direction. He was coming to me. He was. Just put aside all apprehension, I silently begged of him, at least this once. I gripped the smooth railing tightly. I could hear my heart pound, and a little gust of wind blew through my hair and my dress.

3

J ust a few steps before Tom reached me, he stopped and put his
hand on a support post.

"You look better," he said.

Better? What a compliment. I was near death yesterday, and
now I look better. Wow. You sure can't top that as a pickup line.
But it really was not a pickup line, and I knew that.

Everyone knew Tom was no one's fool. And the respect he
gained here did not come from acting rashly.

He had a smile in his eyes and half a grin on his mouth. It was
as if he knew exactly what I was thinking and was laughing at me.
But I hadn't done anything, I told myself. Yet I knew, and he knew.
Tom doesn't say anything because he doesn't have to. He knows.

Urma pushed the door open and said, "Join us for supper," to
Tom.

"K," he said. "Be right back," and he left.

Back inside, Bill took a bath, and Urma set the table and checked
the food.

Soon Bill came out all shaved and in clean clothes.

"So, how's my little mermaid?" Bill asked me. I was not his
anything, never mind a mermaid.

"Fine," I said.

A few minutes later, with one shove, the door was open, and
there was Tom. He had also changed and shaved, and his hair was
still wet.

"Oh, this is great," he said to Bill and Urma.

The next thing I knew, a can of beer came flying through the kitchen, and Tom caught it and opened it.

We sat around the table, and Tom's chair was beside mine.

"Urma has got to be the greatest cook," he told me.

The house smelled fabulous. Urma placed a bowl of cheesy garlic mashed potatoes on the table. Next, a dish of green beans and butter followed. The fish in an onion cream sauce with some tomato slices looked so delicious. Also, there was broccoli and carrots in a cinnamon honey glaze. I could not wait to eat. What was it about the food here? Why does it always taste so good? It must be the fresh air with the lack of pollution.

"So, Addy, what kind of things do you like to do?" Tom asked me.

Then, a huge smile crossed my face. "Oh, you know, gut fish, polish the floors. I make cookies and meatloaf, sort laundry, and knit. I was thinking about taking up embroidery," I said.

"Seriously," he said.

"I like to shop." But somehow, that didn't sound like much. "Well, I'm usually working."

"What are your talents?" Tom asked.

"I jump from planes, then float around in yellow pieces of plastic, but I don't get to do it often," I said.

"So, you don't have any talents," Tom said with a mischievous grin.

"And you? Are you mister talented?" I asked.

"I'm very charming," he said, joking around.

"Well, if I had only known that was included as a talent," I said.

"Also, I'm the greatest fisherman," Tom said.

"Well, second greatest," Bill said.

"I'm a gourmet cook," I said.

"Really?" Urma asked.

"Yes. I serve a plated supper at least once a month," I said.

"What does that mean?" Bill asked.

"Each course is served separately in a very intricately designed composition. In fact, it is like the finest restaurants in the world," I explained.

"Maybe you'll have to show us," Tom said.

"You wouldn't have the ingredients. I use all kinds of exotic things and I shop at specialty stores, mostly."

"Oh, here I thought you were talking about a talent, but it's not a talent to take gourmet foods to make gourmet meals." Tom bugged me. "Urma here does wonders out of nothing. And that is a talent," he said.

"I can't argue with you there," I admitted.

"We don't get much visitors," Bill said.

"That's alright, more attention for me," I said, smiling, and they laughed.

I felt, for the first time ever, that I was a part of a family-like atmosphere and not outside watching. Moreover, I wasn't being treated special here, but just as a member of this little group.

Everything was a lot of fun until Bill asked Urma for another piece of cake, and she got up to serve it to him. I mean, what is wrong with him that he can't get it himself? So, it made me mad because there was no respect for women here.

"You know, you do not exactly have to be served," I said softly. "You are quite capable of getting it yourself." Bill looked at me wide-eyed, unsure of what to say.

"I think if Urma didn't want to get it, she wouldn't have," Tom said. *Yeah right.*

"You guys have women demeaned into not much more than servants," I stated.

"Because they take care of the home?" Tom asked.

"Their only reason for existence is to take care of their husband. Instead of having a purposeful career, they have to do demeaning work."

"So, you don't think that women should help their husbands?"

"There are lots of ways a woman can do that. For example, in Toronto, husbands and wives both work and split the domestic chores," I said.

"And are they all as miserable as you are, viewing men as such a threat instead of being content with who they are? The women here take pride in caring for their household, so there is no room for your feminist and materialistic views here," Tom said.

I almost forgot to breathe. Because no one ever spoke to me like that, and yet for the first time in my memory, I didn't know what to say. I was utterly shocked. And I wasn't wrong. How could I possibly be wrong? Hence, an uncomfortable silence followed.

"You are just very sheltered here," I said finally.

"The cost of living in Toronto is higher," Tom said, "but in Foley's, things are different, so don't voice opinions about what you know nothing about."

"I don't think–" I started.

"It's enough, Addy," Tom said.

He had never once raised his voice, but it carried a firmness I had never felt before. His words kept going over and over as they swam around in my head. From time to time, I was yelled at while working, but I always knew how to retaliate, and it never carried this weight in my mind.

I shouldn't let him have the last word because how dare he? Still, I was unable to say a thing.

What exactly was I trying to say anyway, that women should all work out of the house? So, was I trying to say that women should never cook for their husbands?

Tom managed somehow to change the subject, and gradually they fell into an easy conversation again. But I couldn't even follow it because my mind was swimming.

Had I stepped out of line? Do I really sound feminist and materialistic? Things are so different in Toronto, and I do not belong here.

Bill and Urma must have a lot of respect for Tom because neither said a word when he scolded me. I wondered if Urma understood what I was trying to say. I kept thinking about it.

They played a game, and I watched.

Finally, Tom left and Urma came and sat beside me.

"Do you think I'm unhappy here?" she asked.

Did I? "No."

"Before we moved here, I did have a job. The fishing wasn't very good, so I had to work to help pay the bills. Yet I was stressed out all the time. Bill is not lazy. He used to assist me with the housework, but we were always so exhausted that we even argued a lot.

"When Bill heard that the fishing was so good, we decided to try moving here. And this place was a dream come true, really. All the stress vanished. Bill enjoyed fishing and was proud that he could provide for me, take care of me, and build a house for us. He was so happy.

"I was so proud of him too because he did it all on his own. I was so grateful to be here and to never have to wonder if we would be able to pay rent or buy food."

My eyes started to sting. I had misunderstood the motive behind their little culture here.

"I wanted to keep a nice clean home for Bill and to cook for him and care for him in whatever way I could because he was caring for me. So, I don't mind at all. All things considered, I like doing this because there's no stress involved.

"When Bill comes back from work, we can just relax and be together because all the household duties are done. Bill really appreciates that, and he appreciates me too. I don't feel used at all. In fact, we've been so happy here, Addy, that I can't imagine improving it.

"When I'm doing housework, if you help instead of watching, you'll find it's not that bad."

A tear rolled down my cheek. It made sense when explained like that, and I felt foolish for what I had said. After, Urma gave me a hug, and I hugged her back.

"It's nice that you are here. Stay for a while," she said in such a welcoming motherly way.

I did want to stay.

The phone rang, and it was CBC News. They asked me questions for a report and offered to airlift me out on one of their choppers in exchange for an exclusive interview. After some silence, I told them that I wasn't ready yet. So, they gave me an email address to contact them when I was.

It was odd to talk on a landline. Equally strange that in this day and age, there was no cell service here.

"That's Ok, hey? That I stay a little longer here? I don't want to impose," I asked both of them as they were within earshot of the whole conversation.

"Of course! We're so glad you declined."

"You are going to go out of here like a movie star," Bill mused.

I felt antsy, but at least it was soon bedtime.

33

"Have a good sleep, child," Urma said.

However, I had trouble sleeping. Tom was right, and I wasn't used to being wrong. He was so calm, so collected, and so confident.

Urma was right too. I had just watched her work, and how much better was that? After all they have done for me, the only thing I can do to show my appreciation is to help. Tomorrow I will help, and what else can I do?

I should do something for everyone. Because they have all been so kind to me, looking after everything I need.

I could make them all a meal. After I get home, I can give Urma the money back for the ingredients I used. That would be nice. A fancy-plated supper for all of them. Of course, they don't do a lot of fancy things here, and there is no restaurant anywhere, never mind an elegant one, so it will be something different for them. And I will figure it out in the morning.

WHEN I woke, I ran a bath. The steam rose and swirled around. Baths in the morning are much more relaxing, even a little luxurious. It seemed like something you would never do unless you were on holiday.

Then I had breakfast with them and helped Urma clear the table and wash the dishes.

"I was wondering if you would let me make a meal for everyone here. Because I want to thank them for all their help. So, it would be for you and Bill, Tom, Star and her husband, Becky and her family, and Mac and his wife."

"That's twelve people," she said.

"Well, I usually cook for that many. I would pay you back whatever you think it costs for all the ingredients, and we would need to clear out a bit more room."

"That sounds like a lot of fun if you really want to."

"Yes, I do. Is that alright, though?" I asked.

"Oh, absolutely. You can help yourself to anything at all that you might need, and I'm certainly not going to keep track of the ingredients you use. There is always enough food here, so don't worry about a thing."

To begin with, I repeatedly went through the cupboards, the pantry, and the deep freeze, trying to figure out what I could make. Salads were out of the question, as there were no fresh vegetables. I had never used canned or frozen before. So, this wasn't going to be easy.

Thank goodness for the simplicity of ingredients for crème caramel. But decorating them would be a challenge. I pulled milk out of one freezer and pork tenderloin from another. Urma had three freezers.

I kept being interrupted by news agencies too. A few others phoned, making similar offers, but everyone here was under the impression that CBC did the best job of my story, so I declined all of those.

Finally, I think I had it all figured out. I could do it tomorrow, which would be Friday.

Then I can leave, I guess, on the weekend, but it seemed a little too fast.

Next, there was a knock on the door, and Roxanne came in.

"You still going to braid hair with me, Addy? You feeling Ok?" she asked.

"Sure, yes, absolutely. Should we do it here?"

"No. Come, I'll show you where," she said. She took my hand and led me to the door. Such a tiny hand.

"I don't have any shoes," I said.

"That's alright. The moss is soft. I wouldn't wear shoes if my mom didn't make me."

She had a tiny box with a handle on it. It was made of clear plastic so you could see a child's comb and brush and all kinds of colourful elastics and clips inside. Also, she had a very large hand mirror.

This was the first time I walked off the boardwalk. The moist moss was foreign to my feet. But it was velvety soft, and the rock under was hard and rough.

We had gone to the left, to where the houses ended. This was the only place where you could walk off the boardwalk. You could access some large rocks that followed the shoreline, the dock, or this one and only small flat area. After a few more steps, I set foot in the little field, thick with daisies and the only grass I had seen here.

"This is the daisy field," she explained. "I like to come here sometimes." She walked to the middle and sat down, surrounded by flowers. I came and joined her.

"This is a nice place," I said.

It had been a long time since I last did hair, and it was always just my own. I could remember being in one foster home. The room had been sparse, but there was a large mirror beside my bed. So, I got books on hair braiding from the library and would sit for hours trying different things on myself.

I would do something in Roxanne's hair, and then she would do mine. By the end, she was doing quite well. Finally, we did a braid that goes around the head, not using all the hair but making a crown all the way around.

"That looks pretty on you," Roxanne said when she had finished.

"Does it? Well, I will leave it in then. It also looks adorable on you."

She decided to keep her hair just like mine, and we started walking back. Her mom stepped out, obviously just about to call her for lunch, and smiled when she saw us.

Urma had lunch all ready as well.

"Sorry I didn't help you. I don't know what time lunch is here," I said.

"Since we have breakfast at three-thirty in the morning, we have lunch at nine-thirty." Man, that was early, but I was famished.

It was a terrific soup, and the smell of onions and potatoes filled the kitchen.

As soon as I was done, Ryan was at the door.

"You still wanna go crab hunting with me?" he asked.

"Yes, but let's help Urma with the dishes first," I suggested.

"Ok," he said.

"No. You guys go on," Urma said, and insisted.

"Come on," Ryan yelled as he ran out the door, and I had to run to keep up with him.

He had a large plastic pail, the kind used for paint, and he had two long sticks with grabbers on the ends.

"Oh, you'll need shoes on," he said. "Otherwise, they could grab your toes."

He ran back to his house and brought me a pair of his mom's rubber boots. We headed to the same area, but this time focused on the rocks along the shore.

"Ok. First, we look for them. You may need to move some big rocks to find one," he said, peering between them along the water's edge.

He would poke his stick in every corner. I very cautiously looked around the boulders.

"Here's one!" Ryan yelled.

The thing was huge. And I had no idea we were after something so big. Since it was coming in my direction, I jumped on a rock.

"You just have to grab them with this stick," he said.

"Maybe you should show me how," I suggested while trying to get a bit farther away.

My foot slipped off the rock I was on, and suddenly, this crab came out. It scared me, and I screamed. But Ryan laughed.

"Hurry, grab him," he said.

I had never done anything like this before. This stick was not big enough, was it? I had to get too close for my liking. Besides, was it even strong enough?

Finally, I got him and picked him up, but this looked horrible. The crab was swinging its claws in the air.

"Put him in the bucket," Ryan said.

"How?" I asked.

"Like this." He showed me the pail where the one he caught was now sideways in the bucket, one claw sticking out, still trying to grab at something.

Staying as far away as possible, I somehow managed. Then we looked for more.

One grabbed my skirt, and I screeched. Ryan laughed at me again.

But I was having a blast. Never remembering having this much fun, I was laughing so hard that my stomach hurt. Also, I was out of breath from chasing these things.

After we caught six, we were done, and we both carried the pail with our grabbers back to his place.

"You like eating crab, Addy?" Ryan asked.

"Yes. I do."

"Mom says you can stay for supper cause she's going to cook them all."

"Oh, that would be fun," I said.

"It is so nice to have company for dinner," Becky said when I came inside.

Yet this was very different from the type of company I was used to. I would have the meal all prepared beforehand. After my guests were sitting quietly, I would dish up the first course and decorate the plates. Then I would put the next course on to heat and then bring each one their plate. The wow factor was what I was after. Because I was convinced that everything tasted better when it looked great, but now I was not so sure.

"Have you ever made crab before?" Becky asked.

I had made a crab-stacked salad before, but I confess I had bought it cooked and frozen.

"Never from a live one," I said. I always thought the whole idea of crab and steak to be rather unrefined.

"There are so many crabs here that we can have them as often as we want," she said.

"I had no idea they would be so easy to catch."

"Keep me company while I prepare dinner," she invited me.

"Sure. Just give me something to do so I don't go crazy."

I discovered that both she and her husband had good jobs in Norway, but Ralph was having anxiety and stress issues. So, in their quest to find a simpler option, they eventually found out about the fishing here. Because of his background as an engineer, they were able to immigrate fairly quickly. Foley's Rest needed to be fixed up. Thus, they sold everything and moved here. After a few months of work, he could go fishing every day. Ralph loved it immediately, but it took a while for Becky and the kids to get into the groove.

"It's a tremendous change from a big city with all the culture shock. You must feel it too," she said.

"For sure. I feel pretty out of place here. But there is something about it that I am enjoying."

"Tom's attention, perhaps?" she teased.

"I get way more attention back home. I think it's the warmth of everyone and such a slower way of life. Here, no one is trying to show off. Everything in Toronto seems to be done so that you can prove yourself to those around you."

"Yes, it's so easy to get caught up in that. Somehow, you believe your life will improve with one more purchase, but it never does. There's always something more you think you need."

"I'm learning a lot. All the things I thought I would need to enjoy a vacation are not here. But I am finding that I'm not ready to leave," I reflected.

"That's terrific. We are growing on you then. Maybe you'll come here for all your holidays."

"I'll have to buy a boat." I laughed.

"There are things that I miss, though. Your nails look wonderful. Sometimes it would be nice to be able to get done up. Everything here seems so 'done down,' if you know what I mean."

"Yes. I suppose a person could learn to do their own nails." I wondered aloud.

"Probably, but there are so many things we have to do for ourselves already. Who has the time to learn to do something like that well?"

After talking for a while, it was time to cook the crab. I watched Becky as she dropped them live into a behemoth of a pot of boiling water. They made a sound. It was awful. So, I closed my ears, and Becky couldn't stop laughing.

Then, as the last one was finishing, I heard Ryan telling Roxanne it was almost time. Time for what? Oh, yes. The boats to come in. And how could I forget? The women seem to all prepare supper and then keep it warm while they go out to watch.

Next, the kids showed me their telescope, and they were the first to declare when the boats were coming.

We all stood outside. What a fun day it had been, just like a holiday.

"Can we ask Tom to join us?" Becky asked.

"Sure."

Though it was the strangest thing, I could feel myself getting more excited as the boats drew closer. And it was such a powerful moment when the men walked off the pier into the arms of their wives.

You could tell by the looks on the men's faces that there was no greater reward, no greater feeling of success than to come to their happy wives and for fathers to have their kids run out to greet them.

Tom gave me a little wave and turned to go to his place.

"Would you go and ask him to come?" Becky asked.

"Now?"

"Yes, because he will be washing up right away."

Also, Ralph was getting near.

I ran after Tom.

"Tom," I yelled out, and he abruptly turned around. "Becky and the family want to invite you for dinner," I said.

"Sure. I'll be right over," he said.

"And Tom," I found myself saying, "sorry about yesterday."

"Oh, don't even think about it," he said and waved it away with his hand.

Urma and Bill had finished their greeting, so I slipped inside their place.

"Becky has invited me for supper," I told them.

"I imagine crab is on the menu," she said, smiling. "Have a nice time… and… if our door is shut, just stay out a bit later," she added with a twinkle in her eyes. "I'll open it when we are done."

I got the point. What a funny place this is.

I thought this would also be a good time to invite Star for supper while her husband was washing up. So, I went to the door where I was fairly sure I saw her go in. I knocked on a red house, and a voice from inside said to come in. It sounded like her. Cautiously, I stepped in. Oh good. It was the right place.

"You and your husband are invited to dinner tomorrow, and I'll be cooking it at Bill and Urma's," I said.

"Oh, thank you!" she said.

"What is your husband's name?" I asked.

"Victor."

"So, you will come?" I asked.

"We'd be glad to."

I could see Tom walking towards Becky's, so I guess I will have to invite Mac, the doctor, and his wife after.

When Tom came inside Becky's, the kids ran to him and sort of jumped on him. It was a friendly attack, a bit of a game between them. Tom spun them around, and they screamed with glee. They obviously thought the world of him.

"So, how's my Tuesday's great catch?" Tom asked me.

"Tuesday's? What was your great catch of today, then?" I asked.

"A giant squid," he said, laughing. "But it wasn't alive."

"Addy and I caught the crab," Ryan told Tom. "She's so funny. Every time she saw one, she would scream. You should've seen her when one grabbed her skirt."

"Well, not everyone is as good as you, Ryan," Tom said.

Ralph appeared, said, "Hey man!" to Tom, and gave him a warm handshake. "Welcome, Addy," he said to me.

"Did you see my hair?" Roxanne asked Tom.

"Yes, and I was thinking, *Wow, don't you look like a lady?*" Tom said.

"Addy did it," she said.

"And you two have matching hair do's," he said.

"But guess what?" she said. "I braided Addy's. She showed me how."

"That is amazing. It makes me want to grow my hair out so you can braid it for me," Tom said, and Roxanne giggled.

"Sit down. Sit down, everyone." Becky called out.

Tom was beside me again and I wondered if the people here thought they could set the two of us up. Would that ever be crazy.

The crab was so good it melted in your mouth.

"Oh, you are all invited over to Bill and Urma's tomorrow for supper, as I am going to be making it," I announced.

"That is wonderful. That will be fun. I also heard you are a gourmet cook," Becky said.

"Well, I don't think it will be the greatest here without any stores around, but I'm going to try my best."

"Urma probably needs some extra chairs."

"And tables," I said. "I have also invited Victor and Star, and I want to invite Mac and his wife, everyone who has helped me somehow. So, that makes twelve of us."

"Well, I have six chairs, and I know Urma does, so I will bring them over along with a table tomorrow afternoon if you like," she offered.

"Thank you so much. That will give me one less thing to try to figure out."

"It sounds like you had a full day: planning meals, catching crabs, and doing hair," Tom said to me.

"Yes. Well, I can't sit still for a minute."

"So, tell us about yourself," Ralph said to me.

"I am the chief financial advisor of the largest investment firm in Toronto. I love my career because of all the excitement. There are just meeting after meeting and business lunches, business dinners, and business cocktail parties all the time.

"I have a condo on the harbour front on the forty-second floor. It is not very large, but I have it all decorated Japanese minimalist style. I had these cabinets custom designed to hold all my things, including my bed, which folds out. So, the only thing you would see is a long, shiny black table with a dozen cushions around it and one perfect orchid on top.

"My baby is my yellow sports car. Oh, I love my car. Well, I end up spending a lot of time in it with the traffic the way it is in Toronto.

"Saturdays, I might make a gourmet supper and invite ten or eleven people. Or I would be planning it for another week.

"I love to shop on Sundays. Toronto is a pretty good place for it. They have more European imports than any other city in the country. And there are terrific restaurants where I love to eat or go for a coffee or a special drink," I said.

"I think we would rather hear about you and not just the things you have," Tom said, cutting me off.

My face was burning.

"Are you really in love with your car, Addy?" Ryan said, giggling.

"No."

"Do you have any friends?" Roxanne asked me.

Did I? Of course not. Because I kept people far enough away. Though, I didn't know anyone like this.

I felt kind of sick. I don't need to be here. In fact, they will all be happier when I go back to Toronto.

I wanted to be fuming mad at Tom, but what he said wasn't out of anger, only disappointment.

For now, all I could think of was that I needed to get out of here. We had just finished dessert but were all still sitting around the table. However, there was nothing left for me to say.

Becky changed the subject, and everyone started to talk again, but I was not listening to what they were saying. I have to get out of here.

I pushed my chair back and stood up. Tom reached out and put his hand under my elbow, holding it firmly.

"Don't leave," he said in almost a whisper. "No one wants to hurt you."

4

om didn't let go of me, yet he was not gripping me forcefully. But something made me sit back down.

"There sure isn't any shopping here," Becky said. "It really takes getting used to. Even worse is when you do finally go because you must stock up with two months of groceries. You should see the looks the others give us when they see your grocery cart. And you can't use only one. It is usually easier to fill up your buggy, pay for it, and go back and refill it.

"We eat a lot of eggs, and they go in most things you bake too. Altogether we use a couple dozen a week and go shopping six times a year. That is sixteen dozen eggs. Do you have any idea how many that is to buy at one time?

"Shopping like that takes all day, and that is only for groceries. After you do that a few times, you don't enjoy it as much."

"Then we try to keep it all cool inside the boat," Ralph said.

"The grocery store knows our schedule and puts things aside for us," Tom said. "And we make sure we don't all go at once."

"Yeah, Tom even set up a system because the market in St. John's was unable to keep up. So, now everyone is spaced three days apart," Ralph said.

"It sounds so often, but that only gets us there once every couple of months," Becky said. "We need to own a few freezers and buy plenty of shelf-stable foods."

"We also have to buy fuel for the boats," Tom said.

They made shopping sound about as much fun as going to the dentist. In fact, I'm not sure how they can live like that. What stores could possibly be in St. John's?

"I better get going," Tom said as he stood up. "I've got a bit of paperwork to finish tonight." The rest of us stood up as well.

"Come, Addy," he said to me.

"I'm going to help with the dishes," I said.

"Oh, go on," Becky said. "Don't worry about a thing."

Why had Tom told me to come, and even stranger yet, why had I listened? He was standing by the door, waiting. Slowly, I came up to him, and we left together. We headed toward Urma's.

My feet still felt naked without shoes, but my high heels wouldn't be any good here.

"All I meant," Tom said, "… is that I know you are not really as shallow as that." Shallow? So, now I sound shallow. Who made Tom the living expert on the difference between an empty or fulfilled life? Yet it was shallow because my life was filled with things, only meaningless things.

"I haven't been myself lately," I explained. "I mean, I was close to death a couple of days ago and a near-death experience is sort of shocking."

"Hey, don't feel sorry for yourself," he said, but in a kind and gentle way. "Be glad to be alive."

I am, but that sounded like a dumb thing to say. What was the point of saying anything if he knew everything anyway? This is stupid. I turned to go in, relieved that the main door was open.

"Addy?"

I stopped. Should I just ignore him or turn around? I wasn't even sure anymore, but I twisted around.

"Come for coffee at six," he said.

It was mostly a statement with perhaps a hint of a question to it. Since it was not really a question, I guess I didn't have to answer. I just said, "See you," and went inside.

"You Ok?" Urma asked.

"I really should be heading back home," I said.

"You just got here, dear. Give it a little time. Besides, your body needs a chance to heal itself. It must have gone through quite an ordeal in the sea."

"I think I'm myself again," I said.

"That's good. Then you can enjoy yourself here a bit. You were supposed to be on holiday anyway. Of course, this isn't what you had in mind, but you are here," she said.

"I don't... fit in here, really," I said as I looked out the window.

All the living room windows here seemed to face the ocean, as did the front doors. Their kitchen was behind. The bedrooms and bathroom were on the second floor. It was odd that the windows in the back were very close to the rock, although they let some light in. Nevertheless, Bill and Urma's place had a neat view of both the village and the sea.

"We are a strange bunch, but you'll get used to us," Bill said.

I started planning the supper for tomorrow. Every time I entertained, I would write down the order I'd need to do things to keep it all perfectly organized. I planned which I could do ahead, and which should be done last. Tomorrow will be a busy day.

Oh yes. I better go see the doctor.

"Hello. I'm Adelle Lockheart," I said to the lady that answered the door.

"I'm Jac," she said, giving me a big hug. "Well, Jackie, but everyone calls me Jac. Mac and Jac.

"So, you are Tom's catch, or were you just reeling him in? He is quite the guy, eh?" She turned to Mac, who was coming to the door as well. "She seems to be doing well, wouldn't you say?" Turning back to me, she continued, "It is a miracle that you are alive after so long. So, tell me, what is it like to be saved, especially by a tall, dark, handsome man, might I add."

"Well, I wasn't conscious of too much at the time," I said.

"You must've looked beautiful with your gorgeous hair. And Tom probably thought he was dreaming," she said.

"My hair was up," I said, and quickly added the rest before she started talking again. "I wanted to invite you both for supper tomorrow. It will be at Bill and Urma's for everyone who helped me."

"Oh, isn't that sweet of you? Two days ago, you were close to death, and now you are cooking for all of us. That's some kind of strength you have, amazingly resilient. You must work out and eat very well to have such a healthy body, able to adjust like that. Do you eat lots of fresh fruit and vegetables? You see, we don't get to eat fresh things really, just canned or frozen. However, I heard that frozen fruits and vegetables are actually better because they don't spray them with chemicals to preserve them..."

Does she ever stop? I looked at Mac. He smiled.

Well, there would certainly be no problem with the conversation tomorrow. However, I always wait until everyone is finished with one course before I start the next. But if she keeps talking like this, it will take her hours. Now, they will all need to come back on Saturday to finish eating.

"... then he said, 'Addy is in good hands with Urma. I could do no better.' And so, I see it is. We don't get a lot of visitors here..."

"As you can tell," Mac threw in. He was nearly laughing now.

"Obviously. I mean, who would ever come here? Except for Tom's sister and family, hardly anyone ever comes, so it will be such a treat to have supper with you and get to know you a bit.

"You must tell me all about Toronto and your highfalutin job there. It must be such an exciting place with the traffic and everything. The noise would be nice.

"Here, everything is so quiet that you can hear yourself think. Way too much, if you ask me. Eventually, your mind starts to create different voices, if you know what I mean, but then you probably don't."

Finally, I snuck away. I planned a bit more for supper tomorrow.

"Let's see if you are on the news again," Bill said as he turned on the TV.

It was six o'clock. So, what should I do? I could stay here. Still, Tom seemed like a trustworthy person, but what was his plan? I wondered. Maybe Urma would know.

"Tom invited me over for coffee at six," I said.

"It is six now, dear," she said.

"Yes, I know, but why do you suppose he asked me?"

"Cause he likes you," Bill called from across the room.

"What kind of guy is he, really?" I questioned, ignoring Bill's comment.

"Oh, Tom would do no wrong. He is very respectful and honourable. You need never worry about Tom. He will have someone else there too," Urma said.

47

"Tom believes in not having sex before you are married," Bill said.

"Bill!" Urma said. "That's not what Addy was asking."

"Just as well, it tells you what kind of guy he is. We are glad that we're all married here," Bill said.

"Tom has a lot of family values," Urma said. "That's nice to see in a young person and very rare."

"It's not like he has a choice," I said.

"True," Bill said, smiling. "But once you get to know Tom, you will see that he never compromises on his values. There is a strength of character there—that's for sure."

"Well, I've got myself in enough trouble already," I said.

"Oh, Tom is just a quality-of-life kind of guy. He has no interest in money or what it can buy. He is actually very wise and only wants everyone to be happy," Urma said.

"Go," Bill said. "He's a great guy."

I shouldn't have told them, although it did ease my mind a bit about going to his home.

"I guess we missed it," Bill said. "I heard it was on yesterday again, but we forgot to check."

"Now it's too old for news," I said.

Maybe I'll stand outside of Tom's and listen to see if anyone is talking. Then I would learn if he had someone else there. How would Bill and Urma know? Because I bet this is the first time a single girl has been here, since he arrived.

I walked over but couldn't hear anything. It seemed quiet, but the light was on. Perhaps I should forget the whole thing and go back to Urma's.

At that moment, the door swung wide, and Tom was leaning on it, holding it open. And I could see Victor and Star on the couch inside.

"Hello," I said.

"We thought you weren't going to come," Victor said, getting up to shake my hand as we hadn't been officially introduced yet.

"I was trying to be fashionably late," I said.

Star came over and hugged me. "I know nothing about being fashionable, but it did keep us in suspense, especially Tom," she said, laughing.

"Why? What did I say?" Tom asked from the kitchen.

"Nothing. We were talking about your anxiously looking out the window every two seconds," Victor replied. And Tom just laughed.

Tom's place was what you would imagine a trapper's cabin to be, minus the trophy heads and rifles on the wall. There was a smoky, woodsy smell. But his home was completely uncluttered and very masculine.

He had a wood-burning fireplace covered in stone, with a boat painting above it. The couches were around it. They were dark brown, an espresso colour, all matching and fairly new. In the middle of the sofas were two old fishing crates with a thick piece of glass on top. This was the coffee table, and it looked striking. Also, the walls and floor were all wood. Behind the couch, there was his study. Yet it was a simple desk and almost antique looking. The surrounding shelves were lined with books.

Why have so many books when you can read online? But not that I would know, because I don't read recreationally.

On the wall opposite the fireplace, there was a small table with an old postcard on it with a picture of a boat. Above it, on the wall, was a black-and-white photo of a First Nations man in front of his fishing boat.

"That's my dad," Tom said as he was now behind me. And he handed me a glass of red wine.

For some reason, I wasn't expecting him so close and found myself looking into his eyes for a few seconds before I took it and went to the couch.

Tom also brought a plate of crackers and cheese. I love cheese. There are all kinds that I have tried. After it all, I decided that my favourites were Oka, a mild Brie, Havarti, and Gouda. Artisan bread or sesame rice crisps always go nice with it. However, this was orange Cheddar on soup crackers.

The wine was excellent. Though it was sweeter than I usually had, it had a full body. I imagine that wine, too, tastes better here. Maybe it's because of the wood from all the houses.

"Would you like a fire?" Tom asked me.

"Yes."

It was turning into a cool night, and that sounded perfect. I also never sat in front of a wood-burning fire. Every one I had ever enjoyed was gas because that was what the resorts and restaurants all had.

You could tell that Tom had a system for building one. Everything went just so in this very particular order. Then, after a second of lighting the match, the whole thing came alive.

Wine and cheese seemed a bit out of character for Tom. But what if I was wrong and had prejudged him? This was a nicely decorated place for a guy.

Taking a cracker, I felt this horrible guilt within myself for looking down at this specific type of crackers and cheese. Truly, I was a spoiled brat. There was nothing wrong with anything, and yet, I destroy my own happiness by making stupid comparisons.

It wasn't like I was raised in wealth. So, only in the last few years did I have nice things. But somehow, I had equated everything not expensive to my childhood, and I certainly didn't want to be reminded of that.

I sat close to the fire. Victor and Star were quieter than the other families, which was nice. Now, I could hear it crackle, and I could smell the smoky wood scent. And it was the scent Tom carried with him everywhere.

The cracker tasted terrific and did not bring back any bad memories. I guess I don't eat Cheddar often enough. Perhaps I could even buy soup crackers one day.

This fire was so much wilder than the gas ones and danced around unpredictably. It was strong and rugged like this place, this funny land of the sea.

My hair was soft and curly. I followed a long lock with my hand. Why did I never wear it down? Currently, it was picking up the warmth of the fire and I brought a few waves to my nose. Yes, it was absorbing the smell of it as well.

"What kinds of things do you like to do, Addy?" It was Star who asked now.

"I love to sing," I said, suddenly remembering something I could say.

Which I did. In fact, I would sing when I was sure that absolutely no one could hear me. I thought I actually sounded pretty good and seemed to have no trouble remembering words, either. But I never really considered it as something I like to do, yet it would be alright here. Though no one in Toronto could know.

"That's nice. There isn't enough music here. Jac can play the violin, but that is all, and we rarely get to listen to her," Victor said.

"Can she talk at the same time?" I asked with a grin.

"Oh, I see you've met," Tom said, laughing. "She is so funny, but has a lot of depth."

"You know everyone here very well, don't you?" I asked Tom.

"I like to make people my world," Tom said. "It is more interesting that way."

"Don't you get on each other's nerves, being so close?" I asked.

"Yes, especially in February and March, but we all learn things and cheer up when summer comes," he said. "It is essential to love everyone for who they are."

"I'm not so good with people," I said.

"I'm sure you are, but just don't get a lot of opportunities to be relaxed with others," Tom said.

"You must need to deal differently with others at your job," Victor said.

"People in cities don't make a lot of time for each other, I would imagine," Star said.

This was true. I was never relaxed with people. I was always on edge. Either I was in a business meeting, working, or busy trying to impress others with a gourmet meal. And the few other times I did go out with others, I was still trying to impress them in one way or another.

"That's all true," I said.

"Your hair is beautiful," Star said.

"Thank you."   .

"We are looking forward to dinner tomorrow," Victor said.

"Are you making a real fancy supper?" Star asked.

"I'm trying to make it as fancy as possible," I said.

"That'll be very special because not too much is fancy around here," she said. "I bet we could learn all kinds of things from you."

"Likewise," I said.

The fire filled the whole house with a smoky scent. It was sweet to me and so pleasant, and there was something so comforting about being here. I watched the flames dance around.

Tom came and sat close leaning toward me.

"What are you thinking, Addy?" he asked in an intimate way.

"Not much. I just never sat by a wood fire before. All the ones I've seen are gas fireplaces," I said.

"They don't even smell," he said.

"No. This is nice.

"I have a question," I started with a chuckle, "does anyone here own a cell phone? I take it there is no service here, but my thumbs are in withdrawal."

"Yes, no cell service, but some do. Especially if they have family overseas, then they might get one so they can connect to Wi-Fi and use a messaging app. Not much other purpose, though, cause everything else can be done on your desktop."

"But it's just more convenient. I don't want to boot up my computer all the time."

"All the time? What all do you do on your phone?" he asked.

"Well... order things I need, messaging, social media. I get updates on things, like sales."

"Like shoe sales?" he laughed.

"Sure."

"And here you discovered that you don't even need shoes," he said, looking at my feet.

"Do you even know what social media is?" I teased him.

"Yeah," he chuckled. "It's when you take pictures of what you had for breakfast and put it online for everyone to see."

I had to smile. "I'm guessing you're not on any. It could be a great way to connect with your sister and the kids."

"Margaret isn't on social media either. Doesn't it prevent people from actually talking?"

"I'm sure it does," I said.

"I need to be on for work. Newfoundland and Labrador RCMP. I tolerate it. Occasionally, I'm even forced to post something."

I smiled. "Well, most people do it for the feeling of community, but you have plenty of community right here."

"We do," he said.

"Actually, it's been nice to be unplugged," I admitted.

"You mustn't think I'm against you," he said, dropping his tone in a serious way. I glanced at him. Then I looked into his eyes. Yes,

I knew he didn't have a mean bone in his body. "You upset with me?" he asked.

"Not really. You were right," I said.

"I thought you were a real threat to our community at first, but I was too fast to jump to conclusions. It wasn't appropriate for me to cut you off at Becky's."

"Thanks. I appreciate it."

He smiled leisurely, got up, and poured more wine.

"Tell us how you would describe it here," Star said. "I wonder how an outsider would describe our home."

I thought for a moment. Then, in a slow, poetic style, I spoke.

> *This is the forgotten land. The land of the strong and steady waves.*
>
> *Not many can call this home except those who have the spirit to match. The land and the sea can be tested but never tamed, allowing only the chosen ones to stay.*
>
> *There is a rhythm, a slow and constant beat, bringing the men out to fish and then safely back.*
>
> *A hand slowly pulls you into the warm glow of the lights and the smiles of the people.*
>
> *The salty breezes carry the scent of freshly baked bread and buttery fried fish.*
>
> *The silence is broken only by the sound of the sea and the distant laughter.*

They were looking at me in a sort of daze.

"That's nice," Star said. "Did you just make that up now?"

"Yes."

"You should write it down, maybe," Victor said.

"I'd never remember what I said."

"That's pretty interesting," Tom said.

"You make it sound so... enchanting," Star said.

"Well, it is, really," I said.

"It's a special little place, I guess," Victor said. "It's like our own little world."

"Do you like Toronto?" Star asked after a brief pause.

"A big city is exciting. There is a lot of action and lots to do. But it's hectic," I said. "And it can be stressful."

We talked a bit more and laughed together. Then, when we were leaving, I turned to Tom.

"What kind of wine is this? I like it very much."

He got the bottle and showed it to me.

It was cheap wine. In fact, someone gave me a bottle of it once when they came over for a meal, and I used it for cooking.

"What's wrong?" Tom asked.

"Nothing. Nothing is wrong, and you wouldn't want to know what I just realized," I said.

"C'mon. Tell me."

He may think I'm laughing at him inside if I don't say anything. But if I told him my story, he would think so for sure.

"Well, I just realized that I definitely am a brat," I said, and Tom laughed.

"I thought you said I wouldn't want to know," he said. And I had to laugh too.

THE NEXT day, I started cooking right after breakfast. I knew it would take me longer in someone else's kitchen. Besides, everything had to be perfect.

Dessert would have to be made first so it could cool down. I made the crème caramel and the cinnamon plum sauce to garnish the plates. Then, I had to bake it in muffin tins.

Next was the stacked crab salad. I used a pop bottle to make the moulds. Instead of fresh tomato on the bottom, I had canned red pepper. Rather than yellow teardrop tomatoes, I heated and cooled some frozen squash. Also, there wasn't champagne vinegar to mix with the crab, so white wine vinegar would have to do. Instead of avocado, I would use chopped pieces of Brussels sprouts. It looked better than it sounded. Well, at least it won't turn brown. It is usually garnished with tall sprigs of chives sticking straight up, but I had to use asparagus instead. But it looked perfect as I removed the mould. Now, to make eleven more, but I'll need to do that just before everyone arrives. I blended up more red pepper and oil for the garnishing sauce.

There would be cream of garlic soup which I made up to the last step of adding the cream. But it is such a pain to garnish without fresh vegetables. I finally placed tiny pieces of mozzarella cheese into thawed spinach leaves. Although they were very tough to work with, I finally was able to tie up the ends, making little purses. I tested one in the microwave to make sure they would not explode. This would have to be my decorative element.

Crispy vegetable towers were the only thing I didn't change too much, because it was made with thin slices of potato deep fried and layered with different vegetables. And the garnish is a puree of peas and cream.

My main course would be these little fish parcels with a bit of prune, raisins, and dried apricots inside, along with spices. Lastly, it would be served with pumpkin risotto and some sautéed vegetables.

I spent all day in the kitchen, interrupted only by Becky and Urma asking if I needed any help, and lunch, of course.

There would only be five courses instead of seven, but I can't find any lime sorbet anyhow. Just as well, I think they'll enjoy it.

Finally, I finished folding my last napkin. They were paper, but who says you cannot fold paper napkins? So, everything was done moments before the boats came in.

Anyone who was anyone was outside now. Therefore, I watched the boats arrive. My hair danced around as I shifted from one foot to the next. This whole thing was always so moving.

I stared at Tom. I may as well admit to myself that I found him attractive, but why?

He waved.

For a while, I imagined what it might be like to live here. The pace was slow and steady, almost dreamy. I enjoyed all of today's cooking, but what would it be like to cook every day? I would get restless, being home all the time.

There was a soothing calmness here and even the sea, I felt, should've had bigger waves.

Upon arriving close to shore, I could see that Tom's boat had this absolutely massive fish suspended and hanging up by its tail. And I had never seen anything like it. I didn't know what type it was, but it was huge. Taller than him and weighing a ton, it caused

Ebonene Charles

everyone to clap and whistle. I felt very proud of him, but heaven knows why. A bunch of other guys helped Tom drag it out of his boat. Meanwhile, I slipped inside to start getting the first and second courses ready.

"Wow! You don't get to see one of those every day," Bill said as he came in. "Bluefin are pretty big. Do you know that it weighed in at 967 lbs?"

"I've never seen anything like it," I said.

"How much you miss," he said, smiling. "Hey, are we supposed to eat that or just look at it?"

I was stacking the crab salads. It is too bad there's no more room in the fridge because it ruins the effect if they get to see the course ahead of time. I was almost done when Mac and Jac came in.

"Oh, Addy!" It was a screechy type of scream. The kind that teenagers make. "That's so amazing!" Jackie was saying.

"I think I should be given some credit for the good attentive care I gave her," Mac said jokingly.

"Do you need any help setting the table?" Roxanne asked as she flew in the door.

"No. Thank you. It's already done," I said.

"How's it—My goodness, that is beautiful. I'm never going to want to eat mine," Becky said.

"How do you get it to stay like that?" Ryan asked.

"But there are no plates on the table," Roxanne said.

"I use a mould," I told Ryan. "I am dishing up everyone's plates for them," I added for Roxy.

"You should have a restaurant, Addy. Really you should," Jackie said.

"There are a million of them in Toronto. Trust me. I counted," I said.

"Then you should make one here. There are only forty-four of us here, but we would come all the time. We would just love that, wouldn't we, Mac?" Jackie said. Even she seemed to be at a loss for words.

"You don't expect us to eat that, do you?" Tom joked as he looked over my shoulder.

Soon everyone was seated, and I brought them their stacked crab salads.

They were afraid to touch them because they liked the appearance so much. And they were all pretty excited.

After, I took the plates and served the garlic soup. It got rave reviews as well, and I was really having fun.

No one knew what to do either, so some offered to do dishes for me between the courses. Others wanted to help me clear the table, bring the plates, or dish up. They could not seem to understand that they had to stay seated.

Next, I stacked and served the crunchy vegetable towers. But the women were asking me so many questions. How did I do this? How did I do that? In contrast, everyone was always so quiet in Toronto.

Finally, the main course was served, and I never had guests eat as much as they did. It was great.

Then the dessert was, of course, last.

I had more fun serving them than I ever had before because it was not so special to the people in Toronto. Yet here it was the event of the year.

Jackie was talking a mile a minute, but that didn't stop everyone else from visiting as well.

I would have to leave here soon, I thought, as I watched them all laughing and chatting together. But I realized that I didn't really want to go yet.

I was not as warm of a person as they all seemed to be. Could I ever fit in here? And what difference does it make anyhow? There is no vacant house, so it is not like I could move here, even if I wanted to.

Besides, I don't want to live alone much longer.

I looked at Tom. If only life was that simple.

Try as I might, there was no way to prevent these three ladies from doing my dishes.

"Addy, come walk with me." Tom's voice swept around the corner and landed on my shoulder. Yet no one else heard him at all. He noticed me looking at all the dishes I had dirtied. "They won't let you near them anyway."

I could feel my heart racing. I grabbed a sweater and some shoes Urma found that I could use. What on earth is wrong with me anyhow? Because no guy in Toronto could ever get away with lines like these.

We walked to where the boardwalk connects to the dock along the back row of houses. From this little spot, you could also look east to the horizon. They never get to see sunsets here in the summer, not with the time they go to bed, and of course, they are facing the wrong direction. It was still light out.

"How was it?" I asked.

"It was very fancy."

"But how did it taste?"

"It was so fancy, it made up for the taste," he said with a huge grin. "I'm just kidding. It was good. Everyone really enjoyed themselves, and it was a special memory for them. They'll never forget it."

"Will you make a legend about me?" I asked. He chuckled.

"It wasn't really that good tasting," I said. "I didn't really have the right things, but the most important ingredient I never had." Tom looked at me and waited for me to go on. "Love. Everything here, everything they do, is done with love. It makes ordinary things special. But the converse is also true. Without it, special things are ordinary."

"It wasn't ordinary," he said, looking straight at me.

"Addy, tell me about your past: your childhood, your mother."

"My mother died two years ago," I said.

"I'm sorry," he said.

"Don't be. I'm not. Some people's stories are warm, funny, and full of love. Some are full of tragedy and sorrow. Mine is depressing. After it all, people just shake their heads and say, 'No wonder Adelle is the way she is.'"

"Tell me," he whispered.

5

M y mother's sister apparently set her up with some guy at a bar so he would leave her alone," I started. "So, Mom got pregnant, and she dropped me off at my aunt's place as soon as I was born. My aunt had two children. She hated them and certainly didn't want me. I don't remember too much except that I had nightmares about her and was always hiding. Also, I had to hide from her kids and the men she brought home so they would not beat me up or try to do something worse.

"The neighbours felt sorry for me because I wasn't being fed properly or given decent clothes or a place to sleep. Of course, it's not that they liked me, but they made me a deal. They would feed me, buy me clothes, give me my own room, make sure I got to school, and protect me from my cousins if I did basic chores for them and stayed out of their sight. So, I had to clean their whole home, but it was a much better system than my previous one and they were never harsh.

"When I was around thirteen, though, the man of the house lost his job and started drinking. After that, he began to get violent.

"At fourteen, I ran away and ended up in a foster home. I stayed in a few while working hard at finishing high school.

"When I was done, I got a part-time job, my own apartment, and went to college. After graduating, I landed a career in a large investment firm.

"There isn't really anything else to tell. Oh yes, then two years ago, I received a call saying my mother had died."

"My mother died ten years ago," Tom said. "But I loved her, and she was always good to us. A virus. Then my father passed away seven years ago from a heart attack. He was a great man too."

"Sorry to hear that," I said. "Do you suppose it is better to have loved and lost than never to have loved at all?"

"Yes... just give people a chance," he said.

"Do you have any brothers or sisters?" I asked.

"I have a sister. She lives in Terrace, B.C., with her husband and two kids. She's a good girl and works hard. You would enjoy them. They all came to visit once."

"It must be nice to have family over," I said.

"It is. We have fun.

"You have a lot to give, Addy, so don't be afraid to. You'll enjoy it."

There are valuable lessons to learn in this place. I wonder if I would ever be as relaxed as everyone here because they are so comfortable around others. Also, they are not trying to prove anything or impress anyone. And they are all so warm, and I wasn't sure how to be that way.

Even the ocean was calm and at ease now. The water playfully splashed the rocks and rocked the boats and the wooden platform.

To walk onto the dock was like stepping into another world. One where I felt much smaller. I'd never seen the fishing boats up close before. They looked weathered and worn, tried and tested.

I strolled up to Tom's as it was calling out somehow and ran my hand along the stern. It was rough and strong and painted a dark grey.

I climbed up and stepped inside. Tom was right behind me, although he didn't say a word.

I walked to the end and glanced over the horizon. The excitement of working on a boat and the thrill of the sea seemed understandable. I could feel it now.

"You get a nice view of the ocean from here," I said.

"You bet. I hope I never have to leave."

"Yes. You belong here."

"And where do you belong?" he asked.

"I used to think Toronto."

"And now?"

60

"Now I'm not sure. I didn't even know any place like this existed before," I said. "What is Haida Gwaii like?"

"Lush. It is warmer there, and there are towns where you can get whatever you need. And if you really want to, you catch the ferry to the mainland. It is a huge island. There are many places to see, but it is still very wild and untouched."

"But you prefer it here?" I asked.

"It was harder to make a living there. Here the fishing is plentiful. Of course, this is a much harsher place, but it grew on me, I guess."

"Your dad fished as well?" I asked.

"Yeah. I would go with him even when I was quite young. I never wanted to do anything else."

What must it be like to be convinced of exactly what you want? Right from an early age, he knew what he was after.

In contrast, I never got to try on anything for size. I only wanted a job with authority. Why? Perhaps I desired to get even somehow with the world because I didn't have any control over my childhood.

"Addy, sing a song for me," Tom said.

"I don't just sing for anyone," I said.

"I'm not just anyone," he said with a smile.

"Are you going to fine me with some obscure by-law if I refuse?"

"Surely, you know of a song."

I looked at him, leaning against the side of his boat. He was calm. He was in control.

I sang the first song that came to my mind. It was one with a hauntingly beautiful melody that never had much meaning to me before. My voice carried over the water, and I almost impressed myself, quite honestly. The phrase that particularly grabbed me was when it said, "Now I know, I'm home at last."

He listened very attentively. He didn't fidget or smile or even break eye contact. After, he was quiet.

"I don't want to overstay my welcome here," I said.

"You can't."

"It's like adopting a stray cat," I said.

"No, it isn't. Besides, everyone is just starting to get to know you."

"But I don't know how to fit in here."

"Sure you do. You don't need to be unsure of yourself. They all think you're fascinating," he said.

"Why on earth would they find me fascinating?"

"Because you're mysterious."

"Mysterious?"

"Absolutely," he said.

"You think I'm mysterious too?"

"Not mysterious, but enchanting."

"You think I'm enchanting, and everyone else thinks I am mysterious?"

"Why are you repeating everything I say?" he asked with a chuckle.

"It is funny because it's *this* place that's mysterious and enchanting," I said, grinning, and he smiled back.

"I better get going," I said.

I slowly walked off his boat, off the pier and returned to Urma's, but he stayed there looking over the sea.

"EVERYONE REALLY enjoyed yesterday," Urma said after breakfast.

"Yeah. So, we decided that we are going to keep you," Bill said.

It was Saturday, so no one was heading out to fish.

"I can't sleep on a couch forever," I said.

"No. Only until we can get you married off," Urma said.

It was a good thing that there was a knock at the door right then. It was Jackie.

"We should have a potluck dinner and a dance tonight. You know how we would always dance, and there was no one for Tom to dance with? Now he would have a partner. It would be lots of fun, and we could teach Addy our little dance. It would be something to take home with you. Did you guys have any plans?"

"No," Urma said.

"Would you like to, then?"

"Sure. Just bring anything?" Urma asked.

"Yeah. It will be fun. Great. See you. I'm talking to the others." And she was off.

"Is everyone here invited?" I asked Urma.

"Yes. Absolutely."

That sounded interesting. The whole town or village or hamlet or whatever, together for a dance.

I would get to be Tom's partner. I wonder what kind of dance it is. But I hope it is not some strange, goofy sort of thing.

"Now that we are all aware of your cooking ability, what will you make for tonight?" Urma asked me. "And if it can use potatoes, that would be even better. I have some getting old."

"Do you like pierogi?" I asked her after considering it.

"Oh yes, but no one here makes them."

"I made them once, years ago, but it seemed simple enough."

It was a college party, and I didn't have much money, but I wanted to bring something tasty. Somehow, I also had a lot of potatoes then, but I can't remember why. I do recall it took a long time to make. I boiled them and fried them later, just before bringing them. They were a real hit and certainly better than the frozen ones.

"Everyone would love that," Urma said.

So, we both got busy in the kitchen. First, I found sour cream to thaw and there was bacon and onions. Next, I made a huge pot of potatoes and cheese and a massive quantity of pierogi dough after finding a recipe online. All afternoon I shaped them. Lastly, I fried up lots of bacon and added onion until it absorbed most of the fat. Man, did it smell divine.

Every half hour or so, someone would poke their head in the door and ask for some ingredient they had missed or to see what we were cooking. Then they would give delighted responses after we told them what Urma and I were making. You would think no one ever had pierogi and ham roast before.

The whole town smelled terrific. When I stepped outside briefly, the most amazing scents greeted me. Now I was getting hungry.

Soon I could see everyone starting to carry tables and blankets to the little place where the rock was more flat, kind of. The area of the smooth rock. I laughed to myself. It was beside the daisy field.

This was like a town fair or something, as if the circus had arrived. And excitement hung in the air.

After boiling all my millions of pierogi a bunch at a time, I was exhausted, but getting a bit excited myself.

I put them in the largest dish I came across. It was funny because when I first saw this dish, I thought it was some joke. Because who on earth would have such a large bowl? It looked like a planter, for a tree or something, as it was big enough to sit in. I have never seen this much pierogi in my life.

When I tried to lift the bowl, it was too heavy. I should have put it in two bowls instead. Finally, I was able to slide it off the counter, and I managed, although I surely would have a sore back tomorrow. Of course, there were plenty of strong fishermen around, but I wanted to join the procession of food, carrying what I had made. I slipped my shoes on and convinced Urma and Bill that I was fine and didn't need any help, except with the door.

Then I walked to the little place as the wind played with my hair, and the children laughed and ran all over. The air was full of talking, the scent of the food, and the welcoming saltiness of the sea itself.

I placed the bowl with a bit of difficulty on one of the tables. There was so much food. We had enough to feed hundreds, and there were less than fifty of us.

People spread blankets on the ground, and they stood or sat around talking and laughing while waiting for the others to arrive.

Eventually, everyone arrived. Tom made this loud whistle noise. I had no idea that it was humanly possible to make that blaring sound.

I wonder if it is also some emergency signal for when they are fishing. Surely, if someone were in trouble and whistled like that, the sound would carry over the water, and anybody within a few miles would come to his aid.

But now a silent hush fell over the little hungry crowd as Tom addressed them.

"This is once more testimony of our happy way of life here in Foley's Rest and the wonderful community spirit that makes this home. Thank you all for your very generous support, so please eat and drink and make memories to last during the long winter ahead."

Then Tom stepped back, and everyone took the plates they brought to the tables and began to put as much on as they were able to.

It struck me at that point that he was the leader here. He was the chief. Chief Tom Joseph.

Through all the talking and laughing, the food kept on disappearing. My pierogi got rave reviews, and were also going down fast. By the end of the evening, not one remained.

Everything was incredible. I, too, had to keep coming back to get a bit more of something. But I never enjoyed cabbage this much before. So, what on earth was in there that made it taste so good? These garlic cheese scones were terrific. And the dessert was the same. There were these brownies that had more flavour than this fancy chocolate torte that I used to make.

Finally, everyone finished, but they lingered and went to talk with others while the kids ran around playing.

After a bit, when a breeze started to cool the air, the women packed up the food, and the men folded up the tables. I covered bowls with ill-fitting plates.

Then, as people were carrying their stuff back and I was wiping down tables, Tom came up to me from behind and gave a playful tug on a lock of my hair.

"That was exceptional," he said. "Something tells me you found your secret ingredient."

"Thank you," was all I could think to say as I finished cleaning two tables.

Afterwards, he put them on their sides and effortlessly carried both out, one in each arm.

But it wasn't long before everybody came back for the dance. This was a dance that Ralph and Becky taught everyone to do. It was not from Norway but somewhere else in Europe, passed along from Ralph's family.

Someone brought this old ghetto blaster, and a cassette tape was placed inside. A cassette tape? Then all of a sudden, everybody there, all at the same time, were trying to explain the dance to me.

This dance could only work here, where the men were all solid muscle. Because the guys had to, from behind, lift their partner at the waist as high as possible while the women would reach a leg

65

out gracefully to the side. It sounded interesting and looked even more so. I received plenty of demonstrations and suggestions.

It reminded me of an old-fashioned folk dance. Ralph called out pretty clear commands, and I tried my best to follow them. Although it's an odd feeling, being the only one unaware of how to do something, they were all patient with me. It was special that they wanted me to learn it, like I was being accepted into their culture. After a few practice runs, I had it because Tom had to do the majority of the work and because he was an excellent leader. In fact, a person could dance any dance they didn't know with him because of the control this man possessed.

The dance began, and it was the most thrilling thing. It had to be the closest to flying you could possibly experience. To be whisked off your feet and gracefully lifted in the air was really something. Then I would always land softly because Tom had perfect control.

I never wanted it to end. However, I wasn't the only one out of breath when it did. Nevertheless, everyone danced to it again. I didn't ever remember having this much fun at a party.

Then someone played a slow song and Tom simply took my hand in his and put the other on my shoulder blade. My arm rested on his. He has such large hands. Though he was more awkward at slow dancing, he was still easy to follow.

The smell of his skin and clothes was a scent that always grabbed me somehow. I couldn't imagine a place that I wanted more to be. For this brief time, I was content and happy, carefree and warm. And I only wanted to enjoy the moment and not think of the reality.

Also, it seemed that everyone wanted me here in his arms. It was like I passed some exam and now was deemed worthy of their beloved Tom. Of course, knowing how much they loved and respected him, it would be an honour if they did feel that way, but I was probably jumping to conclusions.

I mean, could I really live this way, so slow and easy? Just spend the day cooking and cleaning, maybe raise a family?

That was the very first time that ever crossed my mind. However, Ryan and Roxanne were not the monsters I thought kids would be.

There wasn't a home with a nicer view than Tom's.

What am I thinking anyway? I live in Toronto. Being here for a few days does not mean I could move here. Because I don't belong here, even if I wished I did.

When I first arrived, I had my nose in the air. I looked down at everything and everyone, feeling sorry for all of them. Here I was convinced I could teach them a few things, yet they were the ones that taught me.

Did Tom still think I was feminist and materialistic? Old traits probably take a while to die, but they would not survive here with nothing to feed them.

The tape went on with another slow song, and I looked into his eyes.

I do have so much to learn, but I will try. I am starting to understand now.

Before long, the song finished, and Tom sauntered over to some others and talked for a while and then left. But he didn't even say goodbye or good night.

He walked away with more determination than usual.

Here, the dance continued. There were some quicker polka-type songs and more slow ones. I danced with Ryan and Tore, another boy there. Later, I made a circle with all six kids, and we spun around as fast as we could. They kept me company.

Finally, everyone got ready to leave. There was nothing left to pack up.

The ground here was funny, being either grass or moss, and all solid rock underneath. Regardless, it was suitable for dancing on. As long as you were careful you didn't twist an ankle.

"So, what do you think of good o'l Foley's Rest entertainment?" Bill asked me as we strolled back.

"It was great, but I would've liked to dance more," I said.

"Yeah, Tom is usually the last to leave. Strange," Bill said.

"He left because he's in love with you," Urma said.

"What?" I asked.

"He is thinking," she said.

I had an assumption that she believes she knows everything about him, but really doesn't.

SUNDAY WASN'T much of a sleep-in morning either. It seems that waking up happens at the same time every day. Breakfast, lunch, and supper all happen at the same hour without any watches or clocks pressuring them. It is all second nature here, a slow and steady rhythm, like the waves of the sea.

It soon became obvious that this was the day for relaxing because Bill was doing a crossword puzzle, and Urma was reading a novel.

"You guys don't watch much TV, do you?" I asked.

"No," Bill grunted. "In a place like this, it would be too easy to watch TV all the time. We used to, as did everyone else, but Tom turned it into something that is frowned upon here. It's not to say we can't enjoy a show, but we slowly found other things we liked to do instead. Now I can tell that we are much happier for it. We were so lifeless before. About a year ago, we cancelled most of our satellite channels because we weren't using them anyhow. Only have a few for the news and the odd game, and most everybody here is the same. It's kind of a positive peer pressure thing."

"Well, that's great, I guess. I'm not much for TV anyway," I said.

Even so, what on earth do I like to do sitting down? I never did get into reading. And now I felt restless.

"I am going to go walk around a bit," I told Urma.

The sun wasn't up yet, but still light enough that you could see.

That turned out to be a good choice because my spirits lifted as soon as I got outside. There is something about the ocean that gives me energy and I always feel excited whenever I'm near it. Maybe it is because of the power that it has.

I walked back and forth along the boardwalk many times. It's not long enough because it only follows all the houses.

Next, I went to the daisy field and sat in the middle of it. I plucked one, then two more.

I wonder if a person could braid these together and make a little wreath of daises? It took me a while to figure it out, but I finally found a way, and I made a circle of them and placed it on my head. I had to giggle at myself. What a silly thing to do. Yet as I stood up and the breeze caused my skirt to dance and my hair to fly, I felt like some enchanted fairy princess.

I walked down to the shore, as it was low tide again, and more rocks were exposed.

I know what kind of clothes would be perfect here. If I only had a very long simple dress, with a cord at the waist and sleeves that widened at the wrist. A cape would work for cooler weather. Middle-age or medieval-style dresses would be ideal for walking by the ocean here.

Beautiful pink colours dotted the clouds and the water in anticipation of the sun.

I walked along the shore, and that was fairly difficult to do because of the large rocks. Stepping onto one, I looked over the sea. I felt mysterious and enchanted, but also carefree, as I jumped onto the next rock. Then another. And I kept skipping from rock to rock as I made my way across the tiny waterfront and back again. After I was basically where I started, I noticed Tom behind on the boardwalk.

When did he get there? I didn't even remember looking in that direction exactly, so he could have been there the whole time. It should've been a bit embarrassing, but it only made some giggles come over me.

"Oh, hi," I said. "How long have you been here?"

"Not much before you came."

So, he did see my entire little dance. That is, if he was even watching.

"Not too much happening today," I said as I continued jumping from rock to rock, coming in his general direction. "I don't mean to interrupt you if you have come to be alone to think. This is a great place for that. I didn't notice you there, but not to worry, I won't bother you." And I turned and started skipping the other way.

"You don't have to leave," Tom said.

"No. After all, you do not own the sea." But I continued hopping along, slowly moving away from him.

"Addy, come here."

I stopped and looked at him, but was unable to read his expression.

He walked towards me after I landed onto a larger rock. I stayed there and watched him coming to me. Yet when he got close, I faced the water instead.

Feeling his grip on my waist, I was whisked up into the air like in the dance. I was a bird flying over the ocean. Then he turned around in a circle before placing me softly on the rock beside him and slowly removing his hands.

The colours were softly fading as the sun poked its bright head up.

"Sing another song for me," he said.

I sang this beautiful sad song about a man very in love with the woman he was to marry. Although she leaves him and is never seen again, he has a dream that she comes back and promises like before that it wouldn't be long before their wedding day.

Tom was quiet for a moment and then asked, "So, how long do you get to stay?"

"I have to be at work next Monday. I'll call the news station soon to see when I can get the helicopter out here."

"I'm glad to see that you recovered so well."

"Yes. I've had such good care. Though I'm going to miss this place," I said.

"Are you?"

"Of course. I have learned so much here. It's beautiful, and the people have been so nice. You have taught me a lot."

"I didn't mean to be teaching you lessons."

"Nevertheless."

The sun was still rising. That was the thing about Foley's Rest. Because they get up at a ridiculous hour and go to bed so early, I am always sleeping before sunset. But since we all faced east, there was a beautiful sunrise in the morning as it poked its head over the water.

An eagle crossed overhead, dived into the ocean and flew away with a fish in its talons. I was amazed, and my eyes followed it as it left.

Tom was watching me, I could feel it, so I just kept looking towards the water. Then, finally, I stepped onto a larger rock.

"What kind of animals live here?" I asked.

"Sometimes puffins nest on the other side of our island. Other than some bird visitors, only the fish of the sea. There are no trees. Eagles, however, can make their nest on the cliffs. But there aren't even insects here, really."

"Not even mosquitoes?"

"There is no still water for them to lay their eggs."

I glanced at Tom. And he leaned against a large rock now and watched me. I tried to see if I could get him to break his gaze, but no. He seemed perfectly content with his eyes on me.

What was he pondering? Was he considering how to ask me out? Was he reflecting on how beautiful I am? How much he wanted me?

Am I conceited or what? He is probably thinking of something entirely different and staring right through me.

However, putting aside whatever he considered now, he might like me. He spun me around and asked me to sing. And he teased me about my cooking and told me I had found the secret ingredient. He pulled one of my curls and danced with me. Also, he invited me for coffee on Thursday, built me a fire and served me wine and cheese. He said I couldn't overstay my welcome and that I was enchanting to him. I'm not ugly. I'm not evil. Tom has no other options. Why shouldn't he like me?

Because I am proud and stubborn, restless, and not accustomed to the way of life here.

Could I honestly, truly, give up everything I have and move here? I might be happy for a while, but I would surely get bored. After everyone gets used to me, they will find me annoying. And I won't know what to do when no one thinks I'm special anymore.

I don't think I am able to ever just fit in somewhere because I like attention too much.

"What are you thinking?" Tom asked.

"That I like attention too much."

"It's not exactly a bad thing. It adds variety around here."

"I may overdo it."

"Just be yourself, and everyone will enjoy your company."

"I don't really know who I am, especially here," I said.

"You do. It just surprises you, that's all."

"Perhaps."

The kids played together in the distance, and the cozy smoke of a fire someone had built drifted through the air.

"You are fortunate that you know exactly who you are, exactly what you want and exactly where you will be ten years from now," I said.

"It's not that hard. I made a decision and stuck to it. I turned it into what I wanted, chose to view things positively, made the best of what I had, and didn't worry about what I couldn't change. Contentment is nothing more than a state of mind."

It all sounded so simple.

A small iceberg floated by.

Yet Tom was still leaning there, watching me.

6

After a bit, I excused myself and walked back to Urma's. She was stirring some soup, and it smelled wonderful. And there were cheese biscuits in the oven.

"Did you have a nice morning?" she asked.

"It was alright."

"I like your crown of daisies."

"Oh my, I forgot about those. It must look a little silly."

"Not at all. It's lovely. Did Tom see you?"

"I ran into him in the harbour. Why?"

"Oh, you just look so pretty.

"You know what I was thinking?" She asked, changing the subject. "We should play a board game after lunch. Do you have a favourite? We have everything."

"I've never played one that I can remember."

"Would you like to?"

"Alright."

After lunch and dishes, Urma, Bill, and I tried a card game. They had to show me what to do, but I think I caught on quickly and it was much more fun than I imagined.

Bill kept pretending to try to see what my card said and when I would look at him, he would study the ceiling and whistle softly. We were all laughing quite a bit. He would always do the funniest things, without any care if it would put him ahead or behind. He didn't seem concerned about winning at all.

When the game ended, Bill suggested a movie and popcorn. I never made popcorn anymore. But it smelled so wonderful and was smothered with butter.

We watched one of the movies they had. Although it wasn't my type, I enjoyed it anyhow.

Afterwards, while we were making supper, Star poked her head in.

"Addy, I wanted to invite you for dinner tomorrow."

"Sure. That would be nice."

"I will invite Tom as well.

"So, how was your day?"

I told her it had been fun, and soon she was on her way.

While we were eating, I heard rain starting to drop on the roof.

"Do you guys get a lot of rain?" I asked.

"Oh, you have no idea," Bill said. "This is nothing."

"Yes, you were here on probably the driest week of the year. August is the driest month," Urma said.

"It rains at least nine months of the year and snows for two."

"And not rain like you would be familiar with. It comes down so hard that you can barely leave the house, and the snow is so wet that it is even worse," Urma said.

So, this place had an evil side. I tried to imagine everyone stuck in their houses.

They would be quietly reading, doing crossword puzzles, watching movies, knitting, playing a game, or doing a puzzle. But I would be pacing the floor and pulling my hair out.

Unless I was with Tom... although, he would be busy doing law enforcement stuff at his desk. But after? That is a crazy thing to think about. I don't even have a hobby. Certainly, I would need to find something to do.

Well, I don't have to worry, as I will not be here during the winter. Not this winter, and not ever again. Perhaps I will visit one day, but I'll do it in August.

MONDAY WAS baking day and the whole place smelled of cinnamon buns. Likewise, Urma was making all kinds of goodies to have for coffee or dessert during the week.

When someone could come and visit you at any moment, you must always be ready. I was beginning to understand that you had to have something in the fridge, cupboard, and deep freeze at all times.

Surely, it would be hard to keep the pounds off here. Yet no one seemed conscious of their weight, but I'm surprised they are as thin as they are.

Especially the men. They were solid muscle. I remembered Tom's colossal fish. It must be tough work fishing for these guys to be able to eat like this and never have any fat on them.

I helped Urma by making this cake with tomato soup, which I never thought was possible. And it was iced with a cream cheese icing. She also prepared a blueberry crumb cake. Lastly, I made a lemon loaf while she started some bread.

After lunch, I headed out to find Roxy.

"I figured out something really neat yesterday, and I wanted to show you," I told her.

"Ok, come and see the picture I'm painting first."

Perhaps I could take up art of some sort and paint or draw. Surely, it is not that hard if you wanted to. Maybe sculpture. Yes, that would be more my style. I will have to try that sometime. However, it is not like I have time for that in Toronto.

Her picture was of a fishing boat in the water. Painting in the background afterwards is not the greatest idea, nor is using such dark colours. And from the angle of the boat, the perspective was all wrong. Probably I couldn't do much better, though.

After I praised her little boat painting, we went to the daisy field, where I showed her how to braid a wreath.

She was quite enthused about it, so we sat in the field making braids of daisies under a cloudy sky. Roxy worked hard on hers until it was just perfect.

"Let's play princess," she said.

"Who is the princess?" I asked.

"We both are."

"Ok, but I must admit, I know nothing about being a princess."

"Well," she said, laughing, "neither do I."

So, I tried to pretend I was a princess in a faraway land. However, it occurred to me that, really, I was.

I seemed to have no problem transforming my imagination. I could see things and hear and smell everything that I imagined should be around me in this story that unveiled itself as we played.

She was my sister, and we lived in a castle, and we heard about some evil plot in the land that we had to try to fix. We rode in a horse-drawn carriage. We got caught, however, by the bad man, despite running as fast as we were able. Next, he put us in the top of a tall tower, and we needed to be rescued by a knight in shining armour and his dragon.

Roxy had no trouble following the whole story. When it was over, she told me I was a very good princess.

Soon, the boats were coming in, and I stood with Becky.

I was restless, though, as if I was in the wrong place. When the specks in the water became visible, I walked to Urma's and joined her. Still, this was not where I belonged. So, I tried the centre where the rest of the women were, but no.

A strong gust of wind came from the ocean and swept over me.

Slowly but steadily, I arrived at Tom's place and stood in front of his home. I put my hands on the rail and looked over the water.

I could make out the figures of the men now, and it was obvious which one was Tom.

Here the breeze was stronger with no other homes to break it.

A sudden notion came over me that this was where I was meant to be. I wasn't going to analyze it right now, but just enjoy the way it warmed my insides. The feeling of being home. The feeling of belonging somewhere and to someone.

At that moment, I wasn't interested in thinking ahead, but doing what felt right to me. What was real was that I was here, and I was falling in love with Foley's Rest and the idea of belonging here.

Standing at his place is more than a subtle hint.

Tom was not one to act rashly, I was aware of that, but he did have about fifteen minutes to think while the boats came closer and closer. Time to consider what it is like for someone to be waiting for him. Time to think what it would be like to greet me, to take me in his arms…

I watched him intently as the breeze threw my hair around. Even though he was now turned my way, I couldn't yet read his expression.

Time seemed to stand still, as it took forever for the boats to come closer. Then, slowly ever so slowly, they came.

Although the expression on his face was clear now, I was unable to make out what he was thinking. However, there was no doubt that he was looking at me.

My heart gradually beat faster as the boats arrived.

They docked, and the men unloaded their catch.

When Tom was done, he locked his eyes with mine and slowly walked over. My heart began pounding. That was all I could hear, and the whole world started to spin. Now everyone was kissing. That much was obvious, but I did not dare look away. And I couldn't.

As he reached the steps, he broke his gaze and looked down. When he wasn't more than a foot from me, he finally looked up.

"This is not a game, Addy," he whispered, and then walked right past me and disappeared behind his door.

Yet I was unable to move. I was stuck staring at his door for a few seconds before I tore my gaze away. Besides, there was Urma, Bill, Star, Victor, Becky, Ralph, Roxy, and Jackie, all watching me. I had an overwhelming urge to run, but forced myself to walk instead. Before my eyes started to burn, I made it to the daisy field.

I wonder if everyone thought I did the wrong thing, or Tom.

Once I was in the middle of the field, I fell to my knees.

The tears were rolling down my cheeks now, and I had a pathetic sense of romance to keep them there and not wipe them away. But I held a few daisies in each hand and let my tears drop on them.

How embarrassing to have everyone see him reject me like that.

I should've known better. In such a small community, nothing is private. So, why didn't I take that into consideration?

Eventually, the tears stopped.

I was invited to Victor and Star's place for supper, and since I had never been there before, it was important to me not to cancel. After a while, I felt that my eyes might not look red anymore, so I slowly walked to their home.

Ok, that was not exactly the most brilliant move. And I knew that. One who has worked so hard to gain the respect of everyone here is not going to throw himself into my arms. At least, not without thoroughly discussing our relationship first.

Still, regardless, that was a blatant rejection, and he was perfectly aware of that. I am strong, and I can take it. Not everything can be perfect here. I can forever carry a bittersweet memory of a special fisherman, the loving, kind people, and the sound and smell of the sea. The strong and steady waves will carry me home and be with me my whole life.

I held my head up, and after knocking, I opened Star's door.

"I'm so happy you could make it," she said warmly.

Tom was there already. I glanced at the clock on the stove and was surprised but glad to notice that I wasn't in the daisy field for that long.

I immediately sensed that Tom was uncomfortable. His head was slightly bent down even when he peered up at me. The look and pose of complete confidence were gone somehow.

And for some evil reason, I found a small comfort in his uncomfortableness. I mean, it was better than seeing him as his usual self, as if nothing at all had happened, as if he didn't succeed in being the first one ever to hurt me.

Even though my heart ached, I kept my head lifted.

"We sure enjoyed supper on Friday," Victor said.

"Thanks. It was a lot of fun," I said.

"You should stay and make a restaurant," Star said.

"You would all have to eat out every second night. Besides, you wouldn't be able to afford me, and where exactly would this restaurant be?"

"We'll build you one," Victor said.

"That still would never work. Could you imagine my grocery shopping?"

"That's true, but we would sure like you to stay."

"Maybe I should get a fishing boat," I said as they laughed, except Tom, who just smiled.

We all sat down to eat, and Tom's place was beside mine, or more likely, it was the other way around. I think everyone here would like to see us get together. Everyone except Tom, that is.

He didn't look at me as usual. But instead, he kept looking straight ahead.

"What are you going to do when you get back?" Star asked.

"Put in my two weeks' notice to quit my job."

"Really? Why?"

"That was something I told myself I would do if I survived. It is time for a change, anyhow. Then I don't know."

"You don't like your job?" Victor asked.

"Oh, I have certainly enjoyed it, but it is all-consuming. I want to take a bit of a breather and get to know myself."

"That is kind of why I came here," Victor said. "Everything was at such a rushed pace. I used to have an office job, but this was different. Things were slow and constant. And moving here was the best thing I ever did. I would say I didn't know myself before, either."

"I don't even have any hobbies or anything. I plan to change my life quite a bit because it has been very empty," I said.

"It's people that make your life full," Tom said.

"I never had any room for people in my life before, but I would like to change that somehow."

We went on to talk about lighter subjects afterwards, and Tom slowly became more relaxed, but he still didn't laugh when we did.

This happened to women all the time in Toronto. They would fall in love with some guy, convince themselves against all conceivable odds that the feeling was mutual, and then be heartbroken to find that it wasn't true.

Tom is a nice guy who cares about everyone here. He cares about everyone that visits here and their friends and family too. He wanted me to learn something here. So, why did I believe that it was more?

After a while, I got restless, so I thanked them for the meal and excused myself.

As soon as the cool air filled my lungs, I had to release some energy somehow, or else I would start crying again. So, I ran back to the daisy field. And if I could just keep moving, I wouldn't get cold.

A song started to play in my mind. It was a fast song without words, but I began to sing the tune anyhow. I sang softly at first, but it made me want to dance, so I did. As I got more and more energy, I started to sing louder and louder and continued dancing and twirling around. All the while, the violin played clearly in my head.

The air was still cool, but I was warm. I was likely singing way too loud, but I didn't care.

The couple who lived the closest stepped outside, but they were smiling, so I didn't stop and knowing I was being watched only gave me more energy. At one point, I saw Mac and Jac. Then Jackie left and came back with her violin. Someone else had some drums that looked like ancient native artifacts.

Soon I had a drumbeat, and Jackie was able to play the song I was singing. Even though she did so a little differently than the one in my head, it still worked.

It wasn't long before the whole town was out, all watching me. Becky and her family, as well as Urma and Bill, were there too.

I remembered the conversation I had with Tom yesterday.

"I was thinking that I like attention too much."
"It isn't exactly a bad thing. It adds variety around here."
"I may overdo it."
"Just be yourself, and everyone will enjoy your company."
"I don't really know who I am, especially here," I said.
"You do. It just surprises you, that's all."

I saw Tom in the distance, leaning on the side of a house on the boardwalk behind everyone else. He was watching me intently and didn't turn away when I glanced at him.

I sang and danced my heart out. When Jackie ended the song, I did a curtsy, and all those gathered clapped and whistled. Then they called out, "One more time."

I was nearly out of breath, but somehow couldn't resist.

We started the song out slowly but gradually got faster. People started tapping their feet and bobbing their heads, and the kids danced around in a circle.

I couldn't for a second forget about Tom. In fact, that was what kept me going. Jackie made the song one big loop, so it didn't end. Finally, when she stopped, I thought I might drop dead.

Everyone clapped and clapped and whistled. It sure doesn't take much to entertain them.

I slowly made my way through the crowd, and Bill put his arm around me.

"Come on, our little dancing queen," he said as we walked back to their place.

IT TOOK me quite a while to fall asleep, and man, was I stiff when I got up in the morning.

After breakfast, I stood outside with my coffee. It was time for me to make plans to leave, but I knew this place would never leave me. It's a strange feeling when you realize your life has changed, and things can never be the same.

I need to be at work by Monday, so I should probably get them to send a helicopter Thursday or Friday.

People walked past and waved. I waved back.

"I guess I should contact CBC News," I said once I was inside Urma's.

"We're really going to miss you."

"Why?" I chucked.

"You have a lot of energy."

"I can't dance like that every night."

"No, but you always have a lot of energy. We get into a rut here, but you are fun because you are so unpredictable."

I smiled. I didn't know that, or at least I never saw myself that way.

"What can I do for you before I leave?" I asked Urma.

"Oh, nothing, dear. Just promise to keep in touch."

"I don't think I can," I said. "I like it too much here. To try and keep in touch would be painful. This is somewhere you need to feel, not talk about. I can't imagine how I could even come to visit ever unless I arrange another plane crash."

"You could fly to St. John's, and one of us would get you there," she suggested.

"And stay on your couch? There is no place for me here, but if that ever changes, then maybe I will be back." She looked at me as if she knew exactly what I meant.

"I'm having trouble accessing my email account from your computer," I said.

"I can't help you there. Usually, Tom gives us a hand with everything that doesn't work. He set it up simple for us."

"There's a security feature on or something, but I don't want to change any of your settings by accident."

"You can use Tom's."

"Surely, Becky, Star, Jac, or anyone else has a computer I can borrow."

"I suppose so."

"How about I make some more pierogi and freeze them so you can have them later? And this way, you guys won't forget about me."

"We wouldn't forget you, but that would be lovely."

Therefore, I got right to work and made lots of pierogi. That is what I did all day long and think.

Exactly a week had passed. However, it felt like only yesterday and yet a lifetime away. And the experience was more interesting than Paris would've been. More life-altering.

I did not want to leave, yet I was excited to change my life and start over. I would quit my job and perhaps even sell my condo. And then? Who knows? It brought a feeling of freedom but also an emptiness that weighed me down.

"Are you doing alright?" Urma asked.

I knew full well what she meant, so there was no use discussing it. "Yes. I guess."

"It's nothing more than a conflict of culture."

I tried to contemplate that, but it didn't make sense, really. How could such an obvious rejection in one culture mean "I love you," in another? What were the cultures being compared? How males think versus females? But it was not location-based because everyone here understood the refusal. I wasn't up to discussing it, so I left it alone.

"Tell me about the winters here," I said.

"They are a tough time for all. If you can make it through the winter without wounds that take all summer to heal, then it is a success story. You can't do anything while it's that cold.

"It rains steady and hard. This is why the houses are all on stilts. The waves are a little stronger, and everything is wet.

"It is dark all the time. The clouds are so heavy that even when it is supposed to be day, you barely notice. It makes everyone depressed.

"You can't just stay in every single day, so you visit, but the others are miserable too, so you make enemies out of your friends."

I tried to imagine. And I wasn't sure I could occupy myself if I were not working, never mind if I had nowhere to go, and it was always dark.

"Summer is August?"

"Yes. That's basically all."

"How can you live here if you are miserable eleven months of the year?"

"Well, it's not all bad. It can be kind of cozy. You learn so much, and this is a very nice community. It becomes a way of life, I guess. Even though there are things that drive you crazy, it's still home, and every year it gets better and easier to deal with. The first one is definitely the worst."

"Do the guys fish through it all?"

"Oh, yeah. Unless there is a terrible storm. Sometimes, maybe once or twice a year, in the evening, the winds will pick up something horrible and toss the boats around. So, as to not let them get damaged, everyone stays up all night holding onto them. Then, the next day, the men will stay home, and only then. In the morning, the sea is always calm, well, calmer anyhow."

"Do you all have... I mean, is someone in charge of this community?" I asked.

"Tom. There is no political structure exactly, but I guess the traditional way is to have a leader, and he fits the description. He does such a good job, so no one complains, except maybe by the end of winter. Tom gets a bit busy then."

"What happens?"

"It's just that boredom causes too much thinking, so someone may decide that they would make a better leader. The only problem is that since no one made Tom the leader, no one can take that away from him either. So, they end up making idiots of themselves and eventually do something illegal, and Tom has to step in. Then things are quiet for a while."

"That's hard to imagine. Everything seems so peaceful here."

"And it is, mostly, but you can't have a life with no troubles whatsoever. Then you would never learn anything."

I finished the pierogi and put them all in the freezer.

The sun poked out of a cloud, and I went outside and walked along the shore.

A lady that I didn't know was coming toward me. "Hi, I'm Jane," she called out. "I've heard you singing here for Tom. I'm in the first house here. You have a gorgeous voice."

"Thank you."

"Have you enjoyed your visit here?"

"Yes. I've learned a lot."

"This is a very different place, but it grows on you. I think you would be able to live here," Jane said.

"There is no place for me here."

"There is. You will see."

"Well, thank you. What makes you think that I could survive?" I asked.

"You are creative with energy and life."

"Why do you say that?"

"Everyone here knows everything that is going on. It all gets around. Anything that is spoken, everyone hears. Anything that is done, everyone finds out about. But we all want you to consider staying because you liven up the place," she said.

"I can't stay."

"Why not?"

"If everyone knows everything, then they all know why," I stated.

"Everyone does know everything, and we all understand Tom a lot better than you do."

"But he probably knows me a lot better than everyone else does."

She actually seemed stumped by that comment.

"We still think you should stay."

"Thank you. I have a condo, a vehicle, and a job. Everything I own is in Toronto, so I can't stay. But perhaps I'll be back one day." I added, to end the conversation.

How could I ever be back? They all want someone new, something fresh. And they all have some crazy idea that Tom likes me, just because there has never been a single girl here before.

I think they would all like to see Tom "settled" and married with children. You can't blame them, I guess. That is what life is about here. And there really isn't anything going on. What else could they possibly find to gossip about?

"I understand that you have things to take care of first. But when you come back, remember that you always have a home here. Everyone wants to get to know you. They all speak well of you, so you can walk into anyone's place here, and you would be welcomed. I wanted you to know that," Jane said.

"Thank you. That means a lot to me." And it did.

"We would've all swarmed you except that we wanted Tom to spend as much time as he wished with you. We'll get to know you better later," she added before leaving.

I can see that when the village decides something, their minds cannot be easily convinced otherwise.

I watched some of the crabs scurry around for a while, and then I saw Tore coming toward me. He is fourteen, the oldest kid here.

"Hey!" he said as a greeting. "How's it going?"

"Fine, I suppose.

"What kind of things do you like to do?" I asked after it became apparent that he didn't have anything he had to tell me.

"I collect and make authentic native weapons," Tore said. "Would you like to see them?"

I admit that I was curious and interested in doing something or seeing something.

I was also interested in being with someone who was not going to give me pep talks about how much Tom loves me. There couldn't be a better choice than a fourteen-year-old boy. All things considered, I nodded, and he led me to his home.

"Hi, Addy. I'm Sylvia," his mom said, giving me a very warm handshake with both of her hands. "It's so nice to finally meet you. Well, I met you at the dance, but you met everyone there, so that doesn't count."

Sylvia was not a bad decorator. Her home was also full of open grain wood, but it was not cluttered like Urma's and Star's. It sort of looked like a cabin. Although it was rather rustic, there was a theme, not just a combination of everything that was collected. There were paintings of birds everywhere.

Tore was waiting patiently for me to follow him into his room.

There I found a massive table with a glass top. And it, too, was made of unfinished wood. Tore raised the glass, which showcased all of his collection. Next, he lifted a stone that was shaped like an arrow and mounted onto a tattered stick of some sort.

"This was the first piece that I found. We don't know exactly how old it is, but this place has not been inhabited for a very long time before this community was established. And this handle is made of bone. This rock must have been shaped this way and used as an arrow," Tore explained.

"What would you shoot it at here?"

"It must have been used for the seals that could come up onto the rock. The only animal that is not in water is the eagle, and the Indigenous people would never shoot at an eagle. Then later, I found this." He held up another rock fashioned with a point much larger than the first. "See the hole that is carved out here? It would have been attached to the retrieving line, and it would've fit into a long stick which all would have decomposed by now, but this must have been a harpoon that would have been used in whale hunts."

"You found all of these things?" I asked.

"No, only these two, although I'm always looking for more. All these other ones Tom helped me make.

"After finding these, we thought, why can't we make weapons just like they did? So, then I would collect rocks and break them open with other ones until I got nice sharp edges. See how sharp this one is? Then we would make handles for them out of sticks that wash up on shore, like this one, or from bone. This bone Tom found. Then if ever I find an eagle feather, I keep it and attach it like this," he said.

"That is really neat."

"I wasn't sure if you would be interested in these, but that is what I like to do.

"See this knife? When I broke one rock, it came out looking like a knife blade, so Tom helped me make a handle for it."

Tore handed it to me to examine. It was neat how the rock was the shape of a knife blade. I ran my fingers down the handle which was so smooth. At the base, it was carved T.J.

"What does this stand for?" I asked.

"Tom Joseph or Tore Johnston."

"What is this handle made of?"

"Some kind of bone. When Tom or Dad are fishing, sometimes they discover a bone in their net from an animal that died."

I was able to carefully examine all of his collection. It was amazing, actually.

Afterwards, I had a quick coffee with his mom.

"It is nice that Tore has such an interesting hobby," I said.

"Yes. It was so kind of Tom to take an interest and get Tore going on this whole thing. He is so good with all the kids, especially the boys, and he spends quite a bit of time with Tore probably because he is the only boy without a brother or sister," Sylvia said.

Soon I had to leave because the boats were about to come in.

But I didn't watch for them. What was the point? That was for lovers, and it would break my heart.

I missed it, though. There was something so moving about it, something that pulled you to be a part of it. Consequently, I felt empty and imagined that I was outside waiting.

We had a nice quiet supper, just Bill, Urma and I. And it was the first time having supper here without Tom.

While we were doing the dishes, there was a knock, and Tom came in. He didn't barge in like usual but stood cautiously at the door. Bill and Urma gave him a warm welcome, and he took off his shoes.

7

"Oh, Tom," Urma said, "Addy needs to use your Internet."

"You're welcome to," he said, holding my gaze.

"That would be good. Unfortunately, I can't access my email on theirs."

"Ah, yes. You can all come to my place if you want," he said.

Everyone seemed to be in agreement, so we headed to Tom's instead.

I was able to sign in on his laptop. But I didn't have a single personal message. It was all just the regular ads of things I had subscribed to. I never checked work emails on holiday, so I wasn't going to that account. Did I have any friends at all? Although, I guess all the people I spent time with were business contacts, and they didn't have this address.

I emailed CBC and requested my helicopter ride on Friday.

Urma and Bill sat on the couches and had a beer.

Tom made me a hot apple cider.

"So, I told them I can leave on Friday," I announced. And they stared at me. "I need to be at work on Monday, so that will barely give me enough time to get used to city life again."

"Are you excited to be going home?" Bill asked.

"No, but I am a little excited about some of the changes I'm going to make. I can't wait to apply some of the things I learned here... I actually have a feeling of freedom."

"Well, that's good, I guess," Bill said slowly.

"In the meantime, you all must decide what gift I can get each of you."

"You don't have to buy us anything," Urma said.

"I know that, but if I do, I might be obliged to bring them."

"If that is what it takes."

Perhaps I could come for a visit. Or just mail everything.

We continued to have a nice evening talking, but Tom still didn't say much.

"Can I check for a response tomorrow?" I asked.

"Sure."

As we were leaving, we ran into Becky and Ralph and the family, so I broke the news.

"Can you get me a really big teddy bear?" Roxy asked.

"Roxy!" her mom scolded.

"How big?" I asked her, and she jumped up to show me. But I reassured Becky that I was glad to know.

Ryan, however, needed some time to consider it.

As I got ready for bed, an overwhelming sense of sadness came over me to think that I was leaving here.

I SPENT the next day at Becky's casually talking and laughing as she did the laundry and hung it to dry on the clothesline outside.

At some point, out of nowhere, Becky asked, "Addy, what do you think of Tom?"

I thought hard.

"I respect him."

"We all respect him," she said in such a way that it convinced me that was not the type of answer she was looking for.

"You saw when I waited for him."

"Tom is a very good guy, so he would never want to hurt you. He is just... well, he's going to do everything right. There was a reason, but it's probably not nearly as bad as you are imagining. Besides, you are romantic and spontaneous, and Tom isn't. Well, he is certainly not spontaneous. We all hoped that he would greet you, but I guess it would go against his character to be so rash, but I'm sure that doesn't reflect what he thinks of you."

89

"On the other hand, I am glad he didn't do anything he would regret later. He always wants to do things right, and I know that he is wise. He knows me, I think, and he also knows what he wants," I said.

"Perhaps, but men aren't as simple as that to figure out. And they see things differently. Tom is especially a lot more practical. What you don't know is what he is thinking."

"Maybe so, but he can tell me otherwise if he feels he left the wrong impression."

"He will, but it'll probably take some time," she said.

"Well, I leave the day after tomorrow."

"He is likely waiting for something. He needs to find out something or be convinced of something."

"You guys haven't seen anyone fall in love here before. So, you don't have any reason whatsoever to believe that Tom has any feelings for me," I said.

"He looks at you differently."

"How many single females around his age visited here in the last five years?"

"That's beside the point," she said, laughing.

"Do you like having children? Did you decide to be a mom?" I asked her. I always wondered about this, but this was the first mother that I really knew.

"Yes. Ralph and I decided to start a family. I always wanted to be a mom. Ralph wanted kids too. It really is a challenge, and I have days that they drive me crazy, but I wouldn't change it for the world. You form a bond with your children that is almost hard to explain.

"It amazes me to no end that Roxy and Ryan are a part of me and the man I love. They are half me and half Ralph. How they grow inside you from nothing, well, that is when you start to love them. You can't help it. They are a very special part of my life and are what make it complete."

When it was time for the boats to come in, I stayed inside at Urma's place, but I felt somehow cowardly for doing so.

All of a sudden, I heard a big commotion. Everyone was whistling and cheering, so I looked out of the window. Thank goodness Bill and Urma live in the centre of this circle.

Mac had some massive beast in his boat. What was it? Oh, just a fish, but it was big. No, it was huge, but it didn't look quite as large as Tom's that one day. Nevertheless, Tom jumped into Mac's boat and helped him haul that thing off.

They should roast it on a spit.

I will never look at tuna the same way again.

"Did you see that thing?" Bill called out to me as soon as they stepped into the house.

"Yes. I looked out the window."

"The fishing here is seriously the best in the whole world," he said. "That's because no one else is crazy enough to come out here.

"We had quite an event today, though. Jim hit an iceberg. He signalled to us, and so Tom, me, Mac, Victor, Ralph, and Cody all went over to his boat, and we were hauling everything to the other side for weight to tip up the damaged part a bit. Then we are all hammering wood boards as the water is gushing in. We got it, though. It was good that we saved the boat. Then we were hauling out water. What a pain.

"It is so hard to dry out the inside of a boat when the water floods in. It often goes mouldy.

"They have their work cut out for them tonight, but Tore is a good kid. He's pretty helpful. They'll take everything out right away and do repairs.

"So, we barely caught anything, but at least Jim still has his boat."

Bill grunted and groaned a bit as he stretched out his arms.

"You're my hero," Urma said to Bill.

"Addy, aren't you proud of me saving Jim's boat?" Bill asked.

"Immensely."

"Well, as always, Tom is the guts and brains behind everything, but we are very supportive.

"I'm starving," he concluded.

We sat down to eat. I was hungry too.

After supper, I walked along the shore for a while to burn the image into my mind so I would never forget it. I wanted to just drink it all in.

I had better check my email too, so I knocked on Tom's door.

"Yeah, come on in. I'm heading out to assist Jim, but help yourself. My laptop is on the desk."

I sat in his empty place, but I still felt him around somehow.

Yes. They responded and told me what time they would arrive. They planned a televised interview at the airport after and then were sending me on a plane home.

So, it was done. And I only had one full day left here.

I closed everything up and stepped out, and there was Tom, Jim, Sylvia, and Tore, busy hauling items out of their boat.

I felt rather dumb just to stand there, so I headed over and helped them fill boxes with things to carry out.

It was only seconds before others came as well, and soon it seemed to me that the whole community arrived.

There could be no mistake in thinking that whenever something needs to be done, Tom was there. Now he was directing everyone. Some were to repair the outside, others to fix the inside. Some were to strip the floor inside and treat it. Others were to wash the things that were taken out.

It was interesting that they had this perfect traffic system because the stair leading down into the boat is narrow and winding, so if someone was going down at the same time that someone else was going up, they could run into each other, literally. To avoid this, they would always call out "going up" or "going down" ahead of them, and the others would wait.

It was neat how it was like a little suite down here. There was a bed and table with chairs, a bathroom, a small sitting area, and a mini kitchen.

There were not many things really, so it didn't take me long to finish packing the boxes.

Tom was carrying out furniture. It was interesting that he carried out items by himself, whereas the other guys always did it in pairs.

"Tom, what should I do now?" I asked as he was walking out with some solid wood cabinet.

"See that mop there? In the pail is a bottle of this mould killer/preventer stuff. If you would be so good as to start mopping the clear areas, that would be great."

The men here probably don't even know how to use a mop. I could sense the fear in their eyes whenever one of them glanced into that corner.

In the little bathroom, I filled up the bucket. I put in the required amount of the "mould killer/preventer stuff", and then started mopping like crazy. The guys continued going up and down, but I wasn't paying any attention.

There was a point, though, when I heard footsteps stop behind me. After a few seconds, I turned to see, and it was Tom, not even a foot from me. I stood straighter.

He reached his hand out and slid it along my chin. It was very rough.

"Don't be mad at me, Addy," he whispered in a sort of groan.

He looked into my eyes for a few seconds and then turned around, grabbed something else, and walked out.

Soon one of the guys came in to fix up the repair on the inside, and my mopping was done.

As I left, Jim, Sylvia, and Tore were thanking everyone for all their help. Sylvia gave me a big hug, and the guys gave me a warm handshake.

The world could learn a lot from this place.

IN THE morning, I went and visited Star.

"We sure are going to miss you. It has been like a vacation since you got here. You make everything seem fresh and new," she said over a blueberry muffin.

"To me, it was."

Then, later in the afternoon, I braved a couple of hours and went to Jackie's. It was a nice change because I had run out of things to say anyhow.

"That was so fun when you were singing outside," she started. "No one will just get up and do things like that here. That was exciting. We care too much, I think, about what others think. Tom is always thinking, but he thinks too much. Sure, he never makes a mistake, but what fun is that? I'm the same too, everyone here.

"People need to do more crazy things and have fun. I had a friend once who you remind me of a bit, except she had a mental condition, so it was a little sad, but she would just do things, as if there was no one else around. One time, in the middle of nowhere, she started dancing. There was no music, but she danced. I thought, why on earth can't we all do that? Why are we, who are in possession of all our mental faculties, unable to express a freeness to express our feelings?" she asked.

I should probably be offended, but I wasn't.

"I was so inspired by you," she continued. "Everyone is.

"You should stay. Well, go set things up and then move here. Of course, you could always stay here, with Mac and me, although everyone would be jealous.

"We would all be so happy for Tom if you did. He is all alone, not that there is anything wrong with being alone, but I think he has had enough aloneness now. There comes a point in everyone's life when you know that you don't want to get old alone. For some people, it takes a while, but Tom is ready now, I can tell.

"He has so much to give, really. We would all be lost here without him because he keeps everything going. He organizes everything and helps everyone.

"You would be perfect for him," she added.

If only he felt that way too.

"You could spend some time with the girls here, as you have with Roxy. It's a little bit of a hard place to grow up. But Tom knows what it takes for a happy community, so he never excludes the kids.

"Why, you might ask, couldn't one of us spend time with them, and we do try, but we don't have the gift that you do.

"Oh, Tom would be so good to you. You would be so happy. No doubt you can see the love he has for you by the way he looks at you.

"Even though it wasn't terribly romantic at the time, you got to admit that you have to admire a guy who is so controlled and so determined to do everything right, and never hurt you, that he didn't greet you when you waited for him. It must've driven him so absolutely crazy that he had to do that," she rattled on.

Interesting perspective.

"Anyhow, when you come back and marry him, you'll have kids, and everyone would be so excited if there were babies around here. Babies always uplift the spirits.

"You would definitely have something to do. So, you wouldn't be as bored as the rest of us. Becky always does very well beating the winter blahs because her kids keep her busy.

"The rest of us are all washed up as far as having kids goes, but this would be a nice place to raise a family.

"You like entertaining, obviously, so that is a good thing because that is something you can always do here. Everyone loved your fancy supper. It didn't taste like anything, but no one minded at all because it was so special," she said.

Again, I should probably be offended, but it was all just too entertaining.

"Nevertheless, you should probably take up another hobby, but not one that takes you away from singing. It is good to have lots of hobbies here.

"It's a certain mindset that is needed, more than anything else. You need the ability to have a creative mind and see everything new. And I think you can do that, so you will be all right here.

"You sure have a beautiful voice. No one else here sings. After hearing you, Mac told me that I should try singing. Can you imagine? I would never sing now because I could never sing like you.

"Mac was sweet to say that, wasn't he? He is a good husband.

"Of course, no one will tell you anything else about their mate because there is this funny love competition here. You don't want to be the first to stop kissing after the guys come back. The women all brag about their husbands to each other. It is so funny but cute.

"Again, that was Tom's doing, really. When he got here, everyone was pretty miserable. He made us all come together, and he gave us a huge lecture on showing love and respect for your mate and how talking bad about them tears down a marriage. Then, if anyone ever made a less than complimentary comment about their mate, Tom would scold them.

"We learned pretty fast, but you know, it's been such a good thing. It made for much warmer winters, if you know what I mean. Everyone has never been so happy.

"We also used to spend all our time just watching TV, and Tom was really against that too. We gradually got off our addiction with much mumbling, but again, it only made us happier.

"Tom is so smart for his age, wouldn't you say? He was raised right, that's for sure," she stated.

How come he was so wise anyway?

"His sister and her family have been here before. They are lovely too. You can tell that even she respects Tom, and her kids think the world of him. Even her husband does. Isn't that something? I tell you, he has won the respect of everyone he has ever met.

"Not every guy is like that, I will tell you now. Addy, you could never do better than Tom, not in the world. Seriously, he is worth sacrificing for."

AFTER SUPPER, there was a knock and Star and Victor came in. They handed me a gift they had made for me.

It was a picture of the shore here that Star had taken with her camera and printed out. And Victor had created a frame for it with stones and things collected from the beach. It was so beautiful that I didn't know what to say.

It wasn't long, and there was another knock, and it was Becky and the family.

She handed me a package wrapped in tissue paper. It was something white, cloth. Pulling it out, it was a dress she had made and embroidered with a long, wide skirt.

"It is so perfect," was all I could say as I held it tightly.

Then Urma passed me a parcel too. It was a beautiful cardigan that she crocheted. It had a lovely large pattern that you would wear over something, like the dress Becky gave.

Ryan then handed me this really neat tiny shell that he had found and, with the help of his father, had drilled a little hole in to be placed on a chain.

Roxy gave me a crown of simple seashells all strung together.

I was very overwhelmed. A tear rolled down my cheek that I could not prevent. Then there were huge hugs from everyone.

They visited for a while, but then left at the same time.

I stood on the boardwalk and waved to them all. Just as I was about to turn back, I saw Tom coming. I was beginning to wonder if I should stay there watching him when he called out.

"Addy, come to the shore with me."

He kept walking towards me until I met him, then turned to go with me to the harbour.

"You excited about going home?" he asked.

"No. I have nothing to go home to."

"You can make your life anything you want it to be. That's a gift you have. You could fill your life with people and enrich their lives, and they would do the same for you. Your strength of character can be used for so much good. Without trying to be heroic or special, you can be.

"Laugh with people. Cry with them. That is what it's all about. You will get hurt, because people are not always the best communicators, but your life will be rich. You won't feel so empty, and you'll learn so much. Don't be afraid of it." I looked at him but had nothing to say. It seemed so deep somehow.

"Sing me one last song," he requested.

The song that came to mind was of a lady's love for her blacksmith, who later turns out to be married. It was a touchy song, and the mood I was in did not help either. I got kind of choked up in the end, but I think I disguised it well.

When I finished, I knew I had to leave, or else I would start crying, so I just said goodbye and turned to flee.

"Wait, Addy." But I was afraid to turn around. *What if the tears wouldn't wait?* "I want you to have this."

Tom handed me something round wrapped in well-used tissue paper. He definitely didn't do a lot of wrapping, as it was not a very elegant job. There was tape everywhere.

My eyes were burning, so I could only say thank you and face away again. I didn't run, but I didn't turn back either.

Tears were stinging my eyes. One tear annoyingly ran down my cheek, but I dared not wipe it in case Tom was still watching.

Urma looked at me but didn't say anything.

I went into the washroom and wiped my eyes. But I didn't want Urma to see what I had in my palm.

I had to rip the tissue and wiggle it out of a part where there was no tape. It was an old compass. I held it up. It was interesting, but why did he give it to me?

Then, left in the wrapping, I saw a note and opened it up.

97

I'm giving you this compass so when you are back in Toronto, you'll be able to know the direction of Foley's Rest. Always remember your friends here and the things you learned about yourself. - Tom Joseph.

I held it for a while in my palm. But it was not helping to keep the tears away. I ran my fingers over the lens. There were little scratches on it.

I wondered where it had been. And I wondered where Tom got it. Did he find it?

For some reason, I found a strange comfort in holding it. It was thoughtful, but it made me sad at the same time.

It was time to move on now. I have to admit that Tom is not in love with me. He is very caring and sweet. But the warmth and consideration he shows for everyone here is evident, and I should be pleased that I was a part of it. And he wanted to enrich my life because he could see the emptiness there. He did it all for me, not for himself. Also, I'm sure he must have expectations for the woman he would open his heart to, ones that I do not meet.

IN THE morning, I stood outside and watched all the men board their boats in the darkness. They had lights on their vessels as well as flashlights in hand, so it was like a little light show. Some clear parts of the sky revealed more stars than black.

Tom was already in his boat before he noticed me. He had on his red buffalo plaid jacket. I think. He bent his head to the side slightly and gave me a wave, which I returned. Continuing to watch until all the men left, their boats became tiny specks disappearing in the darkness.

Of course, I had nothing to pack except the gifts I was given. And I was wearing the dress and the crochet top. The other things all fit inside my purse.

I helped Urma put all my bedding in the laundry.

Soon Star, Becky, and the kids came to give me one last goodbye hug. Roxy also gave me a picture she drew of the two of us pretending to be princesses.

Jackie came over as well to bid me farewell.

Then I could hear the helicopter. It crushed the peaceful calm and silence with its deafening noise. They did some filming from the air of this place as I, and some others, waved from the boardwalk. Then they landed where we had danced.

A cameraman and news anchor filed out and filmed a few shots of Foley's Rest.

Before I knew it, I was heading straight up, and I waved from the window at everyone below until we went over the hill, and they were no longer seen.

The island was tiny. As soon as we were up a few feet, I could see the ends of it. It looked interesting on the other side, the way the rock was. After all the hills, it was rather flat there.

We headed over the Atlantic, and I got a good idea of how isolated this island really was.

After we landed at the airport, they set up a spot to film an interview. Next, they asked me all kinds of questions about the crash and my last two weeks. It was kind of fun, and they were pretty friendly.

Then I boarded a plane and flew to Toronto.

8

T he noise would not stop, not even after the plane did. It was raining and dark.

I used to live here, I thought. It seemed like such a long time ago, as if I was gone for at least a year. Somehow, the streets looked foreign. I recognized them all, and nothing had changed, but it was like stepping back into a past life. It was all ridiculous, really, and I couldn't figure out why I felt the way I did.

I had the taxi drop me off at the bank not far from my condo, where I took out some cash to pay him before walking the last few blocks home.

The streetlamps were reflecting off the wet road, which was still getting rained on lightly. I shivered although it wasn't terribly cold. I used to enjoy all the city lights at night. However, this evening, they didn't seem as welcoming as before.

I was self-conscious, as if everyone was watching me in my white dress and my hair bouncing on my back, but that was ridiculous. But no one cared what on earth I wore. You should see some of the things that people will wear downtown. I didn't stand out in the slightest. Yet it was entirely different from anything else I ever wore here.

I came to my condo and let myself in, where the emptiness greeted me with an icy grin. Again, it felt like something from a past memory and not my home.

I opened a window, but it didn't help. I needed to breathe the fresh air, but instead filled my lungs with a foul, polluted smell that I somehow never noticed before.

Rather than the steady beat of the waves, there was the constant howl of the traffic below. I could see the harbour as well as the downtown from my floor-to-ceiling windows. But the city lights I used to love so much only seemed to close me in now.

I felt so alone.

I took the gift from Star and Victor and placed it on the kitchen counter, as it was the only visible place to put it.

The picture was the only thing on my marble top. There was nothing else anywhere because I had wall-to-wall cabinets that hid everything, including my bed. Only one long black table with cushions around it sat there, along with a single silk orchid in a rectangular glass vase on top.

I opened my cabinet and took out my jewellery box. Why on earth did I have so much? I found a white gold chain, and I placed the shell I got from Ryan on it. I put it on. Then I put on the crown of shells from Roxy.

I noticed myself in the mirror inside of the door. But I looked completely different from before I left Toronto. My skin used to be very pale and even in colour. Now my cheeks were pink and higher than where I placed my blush before. It made my face look rounder. My eyes seemed different also, although I didn't know why. I wasn't wearing eye makeup, so perhaps that's all it was.

I was oddly out of place here in my condo, as well as here in Toronto. It was funny because when I first got to Foley's Rest, I felt entirely out of place there. Now I fit in nowhere.

I thought of the sea, the warm, cozy, colourful homes, the boats, the crabs, Tom. With that, my eyes were burning again.

I requested from my music app the same song I had danced to when I was there, the one that everyone stopped and watched me dance and sing to, even without the melody at first. It must have looked strange. I put the song on. Thus, the tune filled the air and my empty heart, respectively, and I started to dance. When it was over, I pressed repeat so it would just keep playing and playing. I let my hair fly all over, and I sang along.

Hungry now, I searched my kitchen in the hope that I would find something comforting, but there was only gourmet stuff. I wanted a grilled cheese sandwich, even though I had never made that here before. There was a special sourdough bread and some expensive cheese. Even so, this would do. I had no fresh produce left and should have grabbed some on the way in. Additionally, I should start buying some frozen packages. A jar of grilled marinated vegetables smirked at me from the corner. Oh, I froze some leftover rapini that I cooked a while ago.

I ate by myself. There was no conversation around, no atmosphere like a family dinner. In essence, I listened to myself chew.

I really must have so much to learn still, especially when you think that I am the only single girl to go to Foley's Rest in five years and can't impress Tom.

Why do I care anyhow?

Then I took my bath and considered the surrounding bubbles, and how I spent $60 on my bottle of bubble bath. What a waste. I wonder what ordinary people pay these days. Yet somehow, I enjoyed my baths in Foley's Rest more.

I pulled out my bed and climbed in. It was notably huge, and I couldn't believe how large it felt. I guess that's because I was sleeping on a couch for ten nights.

Finally, I fell asleep.

AFTER WAKING up, I stared at the ceiling for a while. What was I even supposed to do today? Then the answer came.

I would buy a gift for everyone in Foley's Rest. I also needed new clothes, as I now hated everything I had. To search in my sterile closet was like being in the lumber section of Home Depot, where you need a trained expert to know the difference. Eventually, I grabbed a navy pair of pants that almost looked like khakis and a sweater.

I decided against my usual shower and took another bath.

Then I went into the kitchen, but after staring at the cupboards for a while, I closed them and decided to eat out.

I drove past my regular commercial district, and instead, headed to a shopping mall, as normal people do. So, I parked and started with breakfast in the mall's food court before heading to the stores. That took me back to the time I was in college. But I was too focused then to have fun. In fact, I don't know if I ever really had any fun.

I started to get into this shopping thing because buying things for other people was much more enjoyable than I imagined. Too bad I've never done it before.

A big teddy made me smile because of its adorable eyes, and it would be perfect for Roxy. I never remember having a stuffy.

There was a doll that I had once. I found it near the dumpster. A few minutes later, when my cousin saw me, he grabbed it out of my hands and pulled the head off without delay.

When I was a bit older, I found a little toy horse in the school playground, the kind with soft hair that you comb. I thought it was so beautiful that I must have stared at it for hours. When I got home, I asked Ann if I could keep it. She was the neighbour who took me in. It was dirty, and she was afraid that it might have germs. But she wasn't mean, just very practical.

Generally speaking, I did everything to make her and her husband happy because I lived in fear that they would give me back to my aunt if I didn't.

I did not have any toys. I never asked for any.

When she took that horse away, I'll always remember that she said when I'm done school and get a good job, I could buy anything I want. Furthermore, they didn't have much money, so it was a big sacrifice for them just to feed me.

Does a child learn to love if they have things to care for?

I stopped feeling sorry for myself and continued with my shopping. Keeping my mind on everyone in Foley's, I tried to find the right gift for each of them.

I found a couple of good frying pans for Urma.

How was I going to bring all these gifts to them? By mail? In my heart, I imagined travelling there to give them personally.

I ran across a clothes store that pulled me inside. My eyes opened wide at all the perfect styles. So many beautiful dresses and sweaters, and the style and setting immediately took me back to the place I had grown to love. Likewise, it almost smelled like the ocean.

The lady working there said they were all Viking-inspired. I loved the natural softness of the fabrics and the cords wrapped around the waist. How many of these dresses could I actually use? But it was hard to narrow it down to just a few choices. My favourite were the ones with sleeves that widened immensely towards the wrists. There were also beautiful capes to go with. Albeit not everything was quite so loud. There were also lovely tops, sweaters that were perfect for oceanside, and even cute-fitting jeans.

Viking. That made sense, as there was a Viking history on the eastern coast of Canada. I wonder if they ever set foot on Foley's Rest. The landscape there certainly lent itself to that, as well as something Celtic or medieval.

Moreover, I must have made the day for the lady working there. Unable to take everything I bought to my car in one trip, I had to do it in a couple of rounds.

When I got home, I wanted to scrap all my old clothes, but I still had two weeks of work left. And I couldn't just show up dressed in my new attire.

THE NEXT day, I wore one of my new outfits. It was a light grey dress with all this ribbon tied at the waist and sleeves that widened to a point. It's true that the sleeves were not very practical, and they would be getting in everything. But the rest was comfortable. And I loved how it felt and how I looked in it.

Then I learned some different Celtic traditional songs that I thought fit Foley's Rest.

Later, at the grocery store, a few people stared at me strangely, but no one said a thing.

THE FOLLOWING day, Monday, I struggled to figure out what to put on. It would not be appropriate to wear what I wanted to—some of my lovely new things. Yet at the same time, I could not dress exactly as I used to. Because it seemed somewhat like a betrayal.

I decided on a grey skirt and a pink blouse. This would have been almost standard for me except that I never left without a suit jacket. Then I didn't apply as much makeup. After not wearing any for a while, it seemed strange to cover myself with it. Finally, I decided to leave my hair down, but I tied a pink ribbon around it at the base of my neck. Next, I put on nylons but later took them off and found a pair of flats.

I thawed a bagel, toasted it, and spread cream cheese on.

Now, there was no compelling need to run out of my condo in some huge imaginary rush. Because no one cared if I ate my bagel here or in my car.

I made some coffee instead of picking some up on my commute. Then I took the time to drink it, although it wasn't nearly as good as Urma's.

I stared at my notice of resignation and finally drove to work.

So, I arrived there exactly when I would've, even if everything had gone exactly as planned. Except, rather than a shopping vacation in Paris, I had a mind-altering experience of a plane crash, a rescue, and ten days in a remote fishing village.

Usually, I would barge through the doors and storm into my office, but today I walked slowly. I looked at the people's faces. Before, I wouldn't have been able to identify the receptionist at the front, as I was always too rushed to glance up.

"Good morning Ms. Lockheart," she said in her usual tone, but after I peered at her as I calmly strolled past, she added. "Sorry to hear about your vacation, but welcome back."

"Thank you."

Slowly, I made my way to the elevator, returning the nods of many who were motioning their hello to me through their glass cubicles.

As I was waiting for it to arrive at my floor, I wasn't looking through my schedule for the day like normal.

A guy that I didn't recognize but obviously worked here said, "You really made the news. We all thought we lost you." There was a pause. "Are you alright?" he asked.

"Yes. Thanks. Why do you ask?"

"Well, you were different before."

"Arrogant and snooty," I said.

"I wasn't going to put it that way," he said, smiling.

When I got to my floor, my assistant jumped up like usual, I guess, and ran to me. However, she abruptly halted when she noticed that I had stopped. Oh yes, I'm supposed to be running to my office with some air of importance.

"My word, you have so much catching up to do. The Hupert account is really not looking good, and the Lancelacks are getting cranky. Those are definitely the two most urgent..."

"Who was handling them when I was gone?"

"Steve, but they are not as confident with him."

"He will learn."

"What?"

"Steve will learn. It takes time," I said, but she gave me a puzzled glance.

"So, can I arrange meetings with Hupert and Lancelacks right away?" she asked.

"Steve can look after those accounts, but I can accompany him if he likes."

"What on earth are you talking about? These are worth billions of dollars."

"I'm putting in my resignation."

She kind of swallowed and didn't know what to say.

I glanced around my office. As normal, there was not a paper anywhere. And there wasn't a single object on my desk. A sure way to intimidate people is to leave nothing around. The windows were large, yet I never looked out. I had everything here except for a bed, although I basically never used any of them.

My assistant, Joan, was still staring at me in disbelief. "What happened?"

"Did you hear about my trip?"

"Yes, but nothing about this."

"It made me analyze my life, that's all. And I discovered that I don't like it, so I'm going to try something else."

"Like what?"

"I'm not sure yet. For now, I will just be cleaning things up so that it can be as smooth of a transition as possible. First, though, I have to see Vince. Can you put me through right away?"

"Sure," she said and left.

Vince was the president, and he would not be too happy. Even though he let me keep my job because I made him lots of money, we never exactly got along. Well, at least ever since I told him to call his own limousine because I was not his receptionist.

Time seemed to pass more slowly now that I was not full of nervous energy.

After I told Vince, he was also shocked and didn't know what to say. I could tell he was torn between being happy that I wouldn't be around and upset that he would have to find a replacement. And it's not that he was short of options, but he knew they were not quite as good as me.

"You'll have to work very hard the next two weeks to tie everything up," he said in his most threatening voice.

I just smiled because what difference would that make to me? Of course, I'll try to be helpful, but he just lost any control he thought he had.

I liked to be in charge, and I usually was while I was working here. But this was the first time that I felt it so thoroughly. I was virtually invincible, yet I still had no idea what I was going to do next.

IN THE evenings, I contemplated selling my condo and my sports car. Perhaps it would be nice to start fresh. But where?

Somehow, I also became almost obsessed with discovering everything possible about the crash. I learned what the experts figured the problem was, and that they located the wreckage at the bottom of the sea. Truly, there was a lot of grief expressed by those who lost a family member or friend.

It was humbling, being the only survivor of an accident that large, especially when I seemed like the only one who didn't have any family. Why me? Probably anyone else would have been a better choice.

One story bothered me more than any other. Because it was a mother battling cancer, and her husband was on my flight. He was travelling for business and then the sole provider for her and their young twin sons. Thankfully, the Canadian healthcare system covers her treatment, but what about her mortgage and other needs? Her sister was taking time off to care for the boys, but even so, this was an irreversible blow.

I still went to work every day, but for the first moment since I started there, I had more important things on my mind. Investing other people's money seemed to pale in significance to everyone trying to rebuild their lives after this crash.

I also needed to figure out what to do with my life. Very casually, I looked at homes for sale in different locations in Newfoundland and Labrador. But was I ready for that?

AS THE days passed, I became more and more convinced that I did want to sell my condo and car. I could get a regular SUV and buy a little house in a smaller town or a quieter edge of a city.

One cloudy afternoon, over a chai tea latte, I stared out of the window of the coffee shop and thought of Tom. Still, I wasn't sure what to buy him, although I had bought something for everyone else.

I remembered the boats coming in. I remembered waiting for them. I remembered the music that played in my heart. After that, those songs were stuck in my head.

That evening, I did a strange thing. I recorded myself singing all the songs that I sang for Tom while I was there. I didn't have the proper equipment, but it would have to do. Also, I wrote him an email saying that I think of Foley's Rest so often and having the privilege of singing there was something I would never forget. Finally, I attached the audio files of my singing to a spot he could link to. Somehow, I just had to do it. Maybe it would help me bring closure to my whole experience there.

At the end of my two weeks, my realtor was showing my suite often, and I was selling my stocks and bonds and closing up my investments. Similarly, I sorted through my things, thinking of what I would keep. Thank goodness I didn't have that many items.

All of my jewellery and almost all of my old clothes, I took to consignment stores. Through with suits, fancy shoes, and all my dress clothes, I was starting over. I basically only kept the items I had bought since I got back and, of course, the beloved dress that Becky made me. My pyjamas, a bit of gym wear, and a couple of evening dresses, I hung onto.

ONE DAY was so hot, sticky and muggy, and that night, wow, what a storm! So, I just sat on the floor and watched it out my window. The weather was like me, restless and irritated.

Then it hit me: I could help that mother. I could. I had some money floating around. Not quite as much as I should for the way I used to spend it, but enough to make a difference in someone's life. Besides, it was looking like my condo was going to sell, so I'd soon have cash from that, and that would be sufficient for me to do what I needed. Something simple. That's what I wanted anyway, and she needed this money far more than I did.

A more settled and content feeling slowly covered me.

Afterwards, the rain slowed down to a gentle drizzle, and I was compelled to go outside. Perhaps it was my endless search for fresh air. Notably, I had on my long velvet cape.

I walked to the harbour. It was nothing like what I wanted with all the lights, boats, and noise. But nevertheless, this was going to have to do. I stood facing the water and started to sing. Everyone thinks I'm an idiot here, but I fit right in with those who burned their minds out on drugs or whatever. It most certainly did not have the same warmth and beauty as in Foley's Rest. In contrast, here I would never draw a crowd because no one cares. There are too many people here to bother.

MY PHONE never rang, not that anyone calls anymore. Of all the people that I would have over, usually business associates, not one of them seemed to care that I was no longer working for that firm. True, I found some emails on my business account when I got back, but no one would miss me if I left the city. And I suppose it was my own fault because I didn't treat any of them personally either.

Although, I really needed to talk with someone. I wanted to call Urma, but what would I say? *Hi, I'm selling everything, and I don't know where to go, but enough about me. How are you doing?*

I just had to end my relationships with everyone there. This way, I at least have a beautiful semi-sweet memory. But I did still have these gifts for them.

I was able to sell my yellow sports car and get an SUV that was a few years old, and even more important, I made contact with that mother fighting cancer. Her name was Laura. The first trip I took with my new wheels was to see her, as I needed to make sure everything looked legit.

Sure enough, my heart broke when I saw how much pain she was in. Her sister moved in and was trying to improve the condition of the house while keeping two very energetic three-year-olds entertained. When I asked if I could help with anything, they simply said to let them know if I heard of any flexible work-from-home offers.

I wrote them four cheques for what I thought would easily take them through the next four months. Then they both bawled their eyes out, and it was so contagious that I had to join in.

I left tired but pleased with myself for the first time.

Then I texted Ann. Perhaps she still had the same number? It was burned in my memory somehow, from elementary school. What will she think of me getting in contact after all these years? I wanted to know if she was still with her husband more than anything else. If she was, then forget it. However, if not, perhaps I could give her something too. It must have cost her a lot to have me living there. Especially considering that since she wasn't my legal guardian, she was never able to apply for a subsidy of any sort.

To my surprise, she responded, and although slightly hesitant, she agreed to meet me. Furthermore, she said she had been divorced for ten years and never saw him now.

Seeing her again after all this time, I realized something. She didn't have normal emotions. She might have had a tragic past, a condition, or both. Ann was stone-faced as always, but accepted my cheque. I expressed appreciation for her protection for many years, as well as for caring for my physical needs. Then she thanked me and left. I'm sure she would like to feel more, but was unable. In conclusion, that explained why we never bonded, and why it was more similar to a business relationship. I walked out of the coffee shop enlightened about a large section of my history.

I started doing all my shopping in regular stores. It was surprising how little I could spend on a bottle of bubble bath. After all, my grocery bill was so much less, and my food only seemed to taste better for some reason.

The only thing is, where would I live? I had an offer for my place, and it sounded like it was going to go through, so soon I got a little anxious about it.

I started looking online at other places across Canada, and there were spots where housing was a lot cheaper, but which should I try? Where would I be able to find a job in due time? In essence, it was overwhelming to think of. All things considered, I needed to find a way to narrow down my search a bit.

THEN THE sale of my condo went through. The good news was that the lady buying it loved my decor so much that she offered me a bit extra to have it all. I didn't want to take it with me anyway, as it would need a moving truck.

The bad news was that she wanted it right away. That came as a real shock to me because I always assumed I'd have lots of time. However, it seemed like a silly reason to decline the offer.

I decided to focus on cleaning out all my things, and once I distil it down to what fits in my vehicle, then I can start anywhere fresh.

It was exciting, but scary too.

I cleaned out my fridge, stove, and cupboards. Then I took all of my dishes, cups, cutlery, glasses, kitchen appliances, and everything and packed them up. It was tough to decide what I wanted to keep, so in the end, I decided to get rid of it all. I brought them all to a second-hand store.

Then I packed away my personal things, which were not too many: my clothes, shoes, bedding, laptop, and the gifts I had for everyone in Foley's Rest. They would easily all fit in my vehicle.

The leaves were starting to turn colour now. It was such a lovely way for them to die.

I would like to end in a beautiful way like that, and I tried to come up with the most romantic way to go. What came to mind was the ancient poem of the lady of Shallot. I could lie on a boat, set it loose and slowly eventually float to my watery grave. After all, perhaps she froze to death. So, that would probably be painful. It would only be noble to die while saving someone else.

Then I remembered what I thought to myself when I was just about dead, floating on the sea. I didn't want to die without learning to love. Maybe I did learn?

No. One week is not good enough for me.

I have to start over and follow Tom's advice. He said that I had the ability to make my life into anything that I wanted and that I could learn to laugh with people and cry with them. And I got a head start. I did the crying part already.

I sat in my empty condo and stared at the walls.

I pulled the compass out of my purse and looked at it. It was funny because it initially took me a few hours to figure out how it works. Before then, I had never seen one before, but now I understand.

I turned and faced Foley's Rest. Tom. If only I could call him and ask him what to do.

Suddenly in an alien world which was foreign to me, I wish I had someone to give me some direction.

I wish that someone could love me. My own mother couldn't. A tear rolled down my cheek, and I had never before shed one thinking of my past. Now I needed a mom to call up and ask for advice.

It could be like the movies. Where I would drive up to my mom's and ring her doorbell, and she would take one look at me and say, "There, there, come in, and I will make you a hot cup of cocoa, and you tell me what's troubling you, and we'll get through it together." Then I would sit in the big warm kitchen, have hot chocolate and cookies, and cry my heart out until I felt better. She would reassure me that I would survive it all and be even happier in the end. Also, she would tell me that she was there to help in any way possible and that I was never alone. And that would be enough to give me the strength that I needed right now. If only I wasn't all alone.

I cried for a while, all by myself.

Then I forced myself to have a bite to eat.

IN THE morning, after grabbing breakfast, I drove to the gym where I had a membership.

I ran on a treadmill for a while, and it helped to release some of my anxieties. Then I took a shower there.

I figured I could eventually get work at a bank. I'm overqualified, but that is probably an average-wage kind of job. That is what I want, something that pays an average wage.

Then I went to my realtor and gave him the keys to my condo, and I had to go over a few things.

I could leave now. And it was the strangest sense of freedom. So, I thought I'd head out of Toronto and perhaps travel a little. I'll start in the Niagara area and find a nice hotel while I decide what to do next.

I bought a sandwich to take with me and was heading to my vehicle when my cell phone rang. Man, I sure hope I don't have more things to do with my realtor. No. It wasn't him. Probably a scam call, but with the various new events in my life, I figured I better answer it.

"Hi. Addy?" I would recognize that voice anywhere. It was Tom.

"Yes."

"It's Tom Joseph. How are you?"

9

"Not too bad," I said.

"I got your songs. Listen, I'm going to be flying out west, and I'll be exchanging planes in Toronto. However, if you are free, I would like to meet you there for coffee," Tom said.

"Sure. When?"

"Well, I am about to book it as we speak, so I thought I would see what's good for you. After six?" he asked.

"Oh, it doesn't matter when, as I'm between jobs right now. So, it could certainly be during the day. Take whatever is best for you, and I'll come see you then. When are you leaving?"

"As soon as I possibly can without paying five times more. My sister and her husband ended up in a terrible car accident. They are both in ICU. So, I'm going to go and take care of the kids."

"Oh, my! What about being an RCMP in Foley's Rest?"

"I don't know. They'll find a replacement... because they'll have to. My sister has no one else. The neighbour has the kids right now. Besides, things really don't look good for Margaret and Brian, so... there's a chance that I won't ever be back here."

"I'm so sorry. Tom... Tom, listen. I have an idea. This will sound crazy, but just hear me out... Why not let me go instead? Right now, I am perfectly free. I've sold my condo, and I don't have a new job yet. I would love to do that for you. So, I would be honoured if you would let me go. I know little about kids, I'll admit, but it can't be rocket science. You can visit anytime, but I could keep you in touch with whatever is going on. After everything you did for me... Tom, you saved my life, and this is nothing compared to that. You can look after the community there and you wouldn't leave them stranded. At least for the time being, until we see how things turn out. Won't you please let me go?"

There was a very long pause, so I used the time to climb back into my vehicle.

"That's a pretty big deal, Addy. Do you realize what you are saying?"

"Yes. But I happen to have the perfect circumstances for it. The coincidence here is amazing. Literally minutes ago, I gave my realtor my keys, and haven't found a new place yet. I was just going to head on the road and stay in a hotel for now. So, a project like this sounds just right for me and will give me the opportunity to learn some things and to figure out what I want to do next."

"But how long after you get there will you need another change?" he asked.

"For four years, I've lived in the same place, so I may sound flighty to you, as if I would leave anything at the drop of a hat for something that sounds better, but that is only if it involves me alone. I wouldn't let you down. Certainly, I'm not going to call you from Vancouver to tell you I have changed my mind. However, I won't promise you that I will spend the rest of my life there."

After a brief silence, he let out a deep breath. "Oh, Addy! You have no idea what that would mean to me."

"I would like to drive, though, but I can leave right away."

"When exactly is right away?" he asked.

"As soon as we are done talking. I'm on a cell phone and in my car. Everything that I still own is in the back."

"How long do you think it would take to get there?"

"I heard about four days. Would that be alright?" I asked.

"I wouldn't have been able to arrive any sooner.

"But why do you have everything you own in your vehicle?" he asked.

"I told you. I quit my job and sold my condo."

"You really are something, you know that? I'll tell you their address, and call the neighbour, Lisa, and tell her what's going on. Addy... Do you think you can handle this?"

I was silent for a bit. *How would I know unless I tried? I wasn't one to give up.* "Do you think I can't?"

"Addy, you can do anything you set your heart to. Anthony and Kimberly couldn't ask for any better. That's the kids' names."

"Well, I'll set my heart to it then. Where do they live?"

"Fourteen Hamburg crescent."

"But where? In B.C.?" I asked.

"Yup. In Terrace. It is close to the coast in the middle of the province."

"Alright. I will just put it in my phone, and then I'll be off."

"Hey, and thanks for the songs. They're great!" he said.

"You're welcome and Tom, I won't let you down."

"I know you won't. I'll keep in touch."

Now I felt free and excited. I went back into the store and got drinks and snacks to hold me over between meals for a few days on the road.

IN MY vehicle, I requested the song I had sung and danced to, and drove off.

A couple of hours later, my phone rang again, and I put the speaker on.

"Hi, Addy. It's Tom. Are you driving?"

"Yes."

"Don't drive too much longer before you get some sleep. Are you going to stay in a hotel?"

"No. I'm planning to pull off at a rest stop for a while."

"Is that safe?"

"Sure it is. I mean, it's right beside the highway. So, if there is a drive-by shooting, I should be fine because I'll be lying down anyway. The bullets should miss me."

He chuckled. "You wouldn't sleep well in your car and with the traffic noise. You should get proper rest."

"Tom... I'll be fine. If I require a proper rest, I know what to do."

"Well, I need you to take good care of yourself, and... I really want to thank you for what you are doing."

"You're welcome, Tom."

By around ten o'clock, I got to a rest stop just past Sault Ste. Marie and slept. I felt like a hotel would waste my time today, but probably tomorrow.

AFTER A coffee and granola bar, I took off. I didn't care for skipping a shower, and of course, I didn't sleep great, so I'll find a place to stay for tonight.

It was a beautiful day for a drive, and I'd never been out here. At this time, the thought of driving across the country was very exciting to me, as was the idea of trying something new.

To assist a family in this way was so personal. And I wasn't doing it for Tom because I needed it more than he did. He would do it all and probably do a better job, but I viewed this as a privilege. Yet this was going to be a challenge for me, as it was so unlike anything I'd done before. Why did I need to do this? It wasn't to have a place to sleep. Was it because I could only help Laura from a distance, and I wanted to be more hands-on? Was it because I found myself in need of being a part of something far more personal?

With meals and washroom stops, I made it to the Manitoba border by nighttime. Stumbling on some cottages in West Hawk Lake, not far at all from the highway, I decided to stop there.

I SAVED my Jacuzzi bath for the morning and then took a little walk to the water.

That Tom trusted me with all this kind of surprised me. Here I was, going to take care of his eight-year-old niece and seven-year-old nephew on the other side of the country, when I expected that I didn't even meet up to his standards yet.

How would coffee with him have gone if he was the one flying out? Did he have something to say to me? I don't think so. Otherwise, he surely would have by now. Although, it was nice that he thought of me.

It was hard for me to understand my feelings for Tom exactly. I am really disappointed that he didn't seem to want to take things any further, but there had to be more to it. I recognized I liked him and possibly loved him. But I think I respected him more than anyone else I knew. He was so crazy different than me, yet seemed so wise. Though I always craved control, it was somehow refreshing to be with someone I admired who *was* in control. It was as if I was relieved of duty. Further, there was a stability to him that I needed.

THE CRISP air of the morning gave me a big appetite, and I found a place to get a real breakfast at Falcon Beach.

Then I drove until Lloydminister. However, that was a tough day of driving because the trees suddenly disappeared, and everywhere I looked, there was... nothing. I'd never seen so much sky in my life. There I ended up in a hotel that included breakfast, saving me a lot of time.

Tom would call at least a couple of times a day to keep track of my location and see how everything was going. I tried to sound very energetic to mask how tired I was now, but he didn't fall for it.

I would prefer to text or message him because that's what I was used to. This phone call thing is new to me. But it's not that I can text while driving, and when I'm done for the day, I have no energy to write anything.

However, when I entered the mountains, it revived me a bit because it was so gorgeous. In B.C., at Mount Robson Provincial Park, I had to stop for a little while just to look up. I wondered why Jasper was so famous, because the scenery only improved as I left the park boundary. It looked so much more lush and wild, and there were pristine lakes right along the highway.

By the time I finished dinner in a lodge at Tete Jaune Cache, I felt done for the day. Also, it seemed like a cute place to stay for the night.

AFTER THAT incredible start of driving through B.C., I guess I had unrealistic expectations. It soon turned into just a highway through trees. There might be a low mountain somewhere in the distance, but that was it. By now, I'd had enough driving, so the final kilometres of the Yellowhead seemed to drag on endlessly. Then, finally, some tree-filled mountains got a little closer, and a few taller ones appeared behind.

There was a neat-looking mountain close to South Hazelton, and soon after, a tiny lake beside the road took my breath away. So, I stopped to stretch my legs and use the washroom at a campground there.

What was I doing? I don't even know how to look after kids. The only children I'd ever been around, were the ones in Foley's Rest. How hard would it be? No, I wasn't that naïve. I knew this would be a real challenge, but I was counting on there being a certain naturalness to it. If I just want to do my best, the rest will come, even if it is exhausting. I hope. When all else fails, I have a healthy dose of self-esteem that prevents me from giving up.

I GOT to Terrace at dinner time and quickly found the house with Tom's instructions. I pulled into the driveway in an immaculately kept neighbourhood. There was green grass as far as you could see, and white bungalows lined up neatly. In the distance were tree-covered hills, and behind them, snow-topped mountains. Various trees were scattered throughout the street, partially covering most of the homes.

This house had two levels, and the white was accented by dark green with the trim and false window shutters. It was a single garage with a couple of hanging flower baskets on each side. There were tall poplars in the back and neatly trimmed bushes in front. I parked and then went to see Lisa next door.

Her place had darker neutral-coloured siding and a peaked roof. She was blond, holding a baby, and close to my age.

"You must be Addy," Lisa at once exclaimed. "Tom described how you look. Come on in."

Two kids appeared at the door, a girl and a boy. "This is Anthony and Kimberly," she added. "We're just having supper. Come on in. Can I get you a bowl too?"

"Don't worry about me. I'm not that hungry."

"Oh, you should have something. Here, hold Devon."

But I had never held a baby before. How does one do it? Well, I guess he is not going to fall out of my arms. He tilted his head and looked at me, looking right into my eyes. It seemed as if this little guy was considering some deep thought. This was really strange. I always thought babies were different, kind of without brains or anything, but Devon was definitely thinking of something.

I glanced at Lisa, who was putting a soup bowl on the table for me. But oh my goodness, it was canned pasta. The kids had the same thing. They were watching me intently with eyes wide open. This took me way back into my childhood, back to parts I tried not to remember.

She lifted the baby from me, and I sat down to eat.

Though the taste wasn't as bad as it looked, it brought some anxiety. All of a sudden, I felt extremely unsure and also noticed that everyone was watching me.

I didn't really know how to look after kids.

"Are you going to marry Tom?" Kimberly asked.

I just about choked. "Well, before you plan to marry someone, you date them, or go out together, and start a courtship. Then you can decide if you want to marry them. Tom and I are not even dating."

"Oh," she said with disappointment.

"So, you have been to Tom's?" Anthony asked.

"Yes."

"When?"

"Well, it is late September now, and I was there at the beginning of August. So, it's about six weeks now, I guess."

"How's he doing?" Lisa asked.

"Oh, good. He is very worried about all you guys, though."

"I wish he could've come," Kimberly said.

"I'm sure he will, but he isn't able to stay as long as I can."

Lisa inquired about my drive, and before I knew it, we were all done.

It was time for me to take this responsibility from her. So, I got the keys and entered into the place that would be my home for a while.

There was a nice, long white kitchen to the right and a comfortable living room on the left. The basement was a great play area for the kids, and the upstairs held the three bedrooms. Behind the kitchen, though, was a beautiful sunroom with wicker furniture.

So, if it's ever possible to get any time to myself, this is where I'll be. The patio was on the side.

I first looked into the cupboards, fridge, and freezer to see if there was something to make breakfast with in the morning. Yes. I think we can survive for now, but I'll try to get some fresh stuff soon. How does a person cook regular food? I'd experimented a bit over the last month, but was still mostly doing takeout. What does one do with ground beef? I thought of Urma's meatloaf.

The house was kind of a mess, so I started to clean up.

The kids were cute, cautious, and curious all at the same time. But they seemed happy to be in their home again and kept themselves occupied while I tidied up a bit.

My, was I tired.

What could I create for breakfast in the morning? I wonder if I can make pancakes. Surely, that's not too hard. I looked for a recipe online and then went to see what the kids were up to.

They practically destroyed the sunroom. Well, they had things all over anyway. They kept missing or forgetting something when I tried to get them to clean it up. I could've done it faster myself. Able to convince them to take baths, I tidied up some more.

What on earth do children do before going to bed? Read a story? I'll read them a story. Thank goodness they didn't look at me like an alien when I suggested that, but off they went to choose one. It took them a while to decide, but finally came with a book.

Before we got all settled, the phone rang, and Anthony ran to grab it with Kimberly at his heels. They still have a landline? It nearly scared me.

It was Tom, and the kids were glad to visit with him. He spoke with Anthony for a while and then Kim. I was expecting I would talk next, but the phone was already hanging up, and she told me that he would call me later.

We read the story, and they settled down to sleep. Well, eventually, after many tries.

Finally, I was able to take a bath too and then changed the sheets on their parent's bed.

I set the alarm and crawled in.

Though I don't know for certain, I get a feeling that this whole mother thing is a bit of work. I hope I have more energy tomorrow.

When my phone rang, I had almost fallen asleep. It was Tom, making sure everything was going alright and to see if there was anything he could do. But I was so tired that I was not much of a conversationalist.

Finally, I got to sleep.

IN THE morning, I dragged myself out of bed.

I tried to comfort myself with the thought of breakfasts in Foley's Rest because the whole village always smelled wonderful in the mornings. I would make a big breakfast like that. One that feeds not just the body but the soul. Hmm. That is almost poetic. Anyhow, that's what my first mission was.

It eventually roused me to a more cognitive state and put me in a better frame of mind. I even felt that it smelled pretty good in here when I woke the kids up. I fried pancakes, sausage, and eggs and served them with some canned fruit salad and yogurt. Anthony and Kimberly seemed really happy about it, so that made my morning.

I threw together some tuna sandwiches, and soon they were off to school.

I quickly took an inventory of food items, took a trip to the grocery store, and stocked up on things we would need for the next little while.

After my lunch, I cleaned up a bit and was still putting groceries away when Anthony and Kimberly crashed through the door. Kim came and gave me a hug, and they hung around for a while to tell me about their day.

It was interesting to be a part of a world that I knew nothing about. It was like getting a taste of being a mom or adopting a family for a while. The only thing was that this was going to be a lot harder than I thought.

I cleaned up some more. The bathroom needed a proper clean.

The phone rang.

"Hi, dear. You must be Addy. I am Debbie, a friend of the family. How are you making out?"

"Good, so far."

"Excellent. Do you need anything?"

"No. Not yet anyway."

"Well, I'll give you my number in case you need something. So, how's Tom doing?"

"Oh, he is fine."

"That's good. I was talking to him the other day, and I can tell that it is just eating his heart out that he can't come. He is so pleased that you are here. He said that we would all like you and that you would be great with the kids. Tom instructed me to make sure you never needed anything. Anyway, I'm so glad that Tom found someone because he is such a wonderful guy. Do you have a paper and pen to take down my number?"

I was kind of stunned. What on earth was I supposed to say? What did Tom tell her? Probably she was just assuming that we were together, but still, she didn't give me a chance to explain.

"How do you know Tom?" I asked.

"He grew up here, dear."

I did not know that. I thought he came from Haida Gwaii. So, probably a lot of people here know Tom. Oh great. Everyone that knows him seems to love talking about him.

"Hey, what's up?" I inquired of the kids, after noticing some glum faces when I was done on the phone.

"We were thinking about Mom and Dad," Anthony said.

"How about we go and see them now?" I suggested, as it was barely after four.

"Sure," they said, but were not excited at all.

When we got there, I instantly understood why.

Funny, no matter how hard they try to decorate a hospital, it is still depressing. There was a particular smell there. Seeing people in wheelchairs and those skimpy robes, slowly and painfully walking the hallways, hauling bags on wheels with a needle jammed in their arm, was enough to make me want to leave.

When we got to see Margaret and Brian, it was very sad because neither were really conscious, and their children could only say hi with teary voices and hug nearly lifeless bodies. There were casts and bandages here and there. I almost started crying as well because my heart went out to these kids.

Finally, we left, but these images kept haunting me. I wonder if I even should bring them here, yet it seemed the right thing to do.

123

Upon returning, I threw a pizza in for supper, but the kids hardly ate anything.

"What do you do when you are sad, Addy?" Kimberly asked.

"I put on a song that I like, and I sing and dance to it. If I don't have something with me to play it from, I hum it to myself, and it makes me feel better somehow."

They wanted me to show them, so I requested that tune, and as always, it grabbed me and made me dance and sing along. Soon they joined in as well, and we all danced around the living room.

Finally, they took baths, we read a story, and I tucked them into bed.

I was ready to crawl into bed myself when I heard something. So, I stepped into the hallway. It was Kim, and she was crying.

I went into her bedroom. What do you do with a sobbing child? I scooped her up in my arms and gently rocked her back and forth. She cuddled up to me and gradually stopped. I had no wise words of wisdom or any comforting thoughts, so I sang three lullabies instead. She crawled into the covers, and I kissed her on the forehead.

I had just returned to bed when my phone rang. It was Tom.

"Is this an alright moment for me to call you?"

"Sure."

"With a four and a half hour time difference and our different schedule here, when I get home, it's nine-thirty in the morning for you. It is three-thirty in the afternoon for you when I go to bed. Now, I'm calling first thing. It is three in the morning here, but is ten-thirty too late to be phoning you?"

"No. It's fine."

"I thought you would be too busy to talk if I phoned earlier in the day."

"Probably. Tom, you lived in Terrace?"

"Yes. We moved there when I was in high school. Soon after I finished, I returned to Haida Gwaii, but I would come to visit Margaret as often as I could."

"We went to see them today," I said.

"How are they?"

"I don't know, really. They are not that aware and pretty banged up. The nurse seemed to indicate that they just might need some time."

"How are the kids taking it?" he asked.

"Well, not too bad, considering."

We talked for a while until Tom said he better get out of bed. So, here I am, lying down in bed talking to Tom, who is also in bed. Isn't that a bit personal?

THE NEXT day settled down a little for me. I did some cooking and baking to freeze some things. This was my first lasagna. It would be handy to have food ready for the days we go to the hospital.

In the afternoon, I worked hard at cleaning and doing laundry so that I could spend some time with them that evening. I figured it would be a good way to break up the trips to the hospital. Every second day would be all we can possibly handle as far as visits go.

When the kids got home, we had a round of hide and seek.

Tom called and spoke to them. Anthony told him about my excellent food, and Kim spoke of reading stories before bed and singing and dancing together. I was glad that they sounded content.

I made them do their homework, and then we played some more until bedtime.

Tom phoned again. Is he going to call every night? I was a little confused because he wasn't showering me with words of endearment, but he wasn't just talking about family business, either.

He talked about the people there, some tough times at sea, his dad, and all kinds of things.

Phone conversations were rather nice for a change. So much more personal. Tom said I could always send him an email if there was something I didn't want to forget. He reassured me that he gets them but never replies unless absolutely necessary.

When I asked him how often I should be taking the kids to visit their parents, he simply answered that he trusted my decision.

He e-transferred me a thousand dollars for groceries etc., even though I tried to get him to hold off a bit, until we could see more clearly where things sat. I felt bad taking it, but I could tell that it was important for him to feel like he was providing something.

The next day, we visited the hospital again, and it was no better.

THE FOLLOWING day, I got a call from the school in the afternoon asking if I could bring Anthony home because he was crying. So, I asked to take Kim out of class too, and maybe we could all go somewhere. I packed up a change of clothes for us, and thankfully the school was very understanding of their situation.

I headed to the coast, as I really wanted to see it, and I thought a change of scenery would be good for the three of us. It seemed to be distracting them.

It was a fantastic drive. Terrace was pretty green, and it continued that way as we drove west. There were mountains everywhere, often with snow on them, and the highway followed the Skeena River and the railway tracks. Sometimes there were walls of rock on the side of the highway, where they were partially blasted away for the road.

Once arriving, we parked and took a walk beside the water despite the fact that it was softly raining. Yet I was surprised that there was no beach to be found, but there were sidewalks following the harbour and wood platforms behind some of the businesses along there. Also, they had a few nice parks, even a little sunken garden.

We ordered pasta from a restaurant right there where we could still enjoy the views. They had some pretty good gnocchi.

It stopped raining, so I bought a Frisbee and we returned to the park and played for a while.

I drove around exploring for a bit because I did not want to go back yet and was curious about the area. There was only one small, nice part of town, which was too bad for being in such a beautiful location. I'd have to stop at the coffee shop there. Prince Rupert sure wasn't big, so I was done in a few minutes.

I passed a campground. "Do you guys feel like sleeping in here tonight?" I asked. Their eyes opened wide. "We could stay at a campground if they have room." They were very willing, so I turned around to check it out. I knew that I still had my duvet and some other blankets stored in my trunk. I'd never actually camped before, but it was supposed to be fun.

The owners were so wonderful and went overboard to make us comfortable. They made some kindling for us and gave us some paper and matches so we could have a fire. Also, they brought some stumps to sit on and even offered more, but I think we had all we needed for one night. The kids loved the fire and thought it was great fun to sleep in my vehicle.

I slept better than the last time I tried that, which was when I first left Toronto. Perhaps it was because it was so quiet here, or all the fresh air made me more tired.

In the morning, we all slept as long as we could and then grabbed coffee and a big pack of cinnamon buns before heading back.

WHEN WE returned, I had the kids take baths while I started laundry and vacuumed my SUV.

The phone rang. "Were you at the hospital all night? How's Margaret and Brian?" It was Tom, of course.

"No, we'll go see them today, but everything was the same on Thursday. Why? Did you hear something from the doctors?"

"No. I thought… I've been trying to call. Were you out all night?"

"Yes. We just got back," I said.

"Where on earth were you?"

"We drove to the coast."

"Prince Rupert?"

"Yes."

"You took the kids out all night?" He was upset. "Did you stay in a hotel?"

"No. We camped."

"Addy, for crying out loud, it's not summer!"

"It's pretty warm here, actually. It was a lot of fun, and we all needed the distraction," I said.

"Let me speak to the kids."

To put it mildly, this angered me a bit. I have sacrificed my whole life to be here, even if it was my idea.

I wanted to tell him that they were busy, which really was true because Anthony was in the bath, but Kim was watching me.

Could I be wrong? Was that irresponsible? I don't know anything about raising kids.

"Kim, your uncle wants to speak to you."

I was worried. What would she report to him? I was just starting to get into the swing of things.

I started making lunch and listened to Kim.

"Hi!" She sounded excited. "Addy took us to the sea... Well, Anthony was crying in school, so they called her to come and get him, and so she asked if I could go too, and my teacher said it was Ok, so we drove to the ocean, and we ran in the rain... It was fun, and then we changed... Addy brought extra clothes, and then we went to a restaurant and had supper... We had something that I can't remember the name of, but it's like pasta balls, and salad, and hot chocolates. Then it stopped raining, so we went back to the park and played Frisbee... No. It was so much fun, but then get this: Addy asked if we wanted to camp in her car... She has a big car, Uncle... No. She had all these blankets, so we made a bed... No. It was warm. Then in the morning, we had to leave to get some breakfast... No. Don't be silly... Uncle, we get sort of sad sometimes, and Addy always makes us happy. She is so much fun. I'm glad that you had her come to be with us... No, but it would be great if you could come too... Well, Addy's more fun. She's really cool... But you said she was good with kids... We're really fine, Uncle."

When Anthony came out of the tub, he eagerly wanted to talk to Tom so he could tell him about the fun day we had yesterday.

I was glad the kids backed me up on this one. What a relief. I got worried for a minute.

I didn't feel like talking to Tom, though, so when Anthony was done and told me that Tom needed to speak to me, I told him to tell him that I was busy making lunch. It was true.

After lunch, Kim pulled out her notepad and asked me to draw the wedding dress I wanted. For a second, I was thinking, *What is it with everyone?* but then I realized that this whole book of hers was full of clothing designs, and this was the wedding dress chapter.

You could tell that she had many people draw in it, no doubt mostly her friends at school.

I drew a picture for her of a dress with sleeves that get wider and wider at the wrists, a thick band at the waist, and a sheer loose cape over that trailed on the floor. It was the wedding dress version of my beautiful new outfits.

The dresses couldn't work while I'm playing mom here, but the Celtic sweaters and tops were working just fine for me.

We had kind of a lazy day and coloured, read, and played. That exercise yesterday was good for us.

Later we returned to the hospital, and that put us all in a bad mood again.

What would happen if they didn't make it?

We watched a movie that evening to try to distract ourselves.

That night when my phone rang, I did not feel like answering it. I turned the ringer down, but I couldn't ignore Tom. This is his family.

10

"Hey, I'm sorry," was the first thing Tom said. I was still a little upset and didn't know what to say. "You must understand that I feel so helpless here. I was really worried that something had gone seriously wrong in the hospital and that you guys were there all night. I almost stayed back from fishing. When I couldn't get a hold of you after I came home, I thought the worst. By the time I got you, I wasn't exactly myself. But I'm sorry that I reacted like that… And you never did anything to deserve that. Do you get what I'm saying?"

"Yes." *I guess it did make sense.*

"When I never reached you on your cell, I eventually panicked."

"There wasn't any service there."

"Man! Addy," he sighed, "you scared the daylights out of me. I should've known better, though. You would've called if something was going wrong, and I should be smarter than to assume anything as far as you are concerned… Anyway, the kids had a blast."

So, we went on to talk. I guess he just assumed that I forgave him, which was, of course, true.

THE NEXT day, Tom was trying to solve how to cover their bills. Now that most are paperless, it made things more complicated, and I felt like a spy looking through the office. I did find the bank they were dealing with and a mortgage statement. I think I had the cell phone company. For electricity and water, we seemed to be able to research the providers for this area, and car insurance is provincial in B.C. But Tom had a lot of places to call tomorrow after work to see what all could be done.

It turns out that, after much effort, we could cancel Margaret and Brian's car insurance and cell phone bills. Tom was going to take care of their utilities. However, the mortgage was more complicated. I had to visit the bank to see what they had to say. Of course, they wouldn't be able to tell me the amount in the account, but I could deposit into it. I was wondering if it was necessary because they might have savings. Eventually, the clerk unofficially mentioned that we better start paying for it, and I knew she meant there wasn't enough money to cover any more. So, I took care of it. Everything should go fine if the other bills were paid before the automatic payments went through.

"I never told you to do that. I wanted to have the information I needed so that I could cover it," Tom said that evening.

"You have all the other bills and you sent us money for food and things. Do you really have cash for it all?" I asked.

"For a while."

"We don't know how long this will go on for, so I thought I'll pay this one, as I still have a bit of savings. Once we are more aware of where things sit, then we'll figure the rest out," I said.

"Something might come up. And are you keeping track of how much you are spending? You have to tell me when you ran out of what I sent. But you can't take care of the mortgage."

"We'll figure it all out later once we know how things will go."

"By looking at your credit card and bank statements since you arrived, you should have a complete record. I need you to analyze everything after you've been there a month and then I can learn how much to budget for," he said.

"Yes, but you have to consider that I eat too, and I'm not paying rent."

"Look, Addy, none of this is your expense. You should be getting paid for this, not just being reimbursed."

"Even with two jobs, do you have enough for the house payments, groceries, and bills every month?" I asked.

"I'll figure it out. There's no problem yet."

"I'm taking care of the mortgage for now. You've got everything else. It's simple for me to manage it at the bank. Eventually, we'll settle the score, but we can't drain all your money so fast."

I could tell he hated me paying it, but also, he didn't have enough needed to cover it all for the foreseeable future.

The next couple of weeks came and went. I had some bad moments with the kids. Sometimes I was ready to pull my hair out because they wouldn't listen to me. But usually, that wouldn't last too long.

ON ONE particularly rough Friday, we arrived at the hospital, and there was good news. Margaret was starting to stir a bit more, and it seemed to the doctors that she was getting more responsive.

That evening, when all was quiet, I was incredibly worn out. When Tom called, I tried to tell him the wonderful news about Margaret, but I broke down crying instead. He would just slowly and quietly under his breath say, "hey, hey," and "Oh, Addy." He told me again and again how much he appreciated me being there. Finally, I calmed down and felt better.

The next day I needed to get out of there, so we took off to see some sights in the area. We went for a walk on Ferry Island and then out for supper. Rather than camping, we filled the living room with blankets and had a slumber party there instead.

THAT WEEK, for the first time, Anthony and Kimberly were able to speak with their mother. So, I told her my name, that Tom let me come although he really wanted to be here, that the kids were fine, and I was staying with them in their home. That was as much as I figured she could grasp. I would imagine that her children's welfare would be the only thing on her mind in her situation.

The kids tried to tell her things that we had done. I don't think she picked most of it up, but by the tone of their voices, she knew everything was alright, so she smiled even as she drifted off again.

Even though it would wake him, I decided to call Tom. I could email him, but he rarely checks them until after work. This would be worth being woken up for.

His voice sounded funny, but it was obvious how pleased he was.

From then on, our visits to the hospital were much more eventful.

That weekend was warm but raining. So, we packed a picnic and spent the day outside under shelters, tarps, umbrellas, or anything. We had a great time.

THE NEXT time I was at the bank to pay the mortgage, I don't remember exactly what happened, but before leaving, I had a job there. Now, as if I wasn't having enough fun already, I would get to play single working mom.

The hours were perfect, from nine till two, so I could be home for the kids when they finish school. I did still have some money saved, but how often does a solution fall in your lap like that? Now I don't have to worry about it running out, and I can see how I enjoy this kind of work.

Right away, we had a family conference where I explained to the kids that I was going to start a job. We would have to split all the chores, so we made up lists of everyone's responsibilities. If I could do this, I could do anything. The bank wanted me right away, which was good, I guess.

I told Tom I was starting a job tomorrow.

"What? Where?" he asked.

"At the bank, and it's close by. So, I still get to see the kids off in the morning, and I'll be back before they are."

"What? Staying home got to you? You needed a change?"

"No. Neither," I said.

"When did you start looking?"

"I didn't. It just fell in my lap after some casual conversation. I was there to pay the mortgage, and it turns out they were looking for help."

"Oh, for heaven's sake, Addy, why can't you plan things first and discuss them with others, like normal people do?"

"By others, you mean you. Maybe I'm not normal, but it was inevitable. It was a perfectly rational decision."

"Give me one reason why it is rational," he said.

"People work, Tom. Think of how long it will be before Margaret and possibly Brian can work again, and how long will your savings hold out? Mine won't last forever, either. It seemed like the perfect thing. How many jobs have such a good schedule?"

"You have enough money, though, right? Other than the mortgage, you aren't paying anything. Are you? And we're going to pay you back every cent. Tell me it isn't necessary to do this."

"Um… I think it's wise if I worked," I said.

"No. I never, ever would've let you temporarily cover the house payments if I didn't assume you had a lot saved up. You do, don't you?"

"Well, I had a decent amount when I returned. Not as much as I would have if I didn't spend so freely. But I wanted to start fresh, sort of, so I gifted a fair sum to a mother whose husband was on my plane. She's undergoing chemo and has twin boys. Then I gave some to the lady who had looked after me for many years. Anyway, I still have a bit, but this way, there'll be something coming in," I said.

"Why didn't you tell me? I would've never let you take on the mortgage."

"Obviously, that's why I didn't tell you. Everything is fine. I just don't want things to get too tight."

"Look, you are not going to work to afford to pay for everything there. That is absurd. I'll give you what you need. I have two jobs, remember?" he reminded me.

"With the vehicle payments, the utilities, and groceries, we require more every month than you have left over. How long can you do that for, Tom?"

"Look, I'll get the money to you, but don't take the–"

"How long? Tom, tell me. How many months can you do this for?" I asked.

"Look, I've got savings…"

"I do too, but for how many months can we do this? We'll prolong it at best, and who knows if I would ever find a job with such good hours again? This will be enough for us."

"That is not your concern. And that is not your problem. Let me handle it," he said.

"For how many months can you keep us here with what you have right now? How many?"

"That is not your concern either, but I'll get it to you."

"Tom, listen, I'm going to start this job tomorrow. There is absolutely no reason to turn this down. I can work. Billions of people do, and I've even done it before. I will survive," I said.

"Addy, I wouldn't be working at all if it weren't for you. I would be there and have to keep everything running. I don't want you to wear yourself out. Because that's too much to ask of anyone. I'll send you the money, but just don't take the job."

"This is what single moms do. There are millions of them."

"You are not a single mom. Those are not your kids. You didn't choose that house or any of the expenses. You take them every second day to the hospital. Soon my sister will be home, and you'll be caring for her too. This is insane!" he said.

"Tom. I'm going to start this job tomorrow. It doesn't matter what you say or think. If you send more money, I will not accept it. I need you to save so that you can come for a visit when Brian finally returns. Because I'll need your help then. And honestly, I probably won't be able to work when Margaret comes home, so let me do this while I still can."

"Addy…" He sighed a long sigh. "You are the most amazing person I've ever met. You *promise* me, you will quit the job if you start feeling even remotely run down," he said.

"I'll do what needs to be done. Although I won't kill myself, but it *will* wear me out and run me down. I wasn't born yesterday. But I will learn. I will learn what many women face every day. So, it's a crash course on single parenting and caregiving. This is not exactly a unique set of circumstances. I didn't survive a childhood of neglect and a plane crash in the Atlantic just to wimp out at the first real challenge put before me. I will promise you if we need something, I will let you know, and you will be the first and only to know," I said.

There was silence for a bit.

"I do want to be your first and only," he said, and the change of his voice sent a little shiver through me.

"Addy... I already think you are amazing. You don't need to become some... superwoman now," he added, back to his regular tone.

"I'm not doing it to impress you."

"If I were there, I wouldn't let you go to work," he said.

"How would you stop me?"

"I would tie you up if I had to," he chuckled. "Oh, for heaven's sake, Addy! Before you left here, I told you that you could do anything you set your mind to. I know you can, and I know your mind is set, but I sure hope it doesn't go on for long."

"Maybe it won't."

THUS, I joined the ranks of the working moms, and it was exhausting, but it sure did teach me a lot. I can't believe some women do this for practically their whole lives. All that work, and it only covered a bit more than the mortgage. I took care of a few other expenses when I could without Tom discovering it. Although there was never any money left at the end of the month, at least everything for Laura was still there. We had enough, though.

The weekdays were painful, and sometimes we were pretty crabby with each other. More often than I'd like to admit, I got a little too hard on the kids.

The weekends were always fun. No matter the cost, no major cleaning or cooking projects were done then. Somehow, I gathered enough energy to start another week.

"So, why RCMP?" I asked Tom when we were talking on a Saturday night.

"My mother had just passed away, and my dad was encouraging me to get some training, so I'd have something other than fishing to support myself. But I couldn't think of anything because that was all I wanted to do. I knew I didn't want an office job. It was Darcy who suggested it. He said everyone always respected me, and I knew how to command attention. Seemed like a natural fit to him. I never really saw myself that way, but my sister and dad felt it would work for me after they gave it some thought too. I researched it, wondering how I was going to afford the training. Dad didn't make much, so I knew that would limit my possibilities. Then I found out that not only was there no cost, but they also provided housing and a weekly allowance, and it was only a twenty-six-week course. Then I started to get interested in it. I took my time to figure out how to apply because it's not so easy to get in. But I did, so I headed off to Regina for six months. Afterwards, I moved back to Haida Gwaii and got my level two constable there and then my level one."

"Do you like serving as a policeman?" I asked.

"Not really, but it seems to work for me. Without it, I would never have got to move here. I wouldn't want to serve in a big city, but there or here not much happens, so I guess it's Ok. Every hick town needs an RCMP officer, so it's good that way. It wasn't as good when I was stationed in Masset or Queen Charlotte because I wasn't allowed to fish when I had a shift," he said.

"But in Foley's Rest, you can?"

"Yup. I'm always on call here, so I don't take any shifts."

It was kind of hard for me to imagine him with a uniform or sidearm. Sure, he could have a commanding, controlling way of talking, but he was mostly calm and benevolent. It was as if he didn't need those things.

MARGARET WAS doing much better. We were able to talk now. Sometimes I was so worn out by the time I got the kids there, that I was near tears.

One day, we were both particularly emotional. She saw the stress in my eyes and was mortified about it. Consequently, she started crying, then I started, and the poor kids didn't know what to do. After a while, I thought about how silly it was, and I started laughing, and then she joined in. Then we were hugging, giggling, and sobbing all at once. Sheesh.

Lisa, the next-door neighbour, also came to be a good friend. When I had all I could handle, she would take the kids for an evening so that I would have some time to myself. I always felt guilty, though.

Brian started to improve too. Now we spent longer at the hospital, but I was not complaining. No way. I was terrified of when

Margaret would come home because she would need my assistance.

Tom still called every night without fail, but I was often too tired to talk with him.

Why wouldn't he ask me out anyway? I don't have time to just chit-chat on the phone when I could be sleeping.

IN DECEMBER, Margaret came home.

She needed help with everything because her body was so weak. She was also getting frustrated with not being able to do anything for herself and frustrated that the kids would, of course, come to me for the things that she used to do, but now was unable. I could understand almost, but it didn't make things any easier. A couple of times, I actually scolded her, as I had no other choice. She wasn't trying to be hard on me, and I wasn't trying to be hard on her, but it was a challenging way to live.

Because the bank was so close, I would come home quickly for my two coffee breaks and lunch to help Margaret go to the washroom or see if she needed anything. So, it seemed to be working out, almost. I was happy that I didn't need to quit the job yet, but she felt terrible about that too.

Sometimes Lisa, or Debbie, that family friend that kept in touch, would bring over a meal for us all. That touched me deeply.

The weekends were tough too now, as Margaret still needed lots of help.

Tom consistently called every day to speak with the kids and his sister in the afternoon. That usually puts them all in a better mood. Often Anthony and Kimberly would grumble, but he repeatedly told them to listen to me. Sometimes Margaret, too, would complain about something I did, but I could tell that he would always kindly remind her of the actual situation. It was good to have him on my side, for sure.

Slowly, Margaret got stronger. Actually, it happened rather quickly when you think about it. It just felt like forever. Before the end of the month, Margaret was doing everything by herself and helping out as well. She only had to learn to take things slowly.

We started getting close, and it was what I imagined having a sister would be like.

THE DOCTOR announced that Brian would be coming home in the new year.

At the same time, we also began receiving financial assistance, and I was able to quit my job. Margaret was anxious to give me all the money back, but I knew there wasn't that extra, so I kept telling her to wait for a while.

Tom had been wanting to come for some time after hearing how miserable we all were in December, but we convinced him to hold off until Brian came home. Now, since it was happening, he got his plane tickets and would soon be flying across Canada.

"Oh, I can't wait to see you," was the last thing Tom said to me before he left.

Maybe he will finally ask me out.

I WAS sitting in the kitchen and had my compass out, as I often did. The kids were in bed, and the house was quiet. I turned to face Foley's Rest, which meant being at the corner of the table.

I was there thinking, and Margaret came to make a drink.

"What is that?" she asked, coming close to see.

"A compass."

Suddenly, something caught her eye, and she picked it up and examined it intently. "Where did you get this?"

"It was a gift."

"From Tom?"

"Yes."

"Did he tell you where this came from?"

"No. He never did."

She touched it tenderly and ran her fingers over the lens, as I often did.

"This was our fathers." I was stunned. "He kept it with him always. Dad used to pull it out of his pocket and show Tom and me how it worked. Then, after Dad died suddenly, Tom always carried it with him. He kept it in his pocket for the longest time."

"Perhaps I shouldn't have it."

"Oh, Tom knows what he's doing. He never does anything rashly. I was just surprised to see it and it was nice to hold it again. If our father were alive, he would've approved of you having it. But that kind of adds more depth to that gift, doesn't it?"

THE MIDDLE of January found Margaret, the kids and I, all at the airport waiting for Tom. Anthony and Kimberly were very excited. So was Margaret. Alright, me too. After finding out that my compass was a family heirloom, it gave me more hope that Tom was finally going to ask me out.

They had all visited Tom a couple of years ago, but this was the first time he was leaving Foley's Rest since he moved there. Well, other than St. John's, but that doesn't count. So, the kids had all kinds of things they couldn't wait to show Tom.

Finally, his plane arrived, and upon sighting him, the kids ran to see him, and he picked them up and spun them around. It was such a happy scene, almost like when the boats would come in.

He had on his red buffalo plaid jacket. The one he wore when he saved my life.

He looked at me many times, but next, he gave Margaret a huge embrace and told her that he had been so worried about her.

Then, as he walked over towards me, I didn't know what I was supposed to do. A handshake was too formal, and yet a hug was too personal. I was frozen, waiting to see what he would do. Finally, his hand extended, and he touched the side of my head and let it drop into my hair.

"Addy," he muttered, and then slid it onto my back and turned. He picked up his duffle bag.

What was going on?

Then everyone was heading out of the airport, and I followed behind. Tom kept turning around to glance at me with a puzzled look and finally just stopped until I was beside him before he continued walking.

"You've done a great job," he said to me.

"She's done a wonderful job," Margaret said. "I don't know what we would've done without her."

140

I was very quiet. Because somehow, I had nothing meaningful to say.

I found myself incredibly aware of Tom's presence and it followed me everywhere. I seemed unable to hear or even think, and I wish I could think.

He hasn't asked me out, yet he touched me in front of his family. I'm making too big a deal out of this. It's not like he kissed me or something. A hug would've been much more, and that was even entirely appropriate. Wasn't it?

I have to snap out of this trance before it becomes obvious. Still, he brought back such memories.

The kids were talking a mile a minute as I watched him walk to the vehicle with them hanging around.

I was reminded of his clumsy yet smooth way of moving. With one swift pitch, the duffel bag landed softly inside after I opened the back.

Tom said nothing about my SUV but sat in the front. Margaret and the kids piled in the back.

"Oh, Margaret, is it easier for you to sit in the front?" he immediately asked.

"No. It makes no difference to me. It's all good."

So, off I drove.

It was great that the kids kept talking because my brain was in a fog. Who was Tom to me anyhow?

All of a sudden, Tom was looking at me with a huge grin, and I knew Kimberly must have said something about me or asked me something, but I had not been paying attention.

"Sorry. I wasn't listening," I said.

"Kim said that you are like a fairy princess."

"Oh."

How am I supposed to respond to that? *I took lessons. I graduated with honours from fairy princess school.*

Anyhow, I tried not to let my mind wander anymore.

The kids had lots to say about the last four months.

Tom looked so large in my vehicle, and it's not like it's that small, either.

We got back and started getting a bit of lunch on while the kids dragged Tom all over the place to show him this and that.

141

When it was ready, Margaret asked Tom to bring a chair, which he did and put it beside mine.

Again, I was transformed back to Foley's Rest, having a meal at someone's home. I could smell the rich, woody, salty scent of his clothes.

I had to restrain myself from throwing my arms around him. And I never threw my arms around anyone.

Afterwards, Tom, Anthony and I left the house to get Brian from the hospital.

As I stepped out, I found Tom standing by the driver's side.

"Is it important for you to drive?" he asked.

I was stunned for a minute. He wants to drive my car? No one else has ever driven my car. He is used to being in charge, but so am I.

"No," I said.

He held out his hands, and I tossed him my keys.

He looked at my keychain. On it was this cute stuffed puppy with a tiny body, a huge head, and massive eyes that Kim had bought for me. There was also a miniature model of a vehicle, just like mine. When you pressed it, the headlights came on. Anthony gave it to me. I never used to have anything on my keychain, but these were such sincere gifts that I had to put them there.

"Nice," Tom said with a smile as he held them up.

Then, he unlocked the car, got in and started it up as if he did this every day of his life. He probably hasn't driven for five years.

"You still have a valid driver's license?" I asked.

"I have a sea vessel license. Boats, cars, they are all the same." He looked at me. "I'm kidding. Of course, I have a valid driver's license. I always renew it... Why are you looking at me like that?"

"Like what?"

"Like I just stole your car," he chuckled. "Does it bother you?"

"It's just different."

"It means a lot to me. I'm used to driving, you know?"

"Of course, I know. *Hel-lo.*" I said, and he laughed.

"Please?" he asked.

And he had these begging puppy dog eyes, so how could I say no? Not that I know what begging puppy dog eyes look like, but they must be something similar to this.

It was strange to be on the passenger side. It's been a long time since I was driven anywhere. Before I drove, I took the bus.

What was I supposed to do? Stare out the window?

He drove just like he walked and moved, clumsy, smooth, and swift, but always with a relaxed determination. It sounded weird but was true. There was no other way to explain it.

It occurred to me that, very soon, this wouldn't be my family anymore. Before long, everyone will be well. In a few hours, the kids would have both their parents home, and Margaret's husband would be there. She was able to do almost everything herself already. Tom would care for the more personal needs of Brian, and between them all, I am basically without a job. So, what do I do now?

I remembered a line from a movie that was becoming a favourite of mine. "You're born into a family. You don't join them like you do the marines."

I was empty all over again. It was true that I learned so much, and it changed me in the process. Nevertheless, after it all, what did I have? Memories and the chance to be a part of a family for a while.

Where do I go from here? My mind drew a blank.

All I could think of was the place I had grown to love in only ten days. That was where my heart was, but that was a dangerous thing to desire, bound to lead to disappointment.

Still, his scent lingered, and his presence was with me all the time. It reminded me of the sea, the boats, the wood fires, the easy conversations, the thick humidity in the air and the necessity within me somewhere to burst into song.

The doctors spent quite a while talking to us about what we would need to know to take care of Brian. How would I have done this without Tom? It was basically the exact instructions they gave me for Margaret.

I had worked seriously hard here for four months straight, and now Tom comes for one week, and he is the hero.

I excused myself to go to the washroom. As I looked at myself in the mirror, I wondered: What is my problem anyway?

I had on an ivory sweater and comfortable blue jeans. I still wore my long Celtic dresses, but not that often. They suited Foley's Rest much better. This was a blue jeans place.

Why, though, do I feel suddenly lost and out of place? I wasn't sure.

When I returned, the doctor was finished, and Tom was waiting.

I grabbed my purse and found my big-headed puppy and miniature SUV attached to the strap. Looking at him, he smiled. "Come on," he said as he got up.

Anthony and I dragged behind as Tom pushed Brian in a wheelchair.

Tom got Brian into the front seat without any trouble, and Anthony and I sat in the back.

I peered at my key chains. I had a feeling that I was not getting them back this week.

Then it dawned on me: Why am I suddenly lost and out of place? I was completely in control the whole time I was here… until now. Make no mistake about it. Tom was in control now.

Upon arriving, I watched him put my keys in his pocket. I smiled to myself. Goodness, what was I going to do with this man?

Then he helped Brian out of the vehicle and settled him on the couch once they were inside.

After Margaret and Kim said their hellos, we all sat in the living room.

"What would you like now?" Tom asked Brian.

"I would love Addy to sing a song. The kids are continually telling me of her songs."

Everyone looked at me. So, I stood up.

The song that came to mind was this long, tragic story called The Highwayman, and a singer put it to music. It's like Romeo and Juliet. They all end up dead in the end. This tune always gives me goosebumps.

I sang, and everyone was motionless and just looked at me with huge eyes. No one stirred until I was all finished. And even then, no one moved.

"That's all," I said.

They clapped.

"That is really something," Brian said.

Margaret started supper. I somehow lost that job too.

The Strong and Steady Waves

"Addy, come walk with me," Tom suggested as he grabbed his buffalo plaid jacket. It was not exactly warm out, but that is not why I shivered. I put on a much warmer coat.

11

T hat was an amazing performance," Tom said as we stepped outside.

"A little over the top?" I asked.

"No. It was incredible, and I could listen to you forever. That song was very moving, and it makes me want to do something heroic," he laughed.

"Oh, give me a break. You are everyone's hero."

"Yours too?"

"You saved my life."

"Well, now that I know you, I understand it wasn't necessary. You would've made it just fine on your own."

We were walking fast so as not to freeze stiff.

"Was something bothering you today?" he asked.

"I was thinking that my job is basically done here. No one really needs me anymore. Soon, I will have to pack up my vehicle and leave."

"Not this week," he mumbled.

When we got back, we had supper, and then Tom helped Brian into bed and then crashed on the hide-a-bed. It would have been the middle of the night at Foley's Rest.

Now I would be sleeping in Kim's room. Here I am again, with no place of my own.

Margaret was reading in the sunroom, which was now pitch dark except for her reading lamp.

It needed candles, so I got the lighter. I sang notes softly to myself of a pretty but sorrowful tune as I lit the candles one by one which I placed here a couple of months ago. She closed her book and watched me as I started another song and now started to twirl around as well. I could feel my hair fly around. She smiled.

"We love having you with us," she said when I had finished.

"My work here is done."

"You've done a wonderful job and I still can't come up with one half-decent way to thank you. What can I give you, Addy?"

"Tom," I said.

And we giggled as teenage girls do. She approved, but had no idea what to say. Margaret was a very loyal person so even though she wouldn't tell me any secrets about Tom, I knew she wouldn't tell him any about me and I could trust her.

"I can't give you what's already yours," she finally said.

But she was only jumping to the conclusion that she liked.

I looked up at the stars, and she did the same.

"Remember when you and the kids pretended we lived in a musical?" Margaret asked.

We laughed. I could remember, alright. Instead of talking, we would sing everything and break into dance as well and we continued for quite a while too. Of course, the songs didn't sound like anything, but we laughed like crazy that day.

"You really got the kids singing," she said.

"We've had countless fun memories together."

"You'll be a wonderful mom."

"I knew nothing about kids until I got here."

"And now?"

"Well, I learned some things," I said.

"They sure learned a lot. I even learned a lot."

"Like what?"

"The importance of giving the kids time and attention and the importance of playing with them. You got them through an incredibly tough time, and they are happier than ever.

"I have never been so entertained in my life. Your positive attitude, your joy, and energy are contagious, and I love how I never really know what you will say and do next."

"No doubt that would drive many people crazy," I admitted.

"For sure." We both laughed.

"Speaking about crazy, remember that mouse we found in the kitchen?" I asked.

"Oh, yeah!" she said, laughing harder. "I nearly split a gut when you started chasing it with a pot yelling 'mouse stew! mouse stew!' Kim was screaming, and Anthony was watching with eyes wide, wondering if he would ever eat stew again."

"You laughed so hard that it made me die laughing too."

"Again, I was not expecting that. How can you even think that fast? I would have watched it run across the room and disappear before I would have realized what happened…

"On a more serious side, remember that page that Kim wrote about a very special person?" she asked.

"That was touchy. I almost cried."

"That was sweet. Remember that play you guys did for me?"

"I have so many memories here now that I consider it."

"There's many more to come."

Finally, we said good night and headed off to sleep. I felt better now. This was a vacation. This was my week off. Afterwards, I will figure out what to do, but not until then.

TOM GOT up before any of us and had the coffee going. When I went down the stairs, I saw him standing in the front window, with his mug and watching the snow fall. It was still dark because the days were so short now.

The smell of the coffee greeted me. It was strong. Everyone in Foley's Rest made strong coffee.

I tiptoed to the bathroom so he wouldn't see my bedhead. I used to stay in my P.J.'s until after breakfast, but this week, I might shower before. So, after I looked presentable but still had wet hair, I came out and headed for the coffee pot.

"Morning," he said.

"Hi." I poured some and added my sugar and cream.

Tom's eyes lingered over me and no one else was up yet. With everything quiet and still dark, my heart started to beat faster. After I fixed it just right, I glanced up and met his gaze.

He wore thick corduroy pants, a T-shirt, and a flannel shirt, which all matched. His eyes were so deep and dark.

I walked toward him. Not that I meant to or planned to, but it was a magnetic force. Why was I still attracted to this guy? I never knew a guy this masculine. Was that the word? Notably, he was in control, always perfectly in control. He is quiet, but everything he says carries weight. He is kind and loving, but you have to respect him. In essence, I couldn't step over him, and I couldn't control him. Because he would never allow it.

"So, does anyone send greetings to me?" I finally asked.

"I didn't tell them you were here."

That was strange. Why not?

"I just really want to thank you for being here for everyone," he said.

"You're welcome."

I wanted to ask about the compass, but maybe Tom would be upset at Margaret for telling me, so I didn't.

"You've done a marvellous job here," he said.

"Thanks."

I ran out of things to say, and perhaps he did too.

He could've asked me out. And if he wanted to, he would have.

Soon Margaret got up, and before I knew it, the day was in full swing.

"I don't have anything to wear," Kimberly called out.

This was her new fixation. She never had anything to wear.

"I'll give you something to wear," I yelled back, and she screeched and ran into her room and shut the door as I chased after her. Because I finally found that the only way to deal with it was to make up these ridiculous outfits. "Hey, let me in. I have the greatest idea."

"No thanks. I'm fine and I remembered what I was going to wear," she called back.

"But I have the best idea. You like hats, right? And socks too. You will be the talk of all the boys."

"No thanks."

"You have no idea of the terrific outfit I have in mind."

"No, thanks."

The phone rang, and Margaret answered it, so I took over stirring the porridge and then started making smoothies. The kids loved them, and I just packed them with fruit.

Anthony came out.

"Who was Canada's first Prime Minister?" I called out because he had a Social Studies test today.

"Addy, did you see my science report?" Kim ran up to ask.

"You left it in the sunroom. Remember I told you to put it away?" I reminded her as she raced to grab it.

"What year did Canada become a country?" I asked Anthony. We studied all of this last Friday.

"Where did you find those socks?" I asked him.

"I don't know."

"You want to have stinky feet? Everyone will think you borrowed them from Gargarath." It was a filthy, dirty character in a story we read sometimes. "Go get clean socks."

"Do we have to go to school today?" Kimberly asked.

"Here, mix this up until it is ready," I told her, leaving her with the blender.

"Margaret, did you sign that field trip admission form?" She was off the phone now.

"Yes. Where is it?"

"You didn't give it to him?"

"No. I put it on the fridge."

"Anthony, do you have your field trip permission slip?" I asked him.

"I don't have any socks."

"There should be lots in the dryer. Find a matching pair. Do you have the slip?"

"Yes, I put it in my backpack."

Tom helped Brian back to the living room couch, and they visited there.

"Mom, do I really have to go to school today?" Kim asked.

"Yeah," Anthony added as he came out. "Andrew missed a test, and the teacher just had him do it the next day in the library."

"Why aren't your socks on yet?" I asked.

"You must go to school today," Margaret said.

"I can't find any," Anthony said, so I went to unpack the dryer.

Finally, we all sat down for breakfast, and things were instantly calmer.

"It's not fair," Kim said. "Uncle came all this way, and we don't get to see him."

"You'll be with him after school."

"Yeah, but you guys will do fun stuff while we are gone," Anthony said.

"What makes you say that?" Margaret said. "We have lots of work to do."

"Cause Addy's always doing fun stuff," he said.

We finished breakfast, and the kids reluctantly put their coats and boots on.

"Can't we stay home today, Addy?" Kim asked.

I sat down on a stool at the entrance, so we were at eye level. "I promise you we will not do anything fun. We must get a lot of things done. But after school, we'll probably be finished, and then we can do something enjoyable together. Is that a deal?"

"Uncle, you promise too?" she asked Tom.

"Promise," he said, and they ran out the door.

"Anthony, a ninety on your test," I called out.

"Eighty-six," Margaret said to me.

"Ninety-two," I said. A couple of weeks ago, we started placing bets on the kids' test marks.

We finished clearing the table as Tom came into the kitchen.

"What are you doing today, Addy?" Margaret asked.

"I'm not sure, but to start with, I should go to the store because I ran out of antiperspirant," I said.

"We need to get a new light fixture, some bulbs, switch plates and a furnace filter. So, I'll take you," Tom said.

"That will work just fine, since we require such similar things," I said sarcastically.

Margaret giggled but stopped abruptly after glancing at Tom. Then he grabbed his jacket.

"Come, Addy," he said, and it sounded very much like a command.

Although not planning on leaving yet, I found myself grabbing my coat anyhow.

He should loosen up.

151

He let me in the passenger side of my car, and we drove off. My keys were definitely confiscated, and my house keys sat on there too, so I had to remember that. Now may, however, not be the best time to ask for them.

"What was that about?" he asked.

"What?"

"The sarcasm?"

"I was just joking."

"It wasn't really funny, Addy."

"Well, I'm sor-ry," I said sarcastically.

He glared at me, and his eyes pierced right through me. Man, that is scary. And how can he convey so much without saying anything?

"I can't see what the big deal is," I said.

"Sarcasm is negative. It is always having fun at someone else's expense."

"You have to learn to take a joke," I said.

"No. Addy, I don't mind if you tease me, but don't use sarcasm. It makes people lose respect for you and others. Additionally, I notice the kids are starting to pick it up, and it will only hurt them in the long run. So, please give a second thought to what you say before you say it."

"Look, after all I have done here, I hardly think I deserve this kind of lecture."

"I understand you like attention. Just don't use sarcasm to get it. In the long run, you could end up hurting someone, and there's more to you than that."

I was furious. *How dare he?* "Everyone else thinks it's funny."

"For now, this conversation is over. But we'll talk about it sometime later, after you've had a chance to mull over it.

"Where would you like me to drop you off?"

This is my car, and he is going to drop me off?

"How long will you be?" I asked.

"Not long," he said.

"Then the drug store is fine."

He dropped me off and drove away with my car.

Being irritated, I located my stuff, but found myself unable to think of anything else. I would understand maybe if we were dating, but for him to come across like this after everything I've done here!

I didn't wait long before he came back.

"Hey!" he said, but I just climbed into my vehicle. "Relax, Addy. You've got to learn to take criticism better than that."

"That would be handy, since you plan on dishing it out every day," I said.

He didn't say anything else during the drive home, but I had lost the argument even though I had gotten the last word in.

When we returned, Tom went into the garage to put the light fixture in, and I was still agitated.

I paced the floor and finally sat close to the couch where Brian lay. He slowly turned his head toward me and he didn't look great.

"How are you doing?" I asked.

"Not good," he whispered. "Something's wrong."

I saw a little trickle of blood coming out of his ear.

"Sit tight. We need one more trip to the hospital."

I immediately called 911. This is not good. Margaret heard me and ran to Brian and after, I ran into the garage to tell Tom.

"I called 911. Brian has blood coming out of his ear. I'm driving to the hospital. You ride in the ambulance with him. I'll see you there."

Tom was inside the house in seconds.

"I need my keys," I said as I heard the ambulance coming.

"You stay, so you are here when the kids come home. Margaret will ride in the ambulance, and I'll drive," Tom countered.

"Margaret doesn't need that kind of stress right now," I said.

"Yes, I'll go with Brian," she said.

Just like that, I found myself stuck there, watching as the ambulance came and took Brian away. Margaret left with them, and Tom took off at the same time.

What is Tom doing, coming here and taking over everything? I've been here through all this, and I know what I'm doing. Besides, mine was the perfect solution.

I finally sat down in the sunroom.

I guess he is Margaret's husband, but she just got out of the hospital herself and watch, she'll relapse now because of all the stress.

153

I don't want to be at home because I won't even know what's going on. Furthermore, I was the one who called the ambulance, and I was the one who found Brian in trouble.

Slowly, I calmed down a bit.

I sure hope he is Ok. That is an extremely bad sign if you are bleeding inside your head.

I guess it would be kind of silly if I travelled to the hospital instead of Margaret. I'm not family. I'm the babysitter.

But I like to be where the action is and want to be involved with everything. I want to be in control. I want to be the saviour.

There was no reason to be sarcastic to Tom as he did nothing to deserve that. Why did I say that anyhow? Maybe he had a point. Because I actually did use sarcasm a lot.

Why won't he ask me out? I could take some criticism if he were mine. Possibly.

What can I do now? I wanted to go somewhere, but Tom had my car. So, I'm stuck here. Why wouldn't they at least call and tell me what was going on? I felt so useless, so I tried to do some cleaning.

As time passed and I still hadn't heard from Tom and Margaret, I worried more. If Brian didn't make it... The last four months were hard enough for me, but I thought of Margaret. Imagine doing all this after losing your closest friend.

After having leftovers for supper, one of the kids started crying. I don't remember who, but the other one immediately joined in, and I was next. So, we sat on the couch and cried together. Moreover, I had no energy for anything else.

Then we eventually drummed up enough strength to build things with this creative toy set they had.

Not much later, we heard them. Soon, all three settled inside, and my heart leapt for joy.

"It turned out it wasn't that big of a deal," Tom said.

"They took him in right away. They were so good," Margaret said. "It ended up just being an infection in his ear."

"That's why I wasn't feeling so great. I was all dizzy from it," Brian said as he got hugs from his kids.

They settled him on the couch. Margaret sat beside him, and they talked softly. Tom joined Anthony and Kimberly on their building project.

I continued cleaning the house, and they all called me to come and join them at one time or another, but I politely declined.

The kids should be with their uncle, who came this far to be with them all, and Margaret should be with her husband.

This isn't my house. This isn't my family. This isn't my boyfriend. This isn't my life.

When I finished cleaning everything that needed to be cleaned, I unpacked Kim's clothes drawers and folded everything all up.

Although, for some dumb reason, when I came across this pair of socks that have five toes shaped like mitts, I started to cry. It reminded me of the time I played around with them and put them on my hands. They laughed so hard back then. This is crazy, I thought as I wiped my tears away. Or was it? I have grown to love those kids and this home. Now with nothing and nowhere to go, what was I going to do?

I pulled out my compass and faced Foley's Rest and I sat like that for a long time until I heard Margaret calling me.

Quickly putting the other clothes back, I put the compass into my pocket and got up.

"Yes?" I said when I reached the living room.

My tears had all dried up now. Funny, I don't ever remember crying before meeting Tom.

"I'm trying to put Anthony and Kimberly to bed, but they want you to sing them lullabies first. So, I wondered if you would sing for all of us?"

The kids sat on the couch by their mom and dad. Tom was on the floor, leaning back on the other chair. The toys still lay everywhere. Everyone waited in silence.

I'd never declined singing before.

"Sing the fish song, Addy," Anthony said.

It made me smile. They thought it was funny that one line in this jazzy song said that the fish are jumping.

That is the song I sang first, like always. Then I sang the next one, about little horses, but again not some corny kids' tune. Lastly, I went onto a song that always touched me because of the beautiful words. They were so sincere, and I guess I only understood their full meaning after coming here. I almost made it through, but my voice cracked on the last line.

I fled quickly to the sunroom without glancing back. It is time for me to leave here. I lay on the swinging bench there and pulled the throw over me. My head was on my arm, looking at the stars.

The light broke as someone came.

Tom sat on the floor beside me. Yet I could only see the outline of his face because of the brightness of the hallway. In here, it was dark. He reached out his hand and ran his fingers through my hair, and a sweet heat tingled inside me.

"Are you alright?" he asked.

If I said yes, it wouldn't be true. If I said no, I still didn't understand how to explain it.

"Tell me what's on your mind," he said.

If he only asked me out, everything would be so very different, but I couldn't tell him that.

"Sometimes, I'm not sure what's wrong with me," I finally said, with no word of a lie.

"I thought about what you said earlier," I started, because all things considered, I would rather talk about that. He waited. "You may have a point."

"You have many points, but don't jab me with them," he whispered.

I wondered if he understood.

"I know what you mean," he said, giving my nose a little tap. "Don't think too much and just enjoy the week. Everything will work out."

Somehow, I felt he read my mind or something.

Why is it that every time I'm finally happy, and like I found a home and belong somewhere, I am torn away? And why is it that Tom is an integral part of both these places? I have to go to a place where he isn't and get on with my life.

But now, with him softly stroking my hair and sitting beside me under the stars, I couldn't imagine anything else.

Soon, I crawled into bed and slept in.

I HEARD when everyone got up, but I kept falling asleep.

Finally, I woke after Margaret came into the room.

"You must have been exhausted. But listen, the kids already left for school, and I'm taking Brian to the doctor soon, so if you and Tom want to go out for a while…"

I sat up. My brain, being rather fuzzy, couldn't figure out what all those things had in common. Not until my shower, did I realize I was not supposed to be alone in the house with him. I smiled. I wondered if she worried more that we might kill each other. But Tom had discussed with me before that he didn't want just the two of us in the home together. And shouldn't that mean something? Regardless, he was a respectable guy.

I found Tom and Brian sitting in the kitchen, drinking coffee. Brian looked much better, and he made it to the table for the first time.

"Hi, sleepy head," Brian said affectionately. Tom smiled.

I got my breakfast from the fridge and sat at the table, but not next to Tom, which had become my place. It would look dumb if we all stayed on one side.

We are supposed to go out together. For one thing, how do you go out with someone that you are not going out with?

I saw Margaret getting ready to leave, so I hurried with my food.

We all left simultaneously, but Margaret and Brian got in Debbie's car and Tom and I in mine, with him driving, of course. She had kindly dropped her car off last night.

"We're banished from the house all day," Tom said, smiling.

"All day?"

"Yup. Don't look so excited about it," he said, laughing.

What would I do with him all day? We have never been together for a whole day, and I've never been with any man all day. Besides, what do men do anyway?

"Tell me something, Addy. What is the maddest that you ever got, and what did you do?" he asked.

"I took a kitchen knife after someone once." Tom struggled not to flinch. "I was twelve, and some guy visiting tried to feel me up."

"What about as an adult?"

"Nothing eventful comes to mind. I screamed at lots of people at work, being part of my job description, but not anywhere else.

Likewise, I've never done anything out of anger that I regretted. But why are you asking me this? What kind of person do you think I am?" I asked.

"Hey, I was just asking. Don't worry. I know you're clean," he said.

"Clean? What? Did you check me for police files or something?"

"Naturally," he said, grinning.

"After I offered to look after the kids?"

"Seemed the responsible thing to do."

"I guess so." And I wasn't sure what I thought of that.

He parked in a part of the shopping area. We just got out of my car when I heard my name being called. Lisa waved while pushing Devon in his stroller as she headed to her car.

"This must be Tom," she said, shaking his hand. "I'm so glad to finally meet you in person."

"This is Lisa. The next-door neighbour and my good friend," I told Tom.

"Oh, I can't thank you enough for everything you did. It took a few days for Addy to get here, and I don't know what we would have done without you. I was going to head over to thank you personally," Tom said.

"You're welcome again. When are you here till?"

"Till Sunday," Tom answered.

"That's not too long. How's Brian?"

"He's home now," I said.

"Oh, good grief. You have all been through so much."

"And this is little Devon," I told Tom.

"Nice to meet you," Tom said as he bent over the stroller, picked up his hand, and gave it a gentle shake. Devon smiled at Tom.

"So, what are you guys up to?" Lisa asked in a much too excited tone.

"Nothing really," I said. "You?"

"Just grabbing some more clothes for him, and now I'm heading to an appointment for my haircut."

"Do you want me to take Devon for you while you do that?"

"Oh. That would be so kind of you, but he would only get in the way."

"No. That's no problem," I reassured her. "He wants to hang out with us," I said as I picked him up, and he gave a happy little screech as if to agree and moved his hands excitedly.

"He just adores her," Lisa told Tom.

"Text me when you are done. We'll be wandering around for a while," I told her.

"Thank you guys so much. It's difficult for him to be in the stroller for that long."

"No problem, and if you need to do anything else without him, you go right ahead."

She gave us his car seat and left. Terrace being a little too small, didn't supply a mall large enough to hang out in for a whole morning. Although all the interesting stores found themselves in the same part of town, I had no desire to stroll between them during winter.

Devon would be a good distraction from my so-called anger problem.

He now refused to go back into his stroller and would scream terribly when I tried. But being cunning enough, he knew how to get what he wanted from me.

"Now Tom, Devon has temper tantrums, but I do not." Looking at the little guy, I said, "You tell Tom. Go ahead and tell him that I don't have temper tantrums."

Because I said it in an excited voice, Devon gurgled out something and excitedly moved his hands and feet.

I didn't look at Tom but put Devon on my hip and pushed the stroller into the large store with a bit of everything in it. I spent plenty of time in the kitchen stuff.

Tom was utterly unsure what to do with himself, and not just because this wasn't his thing. I gave Devon all of my attention and barely even glanced at him.

After that, I had Tom drive to this women's clothing store, and I purposely took longer than I needed to and still completely ignored him.

"Addy, what on earth are you trying to do?" Tom asked as soon as we walked out.

12

I paused and turned to face Tom.

"Look. I'm sorry," I said. "I'll stop acting stupid if you promise to forget it."

"No problem."

Next was a men's clothing store with work clothes, so we walked in. I came across a red buffalo plaid jacket and stopped to touch it. When I glanced up, I saw him looking at me with a puzzled expression on his face.

"I wore a jacket like this one afternoon in August," I said. He gave me half a smile, but looked more confused than ever. "I must have got it all wet for you."

"I just washed it," he finally said. So, he obviously knew what I spoke of, but he still didn't understand. There was no way for him to possibly comprehend what happened to my heart every time I saw him wear it.

I forced myself to move on and look at other things.

The shirts here reminded me of what Tom wore. In view of that, I picked one up. Funny how they suited him so perfectly.

"Hey," I heard him say softly behind me as he once again tried to figure out what on earth I was doing. "You think that would look good on me?"

"No... I mean, yes, of course it would... uh... Sorry."

He laughed and took the shirt from me. "What do you think?" he asked as he held it in front of himself.

"It's great," I said.

"What's on your mind?"

"You," I said after a long pause.

A big grin came across his face as he seemed to relax now, and so did I.

He found some clothes for himself and bought them, including that shirt I had pulled out and stared at.

Then we came across a music store, but Devon started getting cranky, so I brought him to my car and tried to calm him down. I dug around in his diaper bag until I located his juice bottle. After a few tries, he finally took it and quieted down.

Tom soon joined me.

"What did you get?" I asked.

He pulled a CD out of the bag and showed me. "Heard of them?"

"No."

"I think you'll like them," and he slid it back inside.

We entered a women's clothing store next, and they had some things I liked. Tom followed close by, but didn't touch anything. Now, with Devon quiet in his stroller, I wasn't sure what to do.

How does one shop with a guy anyhow?

I was looking at a half-decent top when Tom suddenly walked away to another part of the store and pulled out a shawl. It had simple, beautiful flowers embroidered around the edge, so I came to see it.

"Put this on," he said.

Somehow, I was self-conscious of putting it on in front of him, which made me laugh at myself. Nevertheless, I tried to think of a way to decline as Tom helped me out of my jacket. So, I had no choice really but to put it on.

I looked in the mirror, and it was cute. "And this," Tom said, handing me a matching beret, which formed an adorable outfit. He just smiled.

As I removed the shawl and hat, Tom took them, and while I put my coat back on, he headed to the cashier and bought them for me.

I didn't know what to do. Was I supposed to decline? Now it was too late, anyhow.

Slowly, I walked up to Tom.

I recognized the lady at the cash register because we would sometimes talk when I dragged Anthony and Kimberly around.

"How are the kids?" she asked me.

"Oh, they are fine."

"And their parents?"

"Good. Their dad is home now too."

"That is wonderful. Who is this handsome young man?"

"Tom Joseph. This is... the mom's brother."

"Very pleased to meet you. This is a special gift, isn't it?" she said as she handed the bag to me.

"You know how Kim has always liked that little purse?" she asked me before I had the chance to answer the previous question.

"Yes. You finally sold them all, eh?"

"Well," she said with a mischievous grin, "there was only one left when I got the instructions to mark it down 75 per cent. Immediately, she came to mind, so I tucked it away to ask you first if you wanted it."

"Seventy-five per cent off the last price?" I asked.

"Yes. That makes it only ten dollars."

"Oh, thank you. Of course, I'll take it," I said as she ran into the back to grab it. "That's kind of you."

I paid for it. That sure was a good deal, and Kim will be happy. Perhaps I'll keep it for a goodbye gift. Speaking of gifts... I looked at the bag with my shawl and hat in.

"Thank you," I said to Tom as we walked out, but it just didn't seem like enough to say. No one has ever bought me a present before, except for the key chains from the kids. "I don't know what to say."

"You're welcome."

Lisa texted as we tried to figure out where to head next.

"Let's get out of here," I said. After our goodbye to her, I needed some fresh air.

"Where you wanna go?" he asked.

"I'm not sure. What would you like to see?"

"Can we head to the coast?"

"Yes. Although, there's shockingly not much there."

"Depends what you are looking for, I guess. I love the scenery, and it's a bit warmer."

"True," I said.

"I'd just love to drive and see the trees pass on the highway. Really miss that, living on an island with no roads or trees."

"Try driving across the country. That'll cure you." I smiled. "It's all good now. So, that's fine with me."

"Do you mind that I took over your vehicle?"

Again, I had to smile. "I'm getting used to it."

"I really appreciate it," he said as he gently touched his knuckle to my arm. "Without a car, I feel cornered. I usually borrow Margaret's because this way, I was able to help out. But I do miss being behind the wheel. Didn't realize how much till I got behind yours. Funny, the things you miss."

He stopped to gas it up.

"So, Adelle May Lockheart... How did you get such a pretty name? Who named you?" Tom asked as he drove again.

"I named myself. As soon as I turned eighteen, I had it changed."

"What was it before?"

"Stella Raincliff."

"You certainly don't look like a Stella."

"It brought such terrible memories every time I heard it. So, are you actually a Thomas?"

"No. Believe it or not. My birth certificate says, 'Tom.'"

"Do you have a middle name?"

"Curtis."

"Tom Curtis Joseph," I said as I looked in my purse for a lip balm.

When I did so, somehow, my compass fell on the floor, and I tried to pick it up without drawing any attention.

"You have it with you," Tom said.

"Well, I don't want to lose my direction and end up driving straight into the ocean."

"No," Tom laughed. "Especially if I'm not around to pull you out. Speaking of that, we made a holiday in your honour."

"How do you celebrate it?"

"We... sing."

I had to laugh because of the way he said it.

"What's eating you, Addy? Why does it seem like I have to phone you so that we can have a relaxed conversation?"

163

"I don't know. It's as if I'm not sure of my place now that you are here."

"Your place… is beside mine," he mumbled.

This drive between the two towns took only an hour and a half, yet it really was majestic. With so much rock and trees, it always got warmer and wetter the farther you go.

Beside him… My insides suddenly felt warmer too, especially because his voice went deeper when he said it.

"We are a team, Addy," he added. "We're working together."

A team. I repeated in my mind. I liked the sound of it, but you can get a professional team as well.

"You don't always have to be in control," he said.

"But *you* do," I said.

He turned silent for a bit, and I wondered what he was thinking.

"Is it too much for you?" he asked.

"I'm not sure. I'm just… not entirely used to it. I was in control, and now I'm not. The adjustment is sudden, and it's not only your idea. It's everyone's."

"I'd like to tell you that I'll turn it down a bit… but I don't want to make a promise I can't keep." His voice took on a serious tone and deepened a little again.

"You shouldn't change who you are. That's why everyone loves and respects you. I've just… never met anyone like you before."

"I've never met anyone like you, either. You are strong. You're no pushover, and you meet me eye to eye," he said.

Tom mentioned it all as if it was a good thing, and rare. *Eye to eye…* That means at his level, doesn't it?

"Were you always this way?" I asked.

"No. A bit, but not as much. After my dad died, there was a difference. I didn't have anyone to look out for me anymore. Now I had to care for myself and my sister. Well, Margaret was married already, and it's not like she needed help, but you understand what I mean. When they took away my dad's boat and house, it hardened me a little."

"Why didn't you get his house and boat?" I asked.

He took a deep breath and exhaled slowly without making a sound. "We had to move to Terrace when Mom got the virus. Because she had to be in the hospital there. The move cost a lot, but

Dad wanted to keep his property in Masset so we could return after. But he incurred a debt, so it was nothing illegal or backhanded. By the time he passed away, they were not really his anymore."

"You didn't have parents or a home."

"Nope. But I developed a commanding way of speaking when young. I used to stutter as a small child, and my dad helped me see that everything came out better when I said as few words as possible. It just stuck somehow," he said.

We came to the spot where the snow turned into sleet. Then, a little further is where the rain started.

"You eat sushi?" he asked.

"Sure."

"There's a good spot. Have you been?"

"No."

"Have you seen the sunken gardens?"

"Yes."

"The cannery?"

"No. It's closed till May."

"Take the walk to Butze Rapids?"

"No. I've wanted to, but I didn't bring my raincoat."

"Haida Gwaii is amazing, but Prince Rupert is the second-best thing," he said.

"Go anywhere you like because you haven't been here in a while."

"I wish I could meet up with Darcy. He's my best friend and on the island with his wife and daughter. His daughter, Missy, is almost four now, and I haven't even met her. But it's not a simple thing to ferry over. Eight hours, either all day or all night. I'm not here long enough to get over there, and it doesn't make sense to have him make it all the way to the mainland here just to go for a coffee."

"I guess. It's too bad, though. You are so close, yet so far."

"No kidding. It's frustrating."

"Is he like you?" I asked.

"Thank goodness, no. He's Haida also, but he's got patience that I'll never have. In many ways, he's twice the man that I'll ever be. Missed him when I lived in Terrace cause I've never found another friend as good as him. He's no control freak, but everyone that knows him loves and respects him. After all, he's the stronger man, really."

"What's his wife like?"

"She's great. She is creative like you, but more with things. Makes all kinds of beautiful stuff for their store and does flowers for weddings or whatever. Her name is Snow White."

"Seriously?"

"Yes. Her parents named their three girls Snow, Hale, and Rain. Darcy's last name is White."

"Oh, my." I laughed. "That's neat."

"You would've heard about Rain. She went missing in August with that glacier expedition up north."

"Rain? She was the scientist, right?" My mind travelled back to the news reports. That's what took over from the news of my plane crash. But I remembered the name Rain because it sounded so pretty to me.

"Yup. That's her," he sadly muttered.

"How do you just lose two pilots, a scientist, a guide and twenty-four others up in the north? So, that Rain… is Darcy's sister-in-law?"

"Yes."

"Did you meet her?" I asked.

"Yes. I saw her a few times because she loved being at Darcy's. Would camp on their beach. She was brilliant and compassionate."

"That must be hard on Snow to have no closure. How would you ever give up hope?"

"Exactly."

"So, Snow has a store?" I asked, happy to change the subject back.

"Yes. She had an interior decorating store in Vancouver before they got married. Did their place up gorgeous. And Darcy makes furniture. Amazing stuff."

"An RCMP officer slash fisherman with a carpenter. Something tells me you are not much the same," I said.

"No. But we always got along great. Though… that could be because Darcy can get along with anyone."

I laughed. I'd missed Tom's phone calls since he left home. Because he always sounded so down-to-earth then, but it caused me to almost forget how mighty his presence was.

We had a terrific lunch with a commanding view of the bay. I missed the ocean for sure. Terrace is a pretty nice place with all the trees and mountains, but I missed seeing the water.

"Did you ever meet Hale, the other sister?" I asked.

"Just at the wedding. However, she seemed a little more insecure than the other two. High maintenance but still a great person. But in September, she married a complete stranger who has a piece of land out by Prince Rupert. To say they live off-grid is putting it mildly, according to Darcy. Yet he says they are doing really good now."

"Interesting. It sounds like you and Darcy keep in touch."

"Yes. He's always a good friend to talk to."

"Well, what should we do until the kids get home?" I asked after.

"We have to stay out until supper."

"Why?"

"They probably have a reason," he smiled shyly.

"It's barely raining now, so I'll take you for that walk. Your shoes look like they can handle some mud," he said, looking down at my feet.

"One of the first things I had to do was get practical footwear," I said.

"Well," he said as he stood up, "try keeping up with me."

We left the restaurant and headed to my vehicle.

"How much walking have you done over the last five years? You can't walk anywhere on that stupid island," I said.

Tom looked down, and I realized I'd said the wrong thing. I didn't really mean that Foley's was stupid. I started to try to explain when I heard my name.

It was Declan from the kid's school. Being the only single dad around, I tried to make him feel welcome, and I also loved his Irish accent. So, we'd always talk. He was comfortable to be with, and I enjoyed that. Now, he greeted me with a hug as usual, and I asked him about his reason for being on the coast, and he did the same. If I'd ever wondered if he had any other intentions toward me, which

I never had, but if I did, this would confirm that he didn't. Because he never even slightly flinched at me being with Tom. In fact, he seemed to have a sparkle in his eye, as though he was happy for me. After a little more chit-chat, we parted ways.

Tom was very silent now and couldn't seem to look at me.

"I wanted to say, before we ran into Declan, that I was just joking when I used the word stupid. Because I don't consider Foley's Rest that way. I exaggerated. Maybe it was even sarcastic," I said.

He looked at me thoughtfully, but said nothing.

What am I supposed to say about Declan? I'd already told Tom he was a dad at the kids' school. So, I didn't have to defend myself further, did I? Considering that Tom and I were not dating, it seemed silly to try to apologize for... whatever. I hadn't done anything.

We drove to the trailhead and did a very serious 5ks of walking fast. We were both perspiring and panting by the time we finished. Since conversation had been nearly nonexistent, I guess exercise was a good use of the afternoon.

We got back into my vehicle and headed off.

"There's a bookstore here I would like to go to in Terrace," Tom finally said.

Prince Rupert never seemed that far away before. The ride back took forever. Usually, I loved that drive, but now it was painful. I didn't want a one-sided conversation, but I didn't like quietness. Yet I felt that if I talked, I would break some deep thought of his. Finally, I could stand it no longer.

"Would it bother you if I sang?"

"No."

So, I sang a cute song that told a story. It was of a lady mourning for her lost love. Then, in the end, it turns out that the guy she was talking with was her man in disguise, and it touched him.

After I finished, it remained quiet again until we got into the bookstore.

"Is something wrong?" I had finally had to ask.

"No." And he started looking at books.

I didn't read books. It's not that I don't know how, but they never move fast enough. They are always describing everything instead of just getting to the point.

Tom was considering a biography. Who on earth reads biographies? What could possibly be more boring? *Hi. I'm going to write all about my life and the things I did.* I mean, really?

The winters must be very long in Foley's Rest.

I looked at some cookbooks. Then I realized that there would never be a cookbook where I liked all the recipes, and it's faster to look up what you need online. So, I left to peruse the magazines instead. After about ten minutes, I was done there.

I approached Tom. "Are you nearly done?" I asked.

"Almost." He looked at his watch. "We still can't head back yet, so why don't you do a little shopping? I'll be in the coffee shop reading."

Did he think I was flirting with Declan? But I figured he would just lecture me on how that could cause trouble and make people lose respect for me. This silence, I didn't know how to deal with.

He didn't look mad, though. That's what I really couldn't understand. I tried not to keep going over it in my mind, but it was no use.

I thought about my shawl and hat. That was such a sweet gift. Maybe I didn't show enough appreciation for it, but I knew that wasn't the problem.

I've seen everything this morning already. Because how many stores do you think there are in Terrace? If I had something new to shop for, but my mind was blank.

Finally, it was getting close to the time we could leave, so I headed to get Tom. He was in the coffee shop, sitting in the window with a cup of coffee and a large book. He wasn't reading it, even though it was open. Instead, he stared out of the window, and I had to stop for a second to watch him. Always so calm, so settled, and content, I admired it immensely and sort of wished I was more like that.

"Hello," I said, breaking his gaze.

"Hi." He took a sip of his coffee. "You want something?"

"No. I'm fine. Are you alright?"

"Yup. Do you want to go?"

"You can finish your coffee," I said, sitting down beside him so he wouldn't feel that I wanted him to rush.

I tried to sit still. I tried very hard. But it took all of my concentration right now.

I thought of the kids, because we sometimes had competitions to see who could sit still the longest. And I certainly didn't win all the time.

Just when I felt I would burst into song or something, he finally got up, put his books in his bag and threw his coffee cup out.

We walked silently back to my car.

Eventually, we returned home, and I almost ran inside.

As soon as I opened the door, I saw lots of balloons and paper streamers.

"Surprise!" they yelled.

I was perplexed. What was the occasion?

"It's a thank-you party for you," Anthony explained.

Margaret had made all these wonderful finger foods and there was a cake that said, "Thank you, Addy."

No one ever had a party for me before. I was so touched.

Everyone was in the best of spirits except for Tom, who remained quiet and sort of meditative. They even had gifts for me.

"Uncle, didn't you buy anything for Addy?" Kim asked.

"He already gave it to me," I said as I showed them my lovely shawl and hat. So, they made me put it on.

Tom, of course, said nothing.

I had such a wonderful time, although I was worried that I might have hurt him. Additionally, he went to bed when the kids did. What was wrong?

Margaret joined me in the sunroom.

"So, were you surprised?" she asked.

"Yes. I certainly wasn't expecting that. That was so sweet of you guys. I will remember it always."

"Did you have a nice time today?"

"It started fine, but later Tom got really quiet, like he has been all evening," I said.

"He's thinking."

"Of what?"

"Something that's important to him."

"It's driving me crazy. I can't sit still for a second. I can't not say anything for that long."

Margaret laughed. "Tom can."

"I hope he doesn't stay like this all week. He was quiet with everyone."

"He won't."

"I must have done something wrong," I said.

"He would have told you if you did. So, don't worry, just give him some space."

Nevertheless, I was worried and had trouble sleeping that night.

THE REGULAR crazy rush sending the kids off in the morning didn't excite me very much. I couldn't seem to get into anything.

After breakfast, Tom returned to the garage to finish putting in that light fixture he was interrupted from on Monday.

After pacing the floor for a while, I grabbed my jacket and went into the garage.

"Tom, I don't want you to be upset with me."

He peered down from his ladder. "I'm not."

"Well, you're quiet. But whatever it is, you have to know that your friendship means the world to me. There is no one that I respect and admire more than you."

He looked at me but still said nothing, so I left.

"Thanks, Addy," I heard him say as I reached the door.

I tried. There was nothing else that I could think of to do.

I returned to pacing the floor.

"Addy, would you do me a huge favour and get the groceries for us? I just don't have the energy," Margaret asked.

"Sure." And I was glad to have something to do.

I was satisfied with myself for such a heartfelt attempt at making peace with Tom. It was true what I told him.

Oh yes, keys. In the front closet, I rummaged around in Tom's jacket pockets until I found them.

"ADDY!" SALLY, the woman in the floral department, called out. "Hi, I saw Margaret yesterday, and boy, she is doing good."

"Yes. Oh, you got your lilies."

"Finally. They are a bit late this year."

"Brian's home too. Did she say?" I asked.

"She did. I'm so glad things are working out. Tom is visiting, isn't he?"

"Do you know him?"

"Not well, but I've seen him because I've worked here for quite a while. He is one attractive guy," she said.

"This is true."

"How many would you like?"

"Lots."

She wrapped up a few stems for me. I'll give them to Margaret.

"Hi, Jim," I said to the older gentleman who runs the produce section.

"Well, hello! If it isn't my Addy. How are you?"

"Ok."

"Just Ok? That's not good enough for my Addy."

"Things are fine, actually. Brian is home, and everyone is doing well. Tom, Margaret's brother, is visiting."

"But...?" Jim asked.

"Well, my whole job here is basically done now, and... Tom won't ask me out." My voice cracked.

"Oh. Oh. Hey, Addy, don't you worry. If he is the right guy for you, it will all work out. You let him chase you a bit. If he doesn't, he is crazy, and we'll check him into a mental hospital. However, you'll end up with someone really special. Just wait."

"Thanks. You know how you said that you haven't been able to find those strings for your glasses? Well, I found some."

"Where?" he asked.

"In the bookstore. I guess it's for reading glasses."

"Oh. Why, thank you, Addy. I will go and pick them up."

"You don't need to cause I bought some for you." And I pulled them out.

"Thank you, child. How much did you pay? I'll give it back to you."

"No. It's a gift. They weren't expensive."

"That was so thoughtful of you. This is exactly the kind I'd been looking for, and like I said, I couldn't find them anywhere. Because all the others fall off right away. Thanks so much, Addy."

I grabbed some lettuce.

"And Addy…" he called out. "… you will never be alone."

"Hi, Samantha," I said to the bakery lady.

"Addy, how did you like your cake?"

"It was wonderful. Thank you."

"I've got a fresh batch of those buns that'll be ready in two minutes."

Hmm. I seem to know a lot of people here. A person might conclude that all I do is grocery shop.

"Addy, you've got to try my chicken pot pie," the deli guy said.

"Forget it. You'd think chickens were nearly extinct with the price of that stuff."

"Shhhhhhh," he said, laughing.

Finally, I finished looking for things and felt a little better. I stood in line.

"Hi," the lady said in front of me. "My daughter is in the same class as Kim."

"Oh, you were on that nature field trip."

"Yes. How are the kids?"

"Good. Their uncle is visiting, so they are pretty busy."

"How're their parents?" she asked.

"Very good. Their dad came home on Sunday, and their mom is doing much better. My job is just about done here."

"Where do you live?"

"Nowhere now. I was in Toronto before, but I don't plan to go back," I said.

"How come?"

"It is chaotic and impersonal."

"Oh. Well, it's much bigger than here, that's for sure. This is like a small town," she said.

"Terrace is very friendly."

"I guess it is."

She finished and left after saying goodbye.

"Hi, Addy," the cashier said.

"Hi, Christine. How are you?"

"Alright. Although I had the worst customer today, and it put me in such a bad mood."

"Don't you wish you could just forget about it instead of thinking about it over and over?"

173

"Exactly."

As I packed the groceries in my car, I considered how I changed over the last few months. Because I never used to talk to anyone unless I was working. Now I am more comfortable with parents than with professionals.

"Hi," Margaret said. "Thank you so much. However, I must say that you must be the slowest grocery shopper ever. How're all your friends?"

"Oh, fine. Here are some flowers for you."

"Thank you."

"I'll just grab the rest." As I got more bags from my car, Tom came to help me take some things in.

"I stole my keys," I told him.

He smiled. This was more like Tom.

As soon as we were done, I placed my keys back in Tom's jacket pocket and sat at the kitchen table while Margaret put the food away. I needed to get off my feet.

"Hungry?" Tom asked.

13

"I'm starving," I said.

Tom took a plate out of the fridge and put it in the microwave for me. "Want some tea?" he asked.

"Sure, but I can get it."

"You relax. I can make tea, sort of."

He looked lost in the kitchen. Even though it didn't suit him at all, it was sweet.

"So, tell me about everyone," Margaret said.

"Everyone?"

"Ok, maybe not everyone, but some of the people at the grocery store you talked to." She teased me. "What about the bakery girl?"

"Samantha. She wanted to know how I liked my cake."

"What about the deli boy?"

"Well, Frank wasn't there today, only Harold. He tried to get me to buy his ridiculously expensive chicken pot pie."

"And the flower lady?"

"Sally. She said that you looked very good yesterday."

"Which cashier did you have?" She laughed.

"Christine, but she is having a rough day."

I ate lunch and drank tea while Margaret and Tom sat with me.

"If we took the kids out to dinner, Brian and Margaret would be able to have a little quiet time together," Tom said to me.

"Sure."

"I was thinking of that place with all the games."

"Oh, they love it there," I said.

"Been recently?"

"No. Only once, soon after I arrived."

"So, Addy might not know everyone in sight," Margaret said.

After lunch, I sat on the living room floor beside Brian.

"I didn't forget about you," I told him.

"I was beginning to wonder." He smiled.

"I would go insane if I had to lie on the couch all the time."

"I know," he laughed.

Tom came and sat on a chair.

"What can I do to brighten your day?" I asked Brian.

"Tell me something funny," he said.

I thought about it for a minute. I didn't know any jokes or at least, none came to mind. Then, I remembered a little skit that I had seen somewhere. I guess I could do that.

From the closet and pulled out the longest coat I had, as well as a hat. I returned to the living room and hung it, with its hanger, onto the lamp. I put the hat on top. My coat person was the same height as me, which was important.

Margaret came in and was hushed. So, she immediately sat down and watched. Funny, I never seem to have any trouble getting an audience.

I started wiping fuzz off it and straightening it all up. While still facing it, I put my left arm through the left sleeve to do a better job of cleaning it. As I worked closer toward the shoulder, I moved my left hand and immediately looked down at it, but it was now still. When I didn't look at my hand, I would move it, but as soon as I looked down, I would make it freeze still.

This way, I began to create the impression that this hand was not mine but the coat person's.

So, when I eventually saw the hand move, I pretended to be scared to death. Margaret let out a little giggle every time it moved. Soon, they were all laughing.

I feigned that the hand was going to strangle me, but it turns out that it was only joking. We snuggled together. I got my pockets looted when I wasn't watching. Then we fought but made up.

Everyone laughed pretty hard now.

In the last scene, I purposely became a little too active, and my arm came out of the sleeve. Then I tried to figure out why my coat friend stopped moving and where the hand was. Finally, after great disappointment, I put on the coat and hat and walked out.

They clapped, and Tom whistled.

I wonder what it really looked like because I didn't expect them to laugh that intensely. Indeed, they were still clapping and whistling after I finished putting them both away.

"I would have paid money for that show," Margaret said.

"Oh, man. I haven't laughed that hard since... I can't remember when," Brian said. "You have a gift. I'm sure you are aware of that, but you really have a gift."

"The art of stupidity?" I asked, laughing.

"The art of entertaining. You are the most entertaining person I have ever met," Brian said.

I looked at Tom, who hadn't made any comments yet.

"You never fail to amaze me," he said.

They started talking casually, but I felt antsy, so I got up and went into Kim's room.

I sat on my bed, pulled out a brochure I had for Haida Gwaii and looked through it. Moreover, I actually got a little excited because this sounded just perfect.

I had almost finished with it when Tom came in.

"Hey. What are you doing?" he asked.

"Oh, nothing."

"Why did you leave?"

"No reason. I just... I'm not sure. I couldn't get into the conversation, maybe."

"What do you have there?"

"Nothing. It's only a travel thing."

He came closer to see it.

"That's where I'm from," he said.

"I know. It sounds like a nice place."

"That it is. There is so much sandy beach... everywhere. Forest, mountains. Lots of bears, everything. It's a kid's dream, those islands. And there was always something to explore.

"Our land stretched right onto the sea. My grandfather had built a pier that stretched out, and my dad's boat was on the end."

He became silent for a moment, deep in thought. Of course, it must be nice to have pleasant memories like that.

On the other hand, I probably look the same when I think of Foley's Rest or later when I reflect on being here.

"Do you want to go there?" he asked.

"It would be nice to see."

"A lot more fun there than Foley's Rest."

Is that my cue? I wished there were a way to ask for his opinion of what I should do next because he seems to be such a logical thinker. So, is he trying to warn me never to go back there? In Haida Gwaii, I would only be one ferry away to come visit Margaret and Brian and the kids.

"What are you thinking?" he asked.

"Oh, I don't know. Sometimes I just don't know."

"Well, what I do know is that we're going to have a lot of fun tonight," he said as we heard the kids come home.

"We get to go for supper with you and Addy?" Kim excitedly asked Tom as soon as she got home and found out. "Wow! This will be so fun."

Sometime during the meal, I realized that we must look like a family. Since Margaret is First Nations, but Brian is not, Anthony and Kimberly are only half Native. If Tom and I had kids, they would have similar colouring. Anyhow, what an absurd thought.

Tom was so good with the kids.

I decided that since I would probably never see him again after Sunday, I might as well relax and enjoy his company. Evidently, he was not going to ask me out, but I refused to sulk about that this evening.

The truth is that his friendship changed me. And if it weren't for him, I wouldn't be where I am now, on many different levels.

I never quite understood the special attention he gave me. It somehow didn't seem to suit his character, but I was confident that he would never intend to hurt me in any way.

After the kids got into their games, we talked. Reminding me of the phone conversations we used to have, relaxed and fun. Two good friends. Nothing more. And it was fine this way. Almost. Ok, no. It wasn't.

When we came back, Margaret and Brian's faces looked brighter.

I packed all of my clothes into my suitcase.

"Where are you going?" Kim asked.

"Nowhere."

"Then what are you doing?"

"Everything of mine is all over the place. I'm tidying up. Because it's my own portable clothes closet," I said.

As I lay on my mattress on the floor in Kim's room, I considered what I would do next. I should go see Haida Gwaii while on this side of the country. Who knows? Perhaps I'll even settle there. Moreover, if they have a bank I could work in, that would be good enough for me. Then, I would be by the sea again.

I wonder if I should leave before the weekend to give Tom an opportunity to be alone with his family.

I fell asleep but started to have a bad nightmare. The last time I had a bad nightmare was before my plane crash. But this one was worse because I couldn't wake myself out of it for quite a while.

That guy, the one who came after me when I was twelve, was after me again. It was strange because, in real life, I didn't even feel this frightened. Tom was there, but he refused to help me. I was so mad and screamed his name, yet he just stood there, and finally, he put his arms around me and told me to wake up. The nerve of him. Was he blind or something? This guy is trying to get me, and Tom just held me. I tried to get out of his grasp, but was completely unable. Still, he kept telling me to wake up.

Finally, I did.

I found myself soaking wet.

Tom sat on my mattress and had me in his arms. Kim sat in bed with a frightened look on her face, and Margaret's silhouette was in the door frame. I was trembling. Tom held me tight against him and rocked back and forth slowly.

After I regained a little more awareness of what was happening, I didn't want to get my perspiration all over him.

Besides, he didn't help. Well, it was only a dream. I was mad at him, though. I tried to tell myself it was just a dream, but I was still upset with him.

When I gained more strength back, I slowly pulled away from Tom.

"You alright?" he whispered.

"I think so." A chill now ran through me from my wet clothes. "I need to take a shower and put something else on."

He released me, and I looked in my suitcase for another pair of pyjamas.

Tom got up and leaned over Kim's bed.

"You don't worry, and fall right back asleep," he said, kissing her forehead.

"Did Addy have a bad dream?"

"Yes."

"What could be that awful?" she asked.

"Hopefully, you will never know."

I entered the bathroom, grimacing at the bright light. Although I was freezing, I stopped because I heard Margaret and Tom talking.

"Could you stay up until she finishes her shower? She is so weak that I'm afraid she might pass out in there." Tom asked Margaret.

"Certainly."

"Did she have bad dreams before?" he asked.

"None that I ever woke up for. What kind of upbringing did she have?"

"She never said?"

"No. Once I asked her about her mother, and she said that her mother never loved her and to trust her on that one, as if she didn't want to talk about it," she said.

"Addy had a childhood of abuse and neglect. I'm not sure if she was physically abused, but she was never loved. She ran away at fourteen."

"I shudder to think what she dreamed. But she really did scream your name."

"No fooling. Only it wasn't a *please help me* kind of scream," he said.

I was freezing, so I couldn't wait another minute to start the shower.

Thank goodness I didn't pass out.

I felt better afterwards, but still a little weak and shaken.

When I got out of the bathroom, I heard Tom whisper my name, so I went into the kitchen.

"I made a tea for you."

"Thank you." Come to think of it, I am thirsty.

When I took it into Kim's room, I found my sheets changed.
I sat in bed and drank my tea, which soothed me.
When I finished, I fell right back asleep.

IN THE morning, I woke up tired, but Margaret didn't look so great, so I made breakfast for everyone and saw the kids off to school.

Tom helped me with the dishes.

"Did you sleep well afterwards?" he asked me.

"Yes. Thanks for the tea."

"No problem. If you don't want to talk about it, it's Ok, but why did you scream my name? What on earth did I do?"

"I was mad. This guy was after me, and you were right there and wouldn't do anything."

Tom said nothing for a little while as he dried the frying pan.

"You understand that would never happen in real life, though," he said seriously.

"No. I guess not, but it just seemed so real."

"Hi, guys," Margaret said as she came out. "Sorry for leaving you with all this."

"Don't worry about it," I said.

"How do you feel this morning?" she asked me.

"Tired, but otherwise fine."

"What kind of plans do you guys have for the next few days?"

"I'm taking Addy for supper tomorrow night, but other than that, we don't have any," Tom said.

I said nothing. *He's taking me for supper?* I suppose I'll leave on Saturday then. I like how he makes plans for both of us and doesn't even tell me.

Why am I mad at him anyway? It was only a dream. Tom is everyone's hero, so that would've never happened in real life.

Then Tom went to help Margaret with something, so I went into the living room to keep Brian company.

"I think you guys had too much fun yesterday," I said as a huge grin crossed his face. "You and Margaret have a good relationship, don't you?"

"I think so."

What would that be like? I sort of got a taste of parenting, but what is it like to be married? What would it be like to have a friend for that many years? All the friends I have are only a few months old. But it must be nice to be loved for years and years. What kind of relationship would you have with someone you knew for that long?

"How does your relationship change as time passes?" I asked.

"It just gets deeper, stronger and better." *Wow! That is neat.* "You'll see."

I wish.

Soon Tom and Margaret came to join us.

Tom put in the CD he bought for me to hear. It sounded really great, so I listened and listened, taking it all in.

"I thought you would like it," he said.

"I do. But I never know where to find new interesting music."

We talked the morning away. And it was kind of fun to sit around and do nothing. Maybe I am getting better at sitting still.

"I feel like pasta," I said. "Pasta with a creamy garlic sauce."

So, Margaret and I tried to make some together while Tom helped Brian take a bath.

Afterwards, I told Margaret that I was going shopping for the afternoon. Of course, I'd just been, but now I had decided to buy goodbye gifts for everyone. I had that purse for Kim already. However, Tom overheard and said that he would take me. I wanted to be by myself, actually, but I didn't want to hurt him or anything. But it would make it a bit hard to get a gift for him.

I'll probably leave on Saturday morning. Then, I'll take the ferry to Haida Gwaii, and I wanted to have a gift for everyone before.

"So, what are you shopping for?" Tom asked me once we were in my car.

"Well, I would like to get goodbye gifts for everyone."

Tom was quiet for a moment. "Addy, did you find out anything, by any chance?"

"Find out anything?"

"I was just wondering."

"What do you mean?"

"Hmmm. Don't worry."

Now my mind raced. It made me want to search for something, but I didn't know what to look for. What does that have to do with goodbye gifts? Maybe Tom got a goodbye gift for me.

Now, we had a great time shopping together. Tom was himself, and I enjoyed his company. It turned out nice that we had a second chance at this. In the end, I found everything I wanted to, except that I'll need to look for something for Tom on another occasion.

After we arrived home and everyone got busy, I looked at the ferry schedule to the island. I'd never been on an eight-hour boat ride before. It is reservable, but I decided not to because anything could change at this point, and at the same time, I had no idea what I was doing. Also, it would make for an early morning because I would first have to drive to the coast.

I pulled out my compass. It's funny because Haida Gwaii must be the farthest away from Foley's Rest that you can possibly get within Canada.

Margaret called me because she had put ground beef in a frying pan but felt she had to rest a bit, so I promised to take care of it.

I was trying to smash up this stuff when Anthony needed to go over his next set of words for his spelling test tomorrow. Accordingly, I asked him to spell words while mixing ground beef and answering Kim's questions about a story she was writing.

Next, the doorbell rang, and it was Lisa.

I found her nearly in tears. She had a babysitter for Devon, who cancelled last minute, and she had plans for the evening with her husband.

After all that she did for me by looking after the kids when I needed it most, I certainly wouldn't think of refusing.

As soon as she left, though, Devon started to cry.

Now I had a crying baby on my hip while cooking and helping the kids with their homework.

Tom came into the kitchen.

"Addy, what is another word for mad?" Kim asked.

"N-E-I-G-H-B-O-U-R." Anthony spelled.

"Furious," I told Kim. "Honest. True friends are honest with each other." I told Anthony for him to spell.

As he started spelling that word, Tom came and took Devon from me, who was still crying despite my best attempts to soothe him. But that kid is not happy unless he has all the attention. He kind of reminds me of someone.

I continued with my cooking and homework aid, but now became more distracted by watching Tom. Devon seemed like a big baby to me, but in Tom's hands, he looked so small. Even though Lisa told me he doesn't care for guys very much, as Tom tenderly spoke to him, he calmed right down. Tom held him against his chest with one hand and, with the other, softly stroked Devon's tuft of hair. He barely took his eyes off the little guy, who had his head tilted to look back at Tom until he fell fast asleep.

Somehow, that image stayed in my mind all evening.

The kids finally finished with me and left to go play.

"The dinner is almost ready," I said to Tom, who stood by the living room window, still holding Devon.

He came towards me. "What do you suppose I should do with this thing?" he asked, grinning. I had to smile.

"Well, he's a pretty sound sleeper. If you lay him down slowly, he might not wake up. Why don't you put him on my bed? At least if he rolls off, he wouldn't hurt himself."

He would make a good father. I never wanted children before and never imagined being a mother a year ago. Now, I'm sure I would enjoy raising a family. And If I had a husband like that, I wouldn't be able to resist.

Afterwards, when I began clearing the table, the kids joined me and started singing a song I had taught them. We used to practice it often when we would do dishes together. We would each take turns singing a verse, and we sang the chorus simultaneously. In the end, we sounded pretty good.

Brian stayed at the table listening to us and clapped when we finished.

After supper and dishes, the kids seemed to disappear somewhere. They were very involved with something or other. Margaret and Brian were sitting and talking in the sunroom and didn't seem to need any extra company. Devon still slept. Tom was reading his massive book. I went downstairs to see what the kids were up to, but they barely noticed my presence. So, I started cleaning.

"Addy, what are you doing?" Tom asked when I came within earshot.

"Oh, not too much."

"Do you ever read?"

"Yes. I read to the kids."

"What about to yourself?"

"No, because it would sound really dumb when I do all the voices of the little furry creatures."

He smiled. "Do you do anything in a sitting position?"

"Eating."

"Do you like... comics?"

"I've never read any. Aren't they for kids?"

"For all the kids that buy newspapers," he laughed. "Do you have any hobbies?"

I looked at him. I always thought hobbies were for people who had nothing to do. None of them appealed to me.

"Singing is kind of a hobby for me. I learn new songs sometimes. Does that count?"

"I suppose. What would you do if you were suddenly the only person in this world?"

"I would travel through the world singing. I don't know. What would you do?"

"Go on my boat and read."

"Do you read on your boat while you are fishing?"

"No. I wouldn't mix the two."

"Tom?"

"Yes."

"What is tomorrow about?"

"What do you mean?"

"Supper. Is there a reason?" I asked.

"Does it make you uncomfortable?"

"No, I didn't say that. I just wondered if I missed something somewhere."

"I think we should talk," he stated.

Without warning, I felt my face get flush. It's nothing, I told myself. Yet I was terribly worried he'll tell me once and for all that we are only friends and that he hopes he never left any other impression.

"It's important that we talk," he repeated.

I slowly nodded.

This will work out well because after that I'll want to leave here.

Leaving Saturday morning would cause too much of a stir. I'd better go Friday night after everyone is sleeping. I can stay in a hotel in Prince Rupert.

I continued cleaning some more until Devon started crying.

I got him and spent the evening entertaining him. At least someone wanted to be with me.

I read a story to the kids, and they went to bed.

Margaret and Brian followed soon after.

Devon started getting cranky again. Thus, I tried to calm him down so that everyone could sleep. Tom was the only one up.

Finally, Lisa and her husband came.

Then I took a bath, but I found myself hungry for some reason.

Hoping Tom wasn't sleeping yet, I tiptoed into the kitchen, but the lights were off. I whispered his name very softly so there would be no way he would hear me if he were asleep. He answered.

"I didn't wake you, did I?" I asked.

"Nope."

"I was hoping to make myself a snack quickly. Would it disturb you if I turned the light on for a bit?"

"Go ahead."

So, I flipped the lights on and opened the fridge. There was roast chicken. A sandwich would be so perfect. Therefore, I pulled out mayo and cheese and lettuce and the leftover chicken.

Tom came into the kitchen. I wondered if he might wear something really ugly to bed, like sweats, but he had on cotton pyjama pants and a T-shirt. By all means, he looked good, as always. His hair was slightly tousled, but not enough to look funny. He appeared a little younger now and so attractive that I found it hard not to stare at him.

I did see him last night after the nightmare, but I honestly didn't remember what he looked like at that time.

"Do you want one?" I asked.

"Not really. What are you making?"

"A sandwich."

"I'll have a bite of yours," he said.

Whatever does that mean, a bite of mine?

I made my sandwich while Tom stood there watching me.

"What?" I asked.

"What do you mean, *what?*"

"Why are you watching me?"

"You like an audience," he said as he leaned onto the counter in a relaxed fashion.

What was I to say to that?

So, I finished making the sandwich and put everything away.

Now, how was I supposed to give him a bite?

"Do you want me to cut a piece off for you?" I asked.

"Nope," he said as he took my sandwich with both hands and took a massive bite out of it. He placed it back on my plate. I looked at it.

There is a bite out of my sandwich. About a whole quarter was gone in this circle that was missing.

Tom started to laugh.

What was so funny? Should I make another one? I looked at him, but that just made him laugh harder. He had to swallow quickly so he wouldn't choke on it.

He gave me a light punch in the arm.

"Oh, your face. That was priceless," he said, still chuckling.

I couldn't see what was so funny about this. Eating something that Anthony or Kim didn't touch seemed different, but having something that someone took a bite out of?

"Why don't you finish this? I'll make another." I suggested, but that only made him laugh harder.

"No. The rest is all yours. Are you afraid I left some germs on it?"

"Uhh..."

"Oh, Addy. Relax. Lighten up a bit. It shows how uncomfortable you are with me," he said, getting more serious.

"It does?" This I don't understand.

He took another step closer to me, so he was just centimetres away.

"So, it grosses you out that I took a bite out of your sandwich. Then what do you think of kissing? It's very unhygienic, I know. I wonder who ever thought of that."

My face turned red. *Kissing?* Why is he mentioning kissing anyhow?

I had no idea what to do now. Maybe I should take my sandwich and leave, but that seemed cowardly.

He then picked up my sandwich with both hands and brought it close to my mouth.

"Here, try the opposite end. However, I must warn you that I am touching it with both hands, and they say you transfer more germs with your hands than you do kissing."

So, I had no choice but to take a bite.

"Is that so bad?" he asked but didn't let go of the sandwich.

Is this supposed to be romantic? No, but perhaps it is supposed to be funny.

I should take this sandwich now. He might even be wondering why I haven't. So, I brought my hands up, but his were so big that they encircled the entire thing. He studied my movements. Finally, I put my hands out for him to place the sandwich on top, but he didn't. I looked at him. His expression turned more sombre. What was going on?

"Take it," he said without removing his hands.

How could I? There was nothing left to hold on to.

"You won't take it because it would mean touching me," he said.

14

"No," I said, but I knew that Tom was right.

I had to prove him wrong, so I put my hands on his. They were rough and warm and, of course, enormous. He slowly slid his out while his eyes searched my face.

I placed the sandwich on my plate. Now I could see where each of his fingers used to be.

"Are you going to eat that?" he asked.

"Yes." I reached for the knife and cut it into quarters. Who even wants a sandwich that you have to hold with both hands?

He was watching me still, so I took the quarter where there was almost nothing left from Tom's bite, and I ate it. Then I grabbed the piece that had my bite in it.

"Your bite is so tiny," Tom said.

"Are you going to have nightmares now?" he asked.

"No."

"Are you completely grossed out?"

"No."

He leaned with his back against the fridge and looked up. Man, was he ever one good-looking guy. He watched me finish and put my plate in the dishwasher.

"How come you are comfortable with everyone but me?" he asked, appearing rejected.

I looked at him, but I hadn't the slightest clue what to say.

"You can hug some dad at the kids' school? And every member of my family? The neighbour's husband?" he pointed out.

I'd never even considered that before. I knew Tom better than any of those guys. But he'd never tried to hug me.

"You're at ease with everyone but me. Why?" he asked again.

My face was still red, and I didn't know what to say. But Tom was going to wait till I answered. I speculated if I should tell him it's because he was more intense than everybody else put together. Was that the truth? All of a sudden, I wondered. He was more intense, but he wasn't that bad. So, that couldn't really be the reason.

"Cause you are not like anyone else," I finally whispered.

"That's not really a compliment, is it?"

"Umm. It could be."

"I'm not saying it's your fault. I just want to know what I'm doing wrong," he said.

"You aren't doing anything wrong."

"There has to be something."

"Not that I can think of," I said.

"I don't honestly know what I'm doing," he sighed.

"Oh? You had me fooled."

"Think about it, Ok? Then, let me know what I can do differently so that you are more comfortable with me," he said as he straightened. "Good night, Addy... and if you have any more nightmares, remember... I'm the good guy."

"Good night," I said. "I'm sorry to disturb you."

"Addy," he said, and when I did not look at him, he repeated my name. Then he waited until I stared into his eyes before saying, "You do not disturb me."

I turned out the light and went to bed.

What on earth was that? My head almost hurt from trying to rack my brain that hard over the last few minutes. But likely I'm thinking way too much, and guys are just weird, and that is all there is to it.

Surprisingly, I fell asleep right away.

IN THE morning, I enjoyed the buzz around the kitchen at breakfast. It was always an exciting time getting the kids ready for school. Ok, maybe exciting is a big word, but you could feel the energy, nonetheless. I enjoyed that time, although for a while there, I was too stressed to enjoy it. But now, I soaked it all in.

I started thinking about my sandwich last night. Next, Tom will say, "Here, use my toothbrush. It won't kill you."

Well, I guess I did freak out a little.

I've seen couples share a bottle of pop or the same straw. When you think of the very romantic scene of a woman and man at a fancy restaurant feeding each other, they couldn't possibly grab their partner's fork first. So, taking a bite out of someone's whatever is not supposed to be revolting.

However, the one difference here is that we would be talking about couples in all these instances. Yet Tom and I are just friends. Could you imagine going up to the guy who works beside you and saying, "Here, try a bite of my sandwich?" Perhaps close friends would. I wonder.

Oh well, no point analyzing it any further because I am only here for one more day. In fact, not even. My stomach knotted a bit. I'm leaving tonight. This is it. It's my last day here. Wow! That came up fast somehow.

There are still things I haven't done. With this in mind, there were all these little towns around here that I hadn't seen yet. So, that is what I could do today.

"What are you doing today?" Anthony asked me.

"I think I'm going to take a drive," I said.

"Where to?" Kim asked.

"I don't know. Perhaps around to explore some small towns I haven't been to yet."

"Is Tom going with you?" Anthony asked.

"Of course," Tom said as he came up from behind. "Addy always includes me in her plans."

"Do I detect a hint of sarcasm?" I asked.

"A hopeful suggestion," he said.

"Then you guys are going for supper?" Anthony asked. "Only you two?"

"Yup," Tom said.

"Is it a romantic supper?" Kim asked, smiling.

Tom looked up, paused, and then said, "Maybe."

That made me wonder. What did that depend on?

What on earth was his idea of romance anyway? Last night was probably romantic to Tom. And sharing a sandwich is perhaps as romantic as he gets.

Anyway, this is my final day here. That will be my last supper and last evening here, so what can possibly go wrong?

"Can't we take one day off school?" Anthony asked.

"Yeah. We barely got to spend any time with Uncle," Kim said.

"You guys don't have any tests today, do you?" I asked.

They said no, so I looked at Margaret. It would be great if the kids would take today off and be with me, considering this is my last day here.

Oh, wait. They want to be with Tom because he leaves on Sunday. And they have been with me for the last four months, but him only a few days.

"Would you two like to spend the day, just the two of you?" Margaret asked.

"It would be great if the kids could come," I said, after glancing at Tom.

"Well, alright. You guys don't have to go to school today," she said as they cheered.

"So, can we all go for a drive?" Kim asked.

"Yes. That would be fun," I said.

"So, am I invited or not?" Tom asked.

"Sure."

"Sure, I can come if I want, or sure, you were going to ask me?"

"The idea had just come to my head milliseconds before Anthony asked me. However, I wonder if the kids would like to be alone with you."

"No. Let's all go. That would be fun," Anthony said.

"You guys run off, so you can get somewhere before supper," Margaret said as she started clearing dishes.

I suddenly got kind of worried as we were leaving. What if he lectures me or something? What if I say the wrong thing? What if our being together today somehow ruins our evening? What if we start our deep conversation now, and it lasts all day, and I can't handle it for that long? Because I really need to have a nice day.

"What's up?" Tom asked as he took me by surprise by opening the car door for me.

"Uh, nothing."

"You seem… terrified."

"Sorry. I want to have a relaxed, fun time, so if I end up doing anything stupid or saying something wrong, would you just forget it ever happened?"

He looked me in the eye. "Relax, Addy. We will have a fun, carefree day and talk this evening over supper."

"Ok."

"Are you worried about this evening?"

"Perhaps," I managed to say.

"Well, don't be. I'm not going to hurt you. Things will go exactly as you want them to."

How does he know how I want them to go?

"So, where are we going?" Tom asked.

"Let's go up here," I said, showing him on my phone.

"Sure… and I never meant to freak you out last night."

"I know. I just wasn't expecting that," I said.

"I can tell. It totally threw you. But I was only playing around."

"I know. I'm sorry I was so…"

"Cute. You were cute," he said.

"I was not cute. I am cute, but I was not cute." We laughed.

Tom seemed to relax, and so did I. And the conversation lightened as soon as the kids joined in.

"Oh, look at that sweet bakery. Stop!" I said later, and we all got out.

It was a Swiss bakery all in wood and inside there was apple strudel everywhere. They had coffee that smelled so good as well. The guy behind the counter said hello with a strong Swiss accent and three little tables sat by the window with hand-carved benches and red checkered tablecloths.

Outside, giant snowflakes began to fall.

"Oh, Tom," I found myself whispering because there was nothing else to say. This was wonderful.

Tom smiled a funny smile. He probably wonders what's wrong with me.

"Have a strudel. They are fresh, right out of the oven," the guy said with a huge grin.

"Oh yes, and a coffee too," I said.

"You?" he asked Tom.

"The same and two more strudels for the kids."

The man pulled the pastries out with a wooden paddle and put them on Styrofoam plates. Then he poured coffees into Styrofoam cups. Tom paid, of course.

I took my time getting the right amount of sugar and cream as Tom sat down with the kids and watched me.

"Tell me, Tom, what could be more wonderful than this?"

"I'm… not sure," he said, but he had no idea what I meant exactly.

"You think I'm crazy."

"No. I think you are amazing."

"Amazingly crazy."

"I love your passion for life," he said.

That sounded deep.

I took a bite of my strudel, which was so tasty. I'd never had anything like it before.

"What does passion for life mean?" Anthony asked.

"It means knowing how to enjoy yourself," Tom said.

We talked and watched the snow fall.

Then we drove a few more blocks.

"Oh, this is the main street. Stop here. Look. Look! A general store. Let's go see it."

"I think it is just a tiny grocery store," he said.

"I know. Let's check it out."

Tom looked at me funny and got out of the car slowly. He was taking so long that after he closed his door, I grabbed his arm and pulled him inside. But he started laughing.

The store was adorable. It was neat, all the things they stuffed in there.

"Look. Someone close by makes these candles… by hand, Tom."

"That is… amazing," he said, trying to sound excited.

The kids were happy because they found some different-looking candy they wanted to try.

I dragged them into every store in sight, but there weren't many.

"Now, let's check out this spot," I said. So, off we headed. "Are you having any fun?"

Tom smiled. "Yes. I love being with you." *This was the second time he used the "L" word.* "I love watching you," he added. *Third time. That's a lot of love for a guy.*

This next town was more like a hamlet. There was nothing except a small restaurant, but I was starving.

"Let's eat here. Are you hungry?" I asked.

"Yeah."

We stepped inside and it was sweet.

"We have cream-of-cucumber soup and roast chicken sandwiches," the lady told us, and I guess that must be all because we were not given a menu. We said sure.

"You owe me a bite," I said to Tom after she left, and he grinned.

The lunch tasted excellent. They even used smaller bowls for the kids and made them smaller sandwiches. The "chef" came out afterwards to see if everything was alright.

"So, what do we pay you?" Tom asked after a while.

"Well, that depends," the man said. "What do you think it was worth?"

Tom stared at him.

The soup bowls were huge. The sandwiches were terrific and of a very generous size. So, I offered them a reasonable price with a song.

The man grinned. "A song?" he asked.

"Yes. You need some music. I'll sing you a song."

"It's a deal," he said.

I stood up and sang.

His wife came out again. Afterwards, they clapped.

"Tell you what, make it half that and one more song," he suggested, so I sang another.

"Oh, you sing beautifully," his wife said.

"Do you know more songs?" the man asked.

"Oh, sure."

"How about two more songs, and we'll call it even?" he suggested.

I finished them, and they clapped wholeheartedly after each one.

"What a treat to have all you guys in," the man said. "Come anytime."

Someone else came into the café, and I could hear the lady telling them about us.

"I'll leave a tip," I said and was surprised that Tom wasn't stopping me like usual. I put a twenty on the table.

"Oh, no. Here, let me take care of that," Tom said, waking up from his daze.

"I didn't embarrass you, did I?" I asked. "I don't know anything about small towns."

"Could've fooled me," he grumbled.

"Here, take this back. I just wasn't with it," he said as he attempted to give me a twenty back, but I wouldn't accept it.

Outside, I tried to catch snowflakes with my tongue. Tom watched.

I spun around laughing, letting my hair fly, and the kids did the same.

"The snowflakes taste better here," I called out as I danced through the pines.

"Come on," Tom said, grinning.

"You'll have to catch me first," I yelled and took off. Anthony and Kim also ran into the trees.

Tom was still for a moment, but then started after me. I screeched and ran around. I'm not a fast runner, but I am very agile, so I ducked under branches faster than him. It took him a while before he got too close.

What would he do when he did catch up to me? My question was soon answered when he picked me up and threw me over his shoulder.

I was laughing hard and out of breath. We had white all over us from slipping here and there.

He carried me to the vehicle and then opened the door for me.

Anthony and Kim gleefully followed and returned to catching snowflakes on their tongue.

"You are so covered in snow," Tom whispered once he sat inside. He reached out and ran his hands through my hair. I tried to dust it off a bit.

"Come on, you guys! Get in the car!" Tom hollered at the kids, who slowly and reluctantly got in.

"I was going to change for supper anyhow. What should I wear? What is the dress code?" I asked.

"You can wear anything you like. I will look the same as always."

"Do you own a suit?"

"No," he said.

"Just as well, because I've had enough of fancy places because that was all I used to do before."

"Did you wear evening dresses a lot?"

"A fair bit. There always seemed to be a gala or cocktail party," I said.

"Did you keep them?"

"My evening dresses? Yes, I did. I got rid of all my work clothes, all of my suits and even my casual stuff from before, too, because they were not informal at all. Although, I kept my dresses, because I thought I could surely wear them to more than just snooty restaurants. Once I wore one with the kids. We were having a cocktail party."

"You took them to a cocktail party?"

"No, we had one at home, just the three of us."

"Yeah. That was fun," Kim said. "I was dressed like a lady, and we talked like grown-ups."

"The kids were very fortunate to have you," Tom said.

"We had a blast," I said.

We talked as we headed back, but I made him take a few detours and "shortcuts". I even pulled him out to see a few places.

By the time we returned, I had only half an hour to get changed for our date.

I took out my light green satin blouse because I was thinking today that it would be a sweet top to wear. It brought me back to what the moss-covered rocks would appear like in Foley's in a thick fog. What pants, though? I went through everything I had a few times. Finally, I pulled out some nice fitted black jeans. Actually, it wasn't really denim, but it was styled like it. Before settling on a soft black button-down sweater, I tried on a black cape, a black jacket, and all kinds of options. For one thing, I should put on some kind of jewellery because I usually never think of it. I had some small pearl earrings that softly dropped down.

Man, where is the time going? This is what happens when you never go on dates.

I should wear more makeup, but I tried to hurry.

It was time to go, but my hair was all over. I struggled with a few things and then finally pulled back a bit from above each ear and clipped them together behind my head.

Kim came in. "They are wondering why you are taking so long," she said.

"It takes great effort to look pretty," I said.

All got quiet at that moment, and maybe the refrigerator stopped humming, but I overheard Margaret and Tom.

"She never takes this long to change," Margaret said.

"I know," he said, but instead of sounding concerned, he seemed hopeful.

Finally, I came out. Tom stood up and just watched me.

"You look beautiful!" Margaret exclaimed.

"You look incredible," he whispered as we put our coats on.

Once inside the car, I started to get a little nervous. I might have overdone it with the makeup. Perhaps this wasn't really a date, but a business meeting.

We didn't talk much, and was Tom nervous? So, I had plenty of time to terrify myself about the evening.

Although, it had been a fun day.

It was dark by now, but I could see the log cabin-style building with glowing lights inside. It was set amongst the trees, snuggled up with a snowy blanket. And this was the restaurant.

"How wonderful," I said, but Tom made no reply.

When we entered, he told the lady that we had a reservation for Tom Joseph, and she politely excused herself for a moment.

"Tom!" Came an enthusiastic response from a cute black guy who came running up to us from the kitchen or somewhere. He grabbed Tom's hand and shook it energetically. "Man, it's good to see you!"

"How's it going?" Tom asked him, but the man didn't respond. Instead, he was looking at me. He took my hand but did not shake it.

"This is the most beautiful woman ever to come into my restaurant. Please tell me that she is available," the man said without taking his eyes off me.

"Not a chance. This is my girlfriend, Adelle Lockheart. Addy, this is Simon," Tom responded right away.

"Oh well. Tom does deserve the best. I'm honoured to meet you," he said as he kissed my hand. "Come on. I've reserved the finest table for you two."

My head was spinning. *Not a chance. This is my girlfriend, Adelle Lockheart.*

It finally happened. Did it? When did it happen? Did I miss something? Is this the start?

We were led to a cute table by a window and fireplace.

I had to sit down immediately because I thought I might fall over.

"What can I get you guys to drink?" Simon asked.

"Dark ale," Tom said.

"Of course, and you?"

"Lemonade."

"Would you like to upgrade that to a lemonade margarita?"

"Sure."

"I'll get that for you, and your server will be with you right away."

He could've offered me a glass of toilet bowl cleaner, and I would have said yes. But I shouldn't have got a margarita. I'm already spinning and can't think. Imagine what a margarita would do to me now.

"What's wrong?" Tom asked after a while.

I looked at him but could not hold his gaze. What if we had been dating all this time, and I didn't realize it? I wasn't sure what to say.

"What's wrong, Addy?" he repeated.

I took a deep breath. What do I tell him? My mind was completely blank.

This is my girlfriend, Adelle Lockheart.

"Did Simon embarrass you?" he asked.

"No."

"Did I embarrass you?"

"No," I said.

"Look, Addy. If you want to call it off, you can."

I looked at him. My brain turned off. The screen saver went on, I think.

"Tom…" but the words wouldn't come.

Thank goodness a lady brought our drinks.

"Is there anything else I can get you at this time?" she asked.

"A glass of water, please," I managed, taking a sip of my drink and the wonderfully sour taste helped clear my brain a little.

"Tom…" I tried again. "*When* did we start dating?"

"Well… I figured when you sent me your songs, I had a green light, but… before that, I guess."

My brain turned off once more. *You have performed an illegal operation, and this program will be shut down.* So, I had no option but to hit Ok, closeout and reboot.

I stared at the menu in the meantime. Tom carefully flipped it around because I had been holding it upside down.

"What are you trying to tell me?" he asked.

"I didn't know. You never asked."

"You didn't know what exactly? What didn't I ask?"

"You didn't ask me out," I said.

"What do you mean? I asked you out all the time. Even back home, I asked you to spend time with me. Then I called you every day when you got here… every day."

"I know, but…"

I looked at Tom, and he looked different now. He leaned back in his chair and ran his hand through his hair. He bit his lip and leaned forward again. And this was the very first time I saw him unsure of himself or what to say.

"When I waited for you, for the boats, you didn't even…" I started.

"I wanted to. You've *no idea* how much. But it just wouldn't have been right. You were not mine then because you had to go back. I had to wait until you left to see if I would ever hear from you again."

"You didn't say anything when I left."

"No. I didn't want you to feel bad if you changed your mind. I wanted you to be completely free to make a decision without feeling responsible to me for something. Besides, I had nothing to offer you," he said.

"You never said anything when we talked on the phone." I felt dumb. I felt incredibly stupid. "I just thought… maybe you only wanted to be friends," I said.

"Oh, for heaven's sake…" he groaned and ran his hand through his hair again. "I want more than that. Couldn't you tell? I mean… I was more personal than that."

"I don't know. I've never dated before. I knew you wouldn't want to hurt me, but…"

"Addy, I'm so sorry. I thought you understood," he said.

"I should've known, I guess. But I didn't want to be presumptuous. I'm sorry… That explains a lot."

"Yes… no fooling. If I had asked you?"

"That was all I wanted ever since I saw you," I said.

"Oh, man… All week…"

"Considering that we did pretty good."

"Would you like to order?" The waitress appeared out of nowhere. She glanced at me. "But if you need more time, that's fine."

"I'll have the T-Bone," Tom said. "Medium with garlic mashed potatoes and gravy, a corn muffin, and veggies. Addy will have the arctic char with blueberry salsa, wild rice, stuffed peppers, and orange spinach salad."

"Perfect."

"And if we catch a bit of fresh air, we'll be right back," he told her.

"Certainly," she said, taking the menus.

"I hope you don't mind," Tom said. "My guess is that's what you would have ordered."

"Sounds very possible." And it did sound perfect. Although I had no idea what was on the menu, that is likely what I would have asked for.

"Boy, I feel incredibly stupid," Tom said.

"Me too."

"That would've made me seem like a completely careless flirt."

"I'm sorry," I said.

"Don't apologize. It's my fault."

201

"Not entirely. It took two to mess that up."

"Here I was so confused all week, thinking you might have changed your mind about me, or you were afraid. You seemed so uncomfortable and so distant. I wondered if you needed more time. That's why I wanted to talk."

"No. I do not want more time," I said firmly as Tom smiled.

"If only I could go back..." he muttered.

"It's just one week. So, we have plenty of time."

"If you only knew how much I'm in love with you... You'd probably be sick," he said with a smile.

I smiled too, but the tears came out of nowhere.

"I love you so much that it will make up for all the love you never had," he said in almost a whisper as he leaned forward and took my hand.

The tears came faster now. Boy, the only day I wore mascara in a long time.

"Come. Let's get some fresh air," Tom said, getting up and putting his jacket back on.

He must have known before that I was ready to start crying.

The fresh snow-filled air felt wonderful.

Tom walked to my vehicle, leaned his back against it and took me into my arms. He held me close as I cried. And he kissed the top of my head a couple of times.

Finally, the tears stopped. I took a tissue out of my purse and tried to wipe away makeup smears that would be there.

"But you are leaving on Sunday," I said.

"Yes, but you're coming with me. Because I got us both tickets to fly back. However, if you'd rather wait a bit, I would understand."

15

"**N**o. I've waited long enough. Tom... I'm so in love with you."

He placed both his hands on the sides of my face and kissed me on the forehead. Then he took my hand and led me back inside.

Our food arrived soon after, and it was terrific. We swapped a few bites here and there, and in spite of my sandwich views, it wasn't even remotely gross.

We laughed about all the things we would have changed if we had only known.

"I want to wait," Tom started. "When you were at Foley's, it was summer, but the winters are rough. It's a tough time. So, I would feel better if you'd stay over the winter to see if you really can handle it there. Otherwise, I believe you would be making an uninformed decision. Could we do that?" he asked.

"I guess."

"It would test how much you love me." He smiled. "You have to know what it is like there first. I feel strongly about that. You'll have no end of offers of where to stay in the meantime."

"That would be fine," I said.

"I'll kiss you properly when I propose, and you accept. Because I'd never make it through if I started at this time. Is that Ok?"

"Well..." I wanted him to kiss me now. But that would be a while. "If you insist. I suppose we do have years with which to catch up after, but it'll be a long winter," I said.

"I know. Would you do that for me?"

"Yes."

Then we talked about less serious things and ordered dessert.

I decided to leave my vehicle for Brian and Margaret. Obviously, I will not take the ferry tomorrow and I didn't have to go anywhere tonight.

I was pretty emotional, so I giggled easily, and we visited and laughed until late.

The drive back was rather quiet, but he held my hand the whole time, which felt blissful.

That was my first date.

Margaret was still up when we returned. She took one look at me and gave me a huge hug. Even though she probably knew all about them, I excitedly told her about the plane tickets. And she was delighted for us.

Boy, I had trouble sleeping that night because of being so thrilled to be going back. Tom is mine, and what was more wonderful than that?

I SLEPT in and listened to the birds' chirp. They sounded about as excited as I was.

It amazed me how much had changed over the last twenty-four hours.

I heard Margaret and Kim talking downstairs.

"We're going to lose Addy and Tom at the same time? That's not fair. Everything will be so different. Why can't Addy stay until they get married, at least? They can talk over the phone," Kim suggested.

"Don't be selfish. Addy has taken excellent care of you. Now she would probably like someone to take care of her."

"Don't be silly. Addy won't let anyone take care of her."

"She'll let Tom," Margaret said.

"I don't think so."

"You take care of adults differently than you take care of kids," Margaret laughed. "All I meant was that they would like to be together, and we can't keep Addy forever."

"But why not just until they are married? What is Addy going to do there anyway? She can't go shopping. She can't go for drives.

She can't go out for a meal. She can't even work there. Without us to take care of, she will be really bored. And what will she do while Uncle is fishing?"

"She'll take a holiday, relax, visit other people there. I don't know. What I do know is that she has to decide if she likes living there before she makes the decision to marry Tom and stay in Foley's Rest forever."

"They are not stuck there. And they can always move somewhere else if Addy doesn't like it," Kim stated.

"They just want to find it out before they get married and I think that is very wise."

"I think it's dumb. You don't marry someone just because you like where they live, and you don't not marry someone because you don't like where they live. Besides, aren't you supposed to marry because you love each other?"

"Yes, Kim, but it's not quite that simple. It is good to know as much as possible before getting married," Margaret said.

"I'm telling you that Addy should stay here until they decide to get married. If she is willing to go there with Tom, he should be smart enough to marry her before she changes her mind. But if Addy stays there, she won't like it."

"What makes you say that?" Margaret asked.

"There is nothing to do there."

"You greatly underestimate the power of being in love. Besides, Addy was very good at entertaining you all."

"Here, she had to look after us and you. If she was alone with nothing to do, she would always go somewhere. There she can't, and no one will need her," Kim said.

"Tom will."

"Tom loves her, but it's not the same."

"My dear, you are not the expert on being in love," Margaret said.

"I'm just telling you. Maybe I'll talk to Tom about it."

"He can probably answer your questions better anyhow."

It was obvious that Margaret was actually stumped. As ridiculous as it sounded coming from an eight-year-old, Kim was pretty convincing. However, I was glad that she would be talking to Tom and not to me because I wouldn't know what to say either.

When we are married, I'll have a house to take care of and the evenings to look forward to. We'll probably have children and that would keep me busy.

And what will I fill my time with until then? Given that I'll live in someone else's house and have absolutely nothing to do.

How am I going to spend time with Tom anyway? It will all depend on a family inviting us over, or Tom would have to have people in. We couldn't even talk on the phone comfortably. Because no matter where I stay, I would always be within earshot of someone.

I didn't really understand it either. I liked Kim's idea, because I constantly wanted to go back there, but on the condition that I was Tom's wife. Oh well. A challenge is good. And I'll learn new things like how to entertain myself. After all, I will have no option.

Besides, Tom is very wise. He knows what he is doing. Nothing worthwhile comes for free, and isn't he worth the sacrifice?

I can't blame him because he doesn't want me to feel trapped by marrying him. I have to be able to love him and be alright with living there despite the difficulties. It made perfect sense when Tom first explained his plan.

However, I must admit that after listening to Kim, I liked her idea more. Her description of me seemed rather accurate. I have to be a really complex person to be summed up so easily by an eight-year-old girl.

Well, I better get out of bed.

Margaret had made a huge, incredible breakfast. In the meantime, everyone was talking a mile a minute, all very excited about us.

"Can I have your car to drive when I'm older?" Anthony asked.

"Will you get married there if you decide to get married?" Kim asked.

"I don't know," Tom said.

"It'll be a while before you get your license. I'll leave the vehicle with your parents for now," I said.

There seemed like so much to do… and yet, not really.

I popped next door to visit Lisa while Tom was doing a few more things around the house. She was so happy for me.

Afterwards, I found him sorting through stuff in the basement.

"Did Kim speak with you?" I asked.

"Yes. Did you ask her to?"

"No, but I happened to overhear her talking with Margaret."

"She just sounded so grown up. It's hard to believe she didn't get that idea from someone," he said.

"I know what you mean. What did you tell her?"

"The same thing I told you."

"Was she convinced?" I asked.

"Not at all."

"It is strange, but I almost understand where she is coming from."

"You like Kim's advice?" he asked, as he stopped what he was doing.

"I do, actually."

"I know when you set your mind to something, there is nothing stopping you, and I know that you are willing to take chances, but I don't want to be a chance that you take. You have to fully comprehend what you are getting into. And it's not only about surviving a winter. You have only seen me for two weeks and you really should get to know me better. Besides, shouldn't we finally date?"

"As long as you are very sure about this all. But I was wondering if it would be a fair taste of you and Foley's Rest if I were stuck in someone else's house without a responsibility in the world. Then how would we even talk? Because someone would always be around," I said.

"Addy, we've never even been together with you knowing that we are going out."

"I know. I was just thinking. Another thing I was wondering is how will I get from St. John's to Foley's Rest?"

"With Victor and Star. In their boat. They are the ones that'll be there when we arrive. But I must warn you that you will probably be sick in the boat. I've gotten used to it. If you keep an empty stomach, it would be advantageous," he said.

With that lovely thought in mind, I went through the house, looking for any items that might be mine. I pulled my coats out of the closet. Then, I signed over my SUV. I wasn't as attached to it as my previous vehicle, but it had become a friend, nevertheless.

I found Brian sitting at the table.

"Addy, come here a minute," he said. "I don't want you to ever feel we took you for granted. I plan to give back all the money you worked for and spent on my family. And we want to pay you for your car. Tom, however, wants to take care of you all by himself, and it's true that you can't really spend much when you are there. So, till we both start working again, I have little to offer you, as you know, but I promise you that we won't forget about this. I'll write you a cheque for a wedding gift if I can, for at least some of it. And even though this sounds absurd, if things do not work out and you choose to leave for any reason, you are always welcome here, and you must never think that we would blame you or be upset with you. You are our friend and as much a part of our family as Tom is."

"Thank you." I was touched. "Don't even concern yourself with that for now, because I have no need for anything at this time."

I ended up dancing and singing with the kids for a bit.

Then I gave everyone their goodbye gifts, and they all seemed happy with them.

This was perfect. Soon I was returning to the only place I loved, with the only man I had ever loved.

Tom seemed content, satisfied, and relaxed. He was not all over me or anything, but by the way he smiled at me, it was obvious that he was happy.

THE DAY ended before it even began, and we were at the airport the next thing I knew.

"Is it going to bother you to be on a plane again?" Tom had asked.

"No. I'm fine."

As we said goodbye, everyone got rather solemn, but Tom and I grinned from ear to ear. It was early, but I was wide awake.

I was going to miss these guys, though. I had been a special member of their family for the last four months. It was a treasured memory for me, one I was so grateful for. At the same time, I had no doubt I would see them again soon. Maybe we can arrange for them to be at our wedding. Perhaps we should get married in

Terrace. They were all a part of me now. I belonged to this family, and once I wed Tom, it would be official.

As I walked onto the plane, all of a sudden, I started to panic. I now visualized scenes from my crash. Images I had forgotten entirely. I could hear the sound. I saw the people getting sucked out. I felt the wind that made it impossible to breathe.

Squeezing Tom's hand, I forced myself to follow.

"You Ok?" Tom asked as we sat down.

I nodded.

I wanted out of here. My hands were shaking a bit. I never thought much about the plane crash before, but now it all came back.

"Are you going to be able to handle this?" he asked.

"Hopefully, it will improve," I mumbled.

Tom put his arm around me, and I hid my face in his jacket. It looked stupid, I know, but I felt a little better immediately. In due time I even relaxed slightly... until it took off.

I nearly freaked right out when it did. This is dumb, and I couldn't believe this was happening to me. I'm supposed to be able to handle this, but here I am, like a kid, hiding my face in Tom's shirt again. And he held me tight.

After we were in the air for a while, I started to calm down.

"Man, I got pretty worried there. Do you know how long it would take to drive?" Tom asked. "I guess you do have some idea."

That was a pretty quick flight to Vancouver. The landing proved to be difficult for me, and getting on our next plane wasn't easy either. However, the takeoff from Vancouver was a little better, as was the descent in Toronto. The final liftoff was better yet, and I was almost back to normal by the time we noticed St. John's.

As we came closer, I enjoyed the glow of the lights of the city. Eventually, I could see buildings topped with snow, and I had never seen anything like it. It had a cozy look to it, unlike the larger cities. With the lights reflecting on the harbour around it, it seemed like it should be on a painting.

I was grateful to be done flying. It had been about nine hours of being in the air, not to mention at the airports. But the worst part was the time change because I wanted to have supper, but it was eleven at night here.

I was glad to see where everyone shops and excited about this little city's role in my life, but I was supposed to go to sleep. And without supper too. Tom seemed to think it was important because I wasn't used to the boats, and I'd be sleeping in one tonight.

"What's the weather like in Foley's Rest right now?" I asked as we waited for a cab. "Similar?"

"Wetter," Tom said.

"Then it's above zero, right?"

"Hardly. Real wet snow. Sticks to everything," he said.

Most of Canada was even colder than this. Even so, it was only the ocean that kept us warmer than the interior. It was the same in Terrace and even in Toronto. The only place more temperate was Vancouver and Vancouver Island, and other than their airport, I'd never been.

Victor and Star were going to meet us in the harbour, and I'd spend the night with Star in their boat, and the guys would stay in Tom's.

I have to say that I instantly fell in love with St. John's. I just liked the vibe. It was big enough to be a city, yet had a smaller atmosphere to it. The rock folded and turned like the waves did. At the same time, there was a generous sprinkling of snow, and the warm glow of lights everywhere seemed intimate.

I was happy to see Victor and Star, and their hugs felt so good. But they were tired, so we said goodnight and Star and I headed down into their boat.

I liked it in here because it looked so cozy. She was too sleepy to be much of a conversationalist and was soon fast asleep. I was way too buzzed, but it was necessary, so I tried as I tossed and turned. Indeed, it would've been easier to drift off if I wasn't so hungry. But I enjoyed laying in a room that gently rocked in the water.

I woke nauseous and glad Tom didn't let me have supper. Much to Victor and Star's dismay, we'd slept in a bit. Certainly, this time change would take getting used to again, and their insane hour for waking was only going to make this worse.

We walked to a restaurant for breakfast, but Tom warned me not to have anything but some juice. That was fine to start, but I began to get hungry after not long. Even Star was having toast, and the guy's eggs and bacon looked delicious. I really wanted hash browns. I could practically taste them as I tormented myself with the thought. Nothing is worse than feeling sick in the stomach, but it's hard to imagine when you're ravenous. By the time we left, I wondered if I would pass out from hunger, but I was probably just being dramatic.

I mused at the accent that the people here had. In Foley's Rest, I'd never noticed the same. There were individual accents, but not a general one. But I guess that's because everyone came from somewhere else fairly recently.

IT WAS a beautiful sunny morning, and the snow only reflected it and made everything brighter.

Soon, our boats were heading out. I watched Victor expertly untie his. The temperature wasn't that low, but the wind was biting, and the cold travelled right through me. So, I headed back down.

My goodness, the waters were rough. A short time later, I became utterly sick. And I thought I was going to die. I really did. Having no idea it was humanly possible to be this ill and still be alive, the minutes passed like hours.

Even though I almost convinced myself it would never happen, we did arrive at Foley's Rest. I dragged myself off the boat in my rain jacket with a few layers underneath. Star ensured I was dressed for the wet snow, but I felt too gross to enjoy the scenery around me.

Tom had docked shortly before and was waiting as I got out. Of course, I didn't want to see him or anyone, but I had no choice.

He looked funny in a raincoat.

Where was I even going to stay?

I should have my stuff. I glanced back and realized I should've grabbed them, but Victor came out with my suitcases.

"She can stay with us for now. If that's alright," he said.

"Perfect," Tom said and took my things from him and carried them to their place. Star was following behind.

Once we stepped onto the boardwalk, it was sheltered from the overhang of the roofs, but it was so soggy everywhere, regardless. I'd never seen snow like this before. Any tiny breeze seemed to blow it onto the walk, and then it melted. So, I was glad this was a good jacket because I had water running off me. But my feet got wet, and these hikers are supposed to be water-resistant.

When inside, I used the washroom, and when I came out, Star had almost finished making a bed for me on the couch. I laid down.

I could still feel the boat moving.

Victor brought some things in and left again, then Tom and Star did the same until everything was brought in.

I had gifts for everyone, but I sure didn't want to see them.

After a while, I had improved somewhat. Then, I had a bit of ginger ale and sipped it slowly.

Star had millions of groceries to prepare for the freezer, but I knew I wouldn't be of any help. Even the thought of touching food was just too much.

She would talk to herself and not only when she was counting. It was cute.

Urma knocked and came in.

"No one told me you were coming," she said to me. "You could've phoned," she told Star.

"Tom didn't tell anyone else ahead in case it didn't work out," Star explained.

"I certainly never got a phone call from you telling me you were coming. I guess no one wants me around. That's some appreciation after you stayed at my place the whole time you were here last," Urma said.

I was stunned. Is this for real?

"I only had one day to get ready to leave, and I didn't know it would be that important to phone ahead. I thought I would surprise you. The only thing is that I had no idea that I would be this sick. I'm not quite up to visiting yet," I said.

"Don't worry. I can take a hint," Urma said, and she stormed out.

I looked at Star.

"She has been a real pain this winter," she said. "She is driving me up the wall. The whole world has to revolve around her and pass by her for approval. Just ignore her."

Yet it disturbed me, and I kept trying to think of how I should have responded, but it only ended up making me mad instead.

Roxy came to check how I was doing so she could report back to her mother, and I was delighted to see her. I told her to bring her mom and brother because I had gifts for them. Although I was still not feeling great, at least it would distract me from my stomach and Urma.

They loved their presents, and Roxy looked adorable with her massive teddy that she could barely carry.

By the time they left, I was doing much better.

When it was time for the boats to come in, it wasn't an event here because neither Tom nor Victor were fishing today. Still, I glanced out of the window, and somehow, it didn't even look the same in the pouring rain.

I had a tiny bit of supper with Victor and Star, who were in an especially playful mood with each other. They teased one another and laughed like children.

"We're going to Bora Bora," Star said, gleaming.

"Really? That's pretty exotic."

"Yes," she giggled. "We are booking a five-star, all-inclusive resort for a month."

"Wow. You must have saved up a while for that."

She chuckled some more, and Victor was grinning from ear to ear. "It will be so exciting."

"Yes. It will. I'm happy for you two."

"If you could go anywhere on earth, where would it be?" Victor asked.

I thought and thought some more.

"I don't know. For now, I have little interest in travel, not to different countries anyhow. I've been to a few tropical places: Hawaii, Indonesia, Polynesian Islands. But after a while, they all started to look the same, and I realized that I was searching for something I would never find that way. However, you will have a delightful time if you haven't been anywhere warm and exotic before. I'm not too excited about flying just yet."

"Oh, yeah. I bet. How were your flights here?" Star asked.

"Painful. It proved to be good that Tom was there to hold me down."

"You had flashbacks of your crash?" Victor asked.

"Yes, memories that I didn't even realize I had."

"How awful," he said.

"We haven't been anywhere exciting, so we're really looking forward to it," Star said.

"That's wonderful."

I handed them the gifts I had bought for them, and we were all sitting in the living room when Tom knocked and came in. I went to the door.

"Hey," he whispered.

"Hello."

I felt kind of shy for some reason. I waited while he took off his rain gear and then walked with him to join the others.

"Addy gave us such wonderful gifts," Star said.

"Every time I wanted to shop for you, you were always there," I told Tom.

"Brother," he exhaled loudly, "you've given me more than anyone could've."

He sat on the floor beside the couch I was on. I wondered if I should bring up a chair or something, but he looked very comfortable.

Why was I on pins and needles? I was both excited and nervous. I guess this was the first time we were officially here together.

"So, when are you guys planning this trip?" I asked.

But now there was only silence.

"Oh, whenever," Star said without any interest.

Strange.

"Where are you going?" Tom asked.

"Fredericton probably," Victor said.

"That's always nice," Tom said.

They would not have honestly forgotten that we were just talking about Bora Bora.

Why would they not want Tom to know? I wonder if he has something against exotic vacations. That's dumb. What would he possibly have against a tropical vacation? Maybe he doesn't believe in spending that kind of money on pleasure. But that is a bit unreasonable. I mean, seriously! Surely, if someone has the funds to spend on themselves, they should enjoy it. What is the point of hoarding it all up? It is different if they had their nose in the air, but Victor and Star are so humble, and they've never been on a trip like this. So, that is really cruel of Tom. I can see that too much TV couldn't be good, but isn't that delving too deep into everyone's personal lives? What gives him the right to decide all these kinds of things single-handedly? I think he is going too far with this control thing.

I shouldn't have mentioned anything because it caused Victor and Star to squirm. Now what? Will they have to lie just to make it simpler to go? Will they have to say they are going to Fredericton despite them taking this wonderful trip instead? Then they won't be able to share their photos and stories with anyone.

This made me mad. When Tom left, I didn't see him to the door. I'll have to talk to him about this.

IN THE morning, I was much more myself physically. However, emotionally, I felt a little lost. Now I have to find my place all over again.

A bit of fresh air would be good, Star had said after breakfast, so I stepped out when they did.

It was still snowing like crazy, but not quite as wet. Unfortunately, it was also pitch black.

Star kissed Victor, and he went to his boat. The men were all doing the same, getting kisses and heading off to work with their flashlights in hand.

Some had to walk right in front of me to get around. However, instead of seeing their jeans or corduroys and plaid flannel tops or old grey sweaters with patches on the elbows, all that moved were long rain jackets.

Many smiled and waved at me, even though I didn't recognize some of them. Well, I couldn't see their faces because it seemed like the middle of the night.

Water had somehow splashed all over my legs, and my jeans got wet.

I saw Tom come out. Barely being able to see him in the darkness, I still knew it was him, probably from the height and build. He had on a dark raincoat made of heavy rubber. But the hood was over his head, and it looked funny. Tom looked funny. It took away from that gorgeous manly appearance he always had.

Nevertheless, he glanced up at me and waved, and I waved back. Then he got to his boat and untied the rope. In the rain, his actions were not as smooth somehow. And I could only watch the moving lights dancing around like really big fireflies.

Soon, the boats were off, and I slipped inside.

I was cold. Man, I was freezing! I had to change my jeans and still was unable to warm up. So, I climbed back into bed for a few minutes until Star made me some tea.

The couch was exquisitely nice to sit on, with an old blanket around me and a hot tea in a mug in my hands. I slowly sipped and listened to the sound of Star in the kitchen.

I used the day to deliver gifts to the others and got all caught up with them. Urma was still crabby, so I sure didn't stay at her place long.

I was feeling much better, but seemed displaced now. What was I going to do with all my time?

Soon the boats were arriving.

Tom and I had discussed that I could wait for him in front of his place, but he would just greet me with a hug.

I tried to dress for the wetness without looking like an idiot. Then I walked to his place and waited. The other women waved and smiled at me.

As the boats headed back, I made out which was Tom, but he sure appeared different with that coat on. After all, how can we even embrace through that thing? All the men resembled rubber coats. That is all you could see.

With such heavy clouds, short days, and constant snow, their hoods cast a shadow so that you couldn't even notice their faces. Even though the sleet changed to rain, it was coming down too hard to increase visibility.

The closer the boats got, the more depressing the whole thing looked. It was solemn. So, instead of a look of victory, it was more a look of necessary endurance. The waves seemed almost violent. They were not that tall, but rough.

The men hauled dead fish off their boats in the persistent rain. Yet I watched because what else could I do?

Tom finished and was heading down the boardwalk.

216

I leaned against his door, but I wished I wasn't there. There must be more romantic settings for an embrace, even here. As Tom came near, I clenched my fists behind me. This is not the way it's supposed to be.

16

J ust as Tom was a couple of steps away, he removed his hood and undid his coat. And my breath caught in my chest. His skin glowed, his eyes sparkled, his hair bounced, and why did he look better than ever before?

He took me in his arms and held me tight. I clung to his flannel jacket with clenched fists, holding my face against his shoulder. Filled with the scent of the ocean and his smoky, woody smell, I was overcome with emotion.

"I'm so glad you're here," he whispered, and I wasn't able to say anything. "And the ocean is so happy to see you that it burst into tears, the tears of the sea."

I clung to him, never wanting to let go. He gave me a squeeze and then stepped back.

"How are you doing?" he asked with concern.

"I'm good now."

"What was bothering you yesterday?" he asked.

"Sorry. I was just thinking."

"Of what?"

"Oh, nothing," I said.

I felt bad because this was kind of a lie. What could I say? If I asked him now about exotic vacations, he'd be able to put two and two together. Therefore, I must try not to be so obvious. Why is it he can constantly tell when something is up with me?

"I would like it if you felt comfortable to talk with me about stuff," he said.

"I do."

He was easy to confide in, and I would bring it up as soon as possible.

"Whenever you need, I'm always here for you," he said. His words carried weight because I knew he had proved them to be true.

"Come for coffee at five. I'll invite some others," he said.

"Sure."

I had dinner with only Victor and Star. I wonder why they didn't ask Tom to join us. Maybe they saw too much of him, and it isn't reasonable to expect everyone always to invite him.

Perhaps he is not such an easy guy to be with.

"So, is Tom against tropical vacations?" I asked.

"Yes," Victor said after a long pause. "Don't mention it to him. Alright?"

"No problem."

I was mad now. And I wanted to say something, but I suppose it would seem dumb if I came all the way across the country to a remote fishing village just to be with a guy I was going to cut up in public. Besides, Jackie said no one ever talks against their man.

That, of course, was Tom's rule. No wonder they don't want him over.

I headed to Tom's for coffee. Jim, Sylvia, and Tore were there. Although we had a friendly visit, I still had to get to the bottom of this.

"Have you ever been on an exotic trip, Tom?" I asked.

"Nope."

"Would you like to?"

"Nope," he said.

"Why not?"

"It's not important to me."

"What if it was important to me?" I asked.

"You just got here," he said, staring at me now.

"I'm not talking about anytime soon."

"Haven't you already been?" he asked.

"Yes. It's pretty nice."

"Try and sit still for a little while," Tom said.

"That's pretty expensive, isn't it?" Jim asked.

"Well, yes," I said.

"I'd love to be able to do something like that for my family," Jim said as he put his arm around his wife. She looked at him as if to say that saying that was as good as if he actually took them.

"A fisherman's salary won't allow for trips of that nature," Tom said thoughtfully.

I felt kind of dumb now. How was I going to get out of this one? Of course, I didn't wish to go anywhere. Even more importantly, I didn't want Tom to think I required more than he could offer, and I didn't want everyone to believe there was something out there that would bring them more joy.

He did not seem against vacations like that, but they just couldn't afford it.

How would Victor and Star have the money? But we don't know how long they have been saving up. Or perhaps they received an inheritance.

They did say Tom was against it, though.

"Well, it's not exactly all it's cropped up to be," I said. "You're not missing anything that spectacular. In the end, it's only full of selfish people who love their money and need the world to entertain them."

"But you still want to go?" Sylvia asked.

"No. Not really. It was a hypothetical question."

"We don't need no tropical vacation," Tom said jokingly. "Just look outside," and everyone laughed.

I was a little confused because he didn't seem to be against it. Maybe Victor and Star misunderstood him. Perhaps they don't want anyone else to know they are going because they don't want others to feel bad or like they're missing out. That would be kind of them. Anyhow, I'll leave it alone for now.

A bit later, Tom handed me a key. "Here is a key to my place. You can spend some of your days here whenever you wish, or all of them for that matter, when I'm gone. You may need a little solitude." He touched my chin.

For some reason, this excited me. I have a key to his home. Wow! I don't have to be with everyone else all day. This is so great! I can do my own things, and I don't have to pester someone continually.

Considering this, I could have others in, make supper sometimes, and invite friends over. This is fabulous.

I wonder how particular he would be about me going through his stuff. Just in the kitchen, I mean. Surely, that wouldn't bother him.

THE NEXT morning, I told Star I had Tom's key.

"He's got all his records there," she said.

"What?"

"He's the law enforcement officer."

"Oh, yeah. I suppose."

"That could come in handy."

"Don't be ridiculous." I didn't like the sounds of that. "That would only be illegal, never mind that he could never trust me again. Why would you say that?"

"Relax. I was only kidding," she said.

Nevertheless, she appeared happy that I wouldn't be around her all day.

I went straight to Tom's and, for some reason, just stared out the window. My goodness, it was miserable here. *The tears of the sea.* But they seemed more like tears of agony than tears of joy. Now it was so dark. No wonder everyone is gloomy here. I thought I would be happy to be back, but instead I am depressed.

What am I doing here? Oh, yes. I'm here to be with the man I love. It's just that I have nothing to do all day.

After staring out the window for a long time, I finally got up and sorted through his kitchen cupboards. Yuck. I can't possibly make anything with this stuff. What on earth does he eat? Wieners? The only thing I can do with them, is put them on a stick and roast them in the fireplace. I remember him saying something about a fish and wiener dish. How gross.

Besides, he had all the dishes from last night in the sink, which were still dirty.

I wonder how clean he keeps his place. So, I started to snoop around. But there was no dust that I could find. His bed was made. Also, his floors were good, but his tub needed a good scrub. The kitchen cupboards need to be cleaned inside as well.

Is he expecting me to do his dishes? What if he left them hoping I would do them? Does he expect me to clean his place from now on? What if he stops cleaning now that I have a key? Well, I guess I'll soon find out.

I changed my mind about making supper. Because there was nothing here to be inspired by as far as groceries go. This was crazy, even though I may have learned a lot about cooking in Terrace. I don't know how he eats. When does he get supplies next?

I'm not doing his dishes.

What on earth can I do here except cook and clean? Read. Go online. I really do need a hobby. Learning a song is always an option, but I wasn't in the mood. Additionally, I couldn't come up with anything to search on the Internet. One day, I might have to learn to enjoy a book.

At least I'm able to stay out of everyone's way here, and I'm not imposing on anyone.

When it was lunchtime, I paid a visit to Becky and ate with them, but even that somehow wasn't the same. So, I stayed as long as possible without being a nuisance and then returned to Tom's.

I didn't do anything all day but watch the snow plummet out of the sky. And the only thing I looked forward to was seeing Tom when the boats came in.

That did not disappoint, but then he told me he had something to investigate that evening.

I had an uneventful dinner at Victor and Star's, feeling like they never wanted me there either.

IN THE morning, I headed back to Tom's.

There were no dirty dishes, and on the fridge, there was a note saying, "I love you - Tom."

This is stupid. Surely, I can cook something for supper. So, I got to work and would not give up until I had a menu planned. I had a good idea: I would ask Ryan and Roxy to join us. Their parents would no doubt like some quiet time, so I phoned, and it was all decided. Accordingly, I just cooked all day because what else did I have to do?

When our embrace concluded after the boats came, I thanked Tom for the note, and he smiled.

"I made dinner for you, and I invited Roxy and Ryan over. Is that alright?"

"Wonderful."

We both slipped inside as I saw them coming already. While he was taking a shower, the kids kept me occupied and laughing.

Afterwards, we had a fun supper together.

"I love watching you with children," Tom said.

"Maybe I have too much in common with them." I laughed.

"No, but you would make a great mother and I can think of no greater privilege than to raise a family with you."

That grabbed me by surprise somehow. But I'm not sure why. Because I was certain he would want kids, and I wasn't against the idea, but to have him say it so directly, I guess.

I suggested everyone do dishes together, but Tom dismissed Roxy and Ryan to play while he washed, and I dried.

"If you need anything, you tell me, alright? I can find out who is going to St. John's next, and they will bring you anything you say, and I'd pay for it. Do you need anything?" he asked.

"No, not yet."

"When you do, you tell me, Ok?"

"Sure."

"I want you to be happy here. It's probably even better for most things just to order them online, so if you can choose a new activity to pass the time, let me know. Are you bored yet?"

"Unfortunately, I have had my moments already, but likely only because I'm not used to it," I said.

"No. It'll get worse. Try to come up with something you would like to do."

"I'll try."

It was nice to do the dishes with him as the kids played in the background, and afterwards, we all had an enjoyable time playing a game together.

"Addy, I've still got some research to do and stuff. I hope this doesn't go on too long," Tom said as I left.

Friday was a drag, but at least the weekend was nearly here.

223

BREAKFAST SATURDAY was almost painfully silent. Man, these two were quiet, and I was tiring of hearing myself talk.

I hurried to Mac and Jac's as soon as I finished because that was one place where I wouldn't have to do all the talking.

Unfortunately, their blinds were shut, and I'm sure I heard them inside, although it might have been my imagination.

I guess all the women look forward to the weekends so they can be with their husbands.

I walked down the boardwalk. Many of the blinds were closed. When I got to the end, I came back and straight to the other side, but when I returned to Victor and Star's, their curtains were shut too. I hope it's nothing.

Their door was locked when I tried it.

I headed to Tom's and knocked on his. When he answered, his hair was more all over the place than usual, and he seemed unsure of what to say. He was obviously in the middle of something important.

I asked him to walk with me up and down the boardwalk, which he did, but was quiet.

"Sorry. I've got this issue on my mind. It doesn't look good. Also, I would hate to see the consequences here," he said. "Thanks for Thursday."

He stared out at the sea for a while. "I wish this wasn't happening now. Something like this does not happen often, and if this proves true, this could be the biggest shake-up this place has ever had." He sighed. "Whatever happens, Addy... I might be too busy and disturbed to give you what you need. I might say the wrong things. Please still love me. I'm going to work very hard. Please trust that I'm doing the right thing. Please don't turn on me because I wouldn't be able to take it."

He kind of scared me. What was going to happen? What could go wrong?

I let him get back to his work.

Thankfully, the blinds were now open at Victor and Star's, so I slipped inside.

They never said anything mean to me, but I felt terribly unwanted. In view of that, I should probably stay with someone else for a while, but if people can only stand me for one week, I will run out of places fast.

Maybe I'm not a good guest. It could be my fault. I thought I learned a lot over the last few months, but perhaps still not enough. So, I tried my best to stay out of their way.

It wasn't long after lunch when there was a knock at the door. When Victor opened it, I was surprised to see Tom because he always just walked in.

He didn't look himself at all.

"We need to talk. There is something we must discuss." Tom said to Victor. "Addy, could you visit someone perhaps?" he asked me.

I left and went to Mac and Jac's. In contrast, they seemed happy to have me there, which was a nice change.

A while later, while Jackie was talking, we heard screaming. When we looked out the window, we saw Star throw a pot at Tom. He turned and stared as it dropped into the deep abyss of water.

"Don't ever come back here!" Victor yelled. "You're a traitor to your people! Our forefathers would have burned you alive! Take your white girlfriend and leave us alone!"

Tom just watched and then continued heading home.

"That isn't a good sign," Mac said.

"Does everyone hate me?" I asked.

"Don't be silly. That's not what this is about. It's about something entirely different," Jac said.

"What?"

"I don't know. I really can't imagine."

"I don't want to go back there yet."

"No. Stay here a bit," Mac said.

I had supper with them and a pretty relaxing time, considering.

Later, when I glanced out the window, I saw something in front of Victor and Star's place. It was by the edge of the walk, so it was getting heavily rained on. I looked closer. Yet the sun was low by now, so I couldn't tell what it was, but after turning away for a while, it occurred to me that it might be my all of my belongings.

"I want to go check something," I said, telling them my strange idea.

They decided to come with me, and sure enough, it was all my things. As a result, my suitcases had soaked up the water like a sponge.

I got busy ringing out my clothes, putting them in the dryer, or hanging them up.

Then there was a knock, and Tom came in. He looked at my bags.

"What happened?" he asked.

"It's pretty lousy," Mac said as he gave Tom a beer and explained what we discovered.

"Oh, for crying out loud!" Tom exclaimed, running his fingers through his hair.

"She can stay here if that's alright," Jackie said.

"Sure," I said as I spread out other items of mine which I had dried with a towel. Tom watched me, but I had to keep busy going through my things.

I heard him tell Mac and Jac he wanted to cover my cost of being there. They, of course, were not interested in that, but Tom was quite persistent.

I kind of tuned them out.

"Addy," Tom said.

"Hmmm?"

"Addy..." he repeated. He needed eye contact.

I didn't want to be distracted, but I'm not sure why. I needed time to process all of this. Perhaps I was still in shock from the events of the last few minutes. But Tom came and knelt beside me.

"Are you alright?" he asked, looking genuinely concerned.

"I guess."

"You don't look alright."

"How do I look?"

"Pale. I'm sorry this had to happen to you."

"It's not your fault," I said.

"Probably many here would say it is. But tell me what you are thinking."

"I'm not thinking anything because I don't even know what's going on. I just have to keep busy and want to finish this before mould grows on my stuff."

"There is likely no chance of that happening right away. But listen... I am always here for you. Remember that."

He returned to the couch, and I tried to find something to do. I didn't have many things, but I wanted to work and think.

This isn't a big deal, really. The rain might not have destroyed anything, as I couldn't find any damage. Now that I don't have suits, most of my clothes can probably tolerate water. It wasn't important to stay with Victor and Star anyway. But I should have left sooner.

However, I had this horrible, unsettled feeling that was foreign to me. Maybe I expected too much of this place.

"Addy, come step outside with me," Tom said as he stood up and headed to the door.

The cool, damp air almost felt good.

I leaned against the front of the house. Then Tom put his hands on the wall, one on each side of me.

"Addy, I love you. Please don't be mad at me or blame me." That kind of choked me up, yet the tears didn't come.

He was very concerned about something, even worried, and I was sure it involved much more than I'd seen.

I stepped forward so I could rest my head on his chest, and he held me tight with one arm and touched my hair with the other.

"Please, promise me that you won't turn against me, although I wouldn't blame you. I've brought you to a harsh land. I did it because I want to marry you, but I'm afraid it's purely selfish because you don't stand to gain anything by being here.

"If it gets too much for you, you just say the word, and I will get you out of here and help you start wherever you decide, no questions asked.

"But if you can, please wait until this blows over because things like this don't happen that often. This may be the most disruptive thing to ever occur here.

"Whatever you decide, just please don't turn on me. Please trust I'm doing my best. I will do what's right and get it all done as soon as possible. Promise me."

"I promise," I said and watched him turn the corner to his home.

I was scared now. What on earth was going to happen? I shivered and went back inside.

They had a fire going, and I tried to warm up by it.

After a while, Jackie came, sat beside me, and put her arm around me. I started to cry, although I wasn't sure why. She, for once, didn't say a thing, and I was grateful.

In the morning, I did laps on the boardwalk. It was Sunday, so I decided after a while to see Becky and the family. They would cheer me up.

I knocked and stepped inside. However, the kids slowly crept to the door with strange, guilty looks on their faces. Then Becky appeared out of nowhere, and she was upset.

"So, whose side are you on?" she asked with hands on her hips.

"Whose side of what?"

"Tom's or everyone else's?"

"I don't know the issue at hand," I said.

"Surely, Tom told you the story from his point of view. He must want you to take his side, no matter how stupid it is."

"He didn't tell me what's going on."

"You're lying," she blurted out.

"You know Tom longer than I have. So, you know he wouldn't tell anyone information he shouldn't. There must be privacy laws or something."

"Well, whatever you say, but Tom is after Victor and Star because he says they didn't pay their taxes and are involved with fraud. It's all so stupid. I mean, what on earth benefit do we get from the government? Given that this is such a harsh place to live, if they can manoeuvre things to make life a bit more comfortable, then good for them.

"Tom is a traitor. He should support his people. But he has no loyalties and is only interested in getting his pay cheque from the government."

"That's a dumb thing to say, after all he does here," I said.

"What? You think you know Tom better than we do? You were here for only ten days before."

"True, but everyone had the utmost respect for him then. You know Tom will stand by his word and the law, which is why you respect him. Now your emotions are in the way, and that's all. What is right is right, and fraud is wrong. If he let it slide, everyone would do the same, and no one would respect him."

"So, you take Tom's side," she said.

"I'm not interested in having dishonest friends. If they are not truthful to someone, be it the government or anyone else, they won't be honest with their friends, either."

"That is such a bunch of bologna. We stand up for what is right, true, and fair.

"You know nothing about this life or Tom, but if you choose to be on his side, then I can only say that you will be sorry. Because he will control your life and then turn on you. You should leave while you still can.

"In the meantime, stay away from my kids and our home. I want to teach them about loyalty to your friends and what you believe in."

"Fine," I said. "I just hope you won't need to end up in jail before you realize what true loyalty is all about."

"Oh, I understand true loyalty and when I consider how Victor and Star took you in, well… you make me sick."

"Their goodness to me is completely unrelated to the trouble they got themselves into. Besides, even before I knew what was going on, they were the ones that cast me out."

"Yes. I heard what they did to your stuff, and it serves you right. You've lived in the lap of luxury, and now you will find out what life is really all about."

"Have it your way and see if it makes you any happier," I said and left.

Becky and her family are not even from here.

I walked back to Mac and Jac's.

Jackie was making soup and humming to herself.

"So, is everyone here going to take sides?" I asked her.

"Well, those on Victor and Star's side will think that the others are on Tom's, but there are usually some that don't care and some that have no reason not to trust him."

"What about you?"

"I'm not sure he has to be so dramatic, but it's his job, I guess. Besides, I don't want anyone to end up with more money than we do when we all work just as hard," she said, smiling.

"Becky told me to stay away from her house and her kids."

"Really? Wow! She doesn't usually get involved. I wasn't expecting that."

"Tom seems very concerned," I said.

"Yes, much more than usual, but I thought it was because it was affecting you. Did he tell you the situation?"

"No. Becky told me, from her standpoint anyway."

"Yeah. Tom won't tell you because he's not allowed to. Are you hurt by what she said?" she asked.

"Yes, but I'm more mad. And I am upset at what she said against Tom."

"I'm sure you didn't hear the end of it yet."

"Do you think Tom will control my life and turn on me?" I asked softly.

Jackie looked at me suddenly and was silent for a while as she stirred her soup. For the first time, she didn't know what to say, or at least took a moment to choose her next words.

"If you are unsure of that, you'd better analyze why you are even here," she suggested.

"No, but it's only a question. Becky said that, but I wanted your opinion on it."

"It would be different if you met Tom yesterday because then I could understand you being unsure. But I am afraid you will have to find the answer to that yourself. However, I lost a lot of respect for you just now. Don't you have any loyalty?"

Her words shocked and stung more than Becky's.

"I'll think about that," was all I could say.

I started putting away my items that were not clothes because it seemed they were all dry. At this time, they were unsightly, spread all over the place.

What did she mean? She must be saying that if I loved Tom and knew him at all, I would never have asked that question. Yet I figured she just would've told me it was nonsense, and that Tom is not like that.

Although, it must have sounded kind of stupid coming from the girl who flew across the country to be with this guy.

She must really think highly of him for her to tell me that. But why would she lose respect for me because I asked that question? I was only looking for reassurance. I would like to know if everyone here knows things about Tom that I don't. Is that so unreasonable? And with the horror stories you sometimes hear about women finding out they are married to a monster, a person can't be too cautious. Can they?

Is she overreacting, or am I the one who still has so much to learn? In the end, I suppose there is a lot I need to discover about relationships as everyone has more experience than me.

When I first got here, I thought Jackie was a little crazy, but I was beginning to see that she had depth and perception.

I guess I don't sound that loyal, all things considered. When Victor and Star told me that Tom doesn't agree with tropical vacations, I was inwardly mad at him. However, it wasn't true at all. They didn't want him to know because he would be suspicious about where they got all the money. Victor and Star had lied to me, and yet I believed them. But a loyal friend would've had nothing more than a little question in mind instead of being all upset.

I was sure glad I didn't act angry with Tom for no reason. I didn't, right? Not too much anyway. On the other hand, I never walked him to the door when he left that night, and that was even before Victor and Star lied about him.

Still, I was the one that had already drawn that conclusion. The truth is that I was the one who came up with that idea.

Now when someone tells me Tom will control my life and turn on me, I believe it? I don't think I believed that to be the whole truth, but I guess I was wondering if there was anything true about it. So, does that make me disloyal?

Does that mean I refuse to be blinded by love or that I don't have enough?

If it was the other way around and a person made up a rumour about me and told Tom... I would be distraught if he accepted it at that. Likewise, I would expect him to immediately reject in his mind anything bad that was said about me and then perhaps talk to me later to confirm what he heard was wrong. But I would be upset if he accused me of something that wasn't true just because he heard it somewhere. If he questioned my worth, friendship, character and love because someone full of anger attacked that, I would be absolutely crushed.

Why was I actually considering those things that Becky said about Tom? In fact, why would I even wonder if he would control my life and turn on me? Maybe I do have a lot to learn about loyalty.

17

I did stand up for Tom, and I thought very well, when I was at Becky's. However, I did that for my own pride.

I shouldn't hold him and everything if I have any doubts about him. I shouldn't lead him on if I am still not sure. But I am sure, aren't I?

Becky said he would control my life. Of course, that was out of anger to scare me, and that it did. I guess because I know that Tom is always in charge. He has no problem correcting me, that's for certain. Is he a control freak, though? Not exactly.

Can I live with a man who has such authority? I sometimes wonder if he wouldn't do better with some meek, quiet, submissive girl. Tom wouldn't control my life, but would he try to control more than I could handle? I don't think so. In all the phone calls we shared, I never felt he was trying to manipulate me. On the contrary, he seemed to demonstrate a lot of trust in me and my judgments.

Becky said he would turn on me. I wasn't concerned about that. Tom wouldn't turn on anyone unless they did something terribly wrong. So, that was likely just her anger talking.

So, all things considered, I should never have asked Jackie that. It made me look like a disloyal person.

Lunch was ready, and I sat down with her.

"So, did you get what I was trying to say?" she said, after babbling on another subject for a while.

"Yes. You had a very good point, and it caused me to analyze myself. You were not altogether wrong. I still have much to learn about loyalty, although you would have been impressed at how well I defended Tom to Becky. I think I have real difficulty trusting others in general...

"What about me? Am I unruly or a control freak?" I asked.

"No," she laughed. "Not exactly, but I'm sure you got accustomed to having things your way for a while. But what's important to single people changes as you grow to love someone. Then you become more interested in their welfare than your own, and since it works like that with both husband and wife, it all evens out in the end.

"If you fell in love with a guy who was, well, the opposite of Tom, then you would walk all over him, and it would only make you miserable.

"Most people who like control are motivated only by their insecurities, but Tom is not," she said.

"Is he always right? I am convinced I'm right and have a valid point, but after everything is said and done, why is he always right?" I asked.

"Well, you're not the first to say something similar. He is perceptive. He guards himself well. After all, his job requires that we all respect him. However, I'm sure he wouldn't be able to guard himself at all times and the more you are with him, the more you'll see. But that's Ok because you would be bored if you didn't have a good argument every now and then," she said.

"Sure, but to lose all the time would be annoying."

"The more important question is, how will you react when you realize he doesn't always do everything right?"

I liked Jackie and how she refused to answer my questions for me. It showed real perception.

After cleaning up a bit, I stepped outside, and for the first time since I came here, I felt like singing. However, I wasn't dressed appropriately, so I headed back inside and changed.

I put on a simple velvet dress with a cord for a belt. Finally, I had my warm cape over, with a hood that sat loosely over my head. It was the perfect outfit for here, and I had bought it thinking of nothing else. It was medieval looking, and the dark colours matched the ominous clouds in the sky.

Going back outside, I found a spot suitable for singing. After belting out a couple of tragic songs, they released some of my frustrations so that I felt much better afterwards.

I looked over the rail at the sea. The snow wasn't as intense now, but this sure was a wild place. I could see why all the homes were painted with such bright colours, because in the heavy clouds, they added the only brightness. There was a creaking from the boats as they gently bobbed in the water. They were all huddled together, waiting for tomorrow.

I thought of Tom. I respected him more than anyone, but trust is a bit harder for me. Growing up, I trusted no one, and rightly so. Tom had been such a good friend, the only person who was always there for me. He continually made himself available if I needed advice or just someone to talk to. He always cares about how I'm doing and how I'm feeling. Loyalty was natural to him.

Now he needed me. He needed my support, and he deserved it. Tom could likely use a comforting drink as a little coffee break.

"What is a nice, warm drink? Something special," I asked Jac after stepping inside.

"Ever have a hot-buttered rum?" she suggested after a moment.

I said no, and so she showed me how to make them, and it did have a neat and different taste to it.

So, I put my cape back on and headed to Tom's with two mugs in hand.

"By the way," Jac said as I slipped out, "you look amazing."

I knocked at Tom's door, and it took quite a while for him to answer. Then, when he did, he looked very disturbed.

"Thank goodness it's you," he said. "What a mess," he sighed.

I handed him a mug. "Would you be able to step out here for just a few minutes?" I asked.

"Sure. Thanks so much. I need this."

He put his coat and shoes on, strode outside, realized he had forgotten his drink inside, stepped back in, and searched for it for quite a while.

"You're distracting me," he said when he finally made it back out. "You are gorgeous. Man, you look good!" I may have blushed.

"Well, I've been having a rotten day until now, and I have a feeling yours has been similar," he said.

"Yes, well, this morning anyhow. What did you hear?"

"Becky phoned me, and I have never known her to act this way. She tried to convince me that you said I was a jerk and all kinds of similar stuff."

"She didn't!"

"Oh yeah. I don't even want to mention it all now, but it's hard to accept that she would be so evil."

"I can't believe she would lie to you like that, and furthermore, it was shocking what she told me when I was over. Especially because I wasn't even aware of what was going on until I got there," I said.

"Sorry I couldn't tell you before. You had to hear it from someone else, so no one would be able to blame me for violating something."

"I figured as much."

"It surprised me that you never asked," he said.

"I knew you couldn't tell."

"So, now, tell me honestly what you think of this situation," he said, resting his arms on the rail.

"Well, I don't know much, but I don't believe in dishonesty. What's right is right," I said.

"Do you think we should make exceptions for our friends?"

"Well, if your friends are dishonest, you can't trust them. Who wants friends you can't trust? Besides, with the whole suitcase thing, they made it evident that they were more interested in guarding their wealth than their friendships.

"I am convinced that you have to stand up for what's right, friends or not. They would never respect you if you didn't and I would never go against what I know to be right," I said.

"Thank you for saying that. You have no idea how important that is to me," Tom said.

"Thank you for not believing Becky."

He looked at me funny, as though he couldn't imagine what other option there was.

"Listen, tomorrow when I'm at sea, I want you to go online and buy some things that'll keep you busy. My credit card is already set up to my account. Find a hobby or something."

"I'll try," I said.

"It looks like it will be a rough week and I will need another officer here. If that works out, would you be willing to help me?"

"To do what?"

"If you could just keep us fed and my place in order. We'll have to cram a few weeks of work into only a few days. To keep everything else going for that time would mean the world to me. Would you do that, please?"

"Sure," I said.

"I'll need to depend on you because I can't do it all by myself."

"To make meals for the two of you, do the dishes and tidy up?"

"Yeah. I take forever in the kitchen, but I'd like the other officer to be treated well, as a guest. Would you take care of it all? I just can't manage that while handling this case. I can only do one thing at a time."

"Sure. I can do that."

"I know you can. Then, when this is finally over, I will be able to spend more time with you." He smiled.

"What will we do to celebrate?"

"Well, I'll leave that to you to figure out."

"Tom, what's over that hill?" I asked, pointing to the one behind the houses.

"Nothing. Just more hills and lots of huge boulders. You definitely can't walk to the other side of the island. We can explore there a bit in August if you want, but never during the rest of the year because the rocks are too slippery."

"Have you actually tried?"

"I'm not making this up."

"But how would you know if just over the hills is some really cool spot?"

"Addy, trust me. Do not go there. It isn't safe. You will get yourself killed."

"So, we can't do rock climbing to celebrate?"

"I don't think I need to repeat myself." He was so serious that I had to smile. I batted my eye lashes a few times.

"I'd like to hear it," I whispered.

Tom groaned, smiled and playfully rolled his eyes. "I better get back to work, but thanks for coming and for the drink. It was exactly what I needed.

"I'll let you know as soon as I find out when the officer is arriving." He raised his eyebrows, dropped them, and stepped inside.

I felt better now about everything. Tom never believed Becky, yet it shamed me to recognize that I wasn't as good of a friend to him. However, there's still time to prove my loyalty, by helping out when the other officer arrives.

But most likely, he was a bit overprotective with the whole hill thing. It's not like someone will die from climbing a few rocks. It's not even close to being a mountain.

THE NEXT day I went to Tom's. Although there were papers all over his desk, I figured it must have to do with Victor and Star, and I didn't want to see them by accident. I'm sure he never meant to leave them out. Therefore, I moved his laptop to the kitchen table.

I shopped online for a while but couldn't find anything I wanted to do. I like that Tom trusted me with his credit card. A couple of hours later, I still wasn't able to get something that interested me. So, finally, I cooked supper for him instead.

"I made you some dinner," I told him as soon as he got back, "cause I figured that you'll be working all evening."

"You're a lifesaver," he said as he kissed me on the forehead.

Later, Tom came in as I was doing the dishes with Jac at their place.

"Hey Addy, they are going to send an officer right away. He will get here tomorrow. I'll still fish because he'll likely only come after I'm home anyway, but if he arrives earlier, would you let him in and make him welcome?"

"Yes. I can do that."

"Did you buy something?" he asked.

"No. I just couldn't find anything."

"Addy. I want you to place an order tomorrow because I'd like you to have something after this whole thing blows over."

"I'll try again," I promised.

"Tom, when do you go shopping next?" I asked.

"I just went before my trip."

"But you don't have any food in the house."

"I don't?"

"No. I can't figure out what you eat."

"I dunno."

"If you need anything," Jackie said, "you are welcome to borrow it from me."

THE NEXT day I pulled my hair out, trying to plan supper.

Then I ordered some sculpting clay online. I'll see if I can sculpt something.

When I finished that, I heard the helicopter.

I stepped outside, as did everyone else, and watched it lower itself onto the one flat area where we had danced last summer. There was no question that it was law enforcement, and the whole thing looked intimidating.

A police officer got out. RCMP officer, actually, but there was no difference in the look. I wonder if Tom has a uniform. I waved to him and headed over.

"Are you Adelle?" the man asked.

"Yes. Follow me."

"I'm Joe," he said once we were under the boardwalk and I shook his hand. "They sure picked a day for me to come. I've never seen a storm like this."

"You will tomorrow and the day after that because this is typical winter weather here." I said, letting him inside Tom's.

"Are you hungry?" I asked.

"Not really, more chilled than anything," he said.

"I'll make some hot broth, and you sit here by the fire."

I got the fire going, heated some chicken broth and brought it to him.

"What's with the outfit?" he asked, but he had a massive grin on his face.

"Oh, I just enjoy being dramatic," I said.

"Tom never told me that he was dating the princess of this island. Is that Celtic? Viking? Medieval?" he asked, chuckling.

"Something like that. To me, it seems to suit the place."

"I guess it does, but maybe in another era."

"This sure hits the spot," Joe said as he sipped his soup.

"Did you go through the papers on the desk?" he asked.

"No."

"Cause they are confidential."

"I figured they could be."

"Is this a one bedroom?" he asked.

"Yes."

"I can bunk out here," Joe said.

"No, you'll have the bedroom. There's a double bed. Tom will be staying on the couch." Tom and I never discussed it, but I imagine that's what he would want.

I guess I better change the sheets on there. I wonder if I should do that. It felt personal.

Nevertheless, I excused myself, entered his bedroom, and closed the door. Examining his bed, I was sure, but not a hundred per cent, that these were the same sheets originally there when I first got his key. There has to be some spare ones around here somewhere. There they are, and it's a brand-new package, too, so he must have ordered them for this occasion. Then I stripped down his bed and put the new sheets on, unable to prevent myself from imagining the calm expression that would grace his face in the early morning. Surely, this is part of taking care of everything. The other extra blankets, along with his sheets, I brought out for Tom to use on the couch.

I worked some more on supper, as Joe visited with me a bit. He was from St. John's and had a wife and kids there.

When it was time for the boats to come in, it seemed dumb excusing myself to stand outside.

"He is here," I told Tom. "I wondered if you would be giving him your bedroom, so I changed your sheets and brought out some blankets you could use on the couch. I hope you don't mind."

"That's great. I didn't get that far yet. That's good. Thanks for handling that," he said. "My couch folds into a bed, so that will be fine enough for me."

The guys moved the desk into Tom's bedroom as I got the supper on the table.

"You shouldn't leave this stuff out," Joe said to him.

"Addy wouldn't look through it. I have to leave it out because otherwise, I won't know where I left off."

We had the meal together, and it was a lot of fun. It reminded me of when I first arrived and how everything looked to me then. Joe ranted and raved about my food, although it seemed ordinary to me.

As I did the dishes, the guys disappeared into the room.

After a while, Tom stuck his head out. "Addy, could you make us some tea?"

That is slightly direct, but I did as I was told and took it to them. Slowly it got late, and I was about to leave when they came out.

Tom brought their cups and teapot and put them in the sink.

"Would you be able to give these a little wash?" he asked.

"Tomorrow, while I'm making breakfast," I said, a bit agitated.

"You didn't clean my tub by chance, did you?" he asked when Joe wasn't within earshot.

"No."

"So far, I haven't been able to, but I'd hate for him to have a shower in it like that," he admitted.

I said good night to both of them and left.

WHEN I let myself in the next morning, I smelled the coffee. Tom made the best coffee.

He was sitting across the couch with his mug and going through papers. Joe was still sleeping, I presumed.

"Morning," Tom said, but he looked tired. "Thanks for your help."

I got breakfast started. I decided to do a puffed peach pancake. While it was baking, I cleaned his tub and set out a towel for Joe.

I returned to finishing the meal, and Tom continued going over his papers.

Finally, Joe seemed to be up, and I kept the food warm while we waited for him because I'm sure no one is used to getting up this early.

When I sat in the living room, Tom glanced up for only a split second.

"The tub is cleaned," I said.

"Good," he muttered without looking up.

I clenched my fists. He was making me cranky.

"Can you bring us some coffee at seven-thirty?" Tom said.

"I don't know how to make it in that," I said. Back in Toronto, I had a single-serve kind that used a pod, and in Terrace, they had a French press. But he had one of those old-fashioned drip kinds.

"I think you can figure it out," he muttered without looking up.

I got up and checked the food, but I was mad now. How dare he treat me like that?

We had breakfast. I did the dishes.

When seven thirty arrived, I decided not to start the coffee.

Tom stuck his head out. "Where's our coffee?" he quietly whispered.

"Make it yourself," I said.

He stared at me for a second. Then he marched into the kitchen and prepared it. He disappeared behind his door again, but came out a few minutes later, poured it for them and slipped back inside without a word to me.

I was now a little too cranky to sit still. So, I made some fish chowder and then returned to Jackie's to get the loaf out of the bread machine. This is something I'll definitely need to buy, because bread takes up so much room in the freezer, and is better fresh. I brought it over and then started working on a lasagna for supper.

However, I left a note saying there was bread and soup for lunch and instructions for cooking the lasagna at dinner. I was getting out of here.

Back at Jac's place, I dressed warmly. After that, there were hills that needed climbing.

"Are you going to Tom's?" she asked.

"No," I replied.

She asked nothing more, but watched as I left.

At the edge of the far boardwalk, there was a spot where the rock perfectly touched the rail. So, all I would have to do is climb over. This was convenient because, any other way, I would have to swim before reaching it.

There has to be some option of going for a walk around here. Why do they even have all these houses up against the cliff-type moss-covered rocks? You can't go anywhere. All there is, is that tiny field at the one end, and besides that, only rock, rock, and more rock. Who would ever live in a place where you can't even go for a good walk? How many times can you pace the boardwalk anyway? It is vital for all the inhabitants to find a way to get to the other side of the island. From my helicopter flight out, I remembered how it looked and it would be enough to add some variety. So, I'll just have to discover how.

I had a bit of difficulty getting over the rail and rock, but finally made it.

With my rain suit on, I was completely protected, but still, water was seeping in somewhere, or perhaps it's because it's so damp that your clothes get wet from condensation.

I stood on the large boulder. Now, to go over that mound and see what's on the other side. I carefully watched my balance, but had no trouble whatsoever getting to the top of it. Tom was exaggerating.

When I was on that hill, I could see many more cliffs and rocks and huge boulders and cracks in the rocks. There was a green carpet of moss on some of them, which made for a pretty sight. I surveyed the area carefully for the most gradual slope.

I don't know what he was talking about. The rocks aren't slippery because they are covered with moss. Maybe the parts that didn't have any, but I wouldn't step there. I got down the ridge without any problem. This was really neat and proved that Tom was at least a bit of a control freak. Then I found another gradually sloping hill and walked up.

When just about at the top, the moss I stepped on decided to slip off the rock. I felt myself falling. There was nothing to grab onto, especially because I was tumbling headfirst. My body slammed into various rocks, one after the other. Then I passed out.

When I woke up, there was an intense pain in my head. My neck was throbbing as well. Rain was pouring on my face, as I landed with it up, and it had even filled my hood. My feet were elevated, and way too much blood rushed to my brain. So, I must be laying on a sharp incline with my legs higher.

It took a great deal of effort to move. I had to inch my body around before removing my head from this rock. Wow, did that hurt! Then water shockingly poured down my back from my hood. I was freezing cold. My skull was killing me. I don't ever remember anything this painful. My plane crash didn't even injure me this badly.

As I tried to climb up the same way I came, the moss kept sliding off the rocks, and there was nothing to steady myself with or hold on to.

I needed to stop frequently and lower my head to prevent passing out, and I also started shaking. Also, the rock might have ripped my hood open, although it was hard to tell because my hair was soaked anyway. Persistently, I attempted to get back up the hill until I passed out again. This is dangerous.

Then I found an area in the rocks that was a bit sheltered and climbed inside.

I tried to size up my situation and discovered that my head was bleeding lots in the back. Thankfully, I was wearing a tank underneath my sweater, and I could tie it around at my forehead. Despite my good rain gear, everything was wet, but I was shivering and had no choice but to put it on again. I huddled in the corner, trying to stay warm.

The sun was behind the hill now because the days were still so short. Although I was glad to be out of the rain, I was cold.

With nothing left to do, I started to sing. I sang and sang, going through every song I knew. At least it kept me occupied and conscious, and gave me something to focus on other than my shivering.

"Addy, what on earth are you doing?!!" It was Tom, finally.

I couldn't hear where his voice was coming from, as it bounced off all the rocks, but he was a distance away. He was also angry and screaming.

"Did you think I was lying about this place? Do you think I am stupid? You could've been killed. Do you think this is funny? Because I sure don't. What do you think you'll accomplish by this? Why don't you just listen for once?"

I stopped singing and had nothing to say in reply. In all my life, I had never felt so dumb before. Although I wanted to retaliate in some way, there was nothing I could possibly do to redeem myself from this. From now on, I would be known as the village idiot.

"Can you see this light?" he yelled as I saw it shine down.

"Yes."

"Tell me when it's beside you."

I directed him via the beam to where I was.

"Why did you do this?" he was yelling again. "What were you thinking? I've got critical work to do right now. But instead, I have to come and rescue you because you didn't listen to me in the first place. It is dangerous here. Don't you care about anyone except yourself? Don't you care that you could have gotten killed? I can't believe you would be this foolish."

He kept screaming at me all the way down, saying similar things. I'd never heard him yell before. I was too frozen to move and certainly had nothing to say in reply.

Finally, he stood before me, and I tried to get out of the hole. He shone the blinding light at me.

"For crying out loud, Addy!" he said, but not as loudly. He had a rope tied around him that went straight up.

When I managed to scramble out, he grabbed me and pulled me tight against him. "Hold on to me and don't let go." It was more of a threat than anything else.

He walked, climbed and pulled us out while continuing to scold me, just not at the top of his voice like before. I hung onto him for dear life, and it wasn't easy.

Why *did* I do this? It seemed to make sense at the time, but now it was obvious that it was so utterly foolish. Stupid, in fact. Even though I tried to remember how mad I was earlier, it all was insignificant at the present time. And I wished Tom wasn't angry, but I couldn't blame him.

I was fortunate to be alive.

The words he kept saying reverberated in my mind. *Don't you care about anyone except yourself? Don't you care that you could have gotten killed?* Hopefully, that meant that his anger was more out of concern for me than anything else. At least, I'd like to think that.

I was amazed at how glad I was to be in his arms, even though he was still reaming me out.

When he had me back on solid ground, he dropped me on my feet and immediately left, with Joe following behind.

Mac and Jac were there, and they walked with me into their home. It was convenient that I was staying with the only doctor around. He pulled my makeshift bandage off, and Jackie tried to help me remove all my extra clothing layers as I shivered intensely.

"You need stitches," Mac said and returned with a needle.

When he jammed it in me, and I swear it scratched the bone, I passed out again.

When I woke, I was lying on the couch before a fire, wrapped in blankets, and my head was properly bandaged. I watched the flames.

Jac came by. "Well, how are you doing?"

"Fine, I suppose, and all things considered, I don't think I deserve the right to complain."

"True enough. However, I have to say that no one here has ever seen Tom yell like that. In the end, it was rather entertaining and almost funny to see him so furiously mad."

"It wasn't funny."

"Only because you weren't badly hurt. Only a few stitches and no broken bones. It could have been so much worse."

"I know."

"What possessed you to go there?"

"I was mad."

"At Tom?"

"Yes."

"Well, you certainly showed him," she joked.

"I know, and I'll never be able to live this down. I'm the village idiot now. There is nothing else to say."

"You are very entertaining, but it wasn't necessary to go this far."

"I know. I don't even know why I did it."

"Because Tom told you not to," she said.

"I don't think that's the only reason," I finally said. "Do you suppose he'll ever forget it?"

"How many times, Addy, do you need to get knocked on the head to figure out that Tom is crazy about you?"

"He wasn't so nice to me before," I said.

"Well, I don't know the situation, and I don't want to, but you must learn to communicate better. Talk it over. Tom's been under a lot of stress lately. Can't you see what he is going through? Cut the guy some slack."

"I'm not helping very much."

"No. You're not."

I ate a bit and then drifted off to sleep.

IN THE morning, I felt well enough, considering. I was very bruised, and most movements hurt, but it was time to suck it up. Despite utter embarrassment, I decided I better go to Tom's and make breakfast for them.

As I opened his door, I heard the coffee finishing. Tom was lying on the couch, but the bed was put away, and he was all washed up and dressed. He wasn't doing anything, though.

I didn't say a thing, and neither did he.

After tiptoeing to the kitchen, I poured coffee into two mugs, and I fixed mine up as I liked it. As I came into the living room, Tom just followed me with his eyes.

I handed him his mug, which he took without a word, and I sat on the edge of the same couch he was on. He pulled himself more upright.

"I am sorry about yesterday and my rock climbing. I am mortified, and never wanted to disturb you," I said.

"But why did you turn on me?" Tom asked.

"What do you mean?"

"Very specifically, I asked if you would like to help, a couple of times, in fact. I told you what I needed from you, but you turned on me. Here I was counting on you, and you're not there when I need you the most. Although I've got much more than I can handle alone, I can't even turn to you, and you promised. I'm getting shot at by almost everyone here, but it hurts when it is coming from you," he said with a blank look on his face.

247

18

W hen Tom put it that way, it did make a little sense.
"You were treating me like a servant. I want to help.
I enjoy it, even, but you had no right to treat me like
that," I began. "You were so commanding: 'Addy, make us some
tea.' 'Would you give these a little wash?' 'You didn't clean my tub
by chance, did you? I'd hate for him to have a shower in it like that.'
When I cleaned the tub, you said, 'Good.' 'Can you bring us some
coffee at seven thirty?' 'I think you can figure it out.' 'Where's our
coffee?' It really hurts to be treated like that."

"I wasn't trying to be personal," Tom said. "I was just focused
on what I had to do. Why would you get so hung up on emotions
when there was serious work to accomplish?"

"Because I don't believe in turning off relationships because
there is work to do. You don't turn it on and off like a light bulb
when you love someone. Despite it all, I still made every meal for
both of you. I'm not your girlfriend only when there is nothing else
going on," I said.

"That's not what I meant. I only wanted you to... well, not
question me, give me the benefit of the doubt. But I wasn't trying to
hurt you.

"I didn't know that I sounded that bad. I couldn't believe that
you had got the bed ready and everything. I never intended for you
to scrub my tub. I was only thinking out loud. I felt awful that I
didn't get a chance to clean it myself. In the end, I was so focused I
wasn't considering how I was saying things.

"Addy, what you did was so helpful for me. You wouldn't believe how much. When I got here, you had everything handled so well, and Joe was all taken care of and I was so proud of you, wondering, *Wow, what did I ever do to deserve her?*

"What I could do to be worthy of you, I'm not sure, but please trust that I have more respect for you than that. And I don't have any problem cleaning, doing dishes, or even cooking, so I am genuinely sorry for whatever I said that left the wrong impression.

"I'll try to pay more attention to what I'm saying. Sorry I was unable to figure out what made you so upset with me. I love you. I didn't mean to hurt you. Can you forgive me?"

"Well, as long as you can forgive me."

"I think we have a deal," Tom said, smiling. "But seriously, do you think you can put up with me?"

"Yes, but I think the more important question is: can you put up with me?"

"That's my hobby. There's nothing I enjoy more."

"Even when I do really stupid things, like go rock climbing?"

"Oh, that did take all, Addy. Sorry I got so mad, though. I just lost it because I was so afraid I could lose you. Sorry about all the yelling. I never yell," he said.

"So I've been told. Sorry that I gave the impression that I had turned on you. Honestly, I didn't even realize that what I said would imply that. Also, I didn't think of how that could've humiliated you, but I never thought it would've hurt you."

"It did, but I understand now. Don't give up on me, Addy."

"Never, but I wouldn't blame you if you gave up on me. I learned so much about people since I first met you, but I am finding that I still have to learn how to be loyal."

Then I got up because I needed to make breakfast.

"Well, if you need some reasons to be loyal to me..." He followed me into the kitchen.

"Like?" I said, smiling, as I started putting ingredients together for pancakes.

"For starters, I'm incredibly... good looking." He was trying hard not to laugh. "My muscular build is the envy of all men. I am an RCMP officer. You should see me in my uniform... You will, as I have to be wearing it later. After today you'll be very proud of me, but on the more serious side. I'm tough but sensitive." He said it in such a funny way that I had to chuckle, and so did he. "I have fabulous taste in women. I am charming and affectionate, as you will find out later."

"Here, stir this," I said, still laughing as I handed him the bowl and whisk.

But my skin tingled at his last statement.

"Is this for pancakes?"

"Yup."

"Hey, I'm good at cooking them, but never got them to taste like anything," he said.

"Well, that's convenient because I'm sure mine would taste great if only they wouldn't burn on the outside and be uncooked inside."

"I'll be your flipper. Hey, that means I can totally flip out without upsetting you."

"You're in a much better mood," I laughed.

"Well, yes. Before that, my girlfriend was mad at me, and I didn't know why.

"This whole case thing, though... it's been really tough. But everything is almost all done. In a few more hours, it should be over," he said.

"That's exciting. Will Joe leave tomorrow, then?"

"Today, I think."

"And after, what'll things be like here?" I asked.

"Well... at first, many will hate me and, by extension, you. Then slowly, sheepishly, they will all come around. Finally, they might make an apology of some sort and hope we all forget that it ever happened."

"Is your uniform the same as Joe's?"

"Yeah."

"Do you still have to spend all day in your room?"

"No, but a bit. There are only a couple of things left to do. Since it shouldn't take too long, maybe we can all be together a little while afterwards," he said.

"That would be nice."

"Is that pan for the pancakes?"

"Yes."

"It's too hot. No wonder you burn them," he said, turning it down.

"Hey. This is my kitchen," I said, trying to look serious.

"It is? Wow! Well, that's fine with me. I don't need a kitchen anyway. Would you like me to turn it back up so we can have black pancakes?"

"No," I said, still chuckling as I took mental note of the temperature he set the burner on.

As I got the bacon started, I noticed Tom testing a drop of batter in the pan, tossing it out and waiting some more. He takes his pancake cooking rather seriously.

We talked and laughed.

With one swift move, he would get the pancake to fly in the air, turn around and land correctly back into the frying pan. I always wondered how people could do that.

Soon after the pancakes were done, Joe got up, and we had a nice breakfast.

"I see you have a little memento of yesterday," Joe said.

"It's my new fashion statement." But I'd almost forgotten about the vast bandage around my head.

I did the dishes as they disappeared into the room again.

When I was going to start making pizzas for lunch, the guys surfaced, proclaiming to be all done. So, I suggested a pizza competition to see who could make the most creative yet tasty pizza. They were all for it, and we spent the next hour laughing our heads off. The guys would pull absolutely anything out of the cupboards and contemplate using it. In the end, none of the pizzas were tasty, but we ate them anyway.

Then we all did dishes and sat around talking. I sang a few songs. Tom said there was no need for me to prepare supper.

Tom and Joe put on their uniforms. Man, Tom looked good in his! Then, the boats arrived, and the guys were waiting for something.

After a while, I heard the helicopter coming.

Things happened fast then. The helicopter lowered itself onto the spot, and Tom and Joe knocked on Victor and Star's house. When they didn't come out, they broke the door down.

When they exited, Victor and Star were handcuffed and led to the helicopter.

Soon it lifted straight up, with Victor and Star and Joe inside. Tom just stood on the boardwalk, watching.

After he came over and walked with me.

"I'm sure glad that is over," he said.

"Me too."

"I'll probably be myself again soon. Hey, I'll make supper for you tomorrow," he offered.

"You going to fish?"

"Course."

I had a little bite with Mac and Jac, but a very sombre mood prevailed. I was so glad it was over, but I wasn't as relieved as I had expected.

"That's possibly the most exciting thing that's ever happened here," Mac said.

"Yes, and you survived it," Jac said.

"Not well," I said.

"How's that?" she asked as she ran water for the dishes.

"It would've been a good time to prove my loyalty, but I failed miserably," I admitted as the realization punched me in the gut.

"Because you went where you shouldn't have?"

"Sort of, but more that I promised Tom I would take care of everything. He made me promise that I wouldn't turn on him, yet... I kind of did. Looking back, he was just very focused and disturbed with the job at hand, but I was concentrating on how I didn't think he was treating me respectfully. Because he never treats me so abruptly normally. But I should've known better and been able to see through that and put up with it. Instead, I retaliated and did my stupid rock climbing."

"How did you retaliate?" she asked.

"Well, I told him to make his own coffee, and I took off, though I did leave food for them first. But then I wasted valuable time by needing to be rescued."

"Did you say anything that you regret?"

"No. Only when I told him to make his own coffee."

"Tom's still upset with you?"

"No. No. He forgave me, and I forgave him, but I feel so awful now because I wasn't a loyal friend again."

"You are learning. Everything is going to work out because, thankfully, Tom can see right through you."

I finished drying the dishes and sat on the couch. Although, my head was spinning.

I WAS more positive about things in the morning, but I still had good reason to feel humbled.

I thoroughly cleaned the bathroom for Jackie, bleaching the tiles and everything.

A while after lunch, I was too tired to continue without a nap. But I decided that I would sleep much better at Tom's because, after yesterday's events, Jac couldn't stop talking.

I changed the sheets on his bed again and thought, why not just have a nap here? It seemed a little wrong, but how could it be? I had on this long dress with wide sleeves and a lengthy skirt, so I reluctantly decided to take it off. And that was an interesting feeling, but there was still lots of time before Tom returned.

Man, it's nice to be in a real bed. I fell asleep instantly.

I woke to a knock on the door. Thankfully, I'm not one of these people who can't remember where they are when they wake up. Then I heard it open. So, it must be Jackie.

What time is it? Why doesn't Tom have a clock in his bedroom?

"I'm in here!" I called out as I sat up, keeping the blankets around me tight.

She is so going to laugh when she sees me sleeping in here.

I wonder what she is looking for. I remember putting the paddle back in the bread machine after I washed it, and I'm sure I didn't remove anything from her bathroom.

When the door opened, it was Tom who stood in the doorway.

All of a sudden, my brain kind of went dead. He is going to think I planned this. Did I sleep that late? I shouldn't even be in his bed. I couldn't tell what on earth he thought as he looked at my dress on the floor. What if he thinks I was trying to seduce him? Besides, there is no one else in the house.

"Are you early?" I finally asked after a very lengthy, uncomfortable silence.

"Nope."

"You should have a clock in here. But I can't believe I slept that long. And I shouldn't even be here. I didn't get to greet you. How could I sleep through the boats coming in? I should have asked first…"

I stopped when I saw that he was trying hard not to laugh.

Then he came further into the room, bent down, and scooped up my dress. He took it and left, grinning this mischievous grin.

"Hey!" I called out after him. "Bring that back!" But it didn't make one bit of difference how much I yelled.

I guess he was in the kitchen making supper and occasionally chuckled to himself as I tried to convince him to return my dress.

I was perfectly stumped as to what to do. Finally, I wrapped a blanket around myself and yanked on it until it came out. I ensured that I was well covered, but at that moment, I heard the front door, and some people came in. I froze.

"Make yourselves at home," Tom was saying. "I'll be right back."

He entered the room carrying my dress, but stopped instantly when he saw me. His eyes leisurely travelled up and down my body.

"Man, you are adorable," he said. And my face grew warm, but he didn't move.

"Do you think this is sexy?"

"No," he laughed. "Actually, I don't. Not to embarrass you, but with your head still wrapped up, your cheeks all rosy, and that huge blanket around you, you look so incredibly sweet, like a little girl. Can I take your picture?"

"What? Don't you have company?" I asked.

"Just a second."

He ran into the kitchen, still holding my clothes, did something with the food and told his guests that he would be a minute.

Then he came back, got his camera out, and took at least ten shots of me from different angles.

"Thanks. I wouldn't embarrass you," he said as he handed me my dress. However, I couldn't take it because I would have needed to let go of part of the quilt. "Oh, sorry," he said and placed it next to me.

"It's Jane and Cody that are here, and don't worry about the bed. I'll fix it up later."

Then he left the room, closing the door behind him.

I got dressed but wasn't able to get rid of the colour in my cheeks.

"We wondered if you were sick," Jane said.

"No. I just fell asleep." Yet I felt kind of dumb, not so much for drifting off, but with my head all wrapped up, it also served as a reminder of my stupidity from a couple of days ago.

So that my brain would clear a bit, I sat and talked with them a little, and I stepped into the kitchen with Tom.

"Did I do something wrong?" he asked.

"No, of course not. It just took me by surprise," I said, smiling. I wanted to see if he needed a hand, but he looked like he had everything under control, as always.

It was a lovely evening, but it seemed surreal, as I probably never fully woke up.

The weekend was quiet and calm. Tom came over a few times, and I also had coffee over there.

STARTING ON Monday, though, I began to get bored. I wasn't in the mood to cook all the time. What was I going to do?

The more bored I got, the more cranky I became. The more cranky I became, the more quiet Tom got. The more quiet Tom got, the less I had to look forward to at the end of the day. The less I had to look forward to, the more I began to wonder if I would succeed here.

Eventually, I got my sculpting clay, and it kept me occupied for at least two hours.

One day, out of the middle of nowhere, Tom said, "Addy, I don't want to lose you." Then I was even more disappointed in myself. Somehow, I was going to have to make this work.

I researched rocks, the sea, and other resources in this area, but it was challenging to find any information about this island. Basically, it doesn't exist to the rest of the world.

Jim, Sylvia, and Tore came over one day for supper. They had been extremely distant after the arrest but had since eased up considerably. When we were all sitting around afterwards, I remembered my question.

"Are there any precious gems that can be found in any of the rocks around here?"

"There's quartz and stuff like that," Tom said after looking at me for a bit.

"Has anyone ever looked for it?" Jim asked.

"I don't reckon so. I can't even prove it, but I heard from a reliable source that there could be quartz. There is an old legend about it."

Tom recounted this fascinating tale about someone finding geodes, not telling a soul about it and then dying tragically before he ever sold any of his vast collection that he was keeping secret. The story had a moral to it and everything.

I had to laugh because it suited him to tell a story like that.

"Just don't go climbing behind the hill, although you did look cute with your head bandaged up."

"I won't, but there are lots of rocks around here anyway."

"Plenty enough," Tom said, smiling.

More research revealed that looking for quartz, feldspar, or mica would be my best bet. I wonder if I could make jewellery or something. Finding it would be more entertaining than doing anything with it, but you never know. Although I'd love to see labradorite, I'm not sure what my chances would be.

Tore showed me a way to smash rocks open. I was having so much fun that I didn't care that I wasn't discovering any gems.

The rest of February passed uneventfully, and March was full of torrential rain.

ONE FRIDAY, Tom said he would take me to St. John's the next day. And that was exciting for me. He told me I shouldn't eat breakfast, but we would have a meal there and hang out for a few hours. Even though I wasn't looking forward to the trip, walking around town would be great. Jim, Sylvia, and Tore would come with us but go their own way once we arrived.

Any hopes I had of the boat ride being any better for me were soon diminished. But after being there for an hour, I finally felt good enough to eat.

The air was crisp here, and a colder wind blew, but to have the sun and things to see in every direction made up for it.

There were some cute streets with different coloured buildings. I guess it's an east coast thing, but it was pretty. The larger boats in the harbour looked nice, but really, I was craving... city. I wanted to see people, cars, businesses, retail stores, restaurants, coffee shops, roads, and sidewalks.

Someone walked by with a dog.

"Why are there no dogs in Foley's?" I asked.

"There's no land for them. No yards. The homes aren't very big, and if one started barking... can you imagine? We'd all have to listen. So, we have a no-dog policy."

"Kids can be loud."

"We allow kids," Tom said with a smile.

"What about parakeets?"

"We don't have a law yet... but we can always make one."

"Goldfish?"

"Gregg has fish. Big tank with all kinds. You should see them some day."

We had to go for breakfast because nobody serves lunch at nine in the morning. And it made me wonder how it would ever be possible to go for a romantic dinner. Anyway, it was really nice to sit in a restaurant, even if it was a casual diner.

Afterwards, we could walk into some of the stores. I needed a few things, but we were mostly strolling casually, and I was so happy to be here. It was also terrific to be only with Tom and not entertaining anyone else.

"What are you going to do, Addy?" he asked.

"With my time, you mean?"

"Yes. Besides marry me and have kids."

"Isn't that good enough?"

"For you, it won't be," he said.

"I'm working on it. Probably start a tiny business of some sort. But I just don't know what yet."

"Sounds good."

"This looks like a neat store," I said, finding a little flower and gift shop.

"This reminds me of Snow," he said, smiling after we were inside for a while.

"Snow?"

"Darcy's wife."

"Oh, right. Yes. Sorry," I said, feeling stupid that I had forgotten her name.

"Reminds me of her store... She made one in front of Darcy's wood shop... And she can do amazing things with flowers."

"I hope I get to see it one day."

"I hope so too," he said, looking off into the distance.

We continued strolling down the street.

"So, how does it work when you leave Foley's Rest? They don't have any police now," I asked.

"Technically, I'm still on call."

"If there's a holdup, it'll take you three hours to get there."

"Yeah, I know, but where's he going to go?" he asked.

"I guess. Since it takes three hours to get here, and this is the first land you could reach, no criminal would get very far. All things considered, you are doing well with this job. I mean, they don't even make you wear a uniform?"

"Either uniform or hide the sidearm."

"What? You don't carry a gun," I said, shocked at the idea.

"Always."

"No!"

"That's why I always wear loose shirts," he offered as he stopped walking. His hair gently moved in the breeze, and his hands were casually in his jacket pockets.

19

"Seriously?" I asked.

It just blew my mind. Tom's jacket was open, so I glanced toward his side, but that was where his coat ended, and through all the bulk, I couldn't see a thing. And I've never seen anything. I'd observed him closely on so many occasions, even inside, and never noticed a weapon.

He took my hand, slowly tucked it inside his jacket, and brought it to his hip, but sure enough, it landed on something hard. Although it wasn't cold, because it had taken on the warmth of his body. For some reason, this seemed personal, and his fingers were still on mine as my eyes gradually travelled up his chest towards his. They locked for a few seconds, and Tom lowered his head slightly, but then he released me and stepped back.

When I was able to breathe again, I thought that it all somehow suggested being so deliciously dangerous. Yet really nothing could be farther from reality.

He took my hand, and we continued walking around. Some of the streets reminded me of Europe as they were full of brick buildings. After a while, we went for coffee and then wondered a bit more.

Finally, Tom grabbed a sandwich, and we met up with the others.

I endured the trip home and recovered in bed.

ONE DAY, Tom's boat came in early, and he had Mac and Ralph inside. Mac was tending to Ralph, who was severely injured. When they both carried him on a stretcher, we knew that things were bad. They took him straight to Mac's place, but it was so disturbing to me that I had to leave.

Next, Tom got Tore and Gregg to head out with him to collect both Ralph and Mac's boats. Being only fourteen, Tore was thrilled that he would get to take a boat home all by himself. Of course, Gregg was the only man who wasn't out fishing during the day because he took all the catch afterwards.

Becky was in pieces.

Tom cleaned his boat, and I tried to help, but the sight of blood greatly troubled me.

It turned out that Ralph was injured by some of his equipment that malfunctioned.

When we heard the air ambulance coming, Becky ran frantically to us on the dock.

"Would you look after Ryan and Roxanne?" she asked, screaming over the chopper.

"Sure," Tom said, and she looked at me.

"I've been terrible, I know..." she started as she glanced at the ground.

"No problem," I said, and I stood with the kids in the pouring rain while we watched the helicopter load their parents in and lift off. The dock has the clearest view of that area but isn't covered.

I took them home to change into dry clothes, and then we headed to Tom's.

I felt that Tom was very noble to go through all that, considering how Becky treated us. So, despite my thoughts that they didn't deserve his help, I was proud of him.

Is looking after children going to be my lot in life? I sure hope Becky is not gone too long, although I did enjoy these kids.

"I suppose I should stay with Roxy and Ryan in their home," I said to Tom after we all ate supper.

"You mean you're not all ready to pack up and live somewhere new?"

"Not exactly."

"Well, why don't they just stay here with me?" he suggested, and they were more than agreeable.

Afterwards, Tom got everyone together to clean up Ralph's boat and repair things.

Late that night, the phone woke me up. I figured I was as good as any to answer it, and I was much closer than Mac or Jac.

"Addy," Tom said, "I can't seem to get... I'm having trouble cause... Addy... Roxy's crying."

"Well, maybe we should take them to their own home. I'll meet you all there," I said.

"Addy, I'm sorry."

"It's alright."

I got dressed in something comfortable, but not exactly pyjamas, and packed some clothes and things for tomorrow.

When I arrived there, it had to be the most pathetic but cute scene ever. Tom was on the couch, looking wholly bewildered and out of place. In spite of him having his arm around the kids, neither looked like they wanted to be there. Roxy's eyes were still teary and red, and Ryan didn't look much better.

I held back a smile.

"Hey, guys. What a rotten day." I said softly. "Come here." And I knelt and put my arms out.

They both ran to me, and I held them tight.

Then we all sprawled onto the couch. It seemed wrong to ask them to go to their beds, rather harsh under the circumstances, when both of their parents were suddenly gone.

When we were all settled, Tom leaned over, kissed me on my forehead, and let his lips trace the side of my face until he got to my ear.

"I love you," he whispered, put a blanket on us, turned out all the lights, and left.

Now I was looking after kids again, although I wasn't complaining because I finally had something to do.

"What's up with Urma?" I asked Tom one evening as he was helping me with the dishes while the two played.

"She doesn't have much self-esteem. Never trusts herself or others. She's a terrific person, but sometimes her past catches up with her. Suffered terrible abuses at a residential school. Give her some time. When somebody has been broken, it can be hard to understand their reactions. She'll come around. Just keep being yourself," he said.

It was only a week later when Becky and Ralph came back. He had an operation, and some bones needed to heal, but other than a few scars, it seemed he was going to recover fully.

Becky was now very friendly to me, as if nothing had ever happened, and that was a relief.

I finally found out the whole story about Victor and Star. They had some fake businesses and charities that they were running. They had scammed many of their money, and the list went on and on. Altogether, it was hard to believe.

Urma was coming around too. She was speaking to me now, as was Bill.

Without the kids, I was getting bored again. So, I tried to practice some new songs, have people for dinner, and smash some rocks, but none of that was really holding my attention.

THEN ONE day, I was looking at my nails and wishing there was a way to get them done, and I wondered what it would take to learn to do this. With that in mind, I did research and purchased a few things. After as much learning as possible, and receiving my supplies, I was able to practise. Gel nails turned out to be pretty easy to work with, and I had my first customers before long. It was simple enough that I could set everything out at Tom's but pack it all away before he even got home. And he was happy that I found one thing to do. Even though it wasn't going to make me lots of money, it made me feel like a part of the community.

Having nice nails was trending in Foley's Rest. I sometimes chuckled to myself at the typical ensemble of worn-out sweats and cardigans with nice manicures. I'm sure the popularity will go down with time, but it was fun for now.

It turned out good for me because it brought me closer to all the women. I just didn't care for the gossip that invariably came up. So, I tried to tame it down by offering possibilities for the other side, but that was the most tiring part of my new job.

ONE DAY in April, Tom and I were playing a checker-like game in Mac and Jac's kitchen while they watched a movie.

"So, summer is August, and that's it, right?" I asked.

"Pretty much."

"And if you propose to me then, we'll get married... next year?"

"I don't want to wait that long," he said as he suddenly looked at me with wide eyes. "I just want to make it to a sunny day."

My brain started turning quickly. "So, after we are engaged... how much later did you want the wedding?"

"As soon as I can and still be able to give you the wedding you deserve. You don't want anything big, do you?"

"No. What's neat, too, is that neither of us has parents to take into consideration, so we can do whatever we wish," I offered.

"I guess so."

COME MAY, I realized that the rain wasn't falling as heavily, and the temperature was warmer yet. But it happened so gradually that no one noticed. One corner of the boardwalk had a bit more space, so I placed a couple of fold-up chairs there, which Sylvia lent me. Now I could make hot chocolates after dinner and meet Tom there, and chat while looking at the rain, the rock, and the little water-logged field where the daisies once stood.

"What's bugging you?" I asked Tom because it felt like he'd been miserable for a long time. Everyone seemed to be. In the end, it was the right they'd earned for still living here.

"It's the worst part of the year. There's some trouble... Look, if nobody has anything to do, they are eventually all going to become criminals. This place will sit rotting and empty as every last one of us is incarcerated."

"Pleasant thought."

"It's not healthy. There is nowhere else in Canada where the fishing is this good, but there's a cost to everything. I tried really hard to make this all work, but maybe it's time to give up before it is too late," he stated bleakly.

"Just last month, you were still emotionally attached to this place, and you said this happens every year. But summer is coming soon," I offered.

"It wasn't fair to bring you here."

"Don't be so dramatic because that's my job," I said.

He smiled and casually leaned further back in his chair. "I've racked my brain for five years about how we might build things, or create activities… but I'm not good with ideas."

We watched the rain fall and a puffin fly past.

"Addy," Tom said, suddenly straightening up, "you are creative in ways I could never be. Would you try to think of something that we could do? Without a lot of cost, of course."

"Sure. I'll give it some thought. I didn't want to come here and abound with opinions for change because it would've left the impression that I'm not content."

"I guess, but now I am begging you for ideas. We need something fresh."

"No problem. I'll come up with some options and let you know… Friday," I said confidently.

"Friday it is. And if you don't end up with anything, you wouldn't have failed me because no one has ever offered good suggestions."

A challenge was good and needed. So, I thought and thought and researched and researched some more. Thankfully, ideas were coming to me, though some were better than others. Sometimes I'd be lying in bed at night, and all of a sudden, I would get another notion. Therefore, I started writing out all of my suggestions, including the crazy ones, because sometimes even a ridiculous suggestion can be fuel for someone else to spring a valuable idea from.

"I can't wait to hear what you have for me tomorrow," Tom said after our greeting on Thursday. "I can sense your excitement, and that alone makes me feel much better."

"Yes. Hopefully, some of them are doable."

"I really appreciate this."

My creative schemes excited me, and I poured my heart into it. The more attention I gave them, the greater it all sounded. It wasn't a tourist attraction we wanted to create, just places to go and options to do, some ways to get exercise and events to look forward to. All things considered, we needed to be able to use the whole island and not have to travel by boat for three hours before you could see or do anything.

I was too excited to even enjoy supper.

"You better just leave," Mac said with a chuckle. "And take everyone's good wishes with you."

Tom wasn't there yet, so I rehearsed my proposals in my mind. I looked out onto the little grassy area. Yes, it would be perfect.

"Well, my love... tell me what you got," Tom said as he arrived and plopped himself on his chair. "You have a business proposal," he said, perfectly amused as he noticed my folder.

"Of course. There is nothing more serious than recreation," I joked.

"Shoot. I'm all ears."

"First and foremost, we need a hot tub. It doesn't have to cost much or be big." I handed him a paper with the intended product on it. "This one can easily be plugged into our electrical system here. All it would require is a simple little shelter over it to protect it from the pelting rain. One with a clear plastic roof to still let in all the light. But it is to be located right in the field there, and we'll have a sign-up sheet where everyone can book up to a 90-minute time slot. This is perfect for year-round and all ages."

Tom looked at me, a little bewildered, and glanced at the suggested location.

"That's not expensive... and would be simple to transport and install," Tom said as he thought aloud.

"Oh yes, the regular kind are terrible beasts, but this comes in a very manageable box. I'm sure it wouldn't last forever, as blow-up items tend not to, but just to start. Even if we bought a new one every year, that's nothing per person per month.

"It is hard to plan much for the worst of winter, but we could also have events. Competitions. Like for pie or jam, or cake, or cinnamon buns. Those participating only have to put a sign on their door, and then everyone comes around to try them all and vote for the best. The winner gets a prize. If we had one in December, January, and February every year... I think that would be about right."

"Okay." Tom was already dreaming about the food.

"Then we need to make the other side of the island accessible. I figured a subway would be a little hard, and so would a tunnel or a gondola, but what about a serious staircase? I mean, it's not that high. We just need a safe way, and the exercise would be perfect for most everyone."

"Possible," he said after a long pause.

"There, I'd propose a tiny kids' park: a slide and swing. It would also be a great spot for a badminton net in August. Also, we would have a place for picnics. Since it's pretty flat there, I think it could be useful for all sorts of things if it was just accessible. So, we need a dock there as well."

"It would be nice to make use of it," Tom admitted.

"Then, this is way out there, but because of how the rock is down on this side, but up behind, and the opposite over there, we might be able to put in a couple of ziplines. They would be a thrilling method of travel to the other end and back. It's a little more expensive to get the hardware, but if there is a lot of interest, it would be worth looking into."

"That would be... different," Tom said with a smirk.

"Lastly, we need a farmer's market. Simply a shelf or small table in front of everyone's window would be enough to create a mini version of one that we could run once or twice a month, perhaps, for whoever makes anything."

"You're hired," he said. "These are good ideas. They aren't expensive in themselves, but do you have any idea how to finance them?"

"Well, if we change the structure to a condo board, we could have regular meetings and set up a monthly amount for everyone to pay as we slowly take care of the ideas that get passed. Rather like having amenities at your residence."

"That's brilliant," Tom said after a long pause. "We should have a meeting with all the people here."

"If we shoved your couches in your bedroom for one evening, I'm sure we would get enough chairs in there. And I could make donuts," I said.

"Donuts? You have been holding out on me."

"I haven't made any yet, but I'll find a way."

266

"I'm sure you will. Everyone would certainly come if you mention there'll be donuts," he said.

So, Tom did legal research, and I learned to make donuts, and we invited everyone to our first meeting.

And it went really well. Except for two couples, the others were very excited to start pooling some money and creating some things to do. There didn't seem to be enough takers for the ziplines, but I think all the other options were going to fly.

We appointed a president, treasurer, and secretary, but I would be the amenities and events coordinator.

I was glad to have something to do, but everyone else was excited too. Many of the others seemed to have ideas now as well. Most of them would complicate things too much, but at least they were all brainstorming options. In fact, one suggestion for a pitch and putt or mini golf just might work. Furthermore, Ralph was happy to use his engineering skills again and made plans long before any financial compensation was figured out.

"You know you have single-handedly turned this town around and everybody is looking forward with renewed excitement," Tom said one Saturday afternoon.

"Oh, it's all a group effort."

"Well, everyone wants to help out now, but it was entirely your doing. We all know that. You are incredible, Addy, and you still never fail to amaze me. I'm so honoured that you came here to be with me."

A LITTLE later in the month, Tom and I received an invitation from Becky for a formal dinner that night. I decided to wear one of my evening dresses, and I spent the whole day getting done up for the occasion. It was kind of fun when I had no opportunity to do that for so long. Additionally, I redid my nails and put my hair up.

As soon as Tom got back, I told him.

"You look pretty," he said as he looked straight into my eyes with his head only inches away. "What are you wearing?" he asked, trying to peek into my cape, but I wouldn't let him.

"You'll see."

"I don't own anything fancy," he said.

"Well, do your best, and I'll wait for you to pick me up."

"Pick you up?"

"Yes. This is a formal date. We should arrive together." Well, I thought so anyway.

So, after Tom ducked inside his place, I ran back to Jackie's and waited. She didn't even want to start eating their supper until we left and almost seemed more excited than I was. Ok, maybe not. But she was talking nonstop and was determined to take a picture of us when Tom came.

It took him a little longer than usual.

When he arrived, he did appear more dressy, with a plain blue shirt and light pants. He had a box of chocolates for me.

"I can't really get you flowers," he mumbled by way of apology, but before I replied he said, "You are so gorgeous." And he grabbed both of my hands in his.

Jackie snapped pictures of us. Then I put on my cape, and we walked to Becky's.

The rain was softer now. It happened so gradually that I didn't notice. The temperature had warmed a bit too.

When we got there, Ryan was all dressed up and asked to take our coats. It was so cute because my cape dragged on the floor when he tried to carry it.

Roxy wore a dress, and she escorted us to our table. They had placed a small table and two chairs in the living room window. It had a white tablecloth, two place settings, as well as two tall candles.

As we sat down, Roxy gave us menus that they made.

It was all so sweet. Here they had set everything up just like a little restaurant, and it felt so special.

The food was terrific. They even had an amazing presentation for each course, so I took pictures of each plate. It was the only thing my cell phone was good for out here.

I heard the waves in the background and smelled the ocean. This was my home.

Although the most exciting part was the attention Tom gave me. He was particularly quiet, but his eyes never left me.

I did all the talking, and he listened, sometimes. Other times when I asked him a question, there was simply silence, and I had to repeat myself. He would apologize, but I wasn't upset because it was only me he was distracted with.

After dessert came to its leisurely finish, they put on some slow music for us to dance to. Having previously cleared out the large furniture, there was some floor space now.

Tom took me in his arms, but he barely swayed even. Instead, he kissed each of my fingers in the hand he held and then very delicately placed the tip of one of them in his mouth.

20

The warm, tingly feeling that surged over my entire body came unexpectedly to me. But my breathing became faster, and all words drifted out of my mind.

Tom whispered, "I love you," into my ear and then nibbled on it. Then, he kissed my neck and everything else that wasn't covered except for my lips.

I melted into his arms. In fact, it was more than that, even.

Thank goodness the others would check on us every once in a while, because it was my only link to reality.

"You like my hair up," I whispered to him.

"Actually, I love it down," he said. "But today, this is nice."

We sipped on a liqueur, but I can't remember much more because I was so totally into him that I noticed nothing else.

I don't even think I did a great job thanking them all for preparing such a treat for us.

We quietly walked to Mac and Jac's.

Just as I was about to turn around to face him, I felt the weight of his body pressing on my back, and I was lightly tossed against a support pillar. When my forehead gently touched the wood, he pulled my hood off, gripped my shoulders, and kissed my neck.

"Addy, I love you so much," he groaned.

"What are you going to do about it?" I whispered.

"I'm going to marry you, silly," he said under his breath, "and take you as my wife."

"When?"

"Soon, but not soon enough."

I closed my eyes, becoming absorbed in his embrace. Furthermore, the back of my neck turned out to be more sensitive to the touch.

"It's just a couple more weeks or so," he mumbled, "till we'll see the sun for the first time this year."

As his lips caressed there, I ended up groaning his name.

"Tell me you love me," he muttered.

"I do."

"Then tell me."

"Tom, I love you way more than I could ever tell you."

He held me very tight against him and was silent for a bit. Then he said goodnight and abruptly left.

ABOUT A week later, one night, I heard a loud groan, a bang, and a snap. Soon after, someone screamed.

Mac and Jac bolted out of their bedroom.

"Get dressed!" Mac yelled at me. "We have to hold the boats."

"Dress real warm!" Jac added.

They ran out before I could figure out what was happening. I don't even have a boat.

When I finally got outside, every man was holding the rope to his vessel, along with his wife. It was obvious that it was challenging work by the looks on their faces and the straining of their arms. Because the ocean was trying to take their boats away from them, but they were not going to let it.

Since the boardwalk was ripped apart in one section, a few of the poles the boats were tied to had been torn off. That led some men to be battling the extremely violent sea in small dinghies to try to get the rest of the dock and their vessels back.

At the same time, the wind was so strong that I wasn't able to breathe unless I faced the opposite way. It was ramming rain in my face with the force of a sandblaster.

Tom called my name, so I approached him. Without delay, he had me hold on to the rope as well, and even with Tom's strength, the power of the ocean was still evident.

"This can't possibly be helping you any," I yelled against the howling wind.

"Anything helps," was his reply.

"What did you do before I came?" I asked.

"All the other women are here," he said after a pause.

"What?"

"Of course, I used to do it on my own. Don't you want to help me?" he asked.

Why could he always read my mind? I wasn't enthused about being out here. Who would be? And I figured that if he was so strong and had managed without me before, I didn't need to be here.

But that was rather selfish of me. Why wouldn't I choose to support him? Even if I didn't have much to offer physically, imagine how he would feel if I was the only woman that stayed in while they all slaved away out here?

"Yes, I want to help you," I said.

Slowly the wind eased up, and the couples sort of snuggled together. They were still both holding on to the rope, but the wife was in front and in her husband's arms. They talked softly to each other, and from time to time, you would hear a giggle. Once everyone was like that, Tom pulled me closer to him as well.

"How come you never come to me?" he asked.

The truth was that it never occurred to me to ever make the first move in an affectionate way. So, I recognized immediately the accuracy of that.

"I'm sorry. You are right. Somehow, I figured that it is always the guy's job."

"I can tell," he said.

"Is it that obvious?"

"Probably to no one but me."

"I'll try to keep it in mind. It's not that I wouldn't like to have my hands all over you," I said.

He laughed, and I snuggled against him.

"After we're married, I'm counting on it," he whispered.

"For now, though, what would you like?" I asked. "What would be meaningful? For me, I love every caress of yours. They are all new and exciting, warm and inviting. But I somehow felt that guys were not as sensitive to touch."

"Well, I don't know about that. Maybe tiny, almost accidental touches wouldn't mean too much, but a big hug would be nice. One that came from you with all your heart."

"That sounds good, but we don't seem to have many appropriate opportunities."

"Are you afraid someone will see you?" he teased me.

"No. After the boats come in…"

"*I'm* the one that gives that hug," he said.

"How do you know that I'm not the one giving it?"

"Cause I know. You'll just have to hug me and then feel the difference."

"I will."

"I love that you are here," he said.

"Here in Foley's Rest, holding the boats, or in your arms?"

"All three."

"Well, I love that I'm here too. You've touched my life in a way that no one could have. You have enriched it like I never thought possible. Your love is the truest thing I know, and I deeply respect and trust you."

"Would you be content to live here and be married to a fisherman?"

"No," I said.

"No?"

"When a person gets everything they want, it goes beyond contentment. Being content sounds like merely being satisfied, but I would be much more than that."

We continued to talk until the sea calmed down more, and everyone tied their boats up to whatever they were able to. Then, arm in arm, husbands and wives walked back to their home.

Tom was kneeling down and tying up his boat.

"I think you should run along now," he said.

"Pardon?"

"I don't think I can handle goodnights tonight. I'm way too into you."

"What about that hug was going to give you?" I asked.

"Could you save it for me?"

"I will," I said, stepping back with a grin and blowing him a kiss.

"Go on," he said, smiling.

THE NEXT day, no one went fishing, but we were all tired. Mac, Jac, and I were all hanging out at Tom's, looking at hot tubs online, when we suddenly had to stop. Because we heard the most blood-chilling screams. They were not that loud, but the sound was unmistakable.

Tom was outside faster than any of us could say anything. Hence, we grabbed our jackets and headed out to watch from a very safe distance.

It was evident that he knew where it was coming from, and he was soon banging on the door. The neighbours stepped out with fear all over their faces, and they were excitedly telling him something, but Tom instructed them to go inside. Then he shot at the lock, forced it open and hurried in. The pounding continued over the whimpering.

Tom yelled at the guy to lie down on the ground with his hands behind his head. He hollered again and again before I heard the gun.

Now a man started yelling, but the worst sounds had stopped.

"Mac! Addy!" Tom loudly repeated our names as we both ran over.

And I don't know what I expected, but not the macabre sight in front of me.

"Mac, do what you can and call the air ambulance," Tom said, and Mac immediately ran out.

"Addy, I need you to grab the handcuffs. You've seen where I keep everything."

In a state of shock, I rushed out too. Never imagining domestic violence to be this ugly, I grabbed the cuffs and raced back. The image of Tom with his foot on the guy's back and the gun pointed toward him was one that I knew would never leave me. However, it was the sight of Lucy that would haunt me for the rest of my life. The man's leg bled, but that was nothing compared to the shape she was in.

Mac was there already when I returned. To begin with, he was talking on a cordless phone and pulling out supplies to help get the bleeding under control.

"Do you need anything else?" I bravely asked after Tom slapped the cuffs on him.

"No. You'd better leave," he said.

Although I was grateful for that, I did nothing at Jackie's but sit and stare out the window.

It seemed like forever before the first chopper came, and it was the air ambulance, thank goodness. When two paramedics rushed out, Tore directed them to the home, and they headed in. Soon after, they carried Lucy out on a stretcher.

I didn't know her well, but she always looked nervous to me. Now I understand why.

Tom and Mac never came out until the next chopper arrived, and a couple of RCMP officers came out. Without any delay, they led their man into custody, who now limped with a bandaged leg, to their helicopter. I didn't remember the guy's name, and he obviously wasn't worth it, but he was not making it easy for them.

Tom stood outside against the railing and watched them get the guy inside the helicopter and lift. He was a real mess, but Mac even more so, as he quietly slipped into his place. However, Tom was still standing and staring at where the chopper used to be.

I somehow sensed it was inappropriate to be at Mac and Jac's right now. Because I think they desired some space. Additionally, Tom needed a hand, and I sure could use something to do, so I headed towards him.

"Tom, let's get you showered and changed," I said, giving him a little pull in the direction of his place. And he followed me in body, but not in mind.

"Come," I said once we were inside, and Tom just stood there. "Grab some clean clothes."

I entered his bedroom and grabbed him a shirt, T-shirt and some pants, and he grabbed some underwear. Afterwards, he followed me blindly into the bathroom, where I put his clothes down and left.

To begin, I tried to find some things in the kitchen to make soup with as none of us had eaten supper, and it was quite late.

There was a knock at the door, and it was Gregg.

"How's Tom? Is he alright?" The older man asked. It was sincere and backed with understanding.

"I don't know. Please come in."

It was good to have someone else here, especially a guy who may understand better what Tom needed at this time.

"That was a lot for Tom. He's not in this job for the action. He only wants to make everything right," Gregg said.

"Yes. How can I help him? What can I do?" I asked.

"Just be there for him when he is ready. That's all.

"You must be pretty shaken up too," he added.

"Yes."

I soon had soup simmering, but was unsure what to say now. Thankfully, Gregg didn't look like he needed entertaining. Instead, he grabbed a can of pop from Tom's fridge and sat on the couch.

"Hi," Tom said to Gregg as he came out.

"Hi," Gregg said.

"Thanks," Tom said to me as he saw the pot on the stove.

He leaned on the counter but appeared completely shaken.

"I'm sorry you had to see that," he said to me. "I probably should've called someone else. It's just that… I knew… you would know… where they were." And Tom broke down sobbing.

I threw my arms around him, and he held me tightly through it all.

After he calmed down and stepped back, I poured the soup into mugs for us so we could sit on the couch. None of us were conversationalists, but Tom kept me super close and seemed to need that. Afterwards, we all started nodding off.

"I think I'd better leave. We all need to sleep," I said as I got up and kissed Tom on the forehead.

"You're the greatest, Addy. Don't know what I would do without you," he said.

"She's a keeper," Gregg said. "Someone strong enough for you."

I headed back to Mac and Jac's. They had already gone to bed, and out of sheer exhaustion, I was soon to follow.

The next day, the four of us were still pretty shaken up. Tom felt awful that he didn't arrive at their house earlier, yet he wished he had his handcuffs with him. Mac wondered if things would've been better if he'd bandaged the bleeding before calling the paramedics.

The truth was that everyone did their best, and it seemed to be my job, as well as Jackie's, to tell that to them. Even over and over when needed.

GRADUALLY, WE all got back to normal, but I couldn't say the same about the weather. Quite a few storms followed after that, and one of them took out all of our electricity. So, I learned how to cook over the fireplace. Now I understood why the bedrooms also had fireplaces. It was five whole days before we had power again, but I rather enjoyed it. Anything new was welcome. Before, I had assumed that the worst storms were in winter, but I guess they were in the spring, just before the rain stops.

I often hugged Tom now, and he was right. It did feel different when I gave it.

Then the days seemed to pass quicker, as there was always something to do. It would take a while for our condo board to be registered, but no one wanted to wait, so we moved ahead with the stairs, dock, and hot tub anyway. However, the paperwork would be a nightmare after, so thank goodness I wasn't the treasurer.

Rumer had it that Lucy was doing alright, but neither of them would be returning.

"I JUST received the news," Tom solemnly said one evening in June, "that Darcy's wife is in a coma. Do you remember I was telling you about him?"

"Your best friend in Haida Gwaii?"

"Yes."

"What happened?" I asked.

"I guess they were taking the ferry back from the mainland, and when Snow got out of the truck... she got hit with another. She fell to the ground, and the wheel came in contact with her head. Didn't actually do much obvious damage, but knocked her unconscious, and she's been in a coma since yesterday."

"Oh, no! That's awful."

"Yeah. Darcy doesn't know what's going to happen."

"Is she in the hospital in Terrace?"

277

"No. I guess they moved her to Prince Rupert. More equipment there. At least Snow's sister is nearby, and Darcy and his daughter are staying there for now," he said.

I could tell that it bothered Tom a lot. He kept in contact with Darcy, but over the next couple of days, there wasn't any change. During that time, he had a far off look in his eyes and found it difficult to get into anything. That is when I truly realized how close a friend Darcy was to him.

By the third day, we received the wonderful news that Darcy's wife, Snow, came out of her coma. And she was in good health too. There was only one problem. She lost the memory of the last seven years of her life. Though this improved Tom's mood immensely, he was still full of concern for them.

THEN ONE day, not long after, Tom came over asking if we could talk. We stood outside his place, and notably, it was getting warmer. Chunks of ice in various sizes were floating by, which was a sign of spring for the locals.

"Have you thought about where you would like to go for our honeymoon?" he asked.

"Well, no. I figured it would be a bit premature because you never asked me to marry you."

"Do you doubt I will ask you?" he asked with a grin.

"I like to handle things as they happen," I said.

"But I like to plan ahead. I'm going to put a ring on your finger. We will get married. We'll have a honeymoon. I just want to know where you'd like to go."

"I'm not exactly sure. There certainly isn't much privacy here. St. John's is an option, I guess. The only place I've wanted to see lately is Haida Gwaii, but that is on the other end of the country. Where would we even get married?"

"That would be my other question," he said.

"Your family is out west. They wouldn't all be able to come out here. Although I would marry you in St. John's if that were our only option."

"It's not," he said.

"You would like it if Darcy was there and Margaret. So, what if we had our wedding in Terrace or somewhere out there?"

"Sure."

"Then go to the islands after, or is that not a good idea? I wouldn't know because I've never been."

"I can't think of anything better. It's really interesting that you said that because... Listen, I have something to ask you. This is going to sound weird. In fact, I probably shouldn't even be asking. I'm expecting you to tell me to forget it, so I won't be offended if you do.

"Darcy lives in Masset, which is in the north of Haida Gwaii. He's got the most wonderful property overlooking the ocean. It has a great beach, lots of treed land, so it's very private, and even a little cabin. And he would be thrilled if we would stay there, and they would for sure respect our privacy and give us as much space as we wanted," he said.

"Oh?"

"I know the timing couldn't be worse for you and I, but I would love to see him. I'd like to be there for him because Darcy was always there for me when my parents died and everything."

"How're things going over there?" I asked.

"Truthfully... shockingly good for what they have been through. They are all home, and Snow has taken well to their daughter. It's just that today was a bad day for Darcy. I could sense the heartbreak in his voice, and though he is the most patient guy, he is a little worn out. Nevertheless, they are doing very well. But it sounds to me like they both need someone to talk to and perhaps something else to focus on besides each other."

"What did you have in mind, exactly?" I asked.

"I was wondering if we could get married at their place and then stay in their cabin for our honeymoon. If you don't like it, there are many other options on the island."

"But you would want to spend some time with them."

"Yes, but perhaps a bit before the wedding. I don't know. Maybe we could be alone for a week after and then have a few days with them. For one thing, I'm sure not going to compromise my time with you."

"You said Snow did flowers for weddings?" I asked.

"Yes. She's amazing. I was Darcy's best man when they got married, and I would like to ask him to be mine.

"Just think about it and if you don't feel it's a good idea, just let me know."

I thought about it. After a few hours, I decided to go for it. I did want to see Haida Gwaii. A cabin not far from a sandy beach sounded perfect. We could stay elsewhere if it seemed too close. I would feel bad for Tom if he wouldn't be able to see his friend. My heart went out to Snow as well. It must be the most terrible thing to wake up and not remember anything about your life and who you are supposed to be. She could use a new friend, one that didn't know her from before. I wondered if she would be up to helping me plan my wedding.

Tom was delighted that I was good with the idea.

"Do you think I could ask Snow if she is good enough to help me with our wedding? It's likely too much for her right now, though," I asked.

"I can think of no one better, but I'll ask Darcy's opinion."

"But Tom, by the time we get there, either everything will be fine, or it will be too late."

"Perhaps we can't wait too long."

THE NEXT day was Monday, and suddenly, after dinner, the sun peaked out. It shone through a little break in the clouds in the west but still above the island. Everyone ran outside to catch the rays, and I didn't even stop to grab a sweater.

"Addy, come here." It was Tom, of course.

He had on his red buffalo plaid jacket, and the sun shone directly on him.

I followed him to our corner on the boardwalk.

"This is the first sign that summer will come," he said.

I shivered. I would've grabbed something if I'd realized I was going to be outside for more than a minute.

Tom took his jacket off and put it over my shoulders. I held it, and he held me.

The sun disappeared as quickly as it came, and everyone stepped back inside.

"Addy, there's something for you in my left pocket there."

When I reached in, my fingers touched the ring.

It was beautiful, striking, in fact. It was like a gold cord holding the diamond.

"I had it especially made."

"It is absolutely incredible. It's so perfect. I never imagined a ring to be this stunning," I said.

He took my hand, took the ring, and slid it on my finger.

"Now, I finally get to kiss you," he said.

"Wait, aren't you going to ask me?"

"It's too late. You are already wearing the ring," he said, smiling. "Besides, you should know by now that I never ask when I really want something."

Then he kissed me. He kissed like he did everything else: abruptly, a little clumsy and with a whole lot of determination. But however you would describe it, it sure worked for me.

"I'm going to get us out there as soon as possible," he said. "I'll give you Snow's phone number, and you can plan things with her. Darcy thought it would be the most perfect thing if we got married there, and he said it would be great if you asked her."

"That's wonderful, but… they will be putting up the stairs soon, and the first farmer's market is coming up, and the hot tub arrives in a week," I said, though it sounded funny. Do I not want to leave?

A grin slowly appeared on Tom's face. "That is a shame. It would be nice to be back for August."

"I guess that's true. Everything should be in good hands," I said.

"It's unbelievable how things have changed over the last year, but I'm so happy that I have you," Tom said. "I was always very content until I met you. Then I needed you more than anything, and my world couldn't be complete without you. How did you ever come into my life? What brought you to me?"

"It was the strong and steady waves," I said.

Excerpt from After I Woke

Read Snow's story in

After I Woke

Ebonene Charles

Day 1

I can hear voices in the background–softly talking, occasionally laughing, but usually in solemn tones. But it's too hushed to make out much of what they are saying and seems like they are in the next room or something. Also, there is some faint beeping in the distance.

I want to open my eyes but can't. Where am I? I try to remember the last thing I did, but I'm weirdly unable. To prevent panic from setting in, I calmly go over the details of my existence in my mind.

My name is Snow Blain and I live in Vancouver, Canada. I started an interior decorating store three years ago, and it is now doing well enough for me to start building my life. Recently, I purchased my first home, which was a milestone for me. It's just a little apartment, nothing that exciting, I guess, but I'm doing it all myself, and I'm only twenty-three.

My best friends are my sisters. Although I know this is odd, my name is Snow, and I have a sister named Hale and another named Rain. In brief, my parents are hippies.

I wonder what they are doing right now. My mom is probably going all over Nelson asking her neighbours if she can uproot their dandelions for them to use the roots for making her tea. Because it works perfectly as a coffee substitute. Dad is possibly crocheting those hacky-sack covers for covering bean bag balls so teens can gather outside and hit it around with the sides of their feet. So, he could be crocheting away in their little store while the customers come and go.

I had to smile. Yes, these are my parents. And if you know Nelson, B.C., you'll understand how they fit right in.

Hale has been trying to start a spa and massage business for the last three years, but it hasn't worked out yet. Personally, I think she spends money faster than she can make it and gets herself stuck. In my experience, business took patience and sacrifice, but she has neither. Whenever something doesn't work in one week, she will scrap the whole thing and try it somewhere new. In spite of not wanting her financial troubles, I'll admit I'm slightly envious of her hot car and perfect nails.

She sure can cook, though. I mean seriously. I am talking about freshly made lavender peach jam with orange blossom honey on white chocolate and Earl Grey-infused scones. And that's only breakfast.

Me, I like to decorate, and my condo is starting to look pretty good, but I have plenty more plans for it.

I like making things, which I must get from my mother. She was always creating hemp jewellery and recycling anything she could find to use in some new project. However, I would describe my crafts as more refined, or at least a distinctly modern style. Therefore, they are more formal and elegant, completely lacking in tie-dye and patchouli, but I do like using natural materials. Lately, all of my creative efforts have been for interior decorating, but now that my business is running, hopefully, everything will start to slow down.

Rain, the youngest of us, has a slightly different approach to life. For instance, ever since she was young, she planned to go to university to become a scientist. It wasn't that she craved the knowledge, but more that she wanted to help our earth. She is very smart. Even though Hale and I don't really understand it, you have to respect her for it.

Rain is the easiest to be with, so it was a natural fit to have her stay with me while attending school. She pays me a bit each month, which helps my mortgage for now, and gets her a better deal for rent than she would be able to find anywhere else. So far, everything is going great. Besides, it's a pleasure to live with someone who isn't a complainer but happy-spirited, and who is always thinking of others.

The only problem is that neither of us can cook.

Hale's cooking is to die for, but it's not so easy to live with her. Unfortunately, she has a new idea every minute and can't sit still for a second. Being a passionate person, she is very into the sensual side of things. Therefore, everything to her is about how it feels, smells, tastes, looks, and sounds.

It is all good, though. Because we all get along and seem to know the proper distance to keep so we don't annoy each other but have a great time whenever we hang out together.

I heard something stir beside me. I had no idea there was someone so close by.

"Snow?" It was a man's voice, but not my father's.

There were no other men in my life, as I didn't seem to have any success in love yet. Then again, I always figured I would know what I wanted when I found it, but lately, I have been wondering. If I still haven't met anyone that interests me, does that mean my system isn't reliable?

Whose voice is this?

It seems warm, and there is no breeze, so I must be inside. I guess I passed out. Strange–I've never passed out before. What could've caused that? And why can't I remember what I was doing last? Hopefully, that is common. Also, I must not be lying on the floor somewhere because this is more comfortable than that.

Opening my eyelids just wasn't going to happen yet.

"Snow. Can you hear me?" It was the same voice, and he somehow sounded anxious, hopeful, and nervous. Who was this beside me? For one thing, he knows my name, so why can't I recognize who this is?

Where could I be? But I made a conscious effort not to panic through it all. Soon I will be able to move and open my eyes, and then everything will make sense.

After a few minutes, I was able to shift my hand a bit. This is progress. Everything will be better shortly, I tried to reassure myself.

"Snow," the man whispered and touched my arm, gently rubbing it. Ok. Who on earth was this? Although I wanted more than anything to get away from being subjected to this unauthorized touching, I was still unable.

Then, I heard a speaker system saying, "Paging Doctor Hapokny. Paging Doctor Hapokny." I was in a hospital.

Why was I in a hospital? What happened? I tried to concentrate on each part of my body, but I couldn't find anything that hurt, really. My skin was irritated, and my head felt kind of strange. Additionally, it seemed that my muscles were all stiff. Why would that be? What could a person ever do to end up with every tendon and ligament uncooperative?

"Snowflake, please wake up." Again, it was the same warm voice.

Only my family called me Snowflake. Talk about being over-familiar and touching my arm too—the nerve of this man! To be sure, I'll give him a piece of my mind when I come to. I suppose he must be my doctor, but they don't usually have the time to sit by their patients and wait for them to... what? What did I have to do? Wake up? I felt awake, but I just couldn't move. He's probably waiting for me to open my eyes and speak to him. And then he'd better leave. Could he be the nurse? In each movie I've seen, it's only a close family member that stays by someone's hospital bedside.

Possibly I'll find him a pleasant man and attractive. Still, there is no way that he should be touching my arm like this. And doesn't he have anything better to do than watch me?

I heard footsteps come in. "She is stirring a bit," reported the guy next to me.

"That's an excellent sign. I'll make a note of that," a woman said.

She must be a nurse. Then this man couldn't be a doctor. Perhaps he is the nurse, and she is the doctor. No, this guy beside me wasn't a professional. Somehow, I knew that much. Unless he was the one who found me…

I tried very hard to remember the last memory I had, the last thing I did, but I still couldn't think of anything. In fact, this was beginning to worry me. There is something missing from my mind. I can sense that something is gone, and it wasn't just that I didn't know why or how I was here. But there was something else gone. It was as though I lost a few days' worth of memories. I really don't like not knowing how I got here. It's a rotten way to drift back to consciousness.

"We want you to come home with us. Please wake up."

Ok. This is beginning to freak me out. Why can't I recognize the voice? Who is "we," who is this man, and why did he say, "come home with us"? What would possess someone to say such a thing?

His voice was kind, thick, and emotional. Not professional at all.

Where is my family if I'm in a hospital? Whatever happened must have just occurred, because no one is here yet. Rain should be around, but perhaps her class is not finished. My parents are a day's drive away, but they would head over immediately if this were serious. I suppose they will notify everyone once I can communicate my awareness. It could be that they are all waiting for that, especially if it's been a while. But if I was unconscious for a few hours, someone would be here by now. Since Rain is the only one in Vancouver with me, why isn't she here? Maybe she is, but hasn't said anything? That didn't seem likely. Everything would be better if I could hear her voice, but she wasn't here.

Relax, I told myself over and over and over again. This is all going to make sense when you can open your eyes. I'm just forgetting something.

When they finally opened, only inches away from my face, was a First Nations man looking right at me.

"Snowflake," he whispered in almost a state of shock and swallowed. "How are you?"

This is a hospital, and this strange guy is too close. I wanted to scream.

"I feel fine," I said, though my voice sounded slightly raspy.

Then very suddenly, without any warning, his body came flying on top of me with this hug that went through the flimsy blanket and stunned me. I couldn't move.

Where is everyone? Why are they letting this happen to me?

This man wasn't very tall and wasn't very big. Additionally, he wasn't muscular, fat, or skinny. He seemed an ordinary build, but his grip was solid. Also, his hair was trimmed neatly, and he looked clean-cut but blue-collar.

"Oh, Snow. I missed you so much," he said as he held me tight. And I could feel each word from his breath on my neck.

This was quite the embrace, but what was most terrifying was how genuine he sounded. On the other hand, if he had this evil laugh, it would almost work. But I could tell his hug was a natural reaction, even though it was the farthest thing from natural to me. Although shocked, I couldn't scream or push him away because of the sincerity carried in his voice.

"Who are you?" I finally asked, knowing that this was dropping the bomb.

Then he abruptly pulled back to look at me. His eyes opened wide, and his face drained of colour with his fear unmasked.

I was supposed to know him.

No. This is stupid. He just has me confused with someone else. That's all.

"I'm your husband... Darcy." His voice shook.

A wave of panic set in now, and my breathing increased. No. There is some mistake. This is getting crazy. Sure, I forgot how or why I am here. I might have forgotten someone I met last week, but I would never forget that I got married.

"There has to be a mistake," I whispered.

"No," he said a little loudly.

"You have me confused with someone else who is your wife."

"No. I do not," he said firmly.

"How long have I been here?" I asked, although, with him confusing me with his wife, I couldn't rely on the answer. Maybe the poor guy was here all this time and didn't know. Perhaps my identification was mixed up, and he was told in error...

"Three days, and one day in the Terrace hospital before."

"Why?"

"You were in an accident and ended up in a coma for four days," he said.

"That can't be. Wouldn't I be in pain if it had been that serious?"

"It was just your head, mostly. It's good it doesn't really hurt, and the bump must've gone down over the last four days."

"What kind of accident?" I asked.

"It happened on the ferry."

If I were visiting my parents in Nelson, I would have to take a ferry. I thought about the ferries in the Kootenays back home, and reminiscing brought me some calm. They kept the pace slow. While you couldn't rush anywhere because there was always a ferry to wait for, it contributed to the peaceful and unhurried attitude of the people living in the region. The crossing was consistently beautiful, with the stunning lake stretching around you and mountains framing the picture.

The big ferries went to the island, so perhaps it was on one of them. I'd taken it a few times to Victoria from the mainland. Because they were so much bigger, with more cars, that would be a more likely setting for an accident. Those large ships had a very different feel, like you were heading out on an adventure. Accordingly, an excitement would always accompany the majesty of circumnavigating through the gulf islands.

"You had just got out of the vehicle..." he continued, "... and were walking between the cars when a truck..." And he had to stop for a second to regain his composure. "You slipped, falling to the ground right in front of a big truck, and it slid into your head."

"Wouldn't I be dead?"

"Well, it didn't ride right over you, but it pulled some of your hair out, and the fall caused you to land in a coma."

A nurse came in, took one look at me and bolted out.

"And what, you married me while I was in a coma?" He stared at me, speechless. "Which ferry?" I asked.

"To Haida Gwaii."

"What? Where?"

"The Queen Charlotte Island ferry," he said.

Why on earth would I be there? That is no-man's-land. Nothing but wilderness can be found there. It is something like an eight-hour ferry ride from the mainland, and mainland is an overstatement. If it weren't for the cruise ships passing by on their way to Alaska, no one would ever come in contact with Prince Rupert. Besides the small towns and native reserves, it's only a spot for adventure enthusiasts and backpackers. But a normal person would ever head west to the coast from the interior of B.C. I'm sure it does have more of British Columbia's rugged beauty, but there isn't a good reason to live there. And from there it only gets worse because you need to take this all-day or all-night ferry from nowhere to get to... What did he call it? Haida Gwaii. Is that the Native name? I know it as the Queen Charlotte Islands.

Rain would love to visit there. She loves trees, moss, and rock. I, though, am quite liking living in a larger city.

It is supposed to be beautiful there, but when you live in Vancouver, that is one place you never need to go. Because there is plenty of wilderness right around with no end to all of these gorgeous walks you can take in the deep, moss-covered forests. And the ocean! With any kind of beach or water experience you dream of. The best part is, after no more than a twenty-minute drive back, you are again surrounded by all the modern conveniences of a big city.

I was uncomfortable, so I tried to shift, but it was too painful to move.

"What was I doing there?" I asked.

"We were going home."

"You are trying to tell me you were with me on the ferry?"

"Yes."

"Why would I be going to the Queen Charlotte Islands?"

"We were going home. That's where we live," he said.

"I live in Vancouver."

At that moment, the thick silence seemed to cover me like a blanket. It was also warm, like a blanket. A wool one that was also slightly prickly.

"Before we got married," he softly corrected.

This definitely proved that there was something wrong. For one thing, I would never in a million years decide to move there. After growing up in a small town, I finally transitioned to the city. Also, I'm not even outdoorsy.

Rain is. She loves camping and all that kind of stuff. I could enjoy doing that with her, especially because the price is decent, but I'd rather go to a fancy hotel. Real stuck-up luxury doesn't interest me, but it should have at least some amenities and a nice view.

He didn't seem drunk. This should have been a good sign, but really it was dashing all my hopes. Because it would give me more reason to believe this was some wild mistake if Darcy seemed even a little deranged.

He wore jeans and a jean shirt, which were clean but not pressed. Not the type to hold an office job, I imagined. As I glanced at his hands, which were rough, calloused, and cracked, it was enough to tell me that he must do manual labour. I noticed his boots. Were they for construction?

Where is everyone? And why am I stuck facing this guy alone? If only my parents or one of my sisters were here.

"What are the names of my family members?" I quizzed him. Once he gets them all wrong, I'll be free, and we can finally solve this.

"Your mom is Martha, but calls herself Candy. Your dad is Todd, and your sisters are Hale and Rain."

How did he know that? Now this was even more disturbing. He must have just done research or something. This is a conspiracy. He is an impostor trying to confuse me and take over my business.

"Who is looking after my business?" I asked.

"Well, no one. We just put up a sign... Oh, you mean *Snowhere Like Home?*" he asked.

"Yes."

"You sold it before we got married."

No. I wouldn't do that either because I worked so hard on that store. I spent years planning and collecting and...

"And when did we get married?" I asked sarcastically. Even though this was getting annoying, sooner or later, this scheme had to bust.

The date he gave was one year ahead of what it is now.

"You mean we are engaged?"

"We've been married for six years," he said, looking as if someone had just punched him in the gut.

My brain jumped and then froze. I think I literally felt it leap up and fall back down.

He is saying that it is seven years later.

It looked like a pretty high-tech hospital room with machines everywhere and I was plugged into most of them. There was basically nothing else except for a few chairs. However, the chords and tubes tangling themselves around my bed left the impression that I was secretly being prepared for a Mars mission.

There was a beautiful bouquet of flowers on the window ledge, now looking a little worn. The good old hardy daisies were still standing firm, and one of the lilies must have just opened. But the other lily had seen better days, hung its head down, and started crying, spilling its bright orange powdered insides on the bedside table.

I was sore. Mostly my skin was irritated, and my muscles were tight, but I shifted a little.

"What year is it?" I finally ventured.

I bit my lip after he answered. No. There is no possible way it could be seven years later. I was only in a coma for four days. There has to be a mistake. I am not married, and I don't live in the Queen Charlotte Islands. I am not thirty years old, instead of twenty-three. I didn't sell my business.

A man who appeared to be the doctor came in now.

"Well, Snow White, you have woken up."

"Do not call me that." I was mad. What are all these stupid people up to? Of course, Snow is a different name, but what right does that give a doctor to make fun of it? At school, kids would occasionally tease me about that, but we are all adults here.

"She doesn't remember anything. She doesn't remember me," Darcy told him.

The doctor frowned. "And you have been married for…"

"Six years, and we met the year before… so that's seven years."

"Hmmm," the doctor said. "Well, amnesia can sometimes go away with a bit of time."

"Look, everything just got all mixed up in your records." I tried to explain. "This is not my husband. Somehow, things are messed up. I'm not married… What year is it?"

He gave the same year that Darcy did.

"What year should it be?" the doctor asked, and I told him, but my confidence was waning.

They could still have my life all mixed up with someone else in a coma.

"Bring me my purse. I should have some ID. I'll show you where I live. You just have me confused with a different person."

Of course, my birth date will be the same. Can it really be seven years later? No. Once I get my ID, everything is going to sort itself out, and they'll finally realize they have the wrong person.

This whole year thing might be a mental test of some sort. Currently, they are just trying to see how I respond under pressure and are all lying about the year to see my reaction.

"Where am I?"

"UHNBC, the University Hospital of Northern British Columbia. The Prince George Hospital," the doctor said.

Prince George? Aren't I a world-class traveller? This kept getting worse and worse.

"Where are my parents and sisters?" I asked.

"I'll call your parents right away to let them know you've woken up," Darcy said. "They still live in the same place, but we've been staying with your sister, who lives just out of town here. Thankfully, you were airlifted here from the coast after one day. Unfortunately, they don't have a phone, so the best I can do is page Clint... her husband."

"What? Who lives out of town that you are staying with?" None of that made any sense. Perhaps we are getting closer to the truth.

"Hale."

"Hale isn't married, nor does she live close to Prince George."

"Actually... she does... and is."

Hale in Prince George... and wed? What? I guess you can run a spa anywhere. I wonder what brought her here. Yet she would only go for someone very successful, so perhaps her husband is super wealthy and, for some reason, has an estate here.

"Did she ever get her company going, or did she finally just find a job?" I'll see if any of this links up.

"Neither. Clint got her out of debt when she promised never to enter into business again or work, either."

"Hale is married and debt free. I can't believe it," I said. It sounded like Darcy did know her, or at least Clint did.

The nurse brought a purse and handed it to me.

"That's not my purse," I said, realizing after what a dumb thing that was to say. I most likely would not have kept the same one for seven years.

I pulled out a key chain which had beads and feathers on it. But it was tastefully done, soft and elegant.

I sat up further. Ow. K, that was painful.

Man, I've gotten fat, I thought as I looked at my now ugly stomach, which bulges out slightly. Once, I used to have not a bad figure.

Next there was a fold-up wooden hairbrush that had a tree carved on the handle. I touched my hair and found it a bit longer than I used to keep it, but there was a very short section in the back. Was that where they cut it because it was under the wheel?

My arms were sore from that small activity. And it was as though I had been lifting weights or something. Ones that were too heavy for me.

Next, I located the wallet. I found the driver's license and pulled it out. It did kind of resemble me, but not the picture I remembered. The name was written *Snow Strawberry White*. No. This can't be. Yet the birth date was the same. The address was in Masset, B.C. This isn't mine. This is someone who looks like me, has the same first name, and was born on the same day. Amazingly enough, she also has the same middle name as me. Hmmm.

But you see, I would never marry a guy who had the last name White. If your name is Snow, that is just something you don't do. Yet how many Snow Strawberrys are born on the same day?

I pulled out my birth certificate. This I remembered, and it was exactly how I recalled with all the details correct.

I looked at Darcy. How on earth could he do this to me? I knew I should calm down, but I felt a fury inside me. There was this burning anger that refused to stay submerged.

"Your last name is White?" I asked.

"Yes."

"I would never marry someone with that last name. Isn't that obvious? This is so sick."

"Well, it does make you a princess," the nurse said as she took the wallet from me and put everything back.

"Where's my cell phone?" I asked Darcy.

"... the service is not very good on the island yet."

"The one I used to have?"

"I'm not sure," he said after a pause and a deep breath.

I stared at the door. There was something that just wasn't right here. Why couldn't I prove them wrong? I was so utterly helpless, and it was making me irate.

"I'm going to go and call your parents," Darcy stated, and left.

Rain. I didn't ask about my sister Rain. I wonder where she is right now. After seven years, she would have finished school and been a geologist. She was going to specialize in glaciers, so that must be what she is doing, but would she have to move far away? Although there are many icefields in B.C., there should be other places on this planet, like Greenland, that are the most significant to study. Her work would help the world realize the effects of climate change.

"Well, I think you've had enough excitement," the doctor said as he briefly popped in again. "Why don't you just rest a bit?"

"Oh, sure."

"This will be difficult for you. You may gradually remember more and more, but you may not. This will overwhelm your mind, so you'll have to take it slowly and try not to analyze too much."

I am Snow White. This is not funny. It's a joke gone terribly wrong.

My brain was racing. How can seven years of my life be erased from my memory? I'm married and live in Masset? Where on earth is that? It must be one small village on the Queen Charlotte Islands. My mind was overwhelmed already.

What do I look like now?

I can't be married. I just can't. And I can't go home with some strange man who claims he remembers me.

A new nurse came and removed my IV. Why didn't that hurt?

I tried to rest a bit but kept thinking of questions. If this was true and not some bad dream, why did I make these decisions? What kind of home do I live in? Am I a different person than I used to be? Now, everyone will expect me to be someone I'm not, someone I've become, but don't even know. In the meantime, I could have cooked or acquired some other new talents, but they would all be lost again. What do I do for work? What is Darcy like? What do I enjoy doing in my spare time? What is marriage like?

The thought was repulsive to me. It's not that I was against a lifelong commitment, but why him? Here I felt no attraction to the guy. Considering that I'm not even ready for marriage, what convinced me to devote my life to him?

How much did I sell my business for, and what did I do with the money? What is his family like?

I can't do this. I just can't. Perhaps I'll go back to Vancouver and see if I can start everything over or pick it up where I left off seven years ago. Staying single is an option for now, and I could, if I should later be inclined, slowly get to know Darcy. In the end, time would be needed to figure out why I chose him out of all the men in this world.

If I could only talk to someone I knew.

I'm not going home with him. Why would I date him? Why would I even notice him? If we had children, they would have tanned skin and dark hair. Which would probably be adorable, come to think of it, but they wouldn't look like me. Well, I'm not having kids. I'm certainly not ready for marriage because I am only twenty-three in my mind.

If I only remember my life up to twenty-three, that's all the experience I have. I would be thirty but act seven years younger.

Maybe, if I could go to sleep, I'll wake up to find that this is all a dream.

I wish I never came out of my coma. Then, I wouldn't be in any pain and just slowly drift away.

If this was reality, Darcy must have been through a lot these last few days. Well, I can't feel sorry for the whole world now. Besides, he doesn't want to be married to a stranger, either.

If my parents get here soon, I can go back with them. Hopefully, they still have room for me.

I don't know how to act thirty. That is old. Seven years of my life, and it's like they were all taken away from me.

I hope Hale is happy. I imagined her walking in with her perfect shoes, nails, hair and eyelashes. She would look seven years older but have a more content and settled expression on her face, going wonderfully with her big movie star grin.

I imagined Rain running in to hug me, all clad in hiking gear. With her hair up in a ponytail and a smile so warm and loving, it would instantly make everything seem better. She had no need for makeup. But knowing her made it wrong to call her a blond bombshell because she either didn't know or didn't care that she was gorgeous. When she went out, she put on lip gloss.

I wonder why Darcy never mentioned Rain. I guess I didn't give him much of a chance.

Why did Darcy say "we"? He said, "*We* want you to come home with us." I sure hope we are not living with his mother or something. I wonder if his family lives close by, but I don't want to meet any family I don't remember.

Yes, I think I'll go back with my parents to Nelson for now, and then I'll figure out what to do next.

I don't need all the answers today. At this time, I just have to get through the next day, then the next week, and slowly the month. That is what the doctor meant. I think.

Darcy's taking a while.

Isn't that a girl's name? I guess not in "Pride and Prejudice," but that was the last name. Darcy White. I mean, really. Darcy? As in Mr. Darcy and Jane Austin's literary masterpiece. That is corny. And White? Out of all the last names in the world...

Perhaps he discovered that he had made an enormous mistake, and I wasn't his wife after all. In another room, he and the doctor are splitting a gut, laughing at this nasty joke they pulled on me. I bet this is all a prank.

Yes. Any minute now, someone will come in smiling and tell me that.

Perhaps this is one of those reality TV shows, and they gave him some information about me to make this sound legit. How long would this need to play out?

The nurse came in and took my temperature and blood pressure. "Are you doing alright?" she asked.

"Physically."

"I hear you. This must be a bit of a shock."

"A bit?"

"We are going to move you into another room," she said.

She was Filipino with dark hair, a thoughtful way of smiling and a demeanour that seemed unhurried.

"Darcy must love you very much. He's been here all day, and every day since you arrived," she added.

I tried to think of that, but it was hard to comprehend.

Perhaps she was smiling because this was on television, but where were the cameras? I looked around.

She had a calming effect on me, and I wished she could stay longer. So, I wanted to ask her something about Darcy, but unfortunately, my mind chose that moment to go blank.

She helped me into a wheelchair and the pull in my leg and back muscles was intense. It was only four days! Walking was going to be hard.

Darcy returned, and he grabbed my few things and accompanied me out of ICU to my new sterile compartment. It was a double, but the other side was empty.

It was an ordinary-looking hospital room, and thankfully I was the only one in it, despite it having another bed. Why do all hospital rooms appear the same? There is never any colour except for the odd accent of hospital green. My water pitcher was off white, the same one I've seen in other hospitals. There must have been a sale somewhere, or someone makes hospital water pitchers, and it is the only hospital water pitcher business, so they've got the market covered for the entire country.

"Well, your mom was so happy, she cried," Darcy said after I was sitting in bed and the nurse left us alone.

"Mom cries at everything."

"Do I look even slightly familiar to you?"

"No. How's Rain?"

He looked down suddenly, closed his eyes briefly and then glanced up at the wall. He didn't want to answer. Instead, he took a moment to think of what to say.

"What happened? Where is she?" I demanded.

"Well, it's June now, and last August, she left on an Arctic mission to study a glacier with a whole bunch of others and a very experienced guide, and... none of them were ever seen again."

"What happened? What do you mean 'they were never seen again'?"

"It was strange. It is still some unexplained mystery. All they came up with was that everyone must have been on the plane when it crashed, but the search crews never located it. There was no trace of anyone where they should've been. So, they searched for weeks trying to find any clues, but they never found a thing, not the supplies, the plane, the pilot or anything at all."

"She could still be alive then," I said.

"Yes, but they only had food for a couple of weeks."

"No. She has to be alive. Rain is a survivor, and she is smart. She is still alive. She has to be. As such a hard worker, she would find a way to keep everyone... safe."

Darcy said nothing.

"Are my parents coming?" I asked.

"Yes."

"When?"

"They will arrive tomorrow sometime," he said.

"Hale, is she coming?"

"Yes. Well, I left a page for Clint. They will get here as soon as possible."

"A page? I thought those didn't exist anymore, even from what I can remember." I stated.

"It's odd, for sure. I don't know of anyone else with one, but it still works, and he uses it for business, mostly."

"What is Clint like?" I asked.

"Oh, he's a great guy. He is pretty quiet, though, and doesn't say much. But he is really good to her."

"When did they get married?"

"In September," he said.

"This last September? Just after Rain went missing?"

"What's even more interesting is that she married him the day after she met him. But you know how she likes to act rashly."

"I'm surprised they are still together after nine months."

"Actually, Hale has changed so much. You will find her settled and very happy," Darcy said.

"He must be wealthy."

"No, he isn't."

"How did he get her out of debt, then?" I asked.

"Well... he didn't have a lot of living expenses. They are expecting in August."

"Wow. The first of us girls to have a child," I said.

Darcy looked down.

Two doctors with clipboards came in.

"Can we ask you a few questions?" one asked.

"I suppose."

They asked a million questions about my life as I remembered it while Darcy looked in agony and near tears. Then, finally, they said it would do.

"So, this isn't a joke. I really have amnesia and no recollection of the last seven years of my life?"

"I'm afraid so," the one doctor said.

"This is slightly upsetting," I mentioned.

"I will recommend counselling. This is quite a surge on your brain, and some therapy will prove helpful."

"I'm not going to a psychologist."

"Just rest for now." And they left.

This was not a joke... or a reality show.

One doctor was Chinese, and the other had a faint German accent. The nurses all seem to originate from different countries too. This little hospital is like the United Nations, just as Vancouver was. It is a melting place of people from all over the world, which I always enjoyed about living there. If you go for a walk in Stanley Park or False creek, you hear all these different languages around you, and they only add to the colour and culture of the surroundings.

"Darcy..."

"Yes."

"I hope you can understand, but I'm going back with my parents. All things considered, I can't go home with you yet. Some time on my own to sort things out is reasonable, don't you think?"

"Please, Snow... Please let me help you. Just give it a try. I love you and we share such a beautiful life together." He had a tired sound to his voice, as though it took every last drop of his energy to speak. He did seem worn out, come to think of it.

"I can't leave here with a strange man. It's easy for you to say, but we'll get in touch when I am ready," And I tried to speak as kindly and gently as possible.

"Snow...It is not just me... I don't want to overwhelm you, but... I think you should take into consideration... so that's the only reason I'm telling you this... but we have a daughter."

It gripped me with fear. I am a mother? *No!*

"She's four, and Missy is her name. She thinks the world of you and is such a good girl and so sweet and beautiful," he said.

Read *After I Woke,*
the next book from Ebonene Charles.

Ebonene Charles

Ebonene Charles loves living on the west coast of British Columbia and can usually be found planning vacations within the province. She loves feeding people and going for walks in the forest. Born in Canada, she lives in a small apartment in Burnaby with her two favourite guys, her husband and son.

Connect Online
ebonenecharles.ca
 @author.ebonenecharles

Manufactured by Amazon.ca
Bolton, ON

33440558R00180